A Silence Falling Dark and Deep

K.N. Salustro

NOVA DRAGON STUDIOS, LLC

For Jacki

The exact person you want in your corner when the world goes dark. I am so proud and grateful to be your sister.

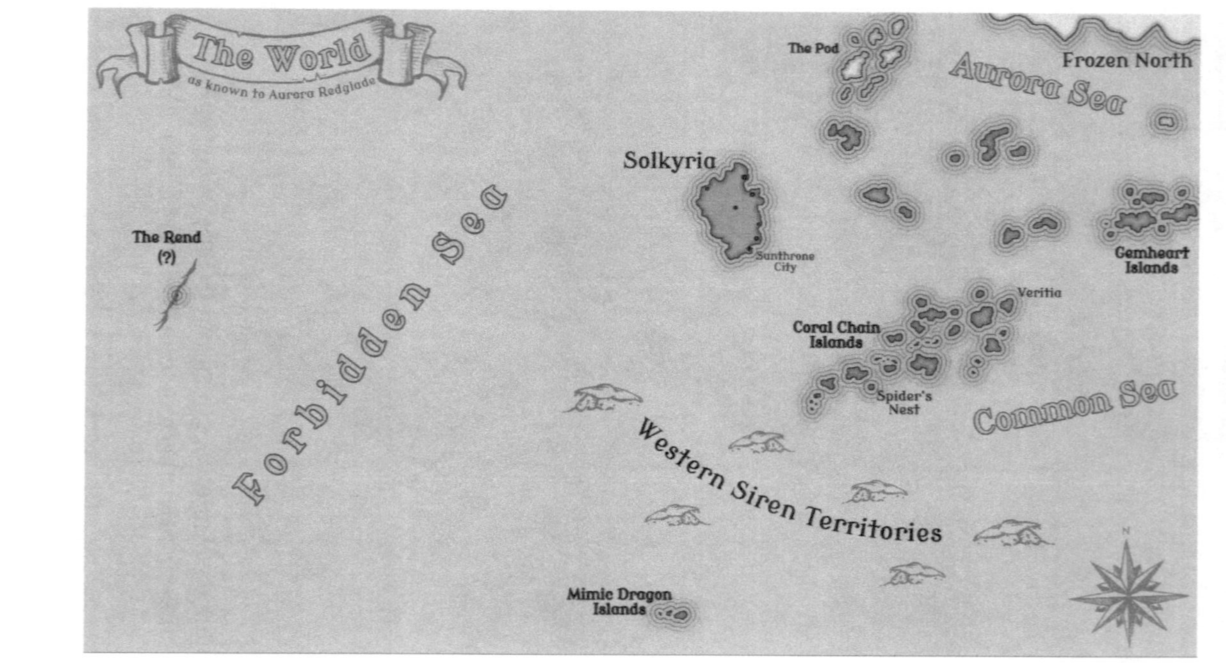

The World
as known to Aurora Redglade
The Rend
(?)
Forbidden Sea
The Pod
Frozen North
Aurora Sea
Solkyria
Sunthrone City
Gemheart Islands
Veritia
Coral Chain Islands
Spider's Nest
Common Sea
Western Siren Territories
Mimic Dragon Islands

Contents

Prologue: Forged in the Storm

Every hand pitched in as the *Southern Echo* skirted the edge of the storm. Dax was no exception. He did not usually handle rigging work, but even this far from the center of the hurricane, the winds were savage, and it was all the crew could do to keep the ship under control. The *Southern Echo* bucked and skipped over the waves, jolting everyone with each crash of her keel against the water, but despite the rough voyage and the hard work of keeping the reefed sails under control, there were smiles across the ship, and Dax could feel the adrenaline and excitement in the rapid drumming of the crew's hearts.

Not so long ago, so many elevated heart rates would have overwhelmed Dax and left him curled on the deck with his hands clamped over his ears, groaning against the splitting pain in his skull as the hammering of his magic overwhelmed him. It had taken a lot of practice and the accidental discovery of the soothing properties of a piece of Solkyrian agate, but Dax finally had a firm grip on his blood working Skill. Or at least a firmer one. His magic could still slip beyond his control if he wasn't careful, but that was more of an inconvenience for him than anyone else. It had been a long time now since he'd accidentally stopped someone's heart.

He could still feel the pulses of the crew even when

the weather was calm and most everyone was bored, but they faded to a dull undertone at the back of his mind instead of a steady thrumming in his ears that made it impossible to sleep. With the storm driving up their adrenaline now, their heartbeats were amplified, but Dax could keep them at bay with a gentle flex of his magic.

He'd come a long way since Iris Arani had found him as a frightened stowaway.

Everyone who sailed the *Southern Echo* had, really.

"Keep steady on the mainsail," the voice of the captain rang out over the howl of the storm. "I want that one fully down before the wind changes."

"Aye, Captain!" came the sturdy response.

What had once been a ragtag group of mutineers had grown to a respectably sized crew, and though rain-lashed and difficult to fully see in the dark of the storm, there was no mistaking the camaraderie that had blossomed across the ship. Of course, that had been buoyed by their recent taking of a good prize under the leadership of Captain Iris Arani and the quartermaster, Will Brownbay.

They make a solid pair, Dax thought.

Old Brownbay's experience and level temper was a good offset to Iris's bold, eager vigor and natural drive to lead. She listened and willingly learned from him, just as the rest of the crew did.

It was a real problem, then, that Will Brownbay wanted to retire.

The whole crew knew that the quartermaster was looking to end his career as a sailor. He often claimed that he wasn't cut out to be a pirate, although his ferocity in battle suggested otherwise. Still, the man had spent a hard life at sea, mostly under the command of imperial officers, and he was ready for a few steady years with his boots on the soil of an island instead of the wooden deck of a ship, his days filled with tending to a small garden and reading until it was time for him to fall asleep in a real bed, not a hammock rocking with the waves. No one begrudged him that quiet dream, but no one was eager to step into his place, either.

Dax did not blame them; the responsibilities and duties of the quartermaster were wide and demanding, and to fill the role was to take on the trust of the crew while commanding their respect and driving their discipline. A quartermaster was a leader, not a friend, and for once, Dax was glad that he had been branded as a Skilled. No Solkyrian-dominated crew would have ever voted a Skilled into such a high position of authority.

On the other edge of that sword, Dax had endured a fair bit of cruel words and gestures, until Iris had rooted out the worst of the antagonists and expelled them from the crew, leaving them to find their own way forward in the pirate haven known as Spider's Nest. That had destroyed the worst of it, although the final blow against the bigotry had only come recently, when Dax had sat for an ink artist among the Leviathan Sea Traders and endured hours of the bite and scrape of a needle against his head. The new tattoos had healed well, although they still itched a little, and Dax had to consciously keep himself from scratching the still-tender parts of his scalp. But getting the large, intricate design had been worth it; now, instead of irritation, the Solkyrian members of the *Southern Echo*'s crew looked at Dax and the twin tattoos flaring out along the sides of his shaved head with reluctant respect tinged with the faintest hint of awe. Dax happily took that over their previous coldness. He still wasn't exactly friends with any of them just yet, save for Iris, but he was making progress.

Dax bared his teeth in a ferocious smile as he hauled

on the ropes with the riggers, furling the ship's sails even more as the wind whipped across the sea. Dark clouds swirled in the sky, dumping cold rain on everyone's heads, but in spite of that, Dax could still feel the steady pulse of the crew's excitement seeping into his skin, brushing against his magic and stirring it into a steady thrum through his own veins.

The plunder from the merchant ship promised to see them well-fed and entertained in the very near future. The small vessel had eluded the *Southern Echo* far longer than anyone had anticipated, but under Iris's relentless determination, the pirate brig had caught up. The fight for control hadn't been so bad, with most of the merchant crew throwing down their weapons and pleading for mercy instead of resisting. Everything had been over fast, and now the *Southern Echo*'s hold bore three small chests of silver coins and several bolts of luxurious cloths that would fetch a handsome price on Spider's Nest.

There was rest and rum and good food and company in their futures, with nothing but a bit of sailing and one bad storm between them and those pleasures.

Of course, *bad storm* was turning out to be a bit of an understatement, but Iris had warned the crew of the dangers beforehand. Under Brownbay's council, she had let them vote to continue the voyage. They were all here now, battling the edges of a hurricane, because the majority of the crew had chosen a swift return over a safer slog around the storm. Iris was on the deck with them now, squinting against the thrashing rain and watching the climbing riggers with genuine concern.

A particularly large wave rocked the *Southern Echo*, and Dax felt Iris's heart leap almost as much as those of the men and women clinging to the ropes above. His Skill responded to their distress, making his head twinge, but he pulled it back, narrowing the channels of his magic as the *Southern Echo* rolled back into balance.

Brownbay came skittering across the soaked deck as the ship righted herself. "Their lives aren't worth that bit of cloth," he shouted to Iris over the wind. "Call them down."

"If the mainsail goes, it's taking everything else with it," Iris called back. "Right now, *all* our lives are worth that bit of cloth."

If Brownbay responded, Dax did not hear it, but he and the quartermaster both knew that Iris had an intimate understanding of the *Southern Echo*'s rigging. She'd climbed and worked it herself long before she'd overthrown the old captain and taken control of the ship. If she thought losing the mainsail was a danger that could not be ignored, it was best to listen to her.

Dax took a deep breath and readjusted his grip on the rope.

Lightning thrashed the sky as the wind howled with a new ferocity, and Dax felt the moment the crew's excitement began to buckle under their fear. Their anxiousness ground against his awareness, gnawing at his control over his Skill, and he grit his teeth as he took a moment to gather himself.

When he felt his magic quiet down to a trickle, he risked a glance over his shoulder at Iris. Her face was still turned up to the mainsail, and she ignored the lashing of her own wet hair against her skin as she watched her crew work. Her mouth was forming what could have been a silent prayer, or a curse upon the gods themselves for the storm; with Iris, it could have gone either way.

For some reason, that gave Dax more comfort than a sudden break in the storm would have.

Iris and Brownbay had both agreed to lower the

topgallant and topsails before the storm had caught the ship, but the mainsail and the foresail had been left to catch what they could of the winds and speed the *Southern Echo* along. The gamble had paid off for the most part, with the ship's mute navigator confirming that they'd sailed much farther than they ever would have if they'd tried to completely avoid the storm, but the hurricane had moved faster than anyone had anticipated. Now those sails needed to come down before the storm tore them away, and Iris and Brownbay had elected to fully lower the yards rather than try to take the sails down separately. The foresail's yard had cooperated beautifully, but the mainsail was fighting back like a distressed animal. The riggers aloft were trying to find the problem, hacking with cutlasses where any other action would have been too slow.

They still weren't fast enough.

The *Southern Echo* rolled under Dax's feet as another massive wave came bearing down on the ship, and he heard the cries of frustration and fear as cold seawater sloshed across the deck. He grit his teeth again and held on to the rope.

A startled shout drew his attention, and he turned to see that Iris had vanished from her place on the deck. Dax's own heart surged as he thought of her being washed over the side of the ship by that last wave, but he caught the flash of her red coat against the darkness of the storm, moving up the shrouds. Dax's heart stopped as he watched Iris scramble into the rigging, a knife clenched in her teeth, but her steps were sure and there was a burning determination in her that Dax could sense even across the distance between them.

She's fine, he told himself. *She knows what she's doing.*

His pulse still jumped as she reached the yard and

joined the two riggers working on the port yardarm.

"Gods above protect that wild girl," Brownbay said as he stepped up next to Dax and the others holding the rope, waiting for the weight of the yard to shift. "And the rest of us from her." The quartermaster tore his eyes away from the captain and called encouragement and adjustments to the sailors on the deck.

Dax responded alongside the others, but he stumbled when the ship rolled again.

"Don't drop that rope, Malatide," Theo Yellowwood shouted down from the rigging.

Dax wasn't the only one who had tripped with that last wave, and he glanced up at the man, not bothering to hide his irritation. His glower under his new tattoos had a satisfying effect; Theo swallowed with visible nervousness and then snapped his attention back to his task. Dax felt a smile rise to his lips, but his stomach flipped as he caught sight of Iris's red coat against the black sky.

Gods above, don't let her fall.

Thankfully, it seemed as though the gods had answered his prayer. The storm did not let up, but within a few minutes of Iris joining the riggers aloft, whatever had tangled the mainsail was dislodged, and the yard finally began to lower. Dax snuck another relieved glance up, proud of Iris, but the feeling twisted into confusion when he saw that she had climbed higher and was staring into the dark clouds. Most of the riggers had descended, but Theo Yellowwood had remained behind. The man hunched on the small platform that surrounded the place where the lower and top mainmasts joined, his face turned up towards the captain. Dax thought that the rigger was calling to Iris, but something had snatched her attention, and she paid him no heed.

"Captain!" Brownbay called, throwing his voice as

far as he could into the wind.

Iris still did not look away from the dark clouds.

"Captain!" the quartermaster shouted again, desperation edging his voice.

Theo looked down, but Iris did not.

"Arani!" Brownbay bellowed, and Iris started and finally seemed to remember that she was up in the ship's rigging while a hurricane thrashed the sky and sea.

She gave a small wave of acknowledgment and began her descent. Theo also started to climb down, and Dax felt his pulse ease.

Then the next wave came, bigger than all the last, and the wall of water was accompanied by an angry burst of wind that nearly ripped Dax from the ship. He wasn't the only one. By the time the water had drained from the deck and the roaring wind was past, nearly everyone who'd been topside had been swept off their feet and carried down the length of the ship. Their lifelines had held, and several people were clinging to the riggers who had jumped down from the rat-lines mere moments before. Dax pushed himself to his knees and looked up, and his heart froze in his chest.

The rigging was empty.

Iris was gone.

Dax was on his feet and moving before he'd had the chance to even begin to think. He untied his life-line, thrust it into the nearest person's hands with garbled instructions he himself only half-understood, and then leapt up on to the railing of the ship. The sea billowed and screamed all around him, but he was diving in before the next bolt of lightning could illuminate that watery hell, plunging straight through the cold surface.

Dax had already been soaked by the rain, so the icy water barely registered against his skin. As he slipped under the waves, however, the world went dark. The rush of the current was the only sound now, other than the beating of his own heart.

His world had not been this quiet for as long as he could remember. For a long moment, Dax hung in the sea, torn between the terror of facing that near-silent world under the water, and the shocked awe of finally being completely alone.

Iris...

Shunting aside his emotions, Dax reached within himself, brushing against his magic. It twisted and surged through his veins, a wild thing that did not fully trust him yet. He felt the same way about his Skill, but he needed it now, needed it to behave and help him where all his other senses failed.

In the darkness under the surface of the water, Dax gathered his magic, widening the channels that were always open to the world no matter how hard he tried to close them. Silence rushed in, and Dax's fear might have claimed him then if he wasn't so focused on the faintest tremors of the water, searching for the beating of another heart.

He found an erratic, terrified pulse off to his left.

Salt stung Dax's eyes as he began to swim, but he kept them open as he went.

I'm coming, Dax thought as he cut through the water. *Hold on, Iris.*

But when another flash of lightning split the sky, illuminating the sea in a wash of gray-green, Dax saw the floundering figure just ahead of him. It wasn't Iris, but Theo Yellowwood.

For one terrible moment, Dax considered turning away. But Iris would never forgive him for letting one of the crew drown. Worse yet, Dax would never forgive himself. Not when he knew he could help. He worried that he had not sensed Iris in the sea yet, but he had to help Theo first.

Thankfully, the rigger could swim, although being thrown off the ship had left Theo disoriented and panicked. He thrashed in the water, his screams for help dying against the waves. He was fighting, but he was going the wrong way, away from the *Southern Echo*.

Dax's arms were already growing tired as he came up near Theo, but he kicked his legs hard as he treaded water. He called to the rigger, but the storm devoured his voice. Theo thrashed and paddled further away. Dax followed him, barely managing to clasp his hand around the other man's arm as a wave lifted them up and then dropped them together.

The rigger screamed and lashed out, striking Dax on the side of the face. Dax yelped in pain as he let go of Theo's arm, seawater rushing in to fill his nose and mouth. Dax choked as he went under again. He felt the pressure of a wave tumble over him and Theo, pushing the rigger beneath the water, too. Dax fought his way back up and took ragged, painful breaths as he coughed up water, but Theo did not surface. Dax did not wait. He drew in as deep a breath as his battered lungs could handle and dove back down.

Theo twisted and fought in the water, but the wave had disoriented him, and his panic was a palpable thing now. Dax reached for him, his magic running along his arm like a natural extension of the limb, and he threaded his Skill into the rigger's racing pulse. Dax's magic rose to meet that frantic rhythm, and without thinking, he pulled it back, slowing the magic and Theo's heart with it.

Dax had not meant to do that, had not even known that he *could* do that, but as Theo's heart calmed, space cleared for something other than panic.

Theo stopped thrashing and started swimming, confusion plain on his face as he turned in the water.

Panic rose again when he saw Dax near him, but he did not resist when Dax got his hands under Theo's arms and pulled him back up.

Their heads broke the surface and they both drew in burning breaths. Theo coughed and retched up seawater, and Dax helped him stay afloat until his lungs had cleared. Lightning flashed as Theo twisted around to see his savior, and recognition bloomed as he took in Dax's face in that brief moment.

"Malatide?" Theo asked, stunned.

"Me," Dax confirmed grimly. He turned in the water. "This way." Dax led the way back to the *Southern Echo*, and Theo did not hesitate to follow.

The gods were kind again. The swim back to the ship wasn't far, although the massive waves made it feel like they were climbing mountains. The crew was on alert, most of them gathered at the railing to search the sea, but it was too dark for them to pick out two faces among the waves, even when Dax and Theo were right up against the hull.

Dax tried to call for help, but the wind and the rain stole his words once more. He reached up to pound on the side of the ship, but only managed a feeble slap before a wave pushed him against the hull. The wood was surprisingly warm despite the chill of the sea, and for some reason, Dax felt a wash of comfort run through him. Above him, one of the sailors at the railing gave a violent yelp and snatched her hand back to her chest, as though something had bit or pierced her palm, but as she peered down, she looked right at Dax, and then she was shouting for the others to bring ropes.

The coils slapped into the water around Dax and Theo, their salvation delivered. Dax grabbed one of the ropes, but he sent Theo up first.

The rigger was exhausted, and he could do little

more than wrap the rope around himself and cling to it while the crew hauled him up. But before he went, he twisted around and said, "Thank you, Dax."

The use of his name instead of the Malatide moniker was enough to catch Dax off guard. He barely managed to nod as he watched Theo get pulled up the side of the ship, nothing but gratitude in the man's eyes. Dax watched long enough to be certain that Theo was not going to fall, and then he returned his attention to the sea, gathering his magic again as his thoughts focused on Iris once more.

It was harder this time, and a bolt of pain lanced its way through Dax's head as he fought for control over his Skill, but he couldn't stop now. He tore his awareness open in a wild rush, letting in everything around him.

The heartbeats of the crew were above him, and there was a faint but steady flicker of something deep within the *Southern Echo*, but the world beyond was cold and empty.

Iris...

She couldn't be gone. She was too bright, too furious to be snuffed out so casually by a fluke of the weather.

But the longer Dax stared at the sea, the more the adrenaline and certainty bled out of him. His arms and legs were heavy, and it was tempting to slip below the surface and rest a moment, floating in that vast nothingness, to feel true aloneness once more.

The rope jerked in the water next to Dax, yanking him back to reality. Lightning cracked across the sky as he started to secure the line around himself, followed closely by the roar of thunder, but there was something off about the sound, something lingering and angry. Dax glanced up at the too-dark sky and thought that he saw something moving within the clouds, but he couldn't trust his sight after that last bolt of lightning. He was about to turn back to the ship when he saw something red plummeting towards the sea, and though he did not hear the splash, he saw the boiling rush of bubbles behind the impact.

Dax let go of the rope and swam for the fallen thing, heedless of the cries from the crew behind him.

Please, he thought as he forced his arms and legs through the water.

He was less than five strokes away when a face broke the surface of the sea, coughing and gasping, and relief pushed strength back into Dax's limbs.

"Iris!" he shouted as he swam closer.

She turned, her skin alarmingly pale and her eyes dazed, but she still reached for him. She let Dax help her back to the ship. It was slower going than it had been with Theo, as Iris was bleeding from a gash on her arm and clutching something in her palm that she refused to let go of, even when Dax pointed out that she'd have an easier time swimming if she opened her hand. Iris bared her teeth and shook her head, kicking savagely at the water as she pulled herself along in an awkward side stroke. Dax stayed with her, making sure she kept her head above water, and then he held her firmly in one arm while the other gripped the rope as the crew plucked them from the sea. They fell over the railing and collapsed side-by-side on the deck, panting hard and staring up at the ring of awestruck faces that surrounded them.

Brownbay shouldered his way through the crowd, shouting for everyone to return to their duties before another wave struck the ship. Iris sat up as the quartermaster dropped to his knees next to her. She did not protest when he took her arm to look at the wound she'd sustained. Dax remained prone on the deck for another minute, letting his exhaustion take hold.

He'd never worked his Skill like that before, and it was claiming the cost now. The piece of agate Dax wore around his neck was hot against his skin, and he could have sworn steam was coming off of his shirt where the wet fabric made contact with the stone. Gradually, the pain from his magic and the heat of the agate began to lessen, and Dax's breathing came easier.

As he recovered, Dax grew aware of Brownbay's scolding voice.

"—doing up there?" the quartermaster was snarling at Iris. He'd knotted some cloth around her arm, although that was doing very little to stop the bleeding.

Iris, however, did not seem to notice that she was injured. "I saw it," she said, almost reverently. "I *touched* it. It's real."

Dax's relief gave way to concern as Iris's expression came into focus. She was staring into the southwest, naked hunger on her face. Her hand was still closed around something, clutching it to her heart.

Frowning, Brownbay turned to follow her gaze, but only swirling black clouds and the core of the storm lay to the southwest.

"How much seawater did you swallow?" the quartermaster asked as he swung back around.

"It's real," Iris repeated, as though she'd found a new religious mantra. "It's real."

"What did you see?" Dax asked as he sat up. He did not like this intensity that had come over her, and he moved slow, lest he startle her into doing something rash.

"Black as smoke," she murmured, drawing a confused frown from Brownbay. "It's out there. It's real."

Dax squinted into the sky. "The storm?" he asked, bewildered.

Iris slowly shook her head and lowered her closed

hand away from her chest. "The dragon," she said, and she let her fingers fall open to reveal the black thing nestled in her palm, its edges so sharp they'd drawn blood.

It was difficult to clearly see the large scale that Iris held, but Dax had the distinct impression of a swirling surface, as though she'd torn off a piece of the storm. Brownbay reached out to touch the strange relic, but Iris closed her hand around it again, snatching it back. She jerked away from the quartermaster, looking at him as though he were an officer from the old merchant crew that had ruled the ship before she'd taken over, and Brownbay drew back as sharply as if she'd struck him across the face.

Iris blinked, and the hunger in her eyes dulled. "Sorry," she said to the quartermaster. "Falling and almost drowning must have rattled me a bit." She frowned then, and looked at her closed hand as though afraid of it. She cracked her fingers open once more, and drew in a sharp breath as she took in the little spot of darkness she'd collected. "That really happened," she whispered as that insatiable gleam began to return to her eye. "Mordanti's dragon is out there."

Dax's stomach flipped. He and Iris had spent many quiet hours trading stories with each other, and the ones Iris always returned to were the tales of Ava Mordanti, the Veritian captain who had sailed hundreds of years ago and defied the Solkyrian Empire until her death in battle. Iris had always spoken of Mordanti as a fixture in history and not a character from a story. She'd also focused on Mordanti's battle records, shunting away mention of a mythical black dragon with a treasure map branded in its wings, but the scale she clutched in her hand now was impossible to deny.

If what she said was true, then Iris had just learned

that some legends were more than real.

"Mordanti?" Brownbay asked incredulously. "The Thief?"

Iris bristled at the Solkyrian title for the Veritian captain, but did not correct him. Instead, she pushed to her feet. "If we could follow it," she began, drifting towards the port railing.

"Captain," Brownbay said sharply, but Dax beat him to Iris's side.

"Iris," Dax said, quiet but firm, "we have to get out of this storm."

She started to pull away. "It was flying southwest. If we could get to the eye of the storm, then maybe—"

"*Iris.*" Dax's voice snapped like a whip this time, but he forced himself to speak calmly when she swung around to face him, a challenge in her eyes. "This is your ship, and your crew," he said. "What kind of captain do you want to be?"

Iris silently repeated the words, but understanding quickly dawned. Her gaze skimmed over Dax's tattoo, right where his Malatide mark was hidden beneath the fresh ink, then across the ship at the toiling crew as they ran to check and secure every last thing on the deck. She glanced down at the black scale in her hand and then gazed out into the storm once more, but there was a defeated slope to her shoulders.

Dax breathed out a sigh of relief and gently touched her arm. "If it's really out there," he said, "we can find it again."

Iris stilled, then nodded slowly. She drew herself up to her full height and scraped the wet hair off of her face, turning away from the southwest and the heart of the hurricane. She still held the stormy fragment of darkness in her hand, but her eyes were fixed on the crew and the ship as she set off across the deck, giving new orders to the helm and moving to help where she saw the need, injured arm be damned.

Dax couldn't help the fond, wry smile that touched his lips as he watched her.

Then Brownbay was at his side. "That was well done," the old man said. "You ever think about being quartermaster?"

Dax gave a hoarse laugh, but stopped when he saw that Brownbay was completely serious. "Me?" Dax said. "I could never do that job."

"You just did the brunt of it," Brownbay noted. "Talking the captain down from bad ideas and looking out for the interest of the crew are the main responsibilities." He nodded in Iris's direction. "You did it far better with her than I ever have."

Dax shook his head. "She'd have realized eventually that we couldn't go deeper into the storm."

Brownbay dismissed the protest with a flick of his hand. "She's got a good head for the most part, but she respects you as a peer where she sees me more like a parent. Someone to listen to, but also defy." The quartermaster eyed Dax thoughtfully. "You just might be exactly what she needs to succeed at this."

"Being a pirate?" Dax asked.

"Surviving," Brownbay corrected.

Dax scuffed his boot against the deck, entirely unsure of how to respond to that. He did not want this, and it was ridiculous to think that it would ever happen. "The crew would never vote for me," he pointed out, grasping at his strongest possible escape. "I'm a Skilled."

"You just saved the lives of a rigger *and* the captain, and probably the rest of ours by convincing said captain not to go chasing shadows deeper into storms." Brownbay sucked his teeth speculatively. "I don't know *what* she saw out there, or what she thinks she's got in her hand, but I know that look she had, and she's going to hold you to whatever promise you just made her." He tilted a glance at Dax. "Best have some authority and the support of the crew before she comes calling."

Dax shook his head again, opening his mouth to protest.

Brownbay cut him off before he could even begin. "You'd certainly have my vote as outgoing quartermaster, and I know the crew will take that seriously. And I wouldn't just throw you to the sharks, lad. I'll teach you what you need to know, make sure you've got your legs under you before I step off this boat for the last time." He held Dax's gaze steadily. "Think about it. Do me the favor of at least that much."

Then he set off across the deck. Dax shivered in the rain as he watched the quartermaster go, but he couldn't say if that was from the cold or the sudden press of a future he'd never so much as glimpsed before.

A pirate ship with a Veritian captain and a Skilled quartermaster, he thought. *I can't think of anything stranger.*

CHAPTER ONE
The Return

NATE WAS AT THE bow as the *Southern Echo* glided around the final coral barriers that shielded the bright blue harbor of Spider's Nest. He wasn't alone; Marcus stood next to him, and several others milled about near the forward railings, leaning out for unobstructed views of the ships in the harbor. For once, the boatswain let them shirk their duties, although the main riggers and the helmsman were still at their tasks; everyone else had been granted unspoken leave to watch for the *Dragonsbane*.

That hated ship had been conspicuously absent from the waters leading back to the Nest, but Arani and Dax had both agreed that Blackcliff would have gone straight for the last pirate haven in the Common Sea to trade his godly gold with Spider. There was simply nowhere else for him to turn. And so, with the head start his ship had taken when leaving the Rend, chances were high that the *Dragonsbane* was already anchored in Spider's harbor, Blackcliff's crew spilled across the island.

And Xander Grayvoice was somewhere among them.

"Not much longer now," Nate murmured to Marcus as the *Southern Echo* glided around the final bit of coral. "Are you ready?"

"Aye," Marcus answered. "You?"

Nate nodded, not trusting himself to withhold the truth. He did not want to face Xander Grayvoice again so soon. The other man was stronger, faster, cunning, and ruthless. Nate had decidedly lost their duel in the gods' temple on the Vanishing Island, and had only come away with his life because Captain Arani had interfered. If they fought one-on-one again, Nate was certain that he would not win.

His heart was beating nervously in his chest as his stomach churned. He wished he had more time to train and prepare, but the *Dragonsbane* had left the Rend ahead of the *Southern Echo*, and it was inevitable that the two ships would meet again here, on Spider's Nest.

Nate was going to face Xander today, whether he was ready or not.

But he had his friends with him this time, and an entire ship of sailors hungry for vengeance after everything Xander and the *Dragonsbane* crew had done, and if they needed Nate to fight, then he would, ferociously and without mercy.

He glanced back to where Eric and Rori stood near the foremast. There was a grim but determined set to Eric's jaw as he waited, cutlass in one hand and heavy carpenter's hammer in the other.

Arani had made it clear before reaching the Nest that they could not outright attack the *Dragonsbane* crew while the ship was in Spider's waters. At least not until she'd sold the drinking horn and secured the funds and supplies they needed to disappear into the east. After that, it would no longer matter if the *Southern Echo* was banished from the Nest. She'd ordered everyone to restrain themselves until then, designating team leaders across the crew to help keep the more zealous members in check, but she had not stopped anyone from arming themselves as the *South-*

ern Echo approached the island.

Just in case.

Next to Eric, Rori waited with a sword belted at her hip, but her arms were crossed against the light shudders that wracked her every few minutes. Anxiousness had plagued her since the Rend, and Nate desperately wished he could soothe it, but not even Luken's presence was helping her.

The bird was perched on Rori's shoulder, a place he'd claimed and refused to leave ever since she'd come back from the Vanishing Island. He shrieked and pecked at anyone who came too close to Rori. He eyed Eric warily now, but the elegant Darkbend was familiar and liked enough to be permitted within a four foot radius of Rori's person. Any closer than that, and Luken voiced his displeasure loudly and assertively.

As Nate gazed at her, another shudder ran through Rori, and she twisted away from something unseen, one hand coming up to close off her ear as though blocking out a voice. Luken chirped and nuzzled her hand, but she dropped it without consoling the bird. Nate could feel the tension in her breathing across the distance between them. Her distress cut ragged lines in the air and sawed against his magic.

A fresh wave of anger heated Nate's chest as he turned back to the island.

He had completely failed Rori on the voyage to the Rend, first keeping her in the dark about the brewing betrayal while he himself willfully ignored the truth, and then losing her to Xander when the Grayvoice had finally made his move.

I'll make it right, Nate vowed. *What he did doesn't go unanswered.*

He edged closer to the bowsprit, straining to see around the edge of the island as the *Southern Echo* slowly completed her journey. When the first ship came into view, Nate's pulse quickened to a roar in his head, but it quieted when he saw that the ship was not the *Dragonsbane*. Neither was the second ship, although that didn't stop Nate's heart from giving another lurch in his chest. He actually felt the anticipation weighing on his shoulders, and badly wanted to break it.

"Where is it?" someone asked as a third innocent vessel slid into sight.

Marcus leaned forward, peering past Nate to the far end of the harbor. "Where is... everyone?"

Nate followed Marcus's gaze, but it took him several moments to register that there were no other ships in the Nest's harbor. A strange tangle of disappointment and relief stole through him, although the feeling quickly gave way to confusion. From the voices picking up across the ship, he knew that he wasn't the only one with questions.

The *Dragonsbane* should have been there. It had left the Vanishing Island ahead of the *Southern Echo*, heavy with as much gold as Blackcliff and his crew had been able to scrape off the beach and out of the shallows before disembarking. Rori had confirmed that the *Dragonsbane* captain and crew had all survived before she'd fled from them, leaving them to revel in the gold coins showering down from the sky. The *Dragonsbane* had been gone by the time the *Southern Echo* had rounded the Vanishing Island and begun sailing east, and they never saw it anywhere on the seas as they came back into the Coral Chain. Blackcliff would have cut straight to Spider's Nest, and he and his hated crew should have been spilled across the island's beaches by now, their spirits and their voices raised high by undeserved triumph.

"They're not here," Nate said.

"Brilliant observation," a voice bit out, stained with

anger.

Nate turned to meet the glare of AnnaMarie Blueshore, the crew's strongest lead gunner now that Jim Greenroot was dead. Every muscle across her thick arms and broad frame was tense as she stared past Nate at the near-empty harbor, as though she could will the *Dragonsbane* to appear.

A retort to her sarcasm rose in Nate's mind, but he pushed it down rather than stoke her ire further. He shuffled out of her way, yielding his place at the bow in favor of tapping Marcus to follow him and join Eric and Rori at the foremast.

Eric had already sheathed his cutlass by the time Nate and Marcus stepped to his side, although he shifted the weight of the carpenter's hammer between his hands as he swept his gaze across the harbor. "This is a surprise," he remarked quietly. "Not sure if it's good or bad."

"Good," Rori said immediately, the word coming out in a sigh that danced away on the breeze as a soft ribbon of relief. For the first time since the *Southern Echo* had left the red world of the Rend behind, Rori visibly relaxed.

Nate's heart lifted a little at that, but Eric looked skeptical.

"This gives us more time to prepare," Nate pointed out. "Maybe Arani can get Spider on our side, stop him before he even has the chance to trade with Black-cliff."

"Maybe," Eric said. His brow was creased into a frown, the white Darkbend tattoo over his left eye sweeping down to underscore the expression. "Unless the *Dragonsbane* was already here and left."

"That's not possible," Nate said. "We would have seen them on their way out." He hesitated, then looked to Rori. "Right?"

The *Southern Echo*'s navigator fidgeted, drawing an irritated chirp from Luken, but the bird refused to leave her shoulder. "If the Rend dropped them closer to the Nest," Rori said, each word slow and reluctant, "then maybe not."

Nate thought of Blackcliff and Xander escaping, their laughter echoing off the shining gold in the *Dragonsbane*'s hold. The idea stoked his anger again, but it was Marcus who spoke up.

"I can't believe the gods would have done that."

Rori's face twisted with bitterness. "That's far from the worst they would do for a laugh."

A troubled light came into Marcus's eyes, but before he could get another word out, AnnaMarie Blueshore stepped into their circle.

"Lowwind," she said to Nate by way of greeting. "Have you been using your Skill lately?"

Nate tensed, not liking where this line of questioning historically led, but he relaxed a little as his friends rounded on Blueshore. He wasn't alone anymore. "No," he answered with flat honesty.

He braced himself for the gunner to demand something of him, or maybe curse him and call him selfish for not using his magic to find their enemies, but Blueshore only gave an impatient nod, ignoring the stares of the other Skilled.

"You sometimes sense things in the wind even when you're not using it?" she asked.

Nate hesitated, but despite AnnaMarie's lingering anger, it did not seem to be directed at him. "Sometimes," he allowed. "Depends what it is and what I'm doing at the moment."

"And you haven't felt any sign of the *Dragonsbane*?"

Nate started to answer, but Rori released a hard breath.

"Shove off it," she growled at the gunner. "They're

not here. Leave it be."

"No," Blueshore shot back. "They need to answer for Jim's death."

Nate and Eric both moved to catch Rori's arms, but she pulled away and squared off against the imposing wall that was AnnaMarie. Luken gave a distressed cry as Rori surged forward, finally relinquishing his place on her shoulder and taking off in a burst of speed, pennant feathers trailing behind him.

"He's not going to track them for you," Rori hissed, not noticing Luken's abrupt departure. Her back was to Nate, but he could easily imagine the way her dark eyes flashed against the imposing design of the dark blue tattoo on her face.

AnnaMarie, however, was not impressed by the Goodtide's fury. "You're not the only one they hurt," she said, her voice low and dangerous. "Just because you were rolling Xander doesn't mean the rest of us have to—"

Nate raised his voice in protest, but Rori moved faster than him, closing the distance between herself and Blueshore with two sharp steps.

She thrust her face close to the gunner's and hissed, "I want to *drown* him."

AnnaMarie recoiled, as did Nate and the two Darkbends. Rori's voice had not sounded like her own in that moment, as though someone or something else were speaking through her.

Rori seemed to realize that, too, for her anger gave way to horror, and she quickly drew back. She pressed the heels of her hands against her forehead.

Nate put a gentle hand on her back, but she jumped at his touch and he withdrew. "Rori," he started, but Eric stepped between them, pushing open the space around the navigator.

"You're safe," Eric told her firmly. "They're not here.

They can't hurt you."

Rori shook as she fought to draw in a deep breath. Her eyes squeezed shut and her teeth clenched so hard, Nate worried they would crack, but she gradually loosened her shoulders and calmed herself.

Some of the ire went out of Blueshore as she watched this unfold. Her gaze slipped to Eric, who gave her a warning shake of his head. Nate shifted his weight, ready to move between the two women and shield Rori, but the gunner rocked back on her heels and waited, not saying a word.

A few moments later, Rori looked up. She was still shaking, but she had regained enough of her composure to speak. "I hate Xander for what he did to me, and to Jim, and everyone," she said to AnnaMarie, sounding like herself once more. "But it's better if we never see him again." She drew herself up and let the anger back into her voice. "And I *never* rolled him aboard the *Southern Echo*."

The gunner snorted. She held Rori's stare for another long moment, thoughts churning visibly behind her eyes, but turned and stomped back to the bow without another word.

Rori gave a defeated sigh as she watched Blueshore go.

Eric came forward and gently put his hands on her shoulders, resting them more firmly when she did not shy away.

"It's all right," the elegant Darkbend murmured as he turned her around. Then he yelped as Luken came ripping back to Rori, sinking his small but sharp talons into Eric's hand. "Damn it, Luken!" Eric spat.

"I'm sorry," Rori said, moving to catch Eric's hand, but he waved her off.

"It's fine." He shook the pain from his hand and tilted his head away from the bow. "Come on, let's you and

I go see what the captain's plans are for our first day back on the Nest." He led her away, shooting a final glare of annoyance at AnnaMarie's back as they went.

Nate slumped against the foremast and ran a hand through his hair, feeling the grit of salt beneath his fingers. "She shouldn't have spoken to Rori like that," he said, "but part of me agrees with Blueshore. What Xander did..."

He did not have the words to finish the thought.

Marcus grunted. "Well, whatever we think, we can't do anything if he's not here." He was quiet for a moment. "I still want to know why *no one* is here, though."

Nate looked at the three other ships anchored in the harbor, finally seeing their details now that the *Southern Echo* had sailed closer. They all bobbed lonely on the water, too much space around them. Nate frowned as he parsed them out.

Two of the ships were nimble pirate vessels, flying the black flags of the *Good Fortune* and the *Screaming Unicorn*. The last was a strange craft, large and stately and painted in the bold colors of a Solkyrian merchant. But instead of the blue-and-gold sun flag of the empire, the ship flew black flags with circular web patterns off of every possible pole, stick, and mast.

"Have you seen that one before?" Nate asked Marcus.

The stout Darkbend nodded. "It's one of Spider's." He pointed at the many flags waving in the wind. "They run up as many of those as they can when they come back to the Nest. That way, no one can say they didn't know what it was when they tried to attack it."

Nate watched the flags for a moment before letting his gaze slide to the empty beach. "And what about that?" he asked, nodding to the much larger flag that hung suspended between two poles staked into the sand, positioned to show the emblem to every ship that came into the harbor.

Marcus eyed the giant black flag. It bore the same circular webbing pattern as the smaller flags on Spider's ship, but this one had a red spider sitting in the middle of its web.

"Don't know," he finally said, the words oddly faint. "I've never seen that before."

Nate frowned when he saw Marcus rubbing his head. "Are you all right?"

Marcus started to nod, but winced. "Just got a headache out of nowhere," he said. "Think I'll be all right once I'm on solid land and get some proper food in me."

"You're going to have to hold off on that," the gruff voice of the boatswain informed him.

Nate and Marcus both turned to see Novachak standing just behind them, his icy eyes narrowed as he stared at the flag on the beach.

"Why?" Nate asked. "What does that flag mean?"

"Nothing good," Novachak answered unhelpfully. His gaze flicked over the empty island and the quiet harbor, and he reached up to absently scratch at his white beard. "Suffice to say, this changes a few things." He turned and stalked off.

Nate watched him go. "You'd think the officers would realize that being intentionally vague only pushes us into deeper trouble," he remarked.

Marcus grunted. "Follow him?"

"Follow him," Nate agreed.

They didn't have to go far. Novachak cut a straight line across the ship to the mainmast, where the captain and quartermaster stood. A small group had gathered around them, including Eric and Rori, and they were all listening raptly as Dax spoke.

"Spider is flying his distress flag on the beach," the quartermaster informed the growing crowd. "Until we know why, no one but the captain and her escort are going ashore."

A few voices rose in protest, but Arani held up her hand.

"I assure you, we won't be there for pleasure." She shifted the bundle of cloth held under her arm, drawing everyone's attention to it. "I need to see what Spider wants, but my priority is to sell the horn and get you all paid. We'll determine what to do from there, whether that's turning you all loose on the Nest—" she cast a narrow glance at the island, "—or restocking and heading east as soon as we can. For now, stay here, until we know what our options are."

The protesting voices fell back to soft murmurs.

Satisfied, Arani began to pick out her escort. "Mr. Redpool, if you are up to the task, I could use your muscle at my back."

The gunner perked up at his name and nodded.

Arani's eyes skipped across the ship, finally alighting on the bow. "Miss Blueshore," she called, "will you come too?"

AnnaMarie did not immediately turn around. The moment stretched just long enough for Nate to exchange a worried glance with Eric. Then Blueshore straightened up and faced Arani. "Of course, Captain."

Arani eyed the other woman, but finally gave a slow nod. "And Mr. Novachak," she continued, "you and I will—"

"No," the boatswain said. He reddened under his perpetual sunburn as everyone turned to look at him. "Begging your pardon, Captain," he said, "but with the crowd as sparse as it is today, a certain someone is bound to pick me out immediately."

Nate blinked, seeing his own bewilderment echoed in Marcus's expression.

Arani, however, was distinctly unimpressed. "This

feud you have with the madame is becoming more and more of a problem," she remarked.

Novachak tilted his head in a solemn nod. "That's why the next time I set foot on that island, I'll do it with a bag of gold bursting at the seams in one hand and my hat in the other."

Arani snorted. "Poetic." She turned to the quartermaster. "Do you have any objections to coming, since the boatswain will be remaining on the ship?"

Dax considered the quiet island. "I will go."

Arani hefted the wrapped drinking horn from the Vanishing Island and led her small shore party to one of the rowboats. When she stepped passed Nate, he felt a muted thrum of power ripple out from the concealed horn, and it was easy to remember how that godly artifact had gleamed under the red sky of the Rend.

He shuddered as he turned away.

None of them knew what power the drinking horn truly held, but no one had been keen to test it. It had come from the gods, yes, but after experiencing firsthand what those gods would do for their own amusement, Nate did not think that anyone from the *Southern Echo* would be sorry to see the relic sold.

He just hoped that it would be enough to start to heal some of the wounds they'd all gotten in exchange for it. His gaze caught on AnnaMarie, and he knew it wouldn't be.

As Nate moved to assist the riggers with the final adjustments to the sails before the ship fully settled in the harbor, he felt the wind play across his skin, bringing the tastes and shadows of the west with it. There were no traces of magic spilling out from a tear in the sky, but there were no wind shadows cast by a ship sailing towards Spider's Nest, either.

That did not mean that Nate could not find one,

however. He was starting to think that he should try, if for no other reason than to make sure everyone was ready for the *Dragonsbane* when it came into port.

And maybe to keep trouble from breaking out among those who actually were ready to see Xander again, but now needed somewhere else to push their anger.

CHAPTER TWO

Spider's Plea

DAX COULDN'T FAULT NIKOLAI for remaining on the ship. He himself had done as much when the island had been too full of life, the beaches packed with Nest inhabitants and visiting pirates alike. That had been largely due to his magic, however, and that felt a bit more justifiable than a personal issue with the madame of the island's pleasure house.

Although, given that Silverdale was the madame in question, that was a bigger problem than it seemed on its surface.

As the rowboat skimmed over the waves, Dax doubted that a single bag of gold was going to be enough to forgive Nikolai's debt. He wasn't sure how much Spider would pay for the drinking horn, but he hoped Nikolai's share would be enough to placate Silverdale. If not, maybe he and Iris could add in a bit from their shares. They'd both offered as much several times in the past, although Nikolai had always insisted that his debts were his alone to pay.

Dax just wished he'd settle them sooner rather than later, particularly when it came to his willingness to go ashore on Spider's Nest.

Even with the emptiness of the island, Dax reluctantly swung himself out of the rowboat and into the cold surf, helping the two gunners push the rowboat up on to dry sand. He'd never liked Spider's Nest all that much, preferring the quiet freedom of the *Southern Echo* and the open ocean to the sweating, drinking crowds on the beaches, in the tavern, on the streets, in the pleasure house, everywhere he turned. But now, with only a scattering of vendors set up on the beach and even fewer people wandering around to look at their offerings, there was a stillness to the Nest that sent a shiver up Dax's spine.

The sooner they sold the horn to Spider and got off the island, the better.

He knew that, but Dax still felt a pang of guilt at the thought of treating a relic from the gods like any ordinary haul taken from any ordinary merchant ship.

For a moment, Dax's gaze settled on the bundle under Iris's arm. A light pulse seemed to emanate from there, raw power making itself known, and Dax closed off the channels of his magic before it could overwhelm him.

Iris led the way from the beach to the little town where Spider had his office. He conducted his business on the upper floor of a two-story building, the lower level of which was dedicated to the tavern where everyone stopped in for food and drink whenever they came to the Nest. Directly across the dirt road was the pleasure house and the bane of Nikolai's existence. Even that, however, was uncharacteristically quiet, with only a few pleasure workers draped across the porch in an attempt to entice customers inside. Their waves of greeting were halfhearted and brief.

"No music today," Iris noted as they turned up the steps to the tavern.

She was right; every other time Dax had been anywhere near the pleasure house, he'd heard piano notes and slurred voices singing along. Today, it was quiet enough to hear the clucking of a chicken scratching in the dirt a ways up the road.

The interior of the tavern was a little more alive, but there were plenty of empty seats and the few patrons that spoke did so with their heads bent close together and their voices low. No one paid much attention to Iris or Dax as they crossed the room and started up the stairs to the second level.

AnnaMarie Blueshore and Julian Redpool settled in to wait for them at one of the tables. The tavern's server was on them immediately, setting heavy wooden mugs of rum before them. Dax peered down at the two gunners from the second floor as they clacked their mugs together and toasted Jim Greenroot's name, throwing back their drinks in one gulp and waving the server back for more.

Dax frowned, wondering if they should have brought along two of the riggers instead of the gunners, but he wasn't going to stop AnnaMarie and Julian from mourning the loss of their friend. Gods knew they hadn't had the proper chance before this moment.

There was a lot of pain seething underneath the crew after everything that had happened in the Forbidden Sea. Dax, Iris, and Nikolai all knew it, but they had to wait for the right time to let the crew release it, and hope it didn't boil over before that moment came.

The first step was selling the drinking horn, and Dax squared his shoulders as he stepped up behind Iris. She raised her hand and rapped on the door to Spider's office, the sound sharp above the quiet tavern.

For a long moment, nothing happened. Dax was about to suggest that Spider might be elsewhere when there was a scuffling sound from the other side of the door, and then it swung open. An exhausted, disheveled man nearly fell across the threshold into Iris. He caught himself on the doorframe at the last moment and brushed his ragged hair out of his face. Iris swayed back, and Dax blinked in surprise as he recognized Spider.

Spider's eyes widened as he took in Iris and Dax standing before him, and then his face crumpled in pitifully obvious relief. "Thank the gods above," he breathed as he moved aside and gestured them into the room.

Dax traded an alarmed look with Iris, and then stepped inside.

"Well," Iris said as Spider shut the door behind them, "you look terrible."

Dax had to agree. In all the years he'd been coming to the Nest, Dax had never seen Spider look anything less than immaculate. Everything—from his tailored shirts and the rich embroidery on his waistcoats down to the careful shine on his shoes—was calculated to put him in the best position for bargains, bribes, and, on special occasions, blackmail. This unkempt creature before them now was a far cry from the polished man Dax had always had trouble reading with his magic; Spider usually kept his feelings close and his heart under control, although Iris had a knack for drawing out his ire. This time, Spider's pulse had leapt at the sight of them, relief and excitement singing in his blood. That combined with his lack of a biting retort to Iris's observation put Dax even further on edge.

"I was afraid you weren't coming back," Spider said as he slipped behind his desk.

"I knew you'd miss us," Iris replied, "but not so much you'd go to pieces." She quirked a wry smile, but Dax heard the slight edge in her voice.

Spider did not rise to the bait. "I want to hire the *Southern Echo* to find something."

There was a heavy pause while Spider looked expectantly between the two of them.

"That's it?" Iris asked. She moved slowly away from the door, the wrapped drinking horn still bundled under her arm. Dax was surprised Spider had failed to notice it thus far, pulsing as it was with unnerving power.

"Yes," Spider said, "specifically, a missing ship, so your Lowwind will be of particular use here, I think. I know you're adverse to renting out his Skill, but I'm willing to hire the full ship and crew for this job."

Another silence fell, with Dax and Iris both staring at Spider with their mouths open.

Something is very wrong on Spider's Nest, Dax thought.

"I think we need to start over," Iris said after a moment. "We're back from the Rend." She placed the wrapped bundle on Spider's desk, careful not to disturb the fortress of paper stacks and ledgers built across its surface. "And we brought this."

Spider started to speak, but the words died on his tongue as Iris pulled the cloth away to reveal the shining drinking horn. She'd polished it herself until it glowed, and given that it had come from the Vanishing Island, that was not the exaggeration Dax normally would have said it was.

The horn gleamed in the candlelight, drinking in the warmth of the tiny flames and magnifying it back into the world. The dragon etched into the silver rim of the horn almost looked alive in the flickering light, and if Dax did not know better, he'd have thought that the rumble of the sea drifting through the open window of the office was the beginning of a dragon's roar.

Spider let out an awestruck breath. "How did you...?" He reached for the horn, but abruptly froze before spinning around and snapping the window shut. He firmly clicked the lock into place, turned back to the desk, then spun again, ripped the curtains closed, and gave a satisfied nod.

Dax traded a bemused glance with Iris.

"This came from the Rend?" Spider asked, snapping their attention back to him.

"Aye," Iris answered. She moved to take her usual seat in front of Spider's desk.

Dax settled in to watch her match wits with Spider, and to provide a looming presence at her shoulder. It was better when he and Nikolai could both be there to loom, but Dax knew that the tattoos that swept along his skull enhanced his glower. Not that Spider had ever seemed intimidated by either of the two men, although if he'd known that Dax could stop his heart, maybe he would have been. After seeing Spider's reaction to Nate's magic, however, Dax knew he'd made the right choice keeping his own true Skill a secret from the man.

Spider ignored him now as he lifted the horn and reverently balanced it in his hands. "How did you get this?" he asked softly.

"It was a gift from the gods," Iris said. Her voice was flat and bitter as she continued, "Apparently, I amused some of them, and they chose to reward me for it." She watched Spider closely as he handled the drinking horn. "You can feel it, can't you?" she asked after a moment. "That thing is not of this world."

"I believe you," Spider murmured as he lifted the horn higher and peered inside. "A new treasure from the Vanishing Island... What does it do?"

Iris shrugged. "I don't know, and honestly, I don't care. I've had enough of the gods and their toys for one lifetime. Let the poor fool who wants to buy it worry about whatever blessing or curse it's carrying."

Spider made a disappointed noise, but wonder and greed danced in his eyes, and Dax felt some of his own tension ease.

For once, this was going to be easy.

Iris leaned back in her seat, a genuine smile touching the corners of her lips. "I'd say that's worth at least as much as the gold the *Dragonsbane* brought back."

It took a moment for Spider to frown. He lowered the horn again and blinked at Iris. "What gold?" he asked.

Iris sighed, but it was Dax who spoke.

"So the *Dragonsbane* hasn't been here yet?"

Spider shook his head.

Dax's mouth twisted into a grimace. He'd been hoping Blackcliff's ship had already come and gone, eliminating the possibility of the two crews clashing in the future. He shared the angry pain that Xander's betrayal had spiked across the *Southern Echo*, but if Iris's pirates ever reunited with Blackcliff's, the world was going to turn red again, this time with blood. Dax didn't want to lose anyone else to that awful feud.

"When Blackcliff returns," Iris said, "he's going to have a hoard of gold that's going to make your head spin. I know you don't have much of a conscience, but I'm going to appeal to what little you do possess and ask you not to trade with him."

Spider gazed at her blankly. "I hardly think a prize from the Gemheart Islands is going to dazzle me."

Confusion rolled over Iris. "The Gemhearts?"

Spider nodded, but his words were slow with wariness. "Last I spoke with him, he was heading north to intercept a fur trader from the Gemheart Islands. He bought that information from me himself."

"Well, he certainly didn't use it," Iris spat, acid in her voice. "He followed us into the Forbidden Sea."

"You're joking," Spider said. He placed the horn back on top of the stack of papers, looking from her to Dax and back again. His expression darkened as he met their frank stares. "You're *not* joking."

Iris flicked a questioning glance up to Dax. In response, Dax reached for his Skill, easing open the channels of his magic. Iris's heartbeat flooded into him, steady and strong, and then came Spider's, ticked into agitated quickness. Dax slammed the channels closed before anything else could brush against his magic.

He gave Iris the smallest shake of his head. Spider's armor-like calmness had been worn away to nothing under his exhaustion, and it had been easy to read him this time; the man wasn't lying.

Iris braced her elbows on the thin arms of her chair and steepled her fingers in front of her chin as she returned her attention to Spider. "I suppose you haven't heard, then, that Xander Grayvoice betrayed my crew, murdered one of our gunners, kidnapped our navigator, and threw himself in with Blackcliff's lot."

Spider sat down heavily. "Gods below," he swore. He swiped his messy hair back from his forehead. "I swear on my mother's spirit, I had nothing to do with that."

"I'm not convinced you wouldn't sell your mother's spirit if it would net you a profit," Iris growled, "but I know you didn't have a hand in this. It was an arrangement made between Xander and Blackcliff, plain and simple."

Spider gave his head a slow, wondering shake. "To think he followed you into the Forbidden Sea..." He was silent for a moment before sitting up with a frown, some of his old vigor returning. "And he had *gold* on his ship? *Godly* gold?"

Iris rolled her eyes. "I can see I've lost your sympathy."

Spider waved away the comment. "I'm simply surprised he did not come back here with a haul like that."

"He's likely on his way," Iris remarked dryly, "and I'm

sure you'll welcome him as a hero when his ship finally does slink back into your harbor."

"Whatever he did to the *Southern Echo*," Spider said firmly, "it was outside of my waters."

"But your island *is* where Xander's alliance with Blackcliff started," Dax put in.

Spider spread his hands in a placating gesture that was anything but. "I can't stop people from talking to each other. If they act, then I can step in, which is exactly what I did when I banished the *Gryphon* and cut their flag. I can't and I won't do the same to the *Dragonsbane*, but I promise you, I haven't had anything to do with that ship since it left a little over a month ago." His frown deepened. "Hold on, how did you get from here to the Vanishing Island and back again so fast? It can't possibly be that close."

"The realm of the gods doesn't play by the rules of the mortal world," Iris said.

Spider tilted his head.

"Magic," Dax clarified.

"Of course," Spider said in a tone that suggested he did not agree in the slightest, but was not in a position to argue. "Well, regardless of what Blackcliff did, his ship isn't the only one that's failed to make an appearance. I trust you've noticed how empty my harbor is?"

"It was hard to miss," Iris said.

Spider gave a grim nod. "Some of my scouts and more than a few of my intel ships have failed to report back to the Nest. The latest one was due back two weeks ago. The last time something like this happened, it was because of a bad storm stalled over the Gemheart Islands, but that only caught a couple of ships, not as many as this. And that was before..."

He swallowed uneasily, then cleared his throat.

"You two know firsthand that the imperial navy has been more active lately, and patrolling farther south.

I'd like to believe that Solkyria is merely shoring up its defenses against Vothein. Their ships have been creeping into the Common Sea, from what little I've heard."

Iris leaned forward with interest. "So the war is turning against Solkyria?"

"It seems to be," Spider agreed, "but I'm concerned that my missing ships could be the work of Prince Trystos's pirate hunters."

Iris sat back, stunned, and Dax marveled that she had not reflexively drawn her saber in response to those words.

"I'm not quite sure what you expect me to do with that information," she said. "Both of those are excellent reasons for me to take my ship and my crew east, before either comes to a head."

"I certainly could not stop you," Spider said wearily.

Dax felt another pause start to rise, but he did not like the calm assurance in Spider's eyes despite his distress over his missing ships. "But?" Dax prompted, ready for the trap to spring.

"But you won't be able to pay your crew or resupply." Spider held up a hand as Iris opened her mouth. "My charitable restocking of the *Southern Echo* has reached its limit. If you want more from me, you're going to have to buy it."

Wordlessly, Iris gestured to the drinking horn still resting in all its godly splendor on Spider's desk.

The man shook his head. "I can't pay you for that right now, unless you're willing to forgo the difference between its worth and one ship's worth of supplies."

A sinking feeling opened in Dax's gut, even as Iris leaned forward to head off the trouble. "Why is it, exactly, that you can't pay for this horn? Gods know you've amassed a fortune from all your operations across the Nest."

Spider gave her a bland twist of a smile. "Most of that fortune has gone into keeping this island alive and safe for you all. The rest went to every willing captain and their crews to find out what's happening to my ships. I'm prepared to do the same for you if you'll join them, Captain Arani."

"Small problem there," Iris said. "I'm not willing to do that, and after everything my crew has just been through, they don't deserve to be thrown back out to sea with nothing to show for their sacrifice." She glanced up at Dax for confirmation, which he gave with a terse nod. "If it's all the same to you," she said as she turned back to Spider, "I'd rather you pay us for the horn and we say goodbye for good."

But Spider was shaking his head again. "I can't. I don't have the money. I can hire you to go out there and learn what you can about my ships, but I can't afford a relic from the gods until some of those ships come back." His gaze touched the drinking horn again, and he sighed. "Either you take my offer so you can pay your crew something, or you take that horn and go with nothing more than what you already have in your hold."

Iris shifted her hand to the hilt of her saber. Dax's magic stirred with the rise of pulsing anger in the room, but he held the channels shut and stepped in before Iris could act.

"You'd pay us for this voyage regardless of whether we found anything or not?" he asked.

Iris looked at him sharply, but he kept his gaze trained on Spider, who nodded.

"Advance payment of one half of the total promised sum," Spider agreed. "The rest given upon your return, regardless of what you return with." He paused delicately. "Less the cost of restocking the *Southern Echo*, of course," he added.

"Of course," Dax said flatly. "I'm only surprised you've offered to pay us at all, instead of holding the agreement over our heads."

Before anyone could conduct business through Spider or on the Nest, they had to sign a contract with Spider pledging to follow the few laws the island had, and to defend the island alongside the other captains if the need ever arose.

The large black flag staked into the beach had suggested that the need had finally come, but Spider only shrugged. "I'm not an unreasonable man. I know this is a bit beyond the purview of 'defend the Nest,' as it were." Then he smiled, and this time, it was closer to its usual slimy caliber. "I also know that the best motivator for pirates is money, and the promise of more if and when they return."

"You know something interesting?" Iris said calmly. "Sometimes, when I'm having trouble sleeping, I imagine punching you in the face. After that, I drift right off."

"Charming," Spider said. "At any rate, that's the only offer I have for you right now. If you take it, I will pay you, and I'll only send you as far as the Gemheart Islands. I've got a couple others scouting up that way, but I want the *Southern Echo* up there, too."

"You mean you want Nate up there," Iris said, "and his wind reading Skill."

Spider gave her a frank nod.

Iris gave him a heavy sigh. "I need time to think on this."

"You can have until sundown today," Spider said. "I need your answer by then, and the *Southern Echo* ready to sail on the morning tide."

This time, Dax's anger rose alongside Iris's.

"Absolutely not," Iris snapped as Dax barked out, "Are you mad?"

They both began to snarl more, but Spider suddenly slammed his hand on his desk and yelled, "I need you!"

Iris and Dax both eyed him warily, anger still racing through their blood, but they closed their mouths and waited as Spider brushed his disheveled hair back once again and straightened the collar of his shirt.

"Captain Arani," he said, "you have led your crew to find the impossible." He gestured from the drinking horn to the chain Iris wore around her neck, the one that held the black dragon scales. "You've done it twice. I'm only asking you now to see what else you can find, even if it's nothing. Gods above, I hope it's nothing, because if it is something, we are all running out of time." He lifted his head and gazed directly into Iris's eyes. "Please."

Iris did not answer. Instead, she looked to Dax. He saw his own reluctance reflected back in her gaze, along with the knowledge that they both shared and understood; they owed it to the crew to put it to a vote.

"The crew needs more than half a day to rest," Dax said, as much to Iris as Spider, although he looked at the man as he said it.

Spider tapped a finger on his desk. "I can give you the rest of today, and tomorrow morning. You'll sail on the afternoon tide."

"That's not enough time," Dax said.

"It's not," Spider agreed, "but it's the best I can do." He stood up, prompting Iris to do the same. "I will still need your answer by sundown today."

Iris gave another tired sigh. "You'll have it." She moved to wrap up the drinking horn, but Spider made a soft noise of protest.

"That should stay with me."

Iris reached for her saber again, and Dax made no move to stop her.

"Just until you've decided if you're going or not,"

Spider added with exasperated quickness. "I can lock it up and keep it safe for you, and I'll hand it back the moment you tell me you are not going to act in defense of the Nest, should that moment come at all."

Iris hesitated.

"I can also start looking for a buyer, if my ships come back ahead of you," he pressed, "maybe even learn something about what this relic can do. Either way, would you rather leave it here, or take it with you to the Gemhearts?"

"Bold of you to assume we're going," Dax said, but he knew how this would end.

If there was anyone they could entrust the horn to, whether a few hours or a few weeks, it was Spider. There were few things in the world that the man held sacred, but business was one of them.

Iris let go of her sword. "I'll speak with my crew," she said. "You'll have your answer well before sundown."

Spider nodded, and Dax was shocked to see that his gratitude was genuine. "Fair winds, Captain Arani," he said, and lifted his hand in farewell as Dax and Iris took their leave.

The drinking horn gleamed on his desk, brighter than anything else in the room.

CHAPTER THREE
Rest and Reparations

NATE'S ATTENTION WAS DIVIDED between the winds playing off the sea and the cards in his hands, his thoughts swirling around the altercation between Rori and AnnaMarie. The gunner had been right when she'd said that Xander had hurt people other than Rori, and that pain had left a crack in their lives as wide and deep as a chasm.

We just came back together, Nate thought tiredly. *Are we really about to break apart again?*

He was fairly certain that the answer was yes, regardless of his own feelings on the matter.

What was worse, he feared that the longer Anna-Marie and others like her went without justice for Jim Greenroot's death, the deeper the schism would grow. Rori, he knew, would not want to hunt the *Dragonsbane*, and it wouldn't be long before fights like the one between her and the gunner broke out among others.

Nate desperately hoped that Arani had gotten the *Southern Echo*'s weight in gold in exchange for the drinking horn; maybe that would patch the divide long enough for it to begin to heal.

Anything would be better than sitting on the ship, trying and failing to distract themselves with games while they waited for the captain to return.

For his part, Nate had been cajoled into a game of Liar's Farm alongside Marcus. Rori, still troubled but not wanting to be alone, had elected to watch rather than play, and that meant that Eric was handily thrashing Marcus and Nate in the game. The elegant Darkbend was about to claim an embarrassingly quick victory in their third round when the call came from the lookout. Nate and Marcus abandoned their cards immediately, sending the painted images of a few chickens and a sea leviathan scattering across the played field of cards.

"This is why neither of you ever win," Eric chided them as they bolted to the railing. "No self-control!"

Nate ignored him in favor of watching the rowboat steadily making its way back to the *Southern Echo*'s side. Dax hailed the ship as it drew closer, but Captain Arani was oddly silent, her gaze locked in a downcast frown at the floor of the boat.

Marcus knocked his shoulder against Nate's. "Captain doesn't look happy."

"No," Nate agreed. "She doesn't."

His heart twisted as he wondered if Spider had not believed the story of their voyage into the Rend and the origin of the drinking horn, but it was impossible to look at that artifact and not believe that it had been crafted by something other than mortal hands. Maybe Spider was a better negotiator than Arani had thought, and he'd taken the horn at a bargain price. Nate hoped not. No one was going to be able to lose themselves in the offerings of Spider's Nest with a meager payout, but he consoled himself with the thought that as long as Arani had sold the horn, something would be infinitely better than nothing, and would give them time to figure out their next move.

"What are we going to do if she couldn't sell it?" Nate murmured to the stout Darkbend.

Marcus made a low noise in the back of his throat, something between a grunt and a growl. "The gunners are all hungry for vengeance. The way Blueshore was talking, I don't know if we'll survive another setback."

Nate turned that idea over, and found it unpleasant all the way around. "I could offer to try to find the *Dragonsbane*. It can't be too far from us now. Maybe Arani would entertain a proposal for a formal hunt over going east." He kept his voice down so no one but Marcus could hear him even as more people jostled at the railings to watch the rowboat crawl back to the *Southern Echo*. "What do you think?"

Marcus made that strange noise again. "It would satisfy the gunners. Probably some others, too." He draped his arms over the railing and squinted up at the sky. "But Rori wouldn't like it, and neither would Eric."

Nate let his breath out in a frustrated huff and raked his hands through his hair. "There has to be an answer to all of this."

Marcus was quiet for a long minute. "I think that no matter what happens next, someone is going to get hurt."

Nate did not have a response, but he knew that he wasn't ready to accept that.

But when Captain Arani climbed back aboard the *Southern Echo*, there was suddenly another matter to contend with when she summoned Nate and Rori to the stern of the ship. The captain led them up to the poop deck, where they could speak without being overheard.

"I hate that I need to ask this of you," she said when they were alone, "but there's something going on that your magic would give us an advantage with."

Rori drew back immediately.

Nate almost reached for her, but stopped himself when he remembered the way she'd flinched at his earlier touch. He did not think it would be welcome now.

"What's happening?" he asked, focusing his attention on Arani instead.

The captain took a few reluctant moments to frame her words. "Your wind reading could help us find a ship for Spider," she said. "If you're willing."

Nate waited, but the captain said nothing more. He blinked in surprise. "That's it?"

Arani nodded and turned to Rori. "As for you—"

"No," Rori said.

Arani spread her hands in a soothing gesture. "I'm not asking you to do anything right now, and I may not ask for anything at all," she said. "I only wanted to warn you that there may come a time when your magic could help the *Southern Echo* escape a pursuer. I wanted to ask if you would be willing to use your Skill then, if it comes to that. But if you're not, simply say the word, and I swear on the *Southern Echo*, I will not look to you."

Rori shifted warily, as though parsing out a trap. "Are you asking me to sink a ship?"

"No," Arani said firmly. "We have cannons for that. I'd only ask you to use your Skill to quicken the currents and get the *Southern Echo* to safety."

Rori bit her lip.

Nate couldn't bear to watch her squirm under Arani's scrutiny and he spoke to draw the captain's attention back to himself. "How far out would I have to range?" he asked.

Rori cut back in. "Really?" she demanded. "Just like that?" There was a hard undercurrent to her tone, but her voice was fully her own in that moment. No trace of a god or otherworldly force trying to speak through her.

Nate turned to face her, careful to keep his expression neutral. "It's my magic, Rori," he said, gentle but firm. "My choice." He returned his gaze to the captain.

"Although, I would prefer not to reenact the dragon hunt," he said, recalling how he'd nearly lost himself in the winds on that voyage.

Arani winced at the reminder. "Not nearly as far as that," she promised. "I won't ask that of you ever again."

She'd proven as much when she'd traded the dragon and her chance at Mordanti's treasure for Nate's life, and he nodded now, believing her earnestness. He also liked the idea of looking for something other than the *Dragonsbane* in the wind, although he supposed there was no reason he couldn't do both. Either way, he was more than willing to use his Skill to help the crew.

When he told Arani as much, her mouth gave a small twist. "In truth, you'd be helping Spider much more than the *Southern Echo*, but if you can sense ships on the wind before they have the chance to spot us, that actually would go a long way towards keeping us safe." She tilted her head to Rori. "And it would mean we may not need Rori's Skill at all, if we can avoid danger."

"Is that even possible?" Rori asked hotly. "Avoiding danger?"

Arani sighed, her hand dropping to rest on the hilt of the saber at her hip. "I'd be a fool to believe it, but I'm certainly going to try."

Rori traded a glance with Nate, and he offered her a small shrug in response. She worried her lip between her teeth before turning back to the captain. "If I say yes, and I start to use my Skill and... something happens..." She trailed off, her gaze darting to the sea.

Nate knew that she was thinking of the *Godfall* again, of something else telling her to use her magic to drown that crew. He didn't stop himself this time when he gently laid a hand on Rori's arm. She jumped a little, and Luken gave a warning squawk from her other side, but she relaxed into his touch and did not pull away.

Nate rubbed her shoulder blade and felt the trembling rhythm of her breath beneath his hand.

"Look at me, Rori," Arani said firmly. She waited until she had the navigator's full attention once more. "I know you, and I know that you would never do anything to hurt this ship, or anyone who sails her. I'm not going to force this on you. If you decide to use your magic, but then need to stop for any reason, even if we're caught in the middle of an imperial blockade, then you stop. It's your Skill, and yours alone."

Rori shuddered, her eyes bright, but she nodded. "I'll consider it," she said softly.

"That's all I can ask of you now," Captain Arani said. She reached out and placed a hand on each of their shoulders. "Thank you, both of you." She drew in a steadying breath before releasing them. "Now I need to break the bad news to everyone, and see which way the crew votes."

"Bad news?" Nate repeated, uneasiness stealing into his voice.

She nodded and beckoned them to the stairs. "I'm telling everyone together, right now. I don't have it in me to say this twice."

"Spider did not buy the horn," Arani said bluntly, standing on the quarterdeck with Dax and Novachak at her sides. The words sounded bitter in her mouth, as though she could not spit them out fast enough. "He could not afford it."

Down on the main deck, Nate felt as though the breath had been knocked out of him.

"That man runs the island," Theo Yellowwood called out. "His entire game is money. How much did you ask that he couldn't afford it?"

Captain Arani shook her head. "We never got to negotiations," she said.

"Where is it, then?" Esmerelda Durmanti asked.

"With Spider," Arani said, spreading her empty hands wide.

More voices rose, and the captain looked to the quartermaster for support.

"Spider has sunk all his resources into finding out what's happened to his scouts and spies," Dax boomed out, his deep voice carrying to every corner of the deck. "He can't buy the horn just yet, but he can afford to hire us to do the same. The captain and I agreed to leave the horn with him until we know if we'll be accepting or declining that offer."

There was a brief pause while the crew murmured among themselves. Nate tried to listen, but he was still reeling from the news and couldn't focus on any one thread of conversation.

So much hinged on the sale of the drinking horn. What were they going to do if they couldn't get any money for their last voyage into hell?

"What does he want us to do?" one of the gunners called.

"Scout around the Gemheart Islands," Arani answered. She hesitated, as though the next words pained her to say. "He's promised us half of the payment upfront, and the rest on our return, whether we've found anything or not."

The mood of the crew immediately lifted.

"That's easy money," Nate heard someone murmur, and soft agreements began to rise.

Arani held up her hand until the deck was quiet once more. "I need you all to remember that the Solkyrian navy has been more active lately, and the Gemheart Islands are firmly under the empire's control. Going there means we'll likely cross paths with a navy ship, probably one much bigger and a lot more heavily armed than the frigate that ambushed us on our way out of the doldrums."

Nate grimaced as he realized what Arani had been asking him to look for in the winds, and why she'd warned Rori that they might need her magic to escape. Gods above and below all knew that Nate wouldn't be able to do anything if a navy ship spotted them.

He remembered the desperate fight between the *Southern Echo* pirates and the navy sailors after the dragon hunt, and how the imperial Highwinds had pulled the wind out of the *Southern Echo*'s sails to leave her dead in the water. The pirate ship had only escaped because Nate had jumped over to the naval frigate and thrown himself—quite literally—against the two superior wind workers. He'd do it again if he had to, but he doubted that trick would work twice. Especially not after the way it had humiliated Nate's brother Sebastian.

Nate could not imagine that his last interaction with his brother had done anything to endear him to his older sibling. If anything, his escape from the navy ship likely would have led to trouble for Sebastian. Nate felt a stab of guilt at the realization, sharp despite all of the lost love between him and his brother, or maybe because of it. He did not regret his choices, but Nate knew that if he ever met Sebastian again, his brother would be out for blood, and maybe not just Nate's.

Arani's voice pulled him out of his thoughts. "What's more," she continued, "Spider is only giving us a day's rest. If we take on his assignment, we sail tomorrow afternoon."

She waited expectantly, but the groans of displeasure were muted compared to what they'd been a few moments earlier.

"But he'll pay us?" one of the swabs asked.

Arani gave a halting nod.

"What happens to the horn if we go?" Rori called out.

The captain lifted one shoulder. "If Spider's ships come in while we're away, he'll look for a buyer. If not, we take it with us the next time we leave."

Thoughtful murmurs rose in the wake of those words, but Nate saw Rori shake her head and mutter something to Liliana that earned a dark scowl from the rigger.

Captain Arani spoke again before more voices could ring out.

"My thoughts on the matter," she said, her expression solemn, "are that we should leave now, and sail east. I know you all have been waiting for long overdue payments, but what Spider is offering is a fraction of what we should get for the horn, and—"

"At least he'll pay us!" one of the gunners shouted, and gruff voices began to rise across the ship.

"And I'll pay you so much more as soon as we sell this horn," Arani shot back before the momentum could build. "Have I ever kept your shares from you before?"

Nate expected to hear reluctant murmurs of agreement, but agreement all the same. Instead, AnnaMarie Blueshore stepped forward.

"A fair share of nothing is still nothing, Captain," the gunner said. Her voice was flat and without any of her earlier anger, but it carried across the deck and commanded everyone's attention just as easily as Arani's. "After what we've been through and what we've lost, we deserve better than that."

Arani stiffened, but she kept her gaze soft and her voice level. "Of course you do," she said. "I swear on everything I hold dear, I'm going to get you what you deserve."

"We know you believe that," AnnaMarie said, "but we don't know who will want to buy that horn in the east, if anyone. We don't know what's out there waiting for us. We've gone with you twice now on that kind of voyage, and all we have to show for it are empty pockets and emptier hammocks where our dead mates used to sleep." The gunner took another step forward, broad shoulders squared and her face tipped up fearlessly at the three officers on the quarterdeck. Her hand was not on the hilt of her cutlass, but her next words cut deeper than the blade ever could. "You tell us that we have the chance for payment now, and the promise of more when we return. Do you stand between us and that?"

Nate felt the collective intake of breath against the light breeze playing across the deck. In the silence that followed, the rigging swayed and creaked gently overhead, and the entire crew waited to see how Captain Arani would respond to the gunner's challenge.

For a moment, it looked as though the captain was going to draw her sword and answer Blueshore's words with steel. Arani's jaw worked beneath her skin as she swept her gaze across the crew, taking in the way AnnaMarie's gun crew had shored up behind their leader. Nate felt the tension turn brittle, and he worried that its broken edges would be sharp enough to spill blood.

Then Captain Arani sighed, quiet but heavy, and said, "No. I am not going to stand between you and Spider's offer. This will go to a vote."

Nate felt the soft rush of released breaths around him as easily as he heard the sounds of relief. What caught his eye, however, was the way Dax visibly relaxed and released the hilt of his own cutlass. He'd been ready to jump in and defend the captain against an uprising.

Given the dissent that had festered on the voyage into the Forbidden Sea, Nate wasn't surprised, but between Arani's ferocious abilities with a sword and Dax's blood working Skill, that would have been a terrifying fight. Thankfully, Nate did not have time to draw an image of that massacre in his mind as the quartermaster was already moving down the stairs, calling for everyone to form up around him in a loose ring. The crew moved, and Nate settled in next to Marcus and Eric.

When Dax had reached the center of the rough circle, he cast a steady gaze at the crew and turned slowly as he spoke. "We're here to vote on whether or not we accept Spider's offer to hire us to scout the Gemheart Islands and bring back whatever information we can about his missing ships. Hands up to cast your vote. You may abstain if you so choose." He raised his right hand and balled it into a fist. "Those in favor?"

Hands went up around Nate, some high and proud, others low and less certain, but it was obvious how this vote would carry. Among the raised hands, Nate counted AnnaMarie and her gun crew, along with all of the riggers, the cook, the swabs, and many more. Even Eric had his hand up, although his was halfheartedly raised and his expression was troubled.

Nate's hand flexed, but he did not lift it.

It took Dax a moment to count the aye votes, and the hands stayed up for as long as the quartermaster held his fist in the air. When he finally lowered it, the hands went down, and though it was unnecessary, his voice rang out again to call for those against.

Much, much fewer hands went up this time, Rori's chief among them. Nate's own hand jerked at his side when he saw hers in the air, but he still kept it down, choosing to abstain along with a couple of others. He had no idea what the right decision was. He did not like the idea of potentially running across the navy again and knew that going to the Gemheart Islands would be dangerous, but the thought of going east now, when the crew was unhappier than ever and the *Dragonsbane* and its hull full of enemies was still somewhere in the wind, made his stomach churn. He had the feeling AnnaMarie had voted for Spider's mission to keep them in the Common Sea, where at least they had a chance at finding Blackcliff and Xander again.

Dax counted the nay votes much faster than the ayes, and then turned to Arani with a sense of formality that seemed both unnecessary and completely appropriate at the same time. "The ayes have the majority, Captain. The crew votes in favor of accepting Spider's offer."

The captain was gripping the railing of the quarterdeck, as though that small part of her beloved ship was the only thing that could ground her in the world. She noticeably deflated as she nodded. "Then accept it we shall. Prepare the rowboats for the return to shore, if you please. All are welcome to disembark this time."

The voices of the crew rose as attentions turned to the boats and the island that awaited them, so Nate did not hear if the captain said anything else, but he thought that he saw her mouth shape the words, *Gods above protect us all.*

True to his word, Spider paid upfront. It was not a grand sum, especially after being divided among the crew, but smiles were coming more easily now that everyone had coins in their pockets and the freedom to spend them. Granted, those coins were mostly copper, so that freedom was more limited than they would have liked. If it had been up to Spider, however, they would have loaded up the *Southern Echo* and set sail for the Gemheart Islands immediately.

The full day's rest Arani had brokered wasn't much, but it was more than what the crew had seen in a long time, and it pacified them for the time being.

The moment their boots touched the shore, the crew splintered under the late afternoon sun. Captain Arani grabbed Novachak by the arm and marched him towards town, telling the boatswain in no uncertain terms that it was time he started making good on his debt to Madame Silverdale now that they were guaranteed to return to Spider's Nest at least once more. He resisted, looking all kinds of panicked, but the captain won that battle. Dax looked after them with fond amusement, but elected to stay with the ship to prepare the *Southern Echo* for her next voyage and hear any further grievances from anyone who wished to air them. The rest of the crew took their money and ran for their favorite spots on the island. For Nate's friends, though, that proved to be a difficult decision.

The journey into the Forbidden Sea had been far shorter than they'd expected, but they had still missed the Dancing Skies Festival by over a week. As the result, much of the traveling festivities were already gone from the Nest. Marcus swore the performers and special vendors had stayed longer in previous years, but the emptiness of the island following Spider's call to action must have convinced them to pack up and leave sooner. Regardless of the reason, the shadow puppet theaters and acrobatic troupe were long gone, the latter of which set Eric at ease.

Marcus tried to tease the taller Darkbend about his previous affair with the obsessive contortionist, but neither of their hearts were in it, and the conversation soon drifted elsewhere, mostly to Eric's surprise that Marcus wasn't suggesting they go to the pleasure house now that they could afford some of the lighter services.

The stout Darkbend shrugged. "Honestly, I thought I'd want to go, too, but I haven't really felt right since the Rend."

"Stomach issues?" Eric asked.

Marcus shook his head. "Something just feels... off. It's hard to explain."

Nate recalled Marcus holding his head on the *Southern Echo* as they'd entered the harbor, and Rori's violent outburst, and Xander pulling her underwater with a sea serpent, and Jim Greenroot's cut throat, and he only came out of the dark spiral when he felt a sharp pain in his palms. He unclenched his hands to see that his fingernails had left tiny red crescents in the flesh, one of which was bleeding. Nate thrust his hands into his pockets and turned to the empty line of the horizon beyond the harbor while his friends continued the debate.

"So if you don't have stomach issues," Rori said, "are we heading for the tavern?"

Marcus made a noncommittal noise. "Maybe later. I'm not hungry right now."

That drew even Nate's eyes to him.

"What?" Marcus asked, frowning at each of them in turn.

"You're always hungry," Eric said. "Your appetite is the one thing we can constantly depend on. If it's gone, the world is probably about to end."

Marcus thought about this for a moment. "I mean, I *could* eat, if it would make you feel better."

Rori huffed a soft, almost-genuine laugh. "You know, I'd actually rather not hole up in the tavern right now." She tipped her face towards the sky and the gentle winter sunlight. "We're not going to see a lot of days like this until the seasons change again."

"Fair enough," Eric said. "Which means there's only one thing we can do." He turned and spread his arms wide, taking in the steady vendors on the beach, the ones who had set up despite the emptiness of the island. "Shopping."

Nate shook his head and turned back to the sea. "I'm good."

"You absolutely are not," Eric said, snatching Nate's arm in an iron grip and yanking him towards a stall with clothes hanging like a proud display of flags. "Your shirts are more patches than cloth at this point, and they smell so bad, rats won't even nest in them."

"It's not *that* bad," Nate protested. He glanced down at his worn clothing. "Is it?"

"Yes," Marcus said, and Rori pointedly did not meet Nate's eye.

Nate stopped resisting as Eric led him to a clothing vendor. Frustration and worry were simmering in his gut, but he had to accept that there was nothing he could do. At least not until the *Southern Echo* was ready to sail again, or something came over the horizon.

He told himself to be patient, but that felt like an ordeal set by a particularly vindictive god at this point.

Marcus and Rori broke away to other stalls that had caught their attention, and Nate halfheartedly submitted to Eric's styling.

Under his friend's critical eye, Nate ended up with a new sturdy pair of trousers and three shirts, one of which was much finer and more expensive than Nate had wanted, but Eric insisted upon. The vendor had been more than happy to sell it, until Eric had turned to the woman with a bright smile and a savage idea about bargaining. Nate had not imagined that such a small person was capable of such loud, vehement swearing, but the vendor had proven him wrong. Eric had let her rage for a few moments, then leaned closer and murmured something that made the vendor's face go pale, and then the woman began thrusting things in to Nate's arms faster than he could get a grip on them. He walked away with all of those clothes for a little more than half of their original price, plus a fine tricornered hat of soft leather, two pairs of shapeless but functional socks, a full set of sewing needles that would be invaluable on the ship, and coins still in his pocket.

By the time all that was done, the *Dragonsbane* had receded to the back of Nate's mind, and he was in genuine awe of the elegant Darkbend.

"How did you do that?" Nate asked as Eric led him to the jewelry stall Marcus had picked out.

"I may have witnessed that particular vendor breaking a special vase in Madame Silverdale's parlor," Eric said. "Nothing to warrant physical punishment, but she would certainly be banned from the pleasure house if the madame ever found out that she was the one who broke it."

Nate blinked. "How long have you been holding that over that poor woman's head so you could get a discount on her wares?"

"Are you suggesting I should have let you pay full price?"

Nate hefted the armful of clothes and pulled his new hat down a little more firmly against his head. "I withdraw the question."

"A wise choice. Marcus, what are you doing with that much agate?"

The stout Darkbend turned as Eric and Nate came up beside him, and Nate saw the piece of green agate he had picked up, large and round as a gold mark.

"I told you," Marcus said, "I haven't really been feeling right." He pressed the agate against his wrist and sighed contentedly. "This helps."

Eric gave the jeweler behind the table a mild look. "And how much are you being charged for that piece?"

"For fresh Solkyrian agate ready to wear," the vendor said, "one silver mark."

Eric opened his mouth to protest.

"Or six coppers, plus the agate the Darkbend's got on him."

Nate's brows rose in surprise. Marcus's agate was considerably smaller than the piece the vendor was looking to trade, and six copper marks made less than half of the silver mark price. Eric looked equally dubious about the offer, his eyes narrowing as he searched for the hidden trap in the vendor's bargain. Before anyone could say anything, however, Marcus had slipped off his hemp bracelet and handed it and the six small coins across the table.

The jeweler smiled as he took Marcus's piece of agate and held it up for Eric and Nate to see. "We don't get rich blue ones like this all that often. It's small, but I can make something special with it."

Eric frowned as he watched Marcus pull the new bracelet around his wrist and tighten the cords. "I can't tell if you just made a good deal or a bad one."

Marcus sighed again as the green agate settled against his skin. "A good one." He set off to find Rori.

Eric gave the little piece of blue agate in the jeweler's hand a lingering look that lasted until Nate nudged his shoulder.

"They're both happy with the trade," Nate pointed out. "That's all they need, right?"

Eric reluctantly turned away from the jeweler. "I'm afraid he's going to regret that. Sometimes, he makes deals without considering the real cost."

Nate watched Marcus take several healthy, steady strides. There was no sign of the Skill sickness coming over the stout Darkbend, so at least the vendor hadn't been lying about the agate being fresh from Solkyria. For reasons no one quite understood, being off of Solkyrian soil caused surges in the magic of the Skilled, leading to dizziness, nausea and vomiting, and sometimes passing out. Nate knew that firsthand. As did everyone else who had been there to witness his first morning aboard the *Southern Echo*, when Nate had tried to take off the gold ring he constantly wore. He still winced with embarrassment whenever he remembered that Marcus had been the unlucky soul the captain had ordered to clean up the mess.

That same ring was still on Nate's right hand, a little dirty and worse for wear, but the Solkyrian sun crest remained irritatingly visible in the metal.

Nate gave the jeweler's table a considering glance, but none of the vendor's offerings were on par with a solid gold ring, and Nate did not have enough money left to outright buy a new piece that could replace the ring as an anchor for his own magic. But there was a thin hemp bracelet with three tiny agate beads on the table, each a varying shade of gray and more like chips of rock than actual jewelry, but they were agate all the same, unmarked by the empire. Nate reached into his pocket and silently counted the coins he had left, then nodded at the bracelet.

"How much for that one?"

The vendor glanced at the piece Nate had indicated, and then at Nate's Skill mark. "That's not going to be enough to anchor you," the man warned.

"I don't want it for that," Nate said.

The jeweler made a thoughtful noise, then shrugged. "Seven copper marks for that one."

Nate snorted. "I'll give you two."

"Five."

"Three."

"Deal."

The coins and the bracelet traded hands, and Nate walked away smiling.

He didn't feel any soothing coolness from the agate beads as he slipped the bracelet on, but their polished surfaces caught the sun as easily as the gold ring, and he felt lighter as he rejoined his friends.

When they found Rori again, she'd traded the silver mark she'd earned as navigator for one thing: a dagger not entirely unlike the one Xander had carried.

Nate burned with questions as he watched her tie the sheath to her belt, and the two Darkbends exchanged a heavy glance, but Rori said nothing, only let her coat fall over the weapon and hide it from view the moment the dagger was secure. She did not speak of it, and Nate and the others did not bring it up again.

By the time they had claimed a spot on the beach to share a good meal and a small bottle of rum they'd bought from the tavern with their pooled remaining funds, the sun was setting.

The liquor burned Nate's throat but settled warm in his belly against the advancing chill of the evening. The sky was burnt gold with no trace of red, and the wind off the sea was calm and heavy with salt. Nate took it all in with a deep, contented sigh as he settled back in the soft sand to watch the stars come out, listening to the steady voices of his friends over the murmur of the surf.

As the wind played across the beach, Nate reached for it without thinking, delving into the clean ribbons of air and searching for the telltale shudder of a shadow. He realized what he was doing a moment later, and pulled his awareness back before his friends could notice.

It amazed Nate how easy it had been to forget about Xander and the *Dragonsbane* for a while, only to slip into action focused around them at the smallest touch of the wind.

He gazed up at the darkening sky and wondered if the rest of the *Southern Echo* crew was having a good evening, if AnnaMarie and the other gunners had let themselves mourn Jim Greenroot, if the riggers had consoled themselves over one of their own turning against them, if Captain Arani could somehow keep them all together once more.

He wondered if he could help.

A inquisitive chirp next to his head pulled Nate out of his thoughts. He looked over to see Luken sitting nearby, eyeing Nate's new hat.

"Absolutely not," Nate said as he sat up. "This one is *mine*, hellspawn."

Luken gave another chirp and flapped back to Rori's side, drawing a laugh from her. It was the first clear, genuine peal of joy Nate had heard from her since the voyage into the Rend.

"There you go," Rori said. "Stand your ground, and he'll learn eventually."

"He's a greedy little thing," Nate noted.

"And water is wet," Rori said as Luken poked his head into her coat pocket and wrestled out one of the dried berries she always carried for him. She gave the bird an exasperated but fond grin as he set to devouring the fruit.

"You do spoil the little thing something fierce," Eric said as he reached for one of the last pieces of smoked meat on the platter resting between them. "And you," he said, turning to Nate before popping the food into his mouth, "had better take good care of that hat. I'd hate to think my hard-won blackmail efforts went to waste."

Nate tipped his hat in salute to the Darkbend, the leather crisp and clean between his fingers. "I'll guard it with my life," he said gravely.

"You'd better," Eric said. "Consider that an early birthday present, whenever that may be."

Nate thought for a moment, trying to make sense of how much time had actually passed since he'd left Solkyria. "How far exactly are we past Dancing Skies?"

Marcus and Eric both shrugged and looked to Rori.

"The last aurora should have been ten days ago," she said.

"Then you're five days late, Eric," Nate said teasingly.

"It's an *extremely early* birthday present," Eric countered, but he turned on his elbow and looked at Nate more fully under the darkening sky. "Shame we missed it. Not that we were in much of a position to celebrate, but still." He passed the rum bottle to Nate. "Happy birthday, Nate."

Marcus and Rori smiled and said the same.

Nate gave them all another salute with the bottle before taking a small sip and handing it back. His head was starting to fuzz around the edges, and that was enough for the night before a voyage.

"How old are you now?" Marcus asked as he took the rum.

"Twenty," Nate said.

"Oh, good," Eric said. "I was worried we'd be in trouble for giving rum to a child."

"I don't look *that* young."

"No, but the empire would have my head for passing liquor to anyone beneath the tender age of sixteen."

"And that's what you're most worried about?" Rori asked. "Not the plundering or living in general defiance of the empire as a pirate?"

"Well, when you put it like that," Eric said thoughtfully, "I'm in a lot of trouble, aren't I?"

This time, Nate joined the others in their laughter.

He looked up at the emerging stars for a moment, words and memories ricocheting inside his chest and demanding to be let out. Nate let them free. "For a while," he said softly, "I didn't think I'd live this long."

Marcus paused with the bottle just touching his lips. "How do you mean?"

Nate waited for the familiar bitterness to wash over him, but to his surprise, it did not come. His voice was steady and even when he spoke again. "I failed my final test at the wind working academy. I was supposed to go to the mines and spend the rest of my life there, which I really did not expect to be very long at all. I had the sealed orders in my pocket the day I met Arani." He nodded to Rori. "I still had them later that night, when I met you and Dax."

There was a soft pause before Rori asked, "What did you do with those orders?"

"I threw them overboard."

"Good," Rori said, and the Darkbends murmured in agreement.

Nate nodded and returned his gaze to the dark horizon. "I've never really been happy about my birthday, since it just marked another year that I'd failed to do anything with my Skill." He drew his knees to his chest and rested his arms across them. "It's a little strange to have forgotten about it this year, but I'm glad I'm here with all of you."

"We are, too," Eric said as he patted Nate on the back. "But I need to be a lot drunker if we're going to be getting sentimental."

"Please don't," the familiar voice of the boatswain said. "Last thing I need is you lot losing all your inhibitions and getting into trouble. We've already got enough of that with the gunners."

Nate turned to see Novachak stepping past their group, heading for the edge of the beach down by the waterline. On his arm was a woman Nate did not recognize, but she was very beautiful. There were age lines on her face and at the corners of her eyes, but they were softened by the fading sunset and only seemed to compliment the paint she'd expertly applied to her lips and eyelids. Her hair was glossy and dark, piled artfully on top of her head and sparking with little beads of crystal that mimicked the necklace around her throat and the earrings that dangled past her chin. Her skin was darker than Novachak's, closer to Nate's own Solkyrian brown, and although it was difficult to say for certain in the dying light, Nate thought that her eyes were blue rather than brown. Her low-cut gown hugged her generous figure, and she offered Nate a slow, languid smile as she caught him staring.

Nate felt the heat rise to his cheeks. He quickly looked away.

"We know we're sailing tomorrow, sir," Rori said easily. "We've no plans to get into trouble."

She was the only one who looked faintly bewildered by Novachack's companion rather than alarmed. Eric was looking back and forth between the two with his mouth hanging open. Marcus was outright hiding behind Rori, although she was considerably smaller than him and therefore not the best barrier against the imposing stranger.

"Thank the Frozen Goddess for you and your level head, my girl," Novachak said. He reached up to lightly pat the hand of his companion where it rested on his bicep, and she snuggled closer against his side. "I have some, ah, business to see to. If the captain or the quartermaster ask, I'll be back within the hour."

The woman tightened her grip on the boatswain's

arm and practically purred against him, "We'll need more time than that. There are a *lot* of lost years between us."

"Two hours," Novachak amended quickly. "No, three. At least."

"Uh-huh," Eric said, his mouth still open.

"We'll tell them if we see them, sir," Rori said. She nodded to the woman. "Madame."

The woman gave Rori what looked to be a genuinely polite smile before pulling Novachak further along the beach. When they were close enough to the water that the waves flirted with their shoes, she brought her lips to his ear and whispered something that made the boatswain stumble and then walk faster. She laughed in delight and caught up the hem of her gown so she could more easily keep stride. The surf washed away the footprints they left in the wet sand.

"Everyone saw that, right?" Eric said once the pair had disappeared from sight. "Nikolai Novachak and Madame Silverdale, strolling arm-in-arm down the beach?"

"*That* was the madame?" Nate asked, remembering Marcus's story of being bodily thrown out of the pleasure house by the very same woman when he'd tried to pay for services with buttons. Evidently, she was much stronger than she looked.

"Aye," Rori said with a thoughtful frown, "that was her."

"Do you think she saw me?" Marcus asked.

No one bothered to answer that.

"I thought she hated Novachak," Nate said.

"She does," Eric affirmed. "He's been avoiding the pleasure house for as long as I've been with the crew, and longer than that. Liliana said she once saw Novachak throw himself into the bushes when he saw Silverdale coming down the street. Somehow, he got up a tree, and refused to come down until after nightfall."

"Seems they've made amends," Rori said, and she sounded more amused now.

"That woman does not do amends," Eric said. "Madame Silverdale would sooner share a passionate kiss with a goat than make amends."

Rori shrugged. "I'm pretty sure she's about to do both with Novachak, and then some."

Eric made a gagging sound. "I don't want to think about Novachak doing that. I *never* wanted to think about that, but now I have a horrible image in my head, and it is all your fault."

"Is the goat there, too?"

"*Rori.*"

She laughed, and Nate grinned, and Marcus eventually decided that the madame was not going to come sprinting back down the beach screaming for his blood, and it took a while but Eric was eventually persuaded to drop the subject. Night had fallen in full by then, pricked by the stars overhead and a few bonfires on the beach, and that was when Dax found them.

"You four all right?" the quartermaster asked as he stepped up to their laughing group.

"Aye," Nate answered. "No trouble here."

"It's been very peaceful," Eric remarked. "Downright boring, actually."

Dax gave a wistful sigh. "That won't last, I'm afraid. I expect we'll see plenty more ships in that harbor when we return from the Gemheart Islands. Whether they're Spider's ships or other pirate crews doesn't matter, the Nest will be swarming again soon enough."

"How many ships did Spider send out looking for his scouts?" Eric asked.

"From what I understand, every one that's put into port within the last week or so."

"Is that a lot?" Marcus asked.

"It's far more than the captain or I are comfortable with." The quartermaster nodded towards the dark sea and the meager spread of lantern lights from the anchored ships. "The ships still in the harbor are some of the slower ones," he continued. "Damaged or in desperate need of a good careening before they go out again. Spider is letting them make repairs, but he's harassing their captains every day to go back out on the water and join the search. Seeing as the *Southern Echo* is fit to sail, I'm amazed Captain Arani got us as much time on the island as she did." He fixed them all with a stern glare made doubly intimidating by the twin tattoos that adorned his skull. "That said, you all are expected to be ready to sail tomorrow."

"We know," Marcus said, yawning. "And Eric's right, there isn't much to do right now, anyway."

Dax kicked lightly at the empty bottle of rum in the sand next to the Darkbend. "That's usually when you two get into trouble."

"We *never* get into trouble," Marcus said, affronted. Then he paused. "Well, 'never' is a bad word..."

"Nate and Rori are keeping an eye on us," Eric cut in. "And besides, we already promised Novachak we'd behave."

Dax brightened at the boatswain's name. "Oh good, you've seen him. When was that?"

"Just before the sun was fully down," Nate said.

"With Madame Silverdale!" Eric said, twisting around quickly enough to splatter sand on to Rori and Marcus. "Now, *I* think that means the sixth hell has broken open, but our navigator here has been suggesting that he's got some hidden charms that I can't see. I don't think she's right, but he's somehow managed to completely beguile the madame. Nate and Marcus are useless on this topic, but maybe you could settle..." He trailed off when he saw the quartermaster's expression.

"Which way did they go?" Dax asked, quiet as the sea before a storm.

Though muted by the rum in his belly, alarm tickled the back of Nate's mind as he took in the horrified stare Dax had fixed on Eric.

Silently, Eric raised his hand and pointed.

Dax turned and began to walk, then jog, then sprint down the beach, kicking sand up with each powerful stride.

Nate exchanged one quick look with the others, then they were all on their feet and running after the quartermaster. Roused from sleep, Luken gave a disgruntled cry as he launched himself off of Rori's shoulder, pennant feathers streaming behind his wings as he flapped overhead. Rori whistled for the bird's attention and made the sign for *follow* with her hands. Luken chirped and took off into the night, soaring after Dax.

The quartermaster and the bird both outpaced them, but the flash of Luken's blue feathers in the moonlight guided them on even after Dax disappeared from sight. They all ran with wild abandon, their breaths loud and heavy in the air and their footprints dark in the sand behind them. No one laughed or so much as spoke a single word; they all knew something was horribly wrong, and Nate could not shake the feeling that they could have stopped it.

They caught up to Dax on a lonely stretch of beach on the northern side of the island. The trees at the edge of the sand were tall enough to throw shadows all the way to the water, turning every piece of driftwood into a monster waiting to ambush its next meal.

"Nikolai!" the quartermaster was shouting into the dark as Nate and the others drew up behind him.

"Answer me!"

Silence answered instead.

Dax's shoulders heaved as he growled in frustration. He dropped to the sand and began taking several long, deep breaths. As his breathing leveled out, he shut his eyes and raised his arms, his hands locking into the position Nate recognized as the one he favored for his Skill use. "All of you," he snarled, "get back *now*."

Nate nearly stumbled in his haste to retreat. Eric caught his arm and kept him steady, but his expression in the moonlight was troubled. Marcus and Rori looked equally perturbed, even as Rori stuck her arm in the air and gave Luken a perch to land on. She bundled the bird close as she moved further away from the quartermaster.

Nate barely dared to breathe as he watched Dax work, even though he knew the quartermaster's Malatide Skill had no ties whatsoever to the wind element. Nate tried to calm the racing of his heart, for he knew that would interfere far more with what Dax was trying to do, but he was no blood worker. He could only stand there, panting and hoping that he and the others had moved far enough away.

Several long, agonizing moments passed, Dax kneeling perfectly still in the sand and Nate and his friends trying to remain as small as possible behind him. Then the quartermaster shot to his feet and ran for a fallen log some distance down the beach, up near the tree line. Nate and the others followed at a slower pace, but as they drew closer and Nate's eyes began to adjust to the darkness of the shadows, he realized that the pale log Dax was turning over was wearing a coat, and very little else. Nate's breath caught in his throat, sharp and hot as the rum he'd swallowed earlier.

"Gods no," Eric breathed.

They took off running again.

Dax was on his knees next to the still form of the boatswain, ordering Novachak in a soft but firm voice to wake up.

Once again, silence answered, but this time, Nate smelled the copper tang of blood.

Rori let out a quiet gasp and pressed her knuckles to her teeth. Luken twittered softly in her other hand, and she drew the bird even closer against her chest. Eric put his arm around her shoulders, but he did not tear his eyes away from the prone form of the boatswain lying naked in the sand.

Novachak's wrists had been bound above his head to a protruding tree root by a short length of rope. His coat had been spread over him as though to shield him against the chill of the night, but Nate could not fathom why.

"Wake up," Dax said again.

Novachak did not move.

"Is he—?" Marcus started to ask, but Nate silenced him with a hand on his arm, afraid that if someone spoke the words, they would become solid and too real.

He's not, Nate thought. *He can't be.* He looked to the quartermaster, but beneath the trees, he could not make out Dax's expression.

He saw it, though, when Dax raised his hand and clenched his fingers, once again using his magic.

A moment passed, and then Novachak groaned.

Four sharp breaths of relief cut the darkness around Nate, mixing with his own.

"Thank the gods above," Eric whispered, and his voice trembled.

In addition to his clothes, Madame Silverdale had taken one of Nikolai Novachak's ears, and she had not been gentle about it.

By the ship's lantern light, Nate could clearly see the dark hole in the boatswain's head even from where he stood at the edge of the galley. He and Marcus were standing by with buckets of freshly boiled water and clean rags, waiting for Eric or Dax to wave them over.

Dax had wanted to take Novachak into town for treatment, but once he was awake, the boatswain had refused to go anywhere but the *Southern Echo*. He'd kept one hand clapped hard against the side of his head and his steps had been weak and unsteady from the blood loss, but he'd managed to keep his feet with Dax supporting him under one shoulder and Marcus the other. Rori had run ahead to find Arani, and Eric and Nate had stayed behind in case Novachak passed out and they needed more hands to carry him. The boatswain had remained conscious, but the rowboat ride back to the ship had been difficult. All the same, Novachak had grit his teeth and insisted they keep going.

"If I didn't bleed out on that beach, I'm not going to do it now that you're using your magic to keep the stuff inside of me," he'd pointed out. Dax had not looked particularly impressed by this argument. "I'm fine," Novachak had insisted, "and I'll be even better once I'm off this frost-touched island."

But he'd still gazed at the lights of Spider's Nest with a wistfulness that Nate did not understand, and something like shame washed across his face before he finally turned away.

Nate wasn't sure if the boatswain had wanted to return to the ship out of a sense of fear or one of embarrassment, but either way, Novachak had relaxed the moment he was back aboard the *Southern Echo*.

He'd directed Nate to bring him new trousers from his possessions, then submitted to Dax and Eric's clumsy doctoring without protest. A few minutes into the process, however, Novachak was talking the two of them through the steps of proper disinfecting techniques, muttering darkly about southerners and their lacking educations all the while.

"We're both Skilled," Dax pointed out when his frustration finally tipped past his concern. "Consider yourself fortunate that we got any education at all. Now stop talking before I have Eric saw off your other ear."

The hole in Novachak's head that had once been surrounded by flesh was still bleeding, and Dax worried that the madame had done something to puncture the eardrum. Novachak confirmed as much, saying she'd stuck the tip of a dagger into his ear before ripping the blade out and using it to claim her grisly trophy.

"You're lucky she didn't take more," Dax said mildly.

"I know," Novachak agreed.

Marcus jerked in surprise. "How in the six hells is this lucky? She *cut off* your *ear.*"

"She could have taken something else," Novachak said, "and been entirely justified."

Nate felt his stomach perform an unpleasant flip.

"Gods below," Eric breathed, "what did you *do* to that woman?"

The boatswain was quiet for a long time, and it seemed that the mystery would survive another night until Nate and Marcus came forward with the buckets and the rags.

"I met Julianna Silverdale years ago," Novachak said as Dax began to wash away the last traces of blood from his head. It was still splattered across his chest, matted in the fine white hairs, but that could wait for the moment. "We were young, wild things," he continued, "drawn together by passion and lusting for each other's bodies like a pair of—"

"Okay," Eric cut in, "I think story time should wait until morning, or any time when I am not in the room."

Novachak chuckled. "You'll understand when you're older."

"I understand *plenty*," Eric snapped. "I just don't want to understand it in the context of *you*."

Novachak shrugged, then winced as fresh rags were padded against the side of his head. "To put it plain, I don't know if it was love, but I know that I wanted Julianna in my life, and I did everything I could to keep her. Gifts, romance, anything to make her smile. It worked, and for a while, I fooled myself into thinking that I could give her a good life. Then I fell into debt."

"You borrowed money?" Nate asked as he lifted the bucket for Dax to rinse a rag.

"No," Novachak said. He thought for a moment, clearly trying to decide how best to phrase the next part, and then gave a resigned sigh. "I lost money. A lot of it. Most of which I didn't actually have in the first place."

"And that," the voice of the captain said from the doorway, "is why there is a strict no gambling rule in our code." Arani was leaning against the frame, Rori hovering anxiously over her shoulder and a few other curious faces peering in beyond her. The captain must have been with some of the crew when Rori found her, for now they were all pressed together and listening close.

Novachak winced again, although Nate did not think it was from physical pain this time. Then he took a breath and kept speaking. "I have always had a problem when it comes to stepping away from cards. I don't play now, and the captain keeps me straight." He nodded to Arani, and she returned the gesture. "But back then, I got myself into the kind of trouble you don't walk away from, and I had to do something to pay off the debts that I owed." He took another shuddering breath, and that wave of shame washed over him once more. "I didn't tell Julianna that I was in trouble, but I still saw her as my way out. She had a different business up and running then, selling clothes she made herself to the wealthy, and she was making decent money. I don't know why I thought she wouldn't notice if I took what I needed, but desperation made me stupid, and one night, while she was sleeping, I took some of her money and used it to pay off the gambling debts. Maybe she really didn't notice, but maybe she did, and she just wanted to give me a chance to make things right because she understood what it was like to be desperate. Then I took more.

"I thought I'd be able to win back what I owed her and then some, but no. Northern winds froze my luck dead and I ended up worse off than where I'd started. I couldn't face Julianna after that so I left. I was a coward. I ran away from her and all my debts, just like I always did.

"I didn't see her again for years, not until I'd joined Captain Arani's crew and came to Spider's Nest. She had a very different business then, and she'd managed to build herself back up, but she never forgot what I did. Neither did I. I've been trying to pay her back, but..."

"But she finally got tired of waiting," Arani said, "and called in that debt."

Someone whistled, low and sad, and Novachak hung his head in shame before glancing at Marcus.

"So, you see," the boatswain said, gesturing to his bandaged head, "that's why you don't run from your debts."

Marcus shuddered.

Nate wasn't sure if he felt pity for Novachak, or for the young Madame Silverdale who could have had a very different life. Either way, the madame Nate had met on the beach earlier that day, bathed in the light of a sunset and so beautiful, had become a monster.

"Well," Eric said after a long moment, "at least now your debts are paid."

But a haunted look came into the boatswain's eye, and suddenly the captain was ushering them all out of the room.

"That's enough for tonight," she said as she pushed Nate and the Darkbends out the door. "Let the man rest, and all of you get some sleep. We have a long journey ahead of us."

CHAPTER FOUR

A Quartermaster's Pledge

AFTER THE TROUBLING EVENTS of the previous night, Dax was more than relieved when the *Southern Echo* slid out of the harbor. It was a clear day with a steady wind from the south filling the sails, and the ship was loaded with fresh provisions of a caliber that spoke to Spider's desperation.

Iris had taken full advantage of his wild need to get her ship and crew back out on the water. Dax was glad she had. The crew would eat better than they had in over a year, even when they could afford meals at the tavern, and as Spider had squeezed them for every last copper mark the entire time they'd known him, it was a refreshing change to see him providing supplies and support without anyone having to blackmail him or threaten his life.

The beginning of a voyage was always the easi-est, but Dax still watched the crew closely as they worked through their assigned tasks. Everyone was tired, which could only be expected after a single day of rest, but their movements were sure and steady all the same. Their mouths were set in hard lines of determination and no one looked despondent.

Dax knew how easily that could change.

Best take a true measure of their morale, he thought.

He started with AnnaMarie Blueshore.

She and her gun crew were resting on the foredeck. After a morning spent hauling supplies and assisting the riggers with lifting the sails, their respite was well earned. As Dax had feared, though, AnnaMarie and the others were quiet, idly playing with short lengths of rope or staring out to sea, ignoring everything else around them. Dax called AnnaMarie over to the port railing and let her talk. It only took a few words to get to the heart of her troubles.

"I've seen my share of blood," she said, watching the coral slide past the hull of the ship beneath the waves. The thick muscles of her arms tightened as she crossed them over her chest. "But I can't stop thinking about Jim's throat opening and all that red coming out."

Dax shifted against the railing next to her, feeling the new strength of the steady pulse that had been running through the *Southern Echo* ever since the Vanishing Island. "It's hard to lose a friend."

"He wasn't my friend," AnnaMarie said, a little too quickly, and then hesitated. "He was like a brother, though. An annoying one, but still family."

"Ah," Dax said. "Losing one of those is damn near impossible."

She nodded. "A lot of the gunners..." She eyed Dax uncertainly, skimming her gaze across the tattoo that covered up and confused his Skill mark. "Never mind."

"Say it," Dax said. "I'd rather you look me in the eye and get it out now than let it fester and hurt something far worse than my feelings later."

AnnaMarie took a deep breath before turning to face him squarely. "A lot of us did not like Xander, and some of us feel like we easily could have been in Jim's place that day, but we were afraid to speak because..." She glanced nervously across the deck.

Dax waited.

"Because Arani shows special favor towards the Skilled," AnnaMarie finished in a rush. She braced herself, as though certain Dax would strike her for that, but her jaw was set and her eyes were hard.

It was Dax's turn to sigh. "I know you well enough to believe that you're not thinking about forcing the Skilled to use their magic," he said, but he still put the lilt of a question at the end of the words.

AnnaMarie shook her head. "I don't care if they do or don't," she said. "But we were afraid to say anything against Xander for fear of what Arani might do. She pretends to be fair but the Skilled are her favorites." She paused again, looking at Dax's tattoos. "The younger ones, I mean. When she took Nate aboard, she could barely be bothered to think of anyone else, and then we gave up Mordanti's dragon to rescue him. Then the boy picked a fight with Jim just before his death, and the worst he got were a few lashes. And then Rori was taken and Arani traded a treasure from the Vanishing Island for her."

If AnnaMarie had ended those words by shouting or dropping her voice to a snarl, Dax would have had some strong words of his own for her. But her voice was level, and her gaze was earnest as she looked at him, trusting him as her quartermaster to hear and listen.

"Would you have preferred if we'd left them for dead?" he asked, but without rancor.

AnnaMarie shook her head immediately. "I'm not saying we did the wrong thing, but we can't help but wonder, if it had been one of us in place of Nate or Rori, would Arani have come to save us?"

Dax knew the answer to that, but weighed how likely AnnaMarie was to believe him. She was an earnest soul, though, and would listen to the truth. "I believe she would," he finally said, "but I have been wrong before."

AnnaMarie blinked in surprise.

"We're all part of this crew, and none of you should feel like your life is worth less than your mate's." He straightened and pulled away from the railing. "I'll talk to the captain about this. I'll leave your name out of it."

AnnaMarie nodded gratefully.

"It wasn't just her fault, though, what happened to Jim," Dax said. "She wasn't the only officer who gave Xander too much leniency. We're all going to live with the guilt of that for the rest of our lives, believe me."

The gunner looked skeptical, but she gave another slow nod.

Dax reached out and put a firm hand on her shoulder. Immediately, he felt the pulse of AnnaMarie's heart through the connection. It was slow and steady, no trace of alarm or deception in the rhythm.

She wasn't happy, but she believed him.

"I'm still your quartermaster," Dax told her, "and I am always going to act in the best interest of this crew. You have my word on that."

AnnaMarie's expression softened. She reached out and clasped Dax's arm, completing the grip of camaraderie. "Thank you, sir," she said, her voice firm.

Dax made to step away.

"I am sorry," AnnaMarie said before she let him go, "about what Arthur said."

Dax remembered standing before the man under a red, magic-soaked sky. *Magic-tainted freak*, Arthur had called Dax, to his face and in front of the crew.

"For what it's worth," AnnaMarie continued in a low voice, "I don't let anyone from my own gun crew talk that way."

"I know," Dax said, "and I appreciate it. I only wish you'd done the same when it came to talk of betraying the captain out on the Forbidden Sea."

AnnaMarie paled, and Dax barely needed his magic to catch the surprised stutter of her heart. "You knew?" she asked.

"I do now," Dax said. He folded his arms and turned back to her. "But I started suspecting your gunners after they accosted Eric."

AnnaMarie flushed with shame. She ran a hand across the back of her neck, brushing aside her short hair. "I did not encourage that, or any of the further talk," she said. "But it died quick, after Rori started finding more of the signs. I swear by all the gods above, no one was ever going to move against Arani in earnest."

"I know," Dax said again. "It's why I'm going to talk to the captain about what you told me instead of having your gun crew keel-hauled." He leaned closer, making sure his next words were for her alone. "But if this happens again, and you do nothing to stamp it out, I will consider you responsible, and you'll go over the side with them. Am I clear?"

"Aye, sir," AnnaMarie murmured. There was no resentment in her voice or her gaze, and she gave Dax a firm, determined nod when he released her to enjoy the rest of the relaxation time she and her people had earned.

Steady on, sailor, Dax thought as he left the gunner.

AnnaMarie was a valuable part of the crew, blunter than a hammer when it came to words, but she was levelheaded, and Dax knew that she'd kept the very worst of Greenroot in check when he'd been alive. She could continue doing as much with several of the other gunners now. He and Iris both wanted to keep her as long as they could. Luckily for them, given how AnnaMarie's heart accelerated every time she looked at Liliana, the gunner had her own incentives to stay, although Dax wasn't entirely sure how Liliana would respond to that, if she ever found out.

AnnaMarie's feelings were fairly obvious to nearly everyone save Liliana, but she'd never exactly been the brightest star in the sky.

The rigger in question was currently aloft, arms and legs hooked through the ropes and a dreamy expression on her face as she let the wind play with her long hair. She wasn't as nimble in the lines as Xander had been, but she was one of the more surefooted riggers, lithe and sinewy as a dancer. She had her fair share of admirers, but always seemed to fix her own attention on sailors she could not hope to win.

Like Eric, who was only attracted to men, and Nate, who currently was only attracted to Rori.

Gods above help these fools, Dax thought. *And if not them, then help the rest of us survive the stupid things they do for love and lust. Speaking of which...*

As though summoned to illustrate the point, Nikolai approached. The boatswain held a small bundle of fresh, clean rags in one hand and an empty bucket in the other.

"Oh, good," Nikolai said with sarcasm-soured cheer, "the noble hero who is going to help me change my bandages."

"I didn't agree to that," Dax said.

"No," Nikolai said, "but you're too kind to refuse." He gestured for Dax to follow him. "Come on, the cook's got some freshly boiled water for me."

Dax rolled his eyes, but he trailed after Nikolai all the same.

Down in the galley, the cook, old Steven Brownsand, did indeed have a pot of boiled water ready. He set it before Nikolai, humming something tuneless but unmistakably happy as he sloshed hot water on to the table.

"You're in a good mood," Dax noted.

The cook gave Dax the biggest smile he'd ever seen from the man. "Fresh food of a quality I haven't seen since I lived in Sunthrone City," Steven said dreamily. "When these hot-tempered fools sit down to eat tonight, I'm going to be their hero."

Dax chuckled and waved the cook back to his work.

Nikolai had started unwrapping the soiled bandages around his head by then. The strips of cloth were stiff with dried blood, and Nikolai winced as the last one reluctantly came away. Dax's nose wrinkled as much from the smell as from the sight, but there was nothing to suggest infection so far. Still, seeing a hole in a man's head instead of the soft shell of an ear was something Dax did not think he would ever grow accustomed to.

Nikolai dropped the dirty bandages into the bucket he'd brought before dipping a fresh piece of cloth in the boiled water and wiping gingerly around the hole. "It's not still bleeding, is it?" he asked.

Dax made himself look closer. There was a fresh trickle of red from the edge of the cut. "Yes," he said, "but not badly."

Nikolai swore and shoved the cloth hard against the side of his head. His free hand dipped into his coat pocket and came out with a surgical needle and a length of thin catgut cord. He extended these to Dax.

"Again, I did not agree to this," Dax said after a moment.

Nikolai waved the medical supplies impatiently.

Dax sighed and accepted them, dipping the needle and his hands into the boiled water to rinse them.

"See?" Nikolai said as he sat down and leaned to the side to give Dax easier access to his injury. "You're too nice."

"Wait until I start the stitches," Dax muttered.

"I'm sure you'll do fine," Nikolai said, and then yelped in pain when the needle went in. "You're stitching, not stabbing, you frost-touched bastard!"

"And you're the one who usually does this," Dax pointed out mildly.

It took several minutes and the resulting stitches were clumsy at best, but the edges of the wound were finally pulled closed and the bleeding stopped. Dax helped Nikolai rewrap his head, making sure the hole and the cuts were firmly covered without obscuring the boatswain's vision.

"Silverdale really didn't hold back," Dax said as he tied the final knot.

Nikolai stiffened at the name, but tried to keep his voice airy when he said, "It could have been worse."

Dax eyed the boatswain, but Nikolai pointedly did not meet his gaze.

"Why did you go off with her?" he asked. "You didn't really think she'd forgive you so easily, did you?"

"I..."

Dax leaned against the table and waited.

Nikolai sighed heavily, then pushed to his feet and began to gather up the unused scraps. "I knew that Julianna was angry," he said, "and she had every right to be. But after I gave her what money I had, we got to talking, and it was so easy, like no time had passed at all. In spite of everything, she seemed genuinely happy to see me."

"And it didn't occur to you that it might be an act?" Dax asked.

"It wasn't," Nikolai said with enough force to surprise them both. Slowly, he relaxed his grip on the rags. "She didn't show it at first, but I know her smiles, and the way she laughs at small things. She was happy to be with me, and then down on that beach..."

"She cut your ear off," Dax finished.

"No." Nikolai paused. "Well, yes, but I mean before that. We're both older but it was still incredible." He fell silent, lost to the memory of what he and Silverdale had done together in the shadows of those trees.

Dax regarded the boatswain for a long moment. "You genuinely love this woman," he said.

Nikolai looked around, startled, and opened his mouth to protest, but no sound came out. For a moment, only the cook's off-key whistling filled the galley, accompanied by the soft bleat of the new dairy goat and the steady sounds of the ship.

"I'd have thought her cutting off your ear would have dampened those feelings," Dax said mildly.

Nikolai frowned at the rag he slowly twined between his fingers. "You know," he finally said, "it might actually be because of that. She held on to that anger, and she acted on it, but she could still smile and laugh beyond it. What I did to her didn't destroy her. It should have, but underneath the hardness that built up over the years, she's still Julianna."

Dax tried to imagine forgiving someone for intentionally inflicting such an injury, or any injury at all. He couldn't. "I don't think I'll ever understand you," he said to the boatswain.

Nikolai gave Dax a sidelong look. "Actually, you do," he said, "far more than you think."

Dax frowned. "I don't—"

"*There* you are," Iris cut in. "I was beginning to think I'd somehow misplaced an entire quartermaster." She looked between Dax and Nikolai, taking in the bucket of bloody rags at the boatswain's feet and the fresh bandaging on his head in one quick sweep. "How's that wound, Nikolai?"

"It could be worse," the boatswain said with a shrug.

"It would also be nonexistent," Iris pointed out, "if you hadn't wandered off with the woman you yourself once described as 'the fury of the Frozen Goddess given form and color.'"

Nikolai grumbled something in reply before busying himself with cleaning off the table and gathering the last of the medical supplies.

Iris shook her head at his turned back before gesturing for Dax to follow her. They took their leave of the boatswain, whose remaining ear was flushed a deep crimson, and headed for the captain's private cabin.

The austere room was as familiar to Dax as if it had been his own. He certainly spent enough time there, pouring over maps and discussing the more inflammatory matters with Iris, away from the rest of the crew. He wasn't surprised to see a few sea charts spread across the long table at the center of the room, already marked by Rori's careful hand to show the best routes through the Gauntlet Reef that twined around the Coral Chain Islands and made those waters so difficult for larger ships to navigate. The *Southern Echo* would have an easier time thanks to her shallow draft, and from the look of the charts, Dax guessed that Iris and Rori had decided to take advantage of that and keep the *Southern Echo* sheltered within the Coral Chain all the way to Veritia and the other northern islands.

From there, it would be open waters until they reached the Gemheart Islands.

And open waters meant imperial naval patrols, which was what worried Dax and Iris the most.

"So it's a mad dash after we pass Veritia, I take it?" Dax asked as he traced the line Rori had drawn.

"Aye," Iris confirmed. "Gods only know what's waiting for us out there, but I'm hoping Nate will be able to sense anything sailing directly for us."

Dax looked around sharply. "Are you going to ask him to read the wind, or order it?"

Iris grimaced. "I'd rather do neither, but if we're going to come back from the Gemhearts without a navy ship in our wake, we're going to need him and his Skill more than ever."

Dax considered her for a moment, taking in the tired slope of her body against the chair she'd dropped herself into. He believed her when she said she did not want to draw on Nate's magic, but AnnaMarie's words from earlier were still fresh in his mind. "It's dangerous to rely on one sailor so completely," Dax said quietly.

Iris's grimace deepened into a full scowl. "If anyone else could do this, I'd ask them. Gods know I'd do it myself if I could."

In spite of himself, Dax quirked a smile as he recalled a younger Captain Iris Arani falling back into her former role as a rigger and scaling the shrouds to handle a particularly snarled bit of rope, much to the distress of the old quartermaster. It had taken a lot of arguing before Iris had finally stopped doing that.

"If Nate agrees to help," Dax said, "you'd best make sure the rest of the crew knows they're going to be compensated equally for the work they do, even if it's not magical."

Iris blinked and tilted her head.

"There's talk that you favor the Skilled over the rest of the crew," he said. "Especially Nate."

Iris's confusion melted into disgust. "Gods below, you treat people like *people* and suddenly you're playing favorites."

"I think some feel that way," Dax allowed, "but for most, it's more of a question of their own value."

The confusion returned.

Dax did not like the feel of the next words on his tongue, but he had to say them. It was his duty to the crew. "You traded two legends for the lives of two Skilled. Some of the crew are wondering if you would have done the same if it was their lives on the line instead."

"Of course I would have!" Iris snapped. She pushed

herself out of the chair and stalked angrily across the room. "I don't know how they could ever think otherwise. I'm not a perfect captain, but I am a fair one." She stopped in front of the windows at the back of the room, where Spider's Nest was receding into the horizon and another island of the Coral Chain was just coming into view at the northern edge of the glass. "Mordanti's dragon was for me," she said softly, "but everything else has been for them. It's why I wanted to go east instead of taking this mad assignment. But they voted in favor of it, and now that we're committed, I will see this through."

"If nothing else, I'm sure Spider will appreciate that," Dax said.

"Gratitude is not an emotion the man is capable of feeling," Iris quipped. "But whatever happened to his ships, it affects all of us." She turned around and gazed at Dax earnestly. "I just hope the answers we find are the silent ones left behind by whatever made them in the first place."

CHAPTER FIVE
Empty Winds

WITH THE FAVORABLE WINDS and the strong currents between the islands, the *Southern Echo* reached the northern part of the Coral Chain within a week. It only took that long because of the hazards beneath the water.

Initially, they took full advantage of the good weather, and it seemed to Nate that the *Southern Echo* was flying past the small, overgrown islands that made up the southeastern edge of the Coral Chain. For a few days, that was all Nate saw off the port railing; uninhabited islands appearing and disappearing so fast it was as though the god of land and mountains had reached into the world and begun to play with it like a child shaping sand. Off the starboard railing was the endless sea, and this was the side Captain Arani asked him to watch.

"Start slow," she told him. "Ten minutes at a time, and rest for two hours before you begin again."

"I can handle a lot more than that," Nate offered, but Arani shook her head.

"You're going to start small, go slow, and avoid burnout," she told him firmly. "This part here is your warmup. If a ship comes for us now, we'll be able to dip into the Gauntlet, so I'm not too worried if you find something close. When we're past Veritia, there's going to be a lot more for you to do."

So Nate began his sporadic wind reading, but even with the short sessions and Marcus eagerly standing by with a bucket of seawater to dump over Nate's head if he overshot the time limit, Rori was agitated. She was back on her navigation duties and didn't have a lot of free time, but she somehow found the space to watch all of Nate's readings with her arms tightly crossed. She was careful to keep her expression neutral, but Nate could sense the unease in her breaths, each one heavy with concern.

At first, Nate tried to ignore Rori, but with the winds dark and clear against his consciousness, barely broken by the faintest tremor of seabird wings, there wasn't much to distract him from the weight of her attention.

There was only so much of that he could endure.

"I'm all right, Rori," Nate told her after he'd made the latest of several very unexciting reports to Captain Arani. "Compared to what I've done before, this is nothing."

Rori shook her head, her arms clenching even tighter across her chest. "It's not nothing. The smallest slip..."

She didn't need to finish the thought for Nate to know that the *Godfall* was back on her mind.

"My magic isn't like yours," Nate said. "I'd have to range a lot farther out before I'd risk losing control."

To his surprise, Rori bared her teeth in a snarling grimace. "Must be nice," she said, her voice low, "to be able to use your Skill so casually."

Nate bristled, a retort rising to his lips, but he stopped himself from speaking it aloud. Instead, he made himself take in Rori's crumpled posture, her uneasy breathing, the nervous way her gaze kept darting to the sea. Her coat was open and had caught on the hilt of the dagger she'd bought from Spider's Nest, still on her hip despite being aboard the *Southern Echo*, the one place she should have felt safe, surrounded by allies.

Their last voyage had destroyed that.

"Is the god still whispering to you?" Nate asked softly.

Rori looked away, but she bit her lip and nodded.

Nate's heart clenched as he let out a slow breath. "That's horrible."

Rori's fingers curled against the sleeves of her coat, her nails digging into the fabric. Nate fought the urge to take her hands and pull them away before she hurt herself; he sensed that this was not the time to try to touch her. Even Luken was shifting uneasily on her shoulder, as though questioning if he should fly or not.

"It's not as bad as it was in the Rend," Rori finally murmured. "On Spider's Nest, it was almost gone, but now that we're back out to sea..."

"Is it all of the time?" Nate asked. "Any quiet moments at all?"

She took a deep, shuddering breath and finally released her sleeves. She rubbed her arms through her coat, soothing back the pain. "Sometimes. It's loudest when I'm angry, like it feeds off of that. I wish I knew a way to make it stop."

Nate hesitated, remembering his earlier conversation with Marcus.

The Darkbend had not believed there was an answer to the problem plaguing the *Southern Echo*, filling the voids carved by betrayal and death, but Nate was starting to think that there was one, after all. The one he'd thought of in the wake of AnnaMarie's anger.

Rori was not going to like it, but if he could convince her to try, maybe it would stop the voice in her ear as readily as a schism through the crew.

He swallowed past the dry lump in his throat and

made himself ask, "Is that why you don't want to see Xander ever again?"

Rori frowned at him. "What?"

He gestured to the open sea off the *Southern Echo*'s starboard side. "The voice gets louder when you're angry, so you're afraid to see the one person you have every right in the world to be furious with. You're afraid you'll lose control over your magic and hurt someone." The gold ring on Nate's hand flashed in the weak winter sunlight. "No one gets to take your anger, Rori, not even a god. I'd be terrified if I was in your place, but from where I'm standing, I think it would actually help you if we found the *Dragonsbane* again."

A silence stretched between them after those words, punctured only by an anxious twitter from Luken.

Then Rori began to shake her head. "No."

"I know you're scared," Nate said gently, "but running away isn't going to solve anything."

"We're not running," Rori said, heat coming into her voice. "We're on assignment for Spider."

"And after that?" Nate asked. "Are you going to live the rest of your life afraid of those men? Of your own magic?"

"There's no reason I ever have to see Xander or Blackcliff ever again," Rori growled.

"Unless our paths cross," Nate said. He knew he was provoking her, but he couldn't stand seeing her buckling under the weight of her own fear. She did not deserve that. Nate could help her face it, and he knew the crew of the *Southern Echo* would be at her back, too. "We're going back to the Nest at least once more before we leave the Common Sea," he pointed out. "The *Dragonsbane* will have probably put into port by now, and Blackcliff's crew isn't going to want to leave in a hurry, not when they have the gold to spend. There's a strong chance we'll find them when we return."

Rori drew back, shaking her head more vigorously. "I don't want that."

"You may not have a choice. Even if we don't find them on Spider's Nest, this will go to a vote before Arani can point us into the east. More than enough people want it." Nate thought of AnnaMarie and the loss of her friend, and of the riggers who'd counted Xander as the next closest thing to family. Then he thought of the looks traded between Rori and Xander on Spider's Nest before the dragon hunt, the easy and familiar way she'd taken the Grayvoice's hand and gone off with him, the way he had let her in close only to drag her beneath the stillness of the Forbidden Sea. That was the greatest injustice of all; that someone Rori had chosen to trust had so completely betrayed her. Nate had to struggle to keep his voice calm when he said, "And I think, deep down, in a part of yourself that you're scared to find, you want it, too."

"I don't!" Rori exploded, sending Luken off her shoulder with a startled cry and drawing the attention of several people on the deck. Angry tears pricked her eyes, but she did not let them fall. "I didn't want it when a god offered it to me on the Vanishing Island, and I don't want it now." She fixed him with a hard, wounded stare. "I thought you understood that."

"I do," Nate said earnestly. "But it may be exactly what you need. What we *all* need."

"No," Rori spat, "it's not. And if you'd ever learned how to be your own person, maybe you'd see that."

Nate jerked back, stunned. "What's that supposed to mean?"

Rori waved a hand, taking him in with one quick gesture from head to toe. "You've spent your whole life trying to make yourself into what you think others want you to be. You had to do it to survive at the academy, but even when you came aboard the *Southern Echo*, you've only ever tried to fit into the mold of other people's wants and dreams."

"That's not..." Nate started, and failed to finish. "I don't..."

"You do," Rori insisted. "You fell hard into Arani's dragon hunt, and then on the Forbidden Sea, you acted more like Xander than yourself, probably because you don't even know who that is."

"That's not fair," Nate snapped. "The dragon hunt taught me how to use my Skill. My *real* Skill."

"And that's fine," Rori said, "but who are you outside of it?"

Nate opened his mouth, but no words were there.

After a few moments, Rori's gaze softened. "I believe going after the *Dragonsbane* is something other people want, but I saw your face when you realized that ship wasn't in the harbor. You can't tell me that's what *you* really want, Nate."

He held her stare for as long as he could, but eventually, Nate dropped his gaze to the deck. "No," he whispered.

"So what do you want? Who are you?" Rori turned away. "And are you brave enough to find out?"

She left him standing alone on the deck, stunned. A long while later, after he'd finally roused himself and gone to help the riggers seek out a better wind to fill the sails, it occurred to Nate that Rori had allowed herself to be furious during their confrontation, but she'd never let the god back in to her voice, and no waves had risen to threaten the *Southern Echo*.

When the *Southern Echo* turned more deeply into the Coral Chain, several things changed.

Most notably, the ship only sailed during the strongest daylight hours, when the jagged teeth of the Gauntlet Reef could be seen through the clear water. When the light shifted and the sea started to darken, the anchor was immediately dropped, and the *Southern Echo* did not move until the next day.

That left Nate with plenty of time to agonize over Rori's questions, which plagued him all through the last hours of sunlight and followed him into the berth. He lay in the dark, listening to Marcus snore in the hammock beneath his, thinking.

Since their last conversation, Rori had stopped hovering nearby every time Nate used his Skill to scout the winds, but her words ricocheted through his skull whenever he caught a glimpse of her moving through her navigation duties, Luken devoutly perched on her shoulder with his pennant feathers trailing down her arm.

She was right, Nate knew. He'd wanted to prove himself for so long that he really had lost himself in his magic. He'd finally learned what his Skill could do on the dragon hunt, and he'd shown everyone—himself included—that he wasn't the useless Nowind the world had called him before he'd joined the *Southern Echo*'s crew. But then, out on the Forbidden Sea, Nate had been at a loss. His Skill had not been needed, and without his magic to define him, he'd thrown himself against the first enemy he could find, only to realize far too late that he'd been blinded by his own arrogance and manipulated by one more person he'd so badly wanted to prove himself to.

That had been for nothing.

Your only worth was finding that dragon, Xander had spat at Nate inside the temple on the Vanishing

Island. *No one needed you to find this place. No one needs you at all.*

And then Xander had almost put a sword through Nate's heart. Would have, if Arani hadn't intervened.

Now Nate was here, aboard the *Southern Echo*, with a captain who trusted him to scout the winds but was not asking him to throw himself dangerously far into his magic, to define himself by it.

Who are you?

Nate caught himself twisting the gold ring on his finger, turning the Solkyrian sun crest around and around. He quickly released it, but the idleness of his hands left him even more restless, until his fingers found the hemp bracelet he'd bought for himself. He began to spin the small agate beads on his wrist, trying to take comfort in their smooth, unembellished surfaces, but it was far from a restful night.

The morning wasn't much better. They had to wait for the sunrise to brighten the sea before the anchor was raised, and Nate was openly fidgeting as he waited for the riggers to begin their search for the best wind. That, however, was a task that was over and done within a few minutes, and the *Southern Echo*'s slow speed meant that there wasn't much else that Nate could help with.

Out on the main deck, trying to wear away the slow minutes, Eric noticed his agony.

"What's wrong with you?" the elegant Darkbend asked.

"Thinking," Nate ground back.

"That's usually only a strenuous activity for Marcus," Eric remarked. He waited expectantly for the stout Darkbend's response.

Marcus did not open his eyes, only continued to lean heavily against the ship's railing and gently massage his temple, distorting the white tattoo over his brow.

Eric frowned before returning his attention to Nate. "What exactly has you so twisted up?"

"Something Rori said," Nate grumbled. The Darkbend made a knowing sound, and Nate flushed. "No, it's—" He broke off, suddenly not wanting to reveal the simple questions she'd posed that had pierced him to his core. "She mentioned that she still hears the god whispering to her."

Eric's teasing grin fell. "How bad is it?"

Nate shook his head. "She said it's not as terrible as before, but it gets worse when she's angry."

Eric gave him a flat look. "So maybe don't say or do anything to upset her."

"Believe it or not, that idea did occur to me," Nate said sourly. "But she can't live the rest of her life afraid of herself."

Eric looked ready to argue, but he paused, and then gave a tired sigh before slumping next to Marcus on the railing. "Going to the Rend was a mistake," he said. "Nothing good has come out of it."

Marcus gave a disgusted huff before Nate could respond. He turned and trudged off without a word, but he did make a point of giving Eric a light shove as he went.

Eric threw up his hands. "Now what's wrong with *him*?"

Nate frowned as Marcus thudded down the stairs that would take him to the berth. "Maybe that agate he bought isn't as strong as he thought it was."

"That's why I didn't want him to buy it so fast. He never thinks these things through." Eric scraped his hands through his hair. "Not that he even needed a new anchor. His Skill is no stronger than mine."

"But he has been saying that he doesn't feel right," Nate pointed out. He wracked his memories of the previous evening, trying to recall the dinner meal beyond his own distracted thoughts. "Did he eat much last night?"

Eric groaned and pushed off from the railing. "He better not have caught something on Spider's Nest. Some illness clawing through the ship is the last thing we need right now."

"Where are you going?" Nate asked as Eric stepped away.

"To find out how worried we should be about the proximity of our bunks to Marcus's," he answered. "Try not to piss Rori off while I'm gone."

"No promises," Nate muttered as he turned to lean over the railing.

Who are you?

He shook his head and distracted himself for a few minutes by peering into the blue water as the reefs slid by. The *Southern Echo* was moving slowly enough that he could follow the brilliantly colored fish swimming through the thick beds of equally vibrant coral, but all those colors were made far less enchanting by the shapes of the Gauntlet.

It had only taken one look at the jagged edges of the reef for Nate to understand the ship's slow forward crawl, and why no one had raised their voices in complaint about the journey's speed, or lack thereof.

The Gauntlet Reef was beyond dangerous, with narrow and twisting passages that the *Southern Echo* sometimes cleared with nothing more than a hand's breadth of distance between her hull and the coral teeth. But just as those reefs could tear apart a pirate ship, so could they rip into a navy vessel. Larger ships with deeper drafts could never have taken the same route the *Southern Echo* was using, and even a powerful Goodtide would have found nothing but trouble within the coral maze. That rendered any advantage the imperial navy might have had over a pirate ship completely moot, and was what kept Spider's Nest so safe despite its location firmly within Solkyrian territory. As long as a pirate crew respected the danger of the reef, they could find safety within it.

As a testament to that respect, Liliana and Theo had both been aloft since the very start of the day, surveying the waters from up high and pointing out the deadly shallows and safer depths. Rori was at the bow, watching the riggers and relaying their signals to Luken, who in turn flitted to the directed spots and flashed his wings at the helm. Captain Arani was at the wheel, her touch light as the *Southern Echo* threaded the coral maze. Over her head, an innocuous flag of soft orange and pink flew in place of the ship's usual standard.

It was strange, almost unnerving to look up and not see the dragon head devouring a golden sun, but Arani was taking no chances now that they were away from Spider's Nest. If they came across another ship, she wanted them to think that the *Southern Echo* was a small merchant vessel picking its way back to the main shipping lanes.

To that end, the captain would likely want a scouting report on the winds soon, and Nate headed for the elevated deck at the stern of the ship to take his measure of the breezes and any shadows they carried.

He hesitated at the stairs, remembering that Marcus had drifted off, but the Darkbend had looked a bit pale and Nate did not want to summon him for bucket duty if he could benefit from a little rest. Nate also wasn't tempted to stray far out on the winds. He may not have known who he was or what he wanted out of his life, but he was certain that he did not want to risk it all by tangling himself in air currents too far away from the ship.

Up on the poop deck, Nate planted his boots firmly on the deck, closed his eyes, and focused on the faint but steady pulse coming up through the wood. He wondered if the dryad knew he was there, if she sensed his magic flaring whenever he slipped into the wind.

He liked to think that she did.

Smiling faintly, Nate drew in a deep breath of air heavy with salt and the earthy scent of the nearby islands, and then released his magic. The world melted into the blues and purples of the winds, each ribbon smearing and folding around him before rushing off on their natural paths. There was a purity to them despite the taste of salt picked up from the water, and Nate let them lift his consciousness into the air.

He stayed close to the *Southern Echo*, dodging around the ship's wind shadow as he searched for the telltale shiver of another craft near the darkness of the waterline. There was nothing, just more empty winds blowing in from the north and the west.

Briefly, he considered ranging out, maybe even tracing the path they'd taken back to Spider's Nest. He knew that he was capable of it; the dragon hunt had taught him as much. He could ride the wind all the way back to the Nest, scout around the harbor, see if a particular ship had finally made an appearance in those waters.

Who are you?

Nate did not know, but he did not think that it was someone moving in lockstep with vengeance.

He returned to his body on the *Southern Echo*, settling in easily and feeling only the slightest bit of warmth from the ring on his hand. He blinked in the winter sunlight, taking a few moments to watch the ship's wake as it spread and faded away. Then he went to report to the captain that, once more, the winds were clear.

The next day, one of the swabs told Nate that Anna-Marie Blueshore was looking for him.

A small surge of unease rose up in Nate's chest, but he remembered what he'd said to Rori about not living in fear, and the decision that he'd made regarding himself and revenge. He steeled himself, and then stole down to the gun deck.

Blueshore was leading her small crew through their daily practice maneuvers and exercises. She worked herself alongside them, hauling on the cannon and lifting weighted barrels until her face and neck were shining from exertion. Nate made no effort to conceal himself, and Blueshore noticed him early on, but she made him wait. When she finally called a halt, her gun crew was breathing hard, the underarms of their sleeves dark with sweat despite the cool air.

"Good work," Blueshore informed them. "We'll run it again at three bells."

A groan went up from the gun crew, but that was their only protest.

Nate stepped out of their way as they jostled past, heading for the galley and the berth. AnnaMarie held back, leaning against her assigned cannon. She folded her arms across her broad chest.

"Lowwind," she said by way of greeting. "Any sign of the *Dragonsbane*?"

Nate froze, then wondered why the question had surprised him.

She's always been blunt, he thought. *Might be best to just speak her language.*

"No," he said. "And I don't think we should go after

it."

AnnaMarie gave him a slow blink.

All right, maybe that wasn't *the best approach,* Nate decided, but he'd already committed and figured he may as well see it through. The worst that could happen was he said the wrong thing and AnnaMarie introduced her fist to his face.

Actually, she'd easily break my nose... Gods below, I should not have come down here alone.

"I know you and your gun crew were hoping we'd find the *Dragonsbane* on Spider's Nest," Nate continued before AnnaMarie could speak again. "Probably a lot of others, too. Gods know there's a part of me that was hoping for it. But I've had some time to think, and I don't know if seeking vengeance is actually going to help anything." He paused, treading carefully around the next words. "It's not going to bring Jim back."

AnnaMarie brought her hands together, knuckles cracking like gunshots.

Absolutely should not have come down here alone, Nate thought as he swallowed past the sudden dryness in his throat.

"Look," he said, trying to find the right words that would keep his bones in the correct places, "if our paths do cross with Xander's again and the need comes, I'll fight with you. He's stronger and faster than me, but I'll stand with the *Southern Echo*'s crew. I'm just not going to use my magic for something like this."

AnnaMarie blinked again. "Oh, is that what you meant?" she said. She rolled her shoulders and began to stretch her arms, completely unbothered by Nate's declaration. "That's fine. I didn't think you would."

It was his turn to blink at her. "You didn't?"

"No. It's your magic, kid." She lifted one arm over her head and leaned to the side. "Do whatever you want with it."

She made it through several more stretches before Nate found his voice again.

"But you just asked me if I'd sensed the *Dragonsbane* in the wind."

"Aye," she agreed, "but I only wanted to know if it was close. I didn't expect you to go ripping off to find it."

"Oh," Nate said lamely. "All right, then." He turned to leave, then turned back. "You're not upset that we didn't find them on Spider's Nest?"

AnnaMarie's face twisted as she bent down to brush her fingers against the toes of her boots. "Of course I am. I watched a traitor slit open the throat of one of my mates, and then get away with it. I liked what Rori said, when she said she wanted to drown the bastard, but all the same." The gunner slowly straightened up. "I'd love to turn the *Dragonsbane* into a pile of splinters, preferably with Blackcliff and that Grayvoice aboard, but until that chance actually comes, there's nothing I can do except be patient and make sure my gun crew is ready."

"They certainly look like they are," Nate said.

Blueshore gave him a malicious grin.

Nate held her gaze for a moment, his mind turning over Novachak's story about unpaid debts and how an untempered hunger for vengeance could unravel and consume someone's life. "What are you going to do if we don't see them again?" Nate asked softly. "If you can't get justice for Jim Greenroot?"

The gunner's smile faded. "We're going to see them again."

The certainty in her voice was hard enough to crack against Nate and drive him back a step. He made himself look her in the eye. "But what if we don't?"

AnnaMarie considered Nate for a long moment, as though trying to decide if she wanted to answer him, or load him into the massive weapon behind her in place of a cannonball. "I suppose I learn how to make peace with that," she finally said. She leaned against the cannon and her expression went cold. "But I'm still pissed at you for what you did on the Forbidden Sea."

"I am, too," Nate said. "But Rori didn't deserve what you said to her back in Spider's harbor."

Blueshore's anger fractured, and she gave him another bemused blink. "Maybe not," she allowed. "The girl expecting an apology?"

"I know she'd appreciate it," Nate said, and it took every bit of strength he possessed to continue holding her gaze.

AnnaMarie blinked again, and then she laughed and pushed off from the cannon. "You know, Lowwind, you're not so terrible." She patted Nate's shoulder as she stepped past him, heading for the steps up to the main deck. The force was enough to make him stagger, and Nate was so relieved, he almost let himself fall to his knees. "I'm glad I didn't let the Grayvoice smother you in your sleep your first night aboard."

"Thanks, I—" Nate broke off as he realized what she'd said. "Wait, what?"

But AnnaMarie was already gone, and Nate began to strongly consider purchasing a dagger of his own when the ship returned to Spider's Nest.

Maybe Rori will let me borrow hers in the meantime.

There wasn't an opportunity to ask, however, as the *Southern Echo* approached the northeastern end of the Gauntlet, moving cautiously under a cloudy sky. The reef thinned, leaving more room for larger ships to maneuver, and Nate began to scout the winds more regularly, until he was reading them every hour of the day the ship was sailing, along with the first hour after sunset and the last one before sunrise. The islands were in a denser cluster in that part of the chain, making the winds trickier to read, but there was nothing for Nate to report until the day before the *Southern Echo* was expected to fully leave the reef, when he picked up the blurry wind shadows of three small ships. None of them were a threat.

Before long, Nate's Skill was no longer needed to detect other ships; there were quite a few sailing the waters beyond the worst of the Gauntlet Reef, and the *Southern Echo* slipped into the known trade route behind them. Arani kept them moving slow to match the pace of the merchants, and for the first time in over a week, the *Southern Echo* sailed during the sunset hour.

Because merchants notoriously sailed with thin crews to fatten their profit margins, half the *Southern Echo* sailors had to wait below deck while the ship crossed the busier lanes, including Nate and all of the other Skilled. That put him face-to-face with Rori for the first time since she'd asked her questions.

Nate still didn't have an answer, but he was glad to see that she looked decently rested. There were no dark circles under her eyes, and she wasn't shying away from anyone who came too close. Luken had also relaxed, and the bird actually let Rori take him off her shoulder and place him on a barrel as she settled in alongside Nate and the others, getting ready to wait out the last of the daylight. For a while, Nate thought that Rori had stopped hearing the god's voice in her ear, that she was finally free and able to relax. Then she abruptly jumped and shuddered, pawing at her ear, a frantic look coming into her eyes. She stopped when she saw Nate, Marcus and Eric all staring at her with open concern, and she flushed under their attention.

"I could really use a distraction right now," she muttered.

Naturally, Eric took the opportunity to bring out his playing cards, although he looked considerably less enthused when Rori asked to be dealt in.

As the first round of Liar's Farm began, Nate tried not to let Rori catch him studying her, but she finally pinned him with a fierce glare over the cards in her hand.

"Well," Nate said, not trying to hide the exasperation in his voice, "now you know how I felt when you were watching me scout the winds."

Rori paused, then dropped her scowl. "I suppose that's a fair point."

"Will you two stop making eyes at each other and focus on the game?" Eric demanded. "Actually, no, keep doing that. It's better for me if she's not paying attention."

Rori gave him a playful shove that sent him sprawling into Marcus, who pushed him right back.

Nate was glad to see that Marcus was feeling better, and for the chance to change the topic. "Is that new anchor finally working for you?" he asked, nodding at the green agate on the Darkbend's wrist.

Marcus considered the large stone piece for a moment. "It's better," he said, "but I wish I'd kept the other one, too."

"There, you see?" Eric said. "That's why you always haggle the price." He lay a card facedown in the middle of the playing field. "Falcon."

"Liar," Rori said.

Eric stared at her for a long moment before flipping the card to reveal a white chicken. "I don't like playing with you," he grumbled.

Rori smirked, and the game went on until the *Southern Echo* had cleared the known naval patrol routes and glided sedately out to sea.

When it was full dark, Dax led the hidden half of the

crew back to the main deck, and then the real work began to catch the winds and bring the *Southern Echo* back up to a respectable speed.

While helping the riggers position the sails, Nate had a good view of the last islands of the Coral Chain receding into the darkness off the stern. One of them had a cluster of lights along its shoreline, where a large town was established.

"That's the Solkyrian naval outpost on Veritia," Theo Yellowwood informed him as they hauled back on a rope together. "A lot of navy ships port there before they go out on patrol. They either leave quick or stay too long ashore, pulled in by Veritian wine. Supposed to be pure ambrosia, that stuff. The more disciplined officers avoid it and get their crews back out to sea before they can get a taste, else they have to drag their sailors back to the boats."

"And the laxer officers?" Nate asked.

"They get in trouble when the next disciplined one shows up."

Nate snorted, wondering what Captain Arani thought of that story.

When he finally picked her out on the dark deck, however, she was facing firmly away from the island. Nate thought about what she'd said to him the night he'd first stepped aboard the *Southern Echo*, about leaving behind everything you knew. He wondered what leaving Veritia had been like for her. Stories passed around the crew claimed that she'd been several years younger than Nate when she'd first gone out to sea, but he'd always known her to be fiercely defensive of her Veritian heritage, if not necessarily proud of it. He watched the captain for several minutes, but she did not once look back at her home.

No, Nate thought, *that's not right. The* Southern Echo *is her home now. Just like the rest of us.*

But there was a stiffness in her posture that betrayed how hard she was fighting not to turn around.

By the next morning, Veritia was nothing but a memory off the *Southern Echo*'s stern, and Arani approached Nate about his wind reading.

"Are you feeling up to ranging further out?" she asked.

"Aye," he answered.

He searched her face for any trace of homesickness, but the captain was calm and unruffled, not a single hair out of place even as the wind tugged at her bun and played with the red feather on her hat.

"If you are willing and able, I'd like you to check each point of the compass," Arani said evenly. "Don't go more than a few miles out from the ship, and take frequent breaks. Marcus is on bucket duty, and he knows exactly how long he's supposed to let you stay out."

Nate stifled a groan and went to work his Skill.

Even with the limitations Arani had set, the work was taxing after so many shorter stints. It took over an hour to check the north, south, east, and west, and Nate's gold ring was hot against his skin by the time he'd finished with the last direction. Some were less challenging than others, depending on the angle and strength of the winds, but no matter what, it was easy to get lost in that world of smeared purples and blues, searching for signs of danger. Three times, Marcus doused Nate with the water after he overshot the time limit Arani had set, and he came back into his own body with a jarring crash and the beginnings of a headache.

"You think I could get a turn with the bucket?" Eric asked after witnessing this.

"Absolutely not," Nate said as he wrung out his soaked shirt. "You'd do it for laughs well before the hour is up."

Eric shrugged. "You're probably not wrong."

The first several sweeps Nate made of the surrounding winds revealed a few ships, but not many. Their shadows cut dark shapes against the lines of the wind down by the hard surface of the water. They all were holding to the expected trade routes and Arani wasn't particularly concerned about any of them, although she still wanted as many details as Nate could give.

"How many masts?" she asked each time Nate came back with a new wind shadow fresh against his skin. "Which way are they sailing? Are they holding a steady course?"

He answered her questions as best he could, and Arani would give a satisfied nod and tell him to rest before his next call to read the wind.

She wasn't alarmed until Nate found a two-masted vessel sailing south. It wasn't on a direct line of intercept with the *Southern Echo*, but Arani had them alter their course and keep the ship Nate had sensed over the edge of the horizon.

"That one is not following any of the trade routes," she told him. "Those are the ones we need to be worried about."

"Could it be one of Spider's missing ships?" Nate asked.

"If it is," Arani answered, "it's not something we need to be concerned with. They'll make their own way back to the Nest, and we'll still be paid for our efforts." She glared out at the horizon and thumbed the pommel of her saber. "But I doubt it's them. I'm not risking the lives of the crew on a gamble like that."

Some of the crew, however, were more willing to take the risk, especially when the *Southern Echo* crossed one of the trade routes from the Gemheart

Islands. Merchant ships ripe for the taking were bleeding their shadows across the wind, but the captain and quartermaster both shot down suggestions that they go after a prize.

"The sooner we complete Spider's assignment, the sooner we'll get paid," Dax said. "If we take a merchant ship, the weight of the cargo will slow us down."

"And who are we going to sell that haul to?" Arani added. "Spider? Who couldn't afford the drinking horn? Who so badly wanted us to take on this job he kicked us off his island before we could spend everything he paid us upfront?" She shook her head. "Best we stay the course, and not damn ourselves with our own greed."

She did not cut her gaze to the boatswain as she said this, but Nate saw Novachak flush all the same, the reddening of his skin made all the more noticeable against the white bandage wrapped around his head.

Days passed without incident, although Arani had them change course twice more to avoid what she suspected were navy ships. Before long, the *Southern Echo* was turning east, heading directly for the Gemheart Islands. They came into sight as jagged splotches on the horizon that solidified into soaring cliffs and tumbles of rocks, each individual island a distinct color that defined its name. To the south was Opal Peak and the Citrine Cliffs, and along the northern edge of the chain, Onyx Island was swept into the embrace of Moonstone Reach. Their rocky lands were considerably duller than their names suggested, but to Nate's eyes, they sparkled with the allure of someplace new. He took in the shapes and colors of each of them, marveling at the abrupt changes between one island and the next.

He was disappointed that the *Southern Echo* was not going to sail closer to them.

The southern islands were the ones Arani intended to scout for Spider from a safe distance. All of the Gemheart Islands were notorious for their rocky coasts, but the north side of the chain had direct exposure to the winter storms that came out of the Aurora Sea. As such, no ships sailed around the northern side of the islands at this time of year. Spider's ships certainly would have kept to the south, and if they'd been unlucky enough to fall victim to the edges of a winter storm, then they had either wrecked or sought shelter within the Gemheart Islands, if they'd been able to get past the rocks.

The captain was not optimistic about that possibility, and after seeing the jagged cut of many different colored rocks rising out of the sea, Nate had to agree with her.

There were considerably fewer ships sailing the waters near the Gemhearts, but Nate still picked up a few wind shadows. Now that they were close to their goal, Arani allowed the *Southern Echo* to edge towards the other ships, until she could confirm through her spyglass that they were not Spider's. She had the crew run up the friendly signal flags in case the other vessels were looking back at the *Southern Echo*, and most of them responded in kind before passing harmlessly along on their way.

Of the two that did not answer the signal flags, one kept on plodding into the west, directly away from the *Southern Echo*. Its sailors likely never saw the pirate ship. The other, however, turned towards the *Southern Echo* and began to pick up speed.

The crew leapt to their tasks when Arani called

for them to move, and Dax and Novachak sent their voices booming across the decks as everyone scrambled to turn the ship and fill the sails. Nate stayed at the captain's side, his awareness flung back into the wind, and he felt a hot spike of panic as he realized the other ship was gaining speed even faster than the *Southern Echo*. When he returned to his body and blinked away the sudden change from the ribboned blue world of the winds to raw daylight, he saw that what had formerly been a small blot of white on the horizon had doubled in size, and there were patches of red among the white sails.

"Oh, it's you," Captain Arani said, sounding distinctly unimpressed as she took in the bizarre display of the sails. She lowered her spyglass and folded it away in a single crisp movement. "Belay the mad dash," she called to the quartermaster and the boatswain, "and run up our colors."

Nate was certain he'd heard that wrong, but Dax and Novachak both took one look at the approaching ship and immediately ordered the wind to be let out of the sails. As Arani's black flag went up, Nate looked out at the other ship, and was surprised to see it answer with one of its own. He squinted, and could barely make out the red symbol against the black field.

"Arm yourselves with cutlasses and your best manners," Arani called as she stepped across the deck. "We're about to parley with the *Red Siren*."

CHAPTER SIX

Parley

IT TOOK AN IRRITATING amount of signal flags, shouted challenges, and muttered curses before the captain of the *Red Siren* finally agreed to come over to the *Southern Echo* rather than the other way around. Dax and Iris both agreed that if Captain Whitebrook wanted to talk to them so badly, he could come to them.

The ships were lashed together without much fuss, and while there were wary glances traded across the railings of the two vessels, there were also a few smiles and waves. Dax relaxed a bit when he saw that. Blackcliff was the only captain that Iris counted as an outright enemy, but away from Spider's Nest, other pirates were rivals at best. When crews crossed, outcomes included everything from shaky alliances that lasted exactly as long as it remained inconvenient to turn on each other, to warily dodging the other ship and minimizing contact. At least here, with the *Red Siren*, there wouldn't be trouble without provocation.

Cedric Whitebrook came across in a flashy leap and swing from a rope, his brown coat whirling giddily around his body. He landed on the deck with a solid thump and smile, already tipping his tricorn hat to Iris. "It's a lovely day to behold an even lovelier sight such as you, Captain Arani," he gushed at her.

Dax noted the man's open shirt—carefully arranged to show off his chest—and thought about how easy it would be to stop his heart. Dax made a point of keeping his hands folded behind his back as Iris stepped forward to meet the man.

"Flattery has never won you anything," she said crisply. "I caution you against it today; I would rather not waste my time."

Whitebrook drew his hands to his chest. "You wound me, my lady."

Dax saw Iris's grip tighten on her saber, and he ducked his head to hide a small smile. He knew she wanted to say something about actual wounds and swords, but she wisely kept the words to herself. Across the way, Dax saw the quartermaster of the *Red Siren* roll her eyes.

Beth Greenwater, he remembered. A stocky, no-nonsense woman that would have been infinitely better for them to speak with, but she'd chosen to let her captain have the honor.

Returning his attention to Whitebrook, Dax watched the man give the *Southern Echo*'s crew a sweeping appraisal. His gaze paused on a few faces, and Dax knew that he was picking out the Skill tattoos. His brows arched with open interest when he saw Rori and Nate. When Whitebrook's gaze slid to Dax, however, it danced along his disguised tattoo, and then wandered away without any sign of recognition.

Dax hid the joyous flare that rose in his chest. He could count on one hand the number of times he and Whitebrook had crossed paths, and it was a relief to know that the man remained unaware of Dax's Skill. Dax had worried that after more than half the crew had left the *Southern Echo* before the journey into the Forbidden Sea, the secret his tattoos covered would have been spread far and wide. If Whitebrook still didn't know, there was hope that others didn't either.

"How did you manage to pick up two young weather

workers, my dear?" Whitebrook asked Iris admiringly as he finished taking in the *Southern Echo* crew. "I've only ever been able to get Grayvoices and Darkbends on my ship, and you know how useless those are." His gaze swung up to the rigging, and for the first time, his smile faltered. "Where is your Grayvoice, anyway? The feral one who liked to swing from ropes?"

This time, Dax had to reach out to still Iris's hand before she could draw her sword. He would have loved to have let her, but it was not the time to cut down a captain in front of his crew and spark a battle between the two ships. He felt Iris's anger pulsing through her, but she took a steadying breath and released her sword after a moment.

"Why are you here, Cedric?" she asked.

Oblivious to the hard edge in her voice, Whitebrook turned another radiant smile on her. "I would ask you the same thing, my lovely flower of the seas."

Beth Greenwater wasn't the only one who rolled her eyes this time. "Get to the point, Captain," the *Red Siren*'s quartermaster shouted.

Whitebrook waved away her impatience, but his smile dimmed and some of the gleeful facade fell away. "It was a surprise to see the *Southern Echo* out here, given your recent troubles with the navy."

Iris did not flinch, although Dax could tell it was a near thing. "Heard about that, did you?"

"Everyone who's been to port on Spider's Nest in the last two months has heard about that," Whitebrook said. "Tangling with the navy twice, and sailing away each time?" He shifted back on his heels, his hands coming to rest at the sword and pistol belted at his sides. "If I didn't know better, I'd think you'd struck up some sort of agreement with them."

"Watch your mouth, sailor," Iris snarled.

Whitebrook's endearing smile returned. "Come

now, Iris, I know you'd never stoop so low, but these are troubling times, and I needed to hear it from you." He leaned in closer again, his voice pitched to an ineffective whisper. "Some of Spider's ships have gone missing, you know."

"We do know that," Dax said before Iris could suggest a creative place to stick his sword. "He's hired us to look for them."

"Oh, you too!" Whitebrook clapped his hands together. "Doesn't seem like he let any of us go without conscripting us for that."

Dax took a moment to eye the *Red Siren*, and he knew Iris was thinking the same thing he was.

Whitebrook and his crew had a somewhat decent record when it came to taking prizes, but nowhere near enough to make them of interest to the Solkyrian Empire and Prince Trystos's pirate hunters. The *Red Siren* itself was larger than most pirate ships, but it was notoriously slow when it sailed under standard rigging. Whitebrook and Greenwater had turned that to their advantage by engineering a special set of rigging that allowed them to bring up additional sails. It put massive strain on the masts, and the *Red Siren* was often beached for repairs when it was in port at Spider's Nest, but it was just enough to give Whitebrook's crew the edge over merchants, and the mere sight of a ship sporting a massive crest of sails dyed blood-red was sometimes more than enough to prompt a surrender.

Whitebrook certainly had a flair for dramatics, but Dax couldn't say it was entirely unjustified.

Still, if Spider had called upon such a slow ship to look for his missing vessels, then this was as serious as Iris had feared.

Something cold crept up Dax's spine even as Whitebrook said, "I know how much you value your time, so I'll give you a little gift and let you know that there's nothing to find here in the Gemhearts. The *Red Siren* has been up and down this chain, and the only thing we've found were a few old shipwrecks from bad weather a few seasons back."

"Really," Iris said.

"Aye," Whitebrook said confidently. "Nothing on the south side worth noting."

"And the north side?" Iris asked.

"Well," Whitebrook said, "there is a more recent wreck off the Ruby Shores that might have been one of Spider's, but it's not worth getting any closer. The rocks make it impossible to get to, and the sea has already claimed part of the hull. Won't be too long before the rest is battered away."

"Did you check for survivors?" Iris asked, and her voice was hard again.

Whitebrook gave her a look of earnest confusion. "If anyone survived that, it's because they had the sense to abandon ship before it slammed into those rocks." His gaze slipped past Iris to the *Southern Echo*'s crew again. "If I had a Goodtide, maybe I'd have braved it, but without one of those, I would have only been wrecking my ship, too."

Iris's jaw tightened, but she said nothing, and Dax took his cue from her.

"If you want to see for yourself, be my guest, but you'll only be wasting precious time that could be better spent in my company." Whitebrook gave Iris an inviting smile that maintained its confidence far longer into the following silence than Dax expected.

He might have been impressed, if he wasn't thinking about stopping the man's heart again.

Out of the corner of his eye, Dax saw Nikolai fighting back a snicker. He glowered at the boatswain, which only made the Northman shake harder with silent laughter.

After a few minutes, Whitebrook shrugged. "I would have enjoyed sailing beside you on our way back to Spider's Nest, but if you insist on going to the Ruby Shores, I'll have to send you off with a wish for better luck than that other ship found." He swept off his hat and dropped into a low bow before Iris. "Fair winds to you, my lady. I look forward to toasting your return when we next see each other."

When Whitebrook was back aboard his own ship, the lines coupling the *Red Siren* and the *Southern Echo* were cut. Beth Greenwater gave Dax and Iris a solemn nod as the two ships drifted apart, and those among the crews who knew each other sent their brief goodbyes across the gap. The *Red Siren* turned south, heading back for the Coral Chain, and the *Southern Echo* swung towards the northern shores of the Gemheart Islands.

"It could have been a storm," Iris allowed once the *Red Siren* was firmly in their wake, "but a wreck off the Ruby Shores at this time of year?" She shook her head, her thumb idly running across the pommel of her saber. "Spider's ships wouldn't have been over there. No one would have, unless they were trying to get away from something."

"So Spider was right, then," Dax said, keeping his voice low. "It's pirate hunters."

Iris was quiet for a long time. "If the gods are kind, it won't be," she finally said, "but we've met those bastards, and they are anything but."

Dax ran a quick prayer through his mind as penance for her sacrilege, but he did not disagree.

CHAPTER SEVEN
The Shipwreck

By the time the *Red Siren* had disappeared over the horizon, the sky had taken on a gray cast and the wind that blew through the sails was pure and cold. Nate shivered as it washed over him. He bundled deeper into his coat, wishing he'd spent his coin on a new one of those rather than the shirts Eric had insisted upon. Although, while bad for his comfort, the breezes were coming in a steady rush, making them easy to catch and hold in the sails and sending the *Southern Echo* along at a swift pace.

But even though the ship had a good wind and the riggers were taking a rest before they were needed again, Nate did not go below to escape the chill. He stayed on the main deck, letting the wind rip through him. It teased at his magic, trying to pull him along, but Nate kept a firm lock on his Skill and did not slip into the element.

Instead, he watched the Gemheart Islands slide past, taking in as much of this new part of the world as he could while his thoughts played over the meeting between the two pirate ships.

Captain Whitebrook had been yet another Solkyrian who had looked at Nate and his friends and only saw their Skills. There had been a few faces aboard the *Red Siren* that had borne the white and black tattoos of Darkbends and Grayvoices, but they had huddled in a close group and stared at the *Southern Echo* crew with the same kind of jealous awe that Nate used to feel whenever he'd seen weather workers dressed in the blue uniforms of the Solkyrian navy. He recognized that sense of inferiority in the presence of perceived betters.

The *Red Siren*'s Skilled sailed under a black flag, but they did not have the same freedom as Nate and his friends.

Nate finally loved his magic and all the things it could do, but Rori had been right; he'd been afraid to understand who he was beyond his Skill. His heart ached for the Darkbends and Grayvoices that sailed with Whitebrook and other captains like him, along with the weather workers serving on Solkyrian ships. That included his older siblings.

He wondered where they were at that moment, if they had found any stolen moments of happiness that day. They were both doing exactly what the empire had said they were born for, filling their assigned places in the world, but Nate felt like he understood a lot more about that world than either of them.

And yet, there was still so much of it he had not seen.

Nate's thoughts turned to the islands he'd glimpsed on the sea charts that Rori and the officers often poured over, tracing out the *Southern Echo*'s future paths and shaping each new tomorrow. When he was much younger and still believed that his Skill would someday secure him a place on a navy vessel, he'd dreamed of seeing the world from the decks of a ship. He was doing that now, as a pirate, but with the future laid open before him, he began to wonder if he could take his own steps forward instead of being swept along. He did not want to leave the *Southern Echo* and her crew, but for the first time, he imagined himself adding his voice to those that charted the next way forward, imagined himself being bold and certain in his choices because he fully understood himself, and if others disagreed and their paths diverged, it would not destroy the very foundation of his world.

But to understand where he could go and who he could be, Nate knew that there was a lot more that he needed to learn. The Solkyrian Empire had consciously held him and every other Skilled back from doing just that, but that could be undone.

And he suddenly knew the perfect way to start.

A few moments later, he knocked on the door to the navigation room. Rori's muffled voice called for him to enter, and he pushed the door open without hesitating.

Rori was in her usual place, bent over the writing desk with a chart spread before her, its corners weighed down by stones. The small room smelled of ink and parchment, the air considerably warmer than it was outside. Small candle flames flickered and danced, bright against the gloom of winter, and their light caught on Rori's cheek and hair as she turned to greet him. She stilled when she realized who he was, but any awkwardness was shattered when Luken gave a joyful screech and launched himself off the table, cutting straight for Nate's head.

Nate managed to duck under the first attack, but the bird was relentless, and he claimed victory by settling into one of the folds of Nate's hat, cooing contentedly as he arranged himself against the leather.

Nate sighed as Luken relaxed, but he let the bird finish before turning to Rori. He pointed up at the back of his hat, where Luken's pennant feathers stuck out. "Answer me honestly," Nate said. "Is there any dignity in this at all?"

It took a moment, but Rori began to chuckle quietly. "Maybe, if the hat wasn't making such adorable noises."

"That's fair," Nate conceded. He waved her off when she made to rise and remove Luken. "The little hellspawn can stay for the moment. There's something I wanted to ask you."

"Does it have to do with your lacking sense of style?" she asked with a growing smirk.

"Don't let Eric hear you say that," Nate warned as he crossed to the desk. "He picked out this shirt, after all."

Rori laughed more earnestly and moved an ink pot aside so Nate could perch on the edge of the desk. He made to do so, but stopped when his gaze caught on the sea chart.

Careful annotations blanketed the page, the script small and neat alongside the precise lines that marked the jagged landmasses that splattered the sea.

"Is that where we're going?" he asked.

Rori grimaced. "Unfortunately." She hovered her hand above the map, careful not to smear the fresh ink as she took in the bulk of the chart with a slow gesture. "The Ruby Shores have one of the most dangerous coastlines in the known archipelago. All these spots here are rocks jutting up from the sea."

Nate studied the map over her shoulder. "We're not really sailing into that, are we?"

"No," Rori said. She skimmed her finger across the bottom edge of the drawn rock clusters. "We'll be over here, keeping our distance, but the captain wanted me to check for any possible spots where a ship could've gone in, accidentally or otherwise."

Nate stared at the map, his eyes drawn to the hand-written script. He drew in a breath, and asked the question he'd come to ask. "Could you teach me to read?"

Rori froze. Her brows were arched and her mouth open in shock when she looked up at him.

"I don't mean at this exact moment," Nate said. "I know you're busy, and will be for a while, but when you have the time, I'd really like to learn." He rubbed the back of his neck as Rori continued to stare at him. "If you're willing, of course. Or maybe I could ask Dax or Novachak."

Rori blinked, and her expression hardened into seriousness. "Didn't you get enough grief the last time you said you were going to ask Novachak for private lessons?"

Nate frowned at her, confused, until he saw the wicked way her eyes danced. "Oh, not you, too!" he exclaimed, his face heating with embarrassment.

"Lily told me," Rori said, now laughing openly.

"She told the whole ship, didn't she?" Nate groaned.

"Well, she was *very* disappointed that you turned her down for the boatswain," Rori said. Then she reached out and caught his sleeve. "But I would be happy to teach you."

Nate sobered, his heart lifting. "Really?"

"Aye," Rori said, holding his gaze and smiling.

They stood like that for a moment, until Rori cleared her throat and reached for his hat.

"I'd better dislodge Luken before he gets too comfortable."

Nate agreed, although the bird did not, and there were a few loose feathers swirling around the navigation room by the time they got him off of the hat. Rori promised to begin his reading lessons once the voyage was over, and Nate left feeling lighter than he had in days. Not even the biting wind could dampen his spirits as he stepped back out on to the main deck.

When the Ruby Shores came into view, however, his elation gave way to a creeping unease.

The main body of the red island was a dramatic jut of cliffs out of the sea, crested with short, scraggly trees that desperately wrapped their roots around whatever rocks they could find. Fog clung to the base of the cliffs, obscuring where they met the water, but tendrils of red rock spiked out of the sea a long way off the shoreline, as though the Ruby Shores were trying to claw themselves away from the rest of the Gemhearts. Waves hammered the reaching rocks, throwing fine mist into the air and filling the world with a low and rolling thunder. The wind swirled and whistled past the spires, tearing itself into a confused mess that Nate could not hope to read.

He was a little afraid to try.

He fiddled with the agate beads on the hemp bracelet he'd gotten from Spider's Nest and consoled himself with Rori's earlier promise that they were not sailing into those rocks.

The majority of the crew was topside as the *Southern Echo* skirted the outer edge of the Ruby Shores. Marcus, Eric, and eventually Rori all joined Nate at the port railing, peering at the jagged rocks with wide eyes.

"Do you think it really was one of Spider's ships that wrecked here?" Marcus asked.

"Hard to say," Rori answered. "It could have been a merchant ship, or even one from the navy. We won't know until we see it."

Eric folded his arms and leaned on the railing. "Would have been nice if Whitebrook had bothered to actually check," he said. "Could have saved us all the trouble, especially after that comment about Darkbends and Grayvoices."

Nate grimaced as he recalled the man's words. *Useless,* Whitebrook had said. Not like weather workers. He'd been looking at Nate's tattoo at that moment.

"No one on this ship is useless," Rori said firmly. Luken gave a soft chirp, as though agreeing with her.

Eric nodded, but he kept his gaze fixed on the spires of red rock. "I know that, but it still hurts to hear."

Nate glanced at the elegant Darkbend, surprised. Eric had never put much value on his own magic, finding pride and confidence in his carpentry skills instead. Nate didn't think one man's ignorance could have pierced that well-earned armor, but clearly it had.

He gently bumped Eric's shoulder. "Whitebrook doesn't matter," Nate told him. "None of them do."

Eric released a soft sigh, but he nodded again and drew himself up a little straighter.

Dax and Arani had the ship hold a steady course as she swept along the Ruby Shores, but no one saw any evidence of a wreck. The *Southern Echo* swung wide, and then skimmed closer to the jutting rocks and began to thread a path through the sparser areas.

"We need to see that wreck. We have to be certain," Arani said, but she did not hide the reluctance in her voice or the way her hand kept moving to the saber at her hip as the island's red claws slid past. She turned to Nate with a beseeching expression. "I don't supposed you'd be willing to see what you could find in the winds?"

Nate eyed the jagged rocks and shook his head. "I'm not going in there," he said. "Those rocks are tearing the winds to shreds, and I don't think I could piece a trail back together. Sorry, Captain."

Arani sighed, but she nodded and went to talk to the riggers about putting more eyes up in the lines.

"I don't blame you," Eric said once she was gone. "Even I can feel how vicious the winds are out here."

"The light is strange, too," Marcus said.

Eric gave the other Darkbend an exasperated look. "You keep saying that. There's nothing strange about the light."

"There is," Marcus insisted. He traced a finger across the piece of green agate he wore on his wrist. "Ever since the Vanishing Island, something's changed." He held Eric's gaze for a moment. "You really don't feel it?"

Frowning, Eric shook his head, but there was an odd undertone creeping into his gaze as he looked at the other Darkbend. "Did something happen on that island?" Eric asked, his voice totally devoid of humor. "Don't lie to me."

Marcus shifted on his feet and pressed the agate even harder against his skin, looking more uncomfortable than Nate had ever seen him.

Eric stiffened, his eyes going wide beneath his white tattoo. "What did you do?"

"Nothing," Marcus said quickly. "It was just, in the temple, there was this presence... I don't know how to describe it."

Nate recalled the probing touch he'd felt on the Vanishing Island, scratching at his awareness and trying to burrow deeper. "Was it like something was trying to grab your Skill?"

Marcus lit up. "Yes, exactly. You felt it, too?"

Nate nodded.

Rori shuddered, giving them both a look suspended somewhere between pity and horror. "That's the touch of a god." She crossed her arms and rubbed her hands over her sleeves. "Trust me, you don't want one of their voices in your head."

"It's not," Nate said. "I haven't felt or heard anything like that since we left the Rend."

"Good," Rori said, but there was a wistfulness to her tone that made Nate step forward and put his hands on her shoulders.

"You shouldn't have to hear it," he told her, "but just because it's speaking, that doesn't mean you have to listen. Your magic is yours, and you're the only one who decides how to use it."

Rori's breath was shaky and uneven, but she gave a brave nod and drew herself up taller.

A shout from the rigging made them all jump.

"Ship ahead," Liliana called, "off the starboard bow!"

Nate swung around, shocked that a ship had managed to sneak up on them out here, but he quickly understood his mistake.

"Gods below," Eric murmured, and Nate had to agree.

There was a wrecked ship ahead of them, but Whitebrook had severely understated the magnitude of its destruction.

It was as if the Ruby Shores had snapped their rock spires around the hull like a pair of jaws, and had no intention of surrendering the vessel until the meal was done.

The tattered ship was lodged between two of the red outcroppings closer to the island, but one of the spires was driven clean through the hull. As the result, the ship was suspended in the air above the waterline, barnacles and sea growth clear to see along the exposed keel. The sea's dark waves barely touched the very bottom of the wreck even when they rose to slap against the rocks and throw spray into the air.

Nate swallowed hard as the image rose clearly in his mind: the ship caught by a storm, massive waves toying with the vessel until it was impaled by the red rocks spiking out of the sea.

He shuddered to think what that would have done to anyone aboard at the time, but Whitebrook was right about one thing; if anyone had escaped that ship alive, they'd done it long before it had wrecked.

Captain Arani ordered the *Southern Echo*'s anchor dropped and the sails furled, and Nate moved to assist the riggers while the captain studied the shipwreck through her spyglass. She was still staring at the wreck long after the *Southern Echo* had come to a halt. Not a word had escaped her, and the crew milled about on the deck as she continued her silent vigil.

Novachak's patience finally wore thin. "Well?" the boatswain demanded. "Is it one of Spider's or not?"

Arani did not lower the spyglass. "I can't tell," she said. "I need to get closer."

"We can't sail much farther in than this," Dax said. "It's too dangerous to bring the *Southern Echo* any closer."

"You're not wrong," Arani murmured, but something in her tone made the quartermaster go rigid, and Nate felt unease begin to simmer in his gut.

He glanced again at the skewered wreck. Tendrils of fog were creeping around the destroyed ship, reminding Nate of the spirits on the Vanishing Island, and he turned away with a shudder. His gaze caught on a small group of people gathered at the railing, locked in a debate. Chief among them were Rori, Roberto Perrani—one of the men who ran navigational assistance for her—and Theo Yellowwood, oldest and most seasoned of the riggers.

Curiosity interwoven with dread moved Nate's feet, and he joined them.

"What's wrong?" he asked as he stepped up next to Perrani. Instinctually, Nate kept his voice low, though he could not say why.

Perrani acknowledged him with the barest of glances. The others kept on staring at the wreck and arguing, as though nothing else in the world existed. Esmerelda Durmanti and another rigger were insisting on a storm, but Theo and Rori were shaking their heads.

"No reason for the ship to be here," Perrani murmured to Nate as the debate continued. His accent was the most pronounced out of all of the Veritian sailors on the ship, and Nate leaned a little closer to be certain that he heard everything correctly. "All sailors know the sea is bad around these islands. Rori and Theo say, if a storm, why sail into danger?"

"You mean, instead of turning out to open sea?" Nate asked.

Perrani nodded grimly and pointed at the jagged teeth of the Ruby Shores. "Rocks are death for a ship. No captain would come here in a storm."

"I suppose not," Nate said slowly, "unless they were looking for something."

"Or running from it," Theo Yellowwood cut in. He still had not turned away from the wreck, but the argument had collapsed during Perrani's explanation. "If something scared you bad enough," Theo continued, "then you might take your chances here, hoping the rocks would protect you if they didn't kill you."

"Like the Gauntlet," Nate murmured. He cut another hard look at the shipwreck. "I don't think that gamble paid off for them. What could they have possibly been fleeing?"

"I think it was less of a *what*," Rori said, "and more of a *whom*." From the set of her spine, Nate could tell that she was thoroughly unnerved.

"The navy?" he asked.

"At least," Rori answered. "Whatever wave picked up that ship, it wasn't natural. Someone did that on purpose."

The wind was thin and cold against the back of Nate's neck as he studied the ruined ship and the harsh spray of the sea against the rocks. He did not know much about tide working, but he knew that water was not like the wind, pliable in a true wind worker's hands. Whenever he'd seen Rori work the tides, she'd struggled hard against them, fighting to turn the currents like they were wild animals bucking against her touch, and the waves she summoned were equally untamed, spreading out from the focal point of her magic to sweep away anything in their paths. Winds could be powerful and dangerous all on their own, Nate knew that firsthand, but nothing compared to the merciless strength of the sea. Nate couldn't help but glance at Rori's Goodtide mark, curling and elaborate, and wonder how much stronger someone would need to be to control the water here, to wreck a single ship and nothing more.

The unease in his gut went from a simmer to a rolling boil.

"Absolutely not," the sharp voice of the quartermaster exploded from the other side of the deck. "That is suicide!"

"It's the only way to be sure," the captain answered, and then there were too many raised voices for Nate to understand the next words.

When he fought his way through the crowd with Rori, Theo, and the others behind him, Nate found the quartermaster glaring daggers at Captain Arani, who was calmly folding her spyglass and putting the instrument away.

"One rowboat, a few volunteers, and a grappling hook," Arani said. "That's all I need."

"You're getting none of those," Dax snapped.

"We'll see," Arani said, then she turned to the crew with a false smile. "Who wants to join me on an adventure through dangerous waters to an even more dangerous shipwreck to find out if said wreck is one of Spider's or not?"

Nate wasn't the only one who stared at her blankly.

But then Rori spoke, and her voice was clear and steady. "I'll go."

"*What?*" Nate blurted, but she was already pushing past him, moving towards Arani. It took him a few tries to get his feet untangled before he could stumble after her.

Arani turned a surprised look on Rori, but there was no mistaking the relief underscoring her expression. "I didn't want to ask this of you," she began.

Rori did not miss a step. "If you're going to survive that, you'll need the water calmed. I'll do it."

"You can't," Nate sputtered as he came up alongside her. "Do you have any idea how dangerous that is, even without—?" He cut himself off before he could say, *Even without a god whispering to you.*

Rori turned to him, and Nate came up short at the swirling war of fear and determination in her eyes. "My magic, my choice," she said, echoing his own words back to him. But her resolve wavered for a moment, the fear winning out. "Right?"

Nate swallowed, fighting every screaming urge to beg her not to go, but instead, he nodded. "Right," he whispered.

"It's too dangerous," Dax cut in, still focused on the captain. "The odds of you coming back from that wreck—"

"I know," Arani cut in. She let out a hard breath. "But we need to know if that's one of Spider's, and if it is, what happened to it." She bared her teeth in a grimace. "And this way, I can bring back proof."

Dax shook his head. "You don't need it."

"It's Spider. Of course I do."

Novachak took a tentative step forward. "I think the captain has the right of it," he said.

Dax whirled on the man as though confronting a traitor, then raked his hands along his tattoos and let out an exasperated snarl. "I'm going with you, then," he said to Arani.

The captain shook her head. "You're needed here." She patted Dax on the shoulder and gave him a twisted smile. "If I go down, the crew will need you to stop anyone else from doing something equally as stupid. The ship is yours until I return. Take good care of her."

"I'm going, too," Eric said, and Nate whipped around to look at his friend in horror. Eric ignored his stare and drew himself up. "If I can examine the damage, I may be able to determine more about what really happened here. If it was just a storm that did that, there should be evidence of it on the rest of the ship, but I'm not seeing it through the spyglass."

Arani nodded. "All right, then. I'll need two strong people on the oars. Who else is willing?"

And so Nate watched in terrified silence alongside Dax, Marcus, and the rest of the crew as a rowboat containing Arani, Novachak, Rori, Eric, and two gunners pulled away from the side of the *Southern Echo*.

Nate's heart was in his throat the entire time the small rowboat fought its way towards the jutting red rocks, lifting and falling with the swells as easily as a leaf caught in a gale. Before long, the boat was too far away for Nate to make out individual faces, and with the way the wind was blowing that close to the surface of the sea, he knew he'd gain nothing useful from scoping out the wind shadow. Dax, Theo, and a couple other seasoned sailors had procured spyglasses of their own, but none of them were inclined to share. Nate squinted into the distance, trying to keep the little boat and its party in sight. He could not do a thing, except stop himself from blinking as he waited for some violent jolt of motion that meant the rowboat had struck a rock or been capsized by a wave or any number of other awful things.

He did not see the exact moment when Rori began to use her magic, but the waves calmed around the rocks, becoming rhythmic and soft if not stopping entirely. It was like looking at the flat and glassy water that had been waiting in the middle of the Forbidden Sea, so strange was that patch of calmness in the middle of all the chaos.

Even with the distance, however, Nate could see the vibrant splotch of red as Arani stood and threw a metal hook up at the suspended shipwreck, a thin line of rope trailing behind it. It took a few tries before the hook successfully lodged itself, and then Arani's red coat was moving up the line, climbing into the wreck. She disappeared inside. Two others went up after her: Novachak and Eric. Once they were gone, the little rowboat moved away, the gunners positioning it back outside the cluster of red rock spires.

The whistle of the wind and the distant calls of unfamiliar birds were the only sounds for the next half hour. Nate braced himself against the railing as he continued to watch the rowboat, and he could have sworn there was an anxious edge to the soft pulse that radiated through the *Southern Echo*, as though the dryad herself fretted over the absence of Arani and the others.

No one was at ease aboard the *Southern Echo*. Everyone was crammed against the port railing, watching the shipwreck. Dax had refused to lower his spyglass, and his mouth was pressed into a hard line as he waited for someone to emerge.

There was a sudden groan on the wind, and the shipwreck shuddered and slid further down the impaling spire.

Nate's heart stopped even as the wreck jerked to a halt. Someone cried out and voices rose in horrified concern, but the wreck did not move again.

Gods above protect them, Nate thought, desperate and helpless. *Please.*

A few more minutes passed before Arani's red coat appeared again, one arm raised to signal the rowboat. Dax let out a hard breath, but he did not lower the spyglass until Arani, Novachak, and Eric had all climbed back down the rope. When the rowboat was on its way back to the *Southern Echo*, he finally lowered the instrument and scrubbed his hand over his face.

The wreck groaned again, and then fell apart around the spire, collapsing into the sea.

Nate cried out with the others this time. He lost sight of the rowboat, and could only think that the wreck had fallen on top of it, taking everyone down with it.

But then there was an unnatural swell of water, and the little rowboat appeared at the crest of the wave, rushing away from the danger.

Nate's knees went weak with relief as several people around him cheered.

When the rowboat bumped against the side of the *Southern Echo*, it was easy to see how pale and shaken everyone looked, even with the ordeal of the wreck firmly behind them. Arani and Novachak both had a grim determination about them that kept them steady on their feet as they climbed up and swung their feet over the railing.

Dax was waiting for them with a glower and his teeth bared in a snarl. "That was beyond stupid," he informed the other two officers.

"Yes," Arani agreed, bent at the waist with her hands on her thighs. "Yes, it was."

Eric came up next, and Marcus extended his hand to help him climb aboard. Rori was close behind, and Nate reached for her, catching her by the arms and hauling her back on to the ship. She fell against him, surprised, but Nate did not let go for a long time, not even when Luken landed on his arm and gave an impatient chirp at Rori's shoulders being blocked.

"I'm all right," Rori mumbled against the collar of Nate's coat.

"You're shaking," he said.

"That's magic burn," Eric said as he reached out and gently untangled Nate's arms from around Rori. "She did good." He gave Nate a flat look as Rori stepped away. "I'm fine too, by the way," he quipped, then dropped his voice lower. "Unless you're done pretending you don't have a favorite person on this ship?"

Nate wasn't sure whether to laugh or take a swing at Eric for risking his own life only to come back and tease Nate, but he settled for releasing his breath in a rush of relief and embracing his friend when Eric opened his arms.

"Well?" Dax asked, drawing Nate's and everyone else's attention. "What did you learn from your very stupid trip, Captain?"

Even though she had not been on the oars, Arani was panting lightly, and her gaze was troubled as she stared down at the *Southern Echo*'s deck.

Novachak supplied an answer during her pause. "There's nothing over there," the boatswain said flatly.

Dax did not manage to fully keep the anger out of his voice. "So you risked your lives and learned nothing?"

"You misunderstand," Arani said. Her voice was quiet but somehow still carried to everyone's ears, and Nate noticed the effort it took for her to straighten up and look Dax in the eye. "There was *nothing* over there. No bodies, no ledgers, not even the last scraps of supplies. All I found were these." She reached into her coat pockets and withdrew two wadded up bundles, shaking them loose to reveal two flags. One was the standard flown by Solkyrian merchants, but the other was black with white lines arranged in a web.

Spider's flag.

"There's another matter," Arani continued. "Eric confirmed that there were no signs of storm damage, and the rowboats were still secured. So unless that ship's entire crew jumped and tried to swim away from the wreck, none of them made it off alive."

Dax frowned. "But there were no bodies?"

"None," Arani confirmed. "Which means that crew was gone from the ship before it wrecked. And no missing rowboats means they didn't leave by themselves."

The *Southern Echo* groaned beneath Nate's boots in the silence that followed the captain's words. He watched Dax, Arani, and Novachak exchange a meaningful look before the captain loudly informed the crew that they would be sailing back to Spider's Nest with all haste. The boatswain and the quartermaster both turned and began to order sailors to their stations, but Arani disappeared beneath the deck before anyone could untangle themselves from the sudden chaos and ask questions.

Nate found himself helping with the rigging next to Theo Yellowwood, and noticed the older man's perturbed expression. "What's happening?" he asked.

Theo leveled one last look at the empty spires where the shipwreck had been. "There's only one thing that would wreck a ship, take its crew, and strip it bare of all records and supplies."

"Pirates?" Nate asked dryly.

Theo shook his head. "Pirate hunters."

Nate jerked on the line, prompting a scolding remark from Theo, but he barely heard it over the pounding of his own heart.

CHAPTER EIGHT

Trick of the Light

SPEED BECAME THE PRIORITY over discretion, and the *Southern Echo* soared back across the Common Sea. Nate devoted his attention to scoping out the strongest and most compliant winds for the riggers to capture, which only demanded his magic for a few minutes at a time. The ring on his finger barely grew warm before he had the best ribbons of wind in sight, and the *Southern Echo* angled across their paths with her usual smooth and easy grace.

With Rori back on her navigational duties and the captain, quartermaster, and boatswain all calling for top speeds, everyone was too busy for much speculation, and then exhausted when they had a moment to rest, but the wreck at the Ruby Shores had left a lasting impression on the entire crew.

"So what do we think?" AnnaMarie asked at dinner. "Terrible storm, or powerful Goodtide?"

Nate pushed his food around with a bit of hardtack as he listened to the argument. A few halfhearted voices answered her, some pointing out that even Rori had struggled with the waters around the Ruby Shores, so the general consensus that Spider's ship had ultimately been taken out by a bad storm continued to reign, even with Eric's firsthand testimony to the distinct lack of storm damage.

"Doesn't matter," one of the swabs said, his head

drooping over his bowl. "It's done, we're going back to the Nest to get what's ours, and then we leave like the captain said."

"Not before we've seen to a last bit of business," AnnaMarie said. Nate lifted his head, but the gunner had her attention fixed on the swab. "If the *Dragonsbane* is there, we move."

"There are pirate hunters prowling these waters," the swab said tiredly. "That means Arani has the right of it, and we need to get out of the Common Sea."

"We will," AnnaMarie said. "After we make them answer for what they did to Jim."

There was a simple factuality to her words, lacking the heat of anger or a warble of uncertainty, and as Nate watched her, the gunner stifled a yawn. He realized that, in AnnaMarie's mind, this was simply something that was going to happen.

Not that anyone looked ready to argue with her, exhausted as everyone was.

Nate was still debating if he should say something or not when AnnaMarie spoke again.

"I would feel better, though, if we knew for sure if the hunters have a Goodtide with them or not."

"But we don't," the swab countered without ire. "We only know it's pirate hunters. Best let it go beyond that." He stood up, ready to head for his hammock in the berth. "Besides, if the empire had a Goodtide that strong, they'd be on the front lines fighting the Vothies, not patrolling the dead side of the Gemhearts."

AnnaMarie paused, considering the point, and made a thoughtful noise. "That's probably true."

"'Course it is," the swab said. "The empire doesn't give up their weather workers so easily, unless they're grossly misunderstood." He gave Nate a light pat on the shoulder as he stepped past. "Or trying to kill everyone, like Rori was."

The remark was light and drew a morbid chuckle from a few people, although Nate tensed as he waited for someone to give voice to hidden fears about Rori they'd been holding since the Forbidden Sea. No one did, however, and Nate gradually relaxed again. But he still pushed the remains of his dinner around his bowl and said nothing as his mind latched on to powerful tide workers and the empire.

It took him a long time to drift off to sleep that night, and when he finally did, his thoughts were still weakly tangled around his older sister Lisandra and the battles she must have been raging on behalf of the Solkyrian empire.

Nate had not seen her in a long, long time, but he was certain that if she'd been the one their father had offered his gold ring to, she would have worn the sun crest with fierce and open pride.

Everyone settled easily into the rhythm of the voyage. Though demanding, there was still a monotony to it, and as the days passed with no sightings of imperial ships—naval, merchant, or otherwise—the sense of urgency began to melt away. Even Arani was mildly impatient rather than panicked, and while she objected to evening music or other loud activities that could have caught the attention of any passing ships in the night, she still found ways to lightly tease the sailors she was more familiar with, drawing brief smiles and laughs whenever she crossed the ship. But that belied the wary expression she wore whenever she thought that no one was watching, and Dax's and Novachak's tempers were running shorter than usual.

Nate helped the riggers as best he could, and then

used his Skill to ride the winds. He started sensing the shadows of other ships as the *Southern Echo* drew closer to Veritia and the northern tip of the Coral Chain. He focused his efforts on parsing out the cuts of the sails and the speeds of the crafts, but he couldn't determine which were harmless and which should be watched. Wind shadows revealed a lot, but not the colors of the flags the ships were flying.

Arani had expected an uptick in ships as they approached the Coral Chain, however. As long as the other vessels paid no mind to the pirate brig sailing under false colors, she only called for small adjustments to the *Southern Echo*'s course to keep them just far enough away to not be worth any special interest.

But Nate still felt a surge of panic whenever he found a new wind shadow, certain that this was finally a ship full of pirate hunters come to destroy the fragile future he'd just begun to reach for, and his nerves were stretched to a breaking point by the end of each day.

This went on until the *Southern Echo* had cut further south, taking the longer but safer passage around the first few islands of the Coral Chain. Arani and Novachak had agreed that they would keep the sails full for as long as possible, trusting the good winds and Nate's ability to find them to help the ship far outpace the speeds they could have safely achieved had they cut into the Gauntlet Reef. Their instincts were right, but as they moved farther away from Veritia, Nate noticed that one of the wind shadows he'd sensed earlier had not disappeared, and instead was following the same wind the *Southern Echo* had in her sails. With his heart leaping against his ribs, Nate alerted the captain to its presence, and she immediately climbed to the poop deck and began to sweep the horizon with her spyglass. Nate directed her to where he'd sensed the wind shadow, but there was nothing there save for the clouded sky and the empty roll of the sea.

"That ship must still be over the horizon line," Arani said as she folded away her spyglass. "We can't see them, but unless the empire has a wind tracker of their own who's learned how to range downwind, there's no way they can see us, either."

Nate thought about crossing paths with Sebastian after the dragon hunt, and could not help but wonder if he'd made an even larger impression on his older brother than he'd initially thought.

The captain saw his growing distress. "Trust me, Nate, they don't have a tracker. No one in that entire godsdamned empire ever thought that what you can do is remotely possible."

"You did," Nate said.

"I am distinctly *not* part of that empire," Arani said. "I hope you didn't forget that just because I don't have the black flag raised."

Nate shook his head, and Arani grunted in satisfaction.

"That ship you sensed is likely heading for the Leviathan Sea," she said. "Whether it's a trader or pa-troller, odds are they have no idea we're out here, but if it will help you rest easier, you can keep a watch on it, as long as you don't wear yourself out. I still want Marcus on bucket duty."

"Aye, Captain," Nate agreed. He turned to descend the steps, but halted when Arani called him back.

"If it's still in our wind when we turn west," she said, "make sure you tell me about it."

Nate nodded and left her gazing pensively off the stern of the ship, at the *Southern Echo*'s churning wake and the waves that smoothed that foaming trail into oblivion.

He knew that Arani was right, the empire could not possibly have a wind tracker. Even if the academy had suddenly recognized that form of wind working, they would have needed to figure out how to train the poor soul and get them ready for a voyage on the open sea. Nate wracked his memories of the wind workers who had been training at the academy while he was still there, and could not come up with a single one who'd struggled to control the wind the way he had. Even the weakest among them had firmly earned their Lowwind marks and been destined for service on ships, with the older ones already scouted for contracts. Maybe one of the younger children had shown signs of a Skill like Nate's, but even then, they were too young to put out to sea.

Rori hid until she was thirteen, Nate remembered. *What if a wind worker did, too?*

But Rori had been caught because of the strength of her magic. A wind worker who could not turn the wind would have been much easier to hide.

The thought struck him with a thunderclap of irony, bringing with it a recollection of the last time he'd spoken with his mother. She'd said that she would have given anything for one child that the empire could not claim. Nate was surprised how much it stung to realize just how possible that might have been, and to think that maybe there really had been too high a price to pay to keep him, after all. It might have saved the Copperrose family so much pain and trouble if only she had been willing to try.

That's not fair, Nate thought. *We were all such good servants to the empire. It probably never even occurred to her.*

There was little comfort in that absolution, though, and Nate's thoughts were stormy enough that he did not realize that Marcus was trying to get his attention until the Darkbend's solid hand came down on his shoulder.

"All right, there?" Marcus asked. "You look like a siren's got ahold of you. I was about to use the bucket."

Nate grimaced. "Nothing so bad as that. Just thinking about the past."

Marcus made a knowing sound at the back of his throat. "I might say that's worse than a siren. No guarantee it's as pretty."

Nate agreed, but he knew to tread carefully with the Darkbend on the matter. Marcus and Eric did not speak of their time at the light bending academy, and for good reason, but it still took Nate some effort to remember and respect that. Thankfully, it had been some time since he'd last put his foot in his mouth, so he counted that as a sign of improvement on his part.

Marcus, though, could clearly see Nate's worry, and he steered Nate to the railing of the ship. "Something you want to talk about?"

"I'm fine," Nate said. "How's your head today?"

"Also fine," Marcus answered, and he did look considerably better than he had yesterday, no hollow sunkenness around his eyes or tired slump to his shoulders, but he would not be deterred. "What's on your mind?"

Nate tried to shrug it off. "It's nothing," he said, and he meant it. His familial problems were small, insignificant things left in the past, and they shouldn't hurt him now.

Shouldn't, but somehow still did.

And Marcus, blunt as he often was, could sense emotional distress like it was a palpable thing, and he refused to let Nate go so easily.

"Really," Nate insisted. He didn't want to talk about his family with Marcus, both out of fear of dredging up something horrible for the Darkbend, and because he did not want to think about it. He could see, though, that Marcus had latched on to his worry like a dog that had been promised a bone and would not leave until it had been given something to satisfy it.

With a small sigh, Nate said, "Ever since the Ruby Shores, I've been thinking about my older sister. She's an extremely powerful Goodtide."

Marcus tilted his head. "Do you think she was involved in the wreck?"

"No," Nate said. He leaned on the railing and took a deep, steadying breath of the salt-heavy air. "She went into service with the navy when she was fourteen."

Marcus gave a low whistle. "Isn't that a bit young?"

"Youngest ever to come out of either weather working academy," Nate confirmed. "I have no idea where she's been since then, but if I had to guess, probably the front line of the war. The empire would have wanted her there."

"Do you miss her?" Marcus asked.

Nate thought about that for a long moment. "Honestly, I don't really remember her all that much. When I think back on my childhood, I mostly remember Sebastian since he was at the wind working academy with me. My sister just... wasn't there." He frowned at the whorls of woodgrain in the deck, trying to recall his sister's face and only seeing Sebastian with longer hair. He startled violently out of that reverie when he realized that he'd brought up his academy life. "Sorry," he said. "I didn't mean to get into that."

"It's fine," Marcus said, and Nate was relieved to see that his friend genuinely meant it. "You're allowed to remember things, and even miss them, so long as you aren't snobby about it."

"I don't miss them, though," Nate said. "I know I had it easy compared to you and Eric, but it was still pretty terrible, being the only one in the wind working academy who couldn't actually work the wind. I really could have used a friend in there."

"No friends, huh?" Marcus asked. "Is that why you were so weird when we first picked you up?"

"Hey, now."

"Don't worry," Marcus said. "You're better. Still weird, but better."

Nate pushed his shoulder, and Marcus responded with a smirk and a light punch to Nate's arm. Nate grinned back and brought his fists up, and then he and Marcus were shadowboxing their way across the deck, laughing quietly whenever one of them tripped into something or an unfortunate someone. Eric was the last one they bumped into. He gave them an exasperated look as they nearly upset the shallow bucket of pitch he'd brought up for his carpentry work on the main deck.

"You two had better stop that," Eric said as Nate helped Marcus untangle himself from the length of rope that had been his ultimate undoing; he'd dodged the pitch bucket, only to get his feet caught in the coil and nearly trip over the railing. "That water's cold. I'm not going in after you."

"That's for the best," Marcus quipped. "I'm a better swimmer than you."

That quickly escalated into an argument that ended with Eric trying to test the theory by grabbing Marcus by the leg and hoisting him over the railing, but the stout Darkbend was better in a scuffle and they both almost went over. Novachak finally broke them apart, looking more tired than annoyed as he did it, and both Darkbends were trying to hide their smiles as the boatswain scolded them.

It was easier after that to ignore the shadow in the wind, even though its blemish remained every time Nate went to check the winds for the riggers. He felt its presence dark and a little cold against his skin as the winds ribboned across his awareness, but it was fuzzy with distance and remained on the other side of the horizon.

The next morning, the *Southern Echo* began to turn west, aiming for the southern side of one of the larger islands of the Coral Chain, where there was more room to maneuver around the Gauntlet Reef. The coral was visible by then, dark and twisting beneath the water, but it was deep enough that there was no concern of running afoul of it.

As per the captain's request, Nate scouted out the ship following the *Southern Echo*, and found it still sailing straight along the line of wind that had been carrying them towards the Leviathan Sea prior to the turn. There were no physical signs of the ship off the *Southern Echo*'s stern, and before long, the wind that carried the shadow was lost behind the jut of the island they sailed around. Relieved, Nate let that stream of wind go, and Arani gave him a firm nod of approval for his work.

But now that they were back in the embrace of the Coral Chain and approaching Spider's Nest, Nate had another worry on his mind.

He found AnnaMarie Blueshore that morning on the main deck, staring off the bow with a hungry expression that betrayed the calm certainty she'd shown a few nights earlier. Nate approached the gunner cautiously, not wanting to startle her, but she did not appreciate his efforts.

"I'm not a wild animal, you know," she informed him without turning around.

Nate froze.

"And you are not stealthy."

He searched for a witty response, but from AnnaMarie's stony expression, he sensed that was the wrong tone. He silently joined her at the bow instead.

"Won't be too much longer before we're back at Spider's Nest," he said, watching the gunner sidelong. "Are you going to be all right if the *Dragonsbane* isn't there?"

AnnaMarie drew in a deep breath and let it out in a slow ribbon of tried patience. "I suppose I will have to be." She rounded on Nate. "Are you going to stand in my way if it is?"

Nate shook his head.

"Good," she grunted. She considered the horizon for another few moments. "I am surprised that you wouldn't want to hunt them down, though. After everything Xander did, I figured you would've thrown yourself into the wind to find him."

Nate crossed his arms against the cool wind blustering across the deck. It lacked the bite of the winds around the Gemhearts, but winter had gripped the Coral Chain as surely as the northern islands. "I thought about it," Nate said. "For a while, I believed it was what I wanted."

"What changed?"

Nate shifted and placed his hand on the railing, feeling the warmth of the wood and the faint presence of the dryad. "Someone asked me who I am beyond my magic. I realized I didn't have an answer."

AnnaMarie's grunt was more thoughtful this time. "And now you know?"

"No," Nate answered truthfully, "but for the first time in my life, I'm looking forward to finding out."

"You still use your Skill," she said.

He nodded. "I love my magic, and I want to use it to help the ship, but I'm going to be the one who decides what that means. No one else."

The gunner was quiet for a moment. "I can't forgive Xander," she finally murmured.

"I can't, either," Nate said, "but I'm not going to let that define me." He fiddled with the agate beads on his hemp bracelet. "When we talked the other day, I meant it when I said that I'll fight if you need me."

AnnaMarie eyed him. "Thanks, but I'd feel better with someone less twiggy at my back."

Nate started to laugh, but stopped when he realized that she was completely serious. He was casting about for something more to say when the gunner spoke again.

"I am glad that you've been honest with me," she said. "And I respect that you don't want to use your Skill to hunt the *Dragonsbane*. I'll make sure there's no talk among my gunners about that." She looked him dead in the eye. "You and me, we're not friends. But we are part of the same crew, and that means something."

"It does," Nate agreed. "I'm sorry I didn't understand that while Jim was still alive."

AnnaMarie made a somber noise in the back of her throat, but she did not say anything else, and Nate left her to her contemplation of the horizon and what waited for them on the other side.

Morning slipped into afternoon without incident, and the *Southern Echo* continued to skirt the edges of the Gauntlet Reef, her sails full. The westbound wind began to slacken shortly after the second bell of the afternoon watch, and Nate climbed up to the poop deck to give himself an easy, unobstructed platform for his next wind reading.

The clouds that had haunted the morning had burned away to soft, cottony wisps against the bright blue of the sky, and the sun was warm on Nate's face as he placed himself at the railing and gathered his magic.

It rose in his chest, familiar as a companionable if

overeager dog, and Nate let it rush through him as he shut his eyes and breathed in the wind. The world melted into the blues and purples of the air, deeper tones streaking in from the north as the colder air currents wound their way along. Nate let them play against his consciousness for a few moments, familiarizing himself with their rhythms, and then he began to look for a steady one heading west. He found it a little north of their current position, closer to the shallower areas where the Gauntlet Reef would be more of a problem, but Arani had told him that they'd gone far enough now that they could afford to bleed off a little speed.

It was a good wind that Nate had found, consistent and reliable.

It also carried the fuzzy wind shadow of a ship.

Nate turned along the line of the wind and began to follow it back into the east. His concern swelled into alarm as the shadow grew stronger, but its edges remained distorted. Still, he could tell the ship's masts were taller than the *Southern Echo*'s, probably balancing a deeper keel. It was sailing straight along the path Nate had picked out, and that line of wind was curving into its sails just a little too perfectly.

Nate rushed back into his body aboard the *Southern Echo* with a gasp. He nearly slammed into Captain Arani as he whirled to where she waited with the allocated bucket of seawater. She jumped at Nate's sudden movement, fumbling the bucket and sloshing water down the front of her clothes.

"Gods below," she swore, "what—?"

"It's back," Nate said.

Arani dropped the bucket and whipped out her spyglass. She had the instrument to her eye and was sweeping the horizon before the first drips of water had fallen from the sleeves of her coat. "I don't see anything," she said after a long moment.

Nate squinted into the distance, but there was no dark splotch to indicate the ship he'd sensed. "It's there," he insisted even as his eyes told him otherwise. "Same one as before. It has to be."

Arani did not lower the spyglass. "Can you go back into the wind and tell how far out it is?"

Nate answered by gathering his magic once more and ranging upwind. He found the smudged shadow soon enough, and followed it back to its source. Here again, though, the edges were blurry, and now that he was closer, he could see that the wind was being shaped into the sails by someone else's magic. The wind glowed faintly where the Skilled had touched and redirected it, and when Nate tried to reach even closer, the magic stung and itched against him.

That was a new sensation. He did not like it.

He quickly withdrew.

Nate came back into his own body more easily this time, but he still had to grip the railing to steady himself. "I can't tell exactly how far it is," he said earnestly, "but it's definitely closer than before, and there's a wind worker aboard. A Lowwind, I think, but their magic is... prickly?"

Arani half-turned to him, a question on her lips, but she stamped it down with a visible effort. "It's coming this way, and you're sure it's closer?" she asked instead.

"Aye," Nate said. "It took me nearly half the time it did to follow the shadow to the source a few days ago."

The captain continued to stare through the spyglass for a long moment. When she finally lowered the instrument, she did so with a frustrated growl. "Why can't I see it?"

Nate worried his bottom lip between his teeth. "I don't know," he finally said. "But I promise it's there." He plucked at the hemp bracelet around his wrist and spun the little agate beads. "Could there be something that the wind worker is doing? Maybe they're manipulating the wind shadow?"

"I don't know that they'd even think to do that," Arani said. "They'd have to first understand wind reading, and then figure out how to push the shadow for you to be sensing it this close."

Nate scratched the back of his neck. "And that doesn't make any sense, does it?" Nate squinted into the distance, but there was still no visible sign of the ship. He could feel its presence against his mind, dark as a true shadow. "Maybe it's not the wind worker doing this," he mused.

Captain Arani did not look around, but her head tilted towards him. "How do you mean?"

"Could it be another kind of magic?" he suggested. "I don't know about the other Skills, but mine doesn't work the way other wind workers' do. Maybe something like that is going on?"

"A unique Skill," Arani murmured. "You have wind reading, and Dax has blood working. I wonder if..." She raised the spyglass to her eye once more, and this time, she did not sweep the horizon, but instead held her gaze steady as she looked off the stern. A full minute passed, and then Arani suddenly stiffened. "Light bending."

She snapped her spyglass shut and surged to the forward railing. "Dax," she called sharply, and then gave a frantic wave. "Bring Marcus or Eric with you."

Nate squinted into the distance again, but could not see what had caught the captain's attention. He was still trying to find it when Dax's footsteps thudded up the stairs, followed by another set that were too light to belong to Marcus.

"Nate will tell you where to look," the captain said. "Hold your glass steady."

Dax stepped to Nate's side, already slipping his own spyglass out of his pocket. Nate pointed him to the spot where he'd sensed the wind shadow of the other ship, and the quartermaster peered through the instrument with a frown. While Dax searched, Nate glanced over his shoulder to follow the conversation between Arani and Eric.

"I know you don't like to talk about it," the captain said, "but I need you to tell me about the light bending academy."

Eric frowned, confused.

"What kinds of things did they teach you to do with the light?" she pressed. "How much could the Brightbends actually do?"

Eric shook his head slowly. "I don't—" He swallowed under the intensity of the captain's gaze, and Nate felt his own skin tingle with goosebumps. "The Brightbends learned the same things we did, but bigger and flashier."

"Did any of them ever learn anything particularly special? How much could they actually bend the light?"

Eric gave a helpless half-shrug.

Next to Nate, Dax made a sound of surprise and almost dropped his spyglass.

"You saw it?" Arani asked.

Dax hesitated, as though not quite sure he believed the answer he was about to give. "Something flickered," he said.

Baffled, Nate looked to Eric, expecting to see his friend equally confused. Instead, Eric was frowning thoughtfully.

"The light flickered?" he asked.

Arani and Dax both nodded.

Eric's jaw flexed. "The instructors always wondered if it was possible, but no one was ever strong enough..."

He trailed off and his gaze went distant as he remembered something. "There was a pair of Brightbend twins," he said slowly. "They were younger than Marcus, but they were strong. Almost as strong as the Brightbends my age. If anyone was ever going to do it..."

"That's good enough for me," Arani said grimly. She moved back to the railing and shouted down at the main deck. "Mr. Novachak, gather the riggers! We're changing course."

There was a brief pause, and then the boatswain's voice rose with fresh orders as he summoned the full rigging crew back to their positions. Nate took a step towards the staircase, but Dax caught his shoulder.

"I think we're going to want you to keep an eye on whatever is out there," the quartermaster murmured.

Then he and Captain Arani were making their way down the stairs, calling to the sailors. Nate heard the door to the navigation room bang open and what sounded like a question from Rori, but the words were drowned out by the sounds of boots hitting the deck and ropes creaking through pulleys.

Nate turned back around to see Eric leaning dangerously far over the stern railing, straining to see something in the distance.

"What is going on?" Nate asked.

"That ship you sensed, the one no one can see?" Eric said. "Captain thinks there's a Brightbend aboard, one strong enough to bend the light around the ship and conceal it from sight."

Stunned, Nate whipped his gaze out to the blue line of the horizon once more. He could not fathom how much magic that would require. "Is that even possible?" he breathed.

"I didn't think tracking something in the wind was possible until I met you," Eric said quietly. "And I didn't think the Rend or the Vanishing Island were possible until we were there." He swallowed again, and his voice was hoarse when he said, "This just may be one more impossible thing Captain Arani has managed to find. I just wish it hadn't been looking for us this time."

Chapter Nine

Pursuit

THEY ALTERED THEIR COURSE slowly, in the hopes of not alerting their pursuers, but as time dripped away and the other ship crept closer and closer on the wind, Iris threw off caution.

"Get us into the Gauntlet," she commanded. "Nate says they've got at least one Lowwind aboard. We can't outrun them, but there's a good chance we can lose them over the coral."

"We could lose our keel, too," Nikolai growled. "These are some of the shallower parts of the reef."

"We're going to have to risk it," Iris said.

Dax and Nikolai wasted no time calling out the new orders, and the *Southern Echo* cut a sharp turn north, directly into the reaching fingers of the reef. Their pace stuttered as they released the old wind from the sails and caught a new one, guided by Nate's reading. That small pause was enough for the alarm to set in among the crew, and Dax winced as their elevated heart rates began to thunder through the ship. He allowed himself a moment to press his hand to his chest, seeking out the soothing coolness of the agate anchor against his skin. He wore his on a heavy cord around his neck, the stone dangling beneath his shirt much in the same way Iris concealed her dragon scales, but he was always aware of its steady presence. It grounded him against the rising pulses of the crew now, and he said a quick prayer of thanks to whichever god above had seen fit to lead him to the discovery that Solkyrian agate could quell the burn of magic. Then he prayed to all the rest of the gods to keep the *Southern Echo* whole and undamaged as they fled into the Gauntlet.

At the bow, Iris had Luken with her, ready to send the bird up for signals to Rori back at the helm, but her attention was locked on the platform nestled between the sails of the foremast, where Liliana perched. The rigger swung fearlessly against the ropes that held her in place, peering anxiously over the sides and bow of the ship at the ridges of coral beneath the water. She scanned their path forward as quickly as she dared, then called down her warnings and guidance to the captain.

Iris tossed Luken into flight and began to use the navigational hand gestures the bird had been trained to recognize. Luken responded by weaving and bobbing through the air, flashing his brilliant pennant feathers across the bow of the ship whenever the *Southern Echo* needed to turn. Rori answered from the helm with a light touch on the ship's wheel. Before long, the ship was fully cradled within the reef. Nikolai called for more wind to be let out of the sails, forcing the *Southern Echo* to an even slower pace, but they couldn't risk going any faster now.

Beneath the gentle waves, Dax could easily see the jagged shapes of the coral reaching for the ship's vulnerable keel, but all he heard was the rush of the water against the wood, no scraping or tearing. He forced himself to look away. He followed the wide line of the *Southern Echo*'s dissipating wake to where Nate had said the pursuing ship had been, but there was still nothing to see save for the sea and the sky and the nearby islands.

Then there was a shimmer of light, just the smallest

flicker of distortion, and Dax had to calm his own jumping pulse as he wondered how close that enemy ship had come if he could see the work of the light bender without the aid of a spyglass.

Time to tell the gunners to be ready, he decided.

AnnaMarie Blueshore and Julian Redpool were quick to answer Dax's command, gathering their respective gun crews and descending to arm their cannons on the gun deck. They moved quickly, but worry was plain on their faces as they fretted over hitting a target they could not see.

Dax was just starting to wonder how to best help Blueshore and Redpool overcome that problem when the distant *boom* of a cannon sounded. Moments later, a spray of water erupted from the sea off the *Southern Echo*'s starboard railing. The shot had landed a somewhat comfortable distance away, not even hitting the decks with a fine mist, but whether it was a warning or a miscalculation of the distance, the jolt of fear across the ship hit hard against the walls Dax had raised around his magic.

To the crew's credit, no one dropped their tasks. Several people flinched, and anxious glances tipping into fear were flung into the east, but they all kept working.

"Steady," Dax called across the ship. "We're getting through this."

"Aye, sir," came the rallying reply, and the *Southern Echo* sailed on.

Dax turned his attention to Iris at the bow, and knew what she was thinking from the grim expression she fixed on him.

They're almost in range, he could practically hear her saying. *A few more minutes and they can blast us into splinters. We have to move faster.*

Dax shook his head. The Gauntlet was far too dangerous. If they picked up more speed, the *Southern Echo* was bound to take damage.

Iris knew that. Dax *knew* that Iris knew that, but she set her jaw and gave Luken another signal. *We have to risk it,* her dark eyes seemed to say. Then she swept her attention across the ship until she found Nikolai near the mainmast. "More speed, Mr. Novachak!" she called.

Nikolai hesitated, glancing at Dax as though seeking permission to argue, or at least someone to agree that more wind in the sails was a terrible idea.

But Dax only nodded.

Their ship was officially locked in conflict, and total command fell to the captain.

If anyone could get the *Southern Echo* through these next few minutes, it would be Iris, but Dax desperately wished that she'd left the Vanishing Island on better terms with the gods.

He did not think that he could ask for their protection now.

"May our fate be our own," Dax murmured.

The riggers scooped more wind into the sails, and the *Southern Echo* began to gather speed once more, although Nikolai had the good sense not to let the ship go too fast. Dax's magic quickened as Rori's distress heightened at the helm and the rigger's hearts seemed to answer in kind, but training and level heads prevailed, even with Liliana's calls coming fast and sharp from the foremast.

Dax heard another cannon blast somewhere in the east, clearer now, and the shot landed just shy of the *Southern Echo*'s stern, throwing up another column of water that splashed the deck this time. That shot might have hit them, if they hadn't taken more wind into the sails and sped up, but Dax took little comfort from the thought as Liliana shrieked to cut to port.

The ship banked sharply, but not far enough. Dax felt the scrape and shudder of coral against the bow. He ran along the railing, searching for the telltale bubbles that would signal the ship's hull had been breached. The foam stirred up by the prow of the ship was too thick for him to be sure, and Dax turned to scan the deck for Eric.

The young carpenter was already running for the stairs, heading below to assess the damage. Dax called for two others to help him, and they disappeared under the deck.

There was a sudden roar of cannon fire, and panic surged through Dax as he sought out the flickering light again, wondering how the enemy ship had come so close so quickly. But he saw the distant spray of water thrown up by the cannonball, and he realized that Blueshore and Redpool had finally answered with a shot of their own.

It did not hit anything solid, but there was a larger, more violent flicker in the air just to the left of where the shot had landed. Calls drifted up from the open gun ports on the deck below, correcting the aim of the second cannon, and another shot blasted out from the *Southern Echo*.

This one sailed straight into the space where the light had warped, vanishing for less than a heartbeat before wood chipped and splintered into the air.

The light danced and wavered, and then fell away in a shimmering sheet from the enemy ship, revealing the frigate in all its terrible glory.

It was a lot closer than Dax had anticipated, and so much closer than he'd dared to hope. He could see the imperial flags snapping in the wind, the golden sun of Solkyria on full display against the sky. He also saw that the *Southern Echo*'s cannon shot had left a sizable hole in the frigate, but one that was well above the waterline and would not be slowing the ship in the least.

From the gun deck, he heard AnnaMarie Blueshore barking out orders as her crew swarmed their cannon, cleaning and reloading with the smooth ease of practiced muscles, but Dax knew they wouldn't be quick enough.

The frigate bore down on them, and he suddenly knew beyond all doubt that both of its earlier shots had intentionally missed the *Southern Echo*.

They're trying to capture us, Dax realized, *not sink us.*

He was not sure which prospect was worse.

"Full sails!" Iris bellowed from the bow. "Now!"

Apparently, she'd rather we sink, he thought wryly.

But he still felt a small thrill of pride in Iris Arani for refusing to give up.

That feeling was followed by a fresh wash of panic from across the ship as Nikolai directed the riggers and Rori jostled with the helm. Liliana's calls from above were frantic now, and Luken's wings flashed as he darted back and forth under the steady stream of commands.

Nothing for it, Dax thought.

He took a firm grip on the *Southern Echo*'s railing, feeling the calm pulse of the dryad within the wood, and braced himself. The sun was warm on his skin, the winds steady, and the water sloshed with an easy rhythm against the ship. There were probably worse ways to leave this world, he decided.

The first coral strike hit the port side of the ship. Dax pitched forward into the railing, grunting against the pain in his gut as the *Southern Echo* lurched past. Fear washed across the ship, spiking the crew's heart rates even higher, but they sailed on.

The next strike was gentler, more of a glancing

bump, and Dax saw coral pass directly beneath the ship. The gods above must have shown them a little mercy, because the water was deep enough that the *Southern Echo* went over that bit of the reef without further contact.

The ship cut west again, narrowly missing another collision with the coral, and Dax looked up to see that the navy frigate had started to angle itself into the Gauntlet, still chasing the *Southern Echo*. But even as he watched, the frigate seemed to hesitate. Then it turned and skimmed away, well clear of the edges of the reef, searching for a wider and deeper channel to sail through.

They weren't going to find one for a long time, Dax knew. Iris had been right about the *Southern Echo* having an advantage with her shallower keel.

"Gods damn that woman," he breathed. "She's going to be so smug about this."

The ship rattled again as more coral assaulted the hull, but they were finally putting distance between themselves and the navy frigate, and Iris called for some of the wind to be let out of the sails. The navy ship fired one last shot at the *Southern Echo*'s stern, but they had pulled out of range, and the shot landed harmlessly in their wake, tossing up water and bits of coral.

There were no cheers as the *Southern Echo* pulled inevitably away from the navy ship, but Dax felt the collective rush of relief across the ship, save for down in the hold where Eric and the others worked. He turned and headed for the stairs to go see the damage for himself. He caught Iris's eye as he went, and between her panting breaths, she smiled at him.

"So smug," he muttered.

But he was still proud of her, the ship, and the crew.

Later, after Eric had confirmed that the damage from the coral was minor and had quickly been patched up, and after the crew had been moderately soothed with promises of answers to their questions, Dax met with Nikolai and Iris in the private captain's cabin.

"You saw the flag, right?" Dax asked the moment Iris had shut the door.

She nodded tiredly, her earlier bravado gone now that she was no longer in front of the crew. She slumped into one of the chairs with a bone-weary sigh.

"They all saw it," Nikolai said. "Hard to miss the Solkyrian sun when it's bearing down on you, especially when the flag is almost the size of the topsail."

Iris gave him a wry, sideways grin. "I swear their flags get bigger every year, but he meant the smaller one, with the silver border and the hollow sun."

Nikolai's white brows came together over his pale eyes. "A royal flag?"

"The personal standard of Prince Trystos," Dax confirmed. He was too agitated to sit, and began to pace the length of the room. "He rarely leaves Solkyria himself, but his hunting ships all fly his flag."

The Northman sat back and let out a long, slow breath. "So do we think his personal hunters were involved with the Ruby Shores wreck?"

Dax remembered the utter stillness of that destroyed ship suspended above the water, pierced through by the rock. He and Iris had both had their suspicions, but they'd kept those thoughts from the crew in favor of not sending them spiraling into hopelessness. And there had been the chance that they'd been wrong, and it really had been a bad storm that had wrecked Spider's ship, or even just a pirate hunter that was unaffiliated with the prince. At least then, the hunting ship would have been on its own, not part of a larger, more dedicated operation.

That small shred of comfort had all but been incinerated by that royal flag.

"I think we're firmly past possible and into probable," Dax said darkly.

"Agreed," Iris said. "If that ship was willing to chase us this far, I think we can assume that Trystos is looking to move against Spider's Nest."

A long silence followed those words, and Dax found himself staring out the windows at the back of the room, noting the slant of the late afternoon sunlight on the water. Miraculous as their escape had been from the pirate hunter frigate, they could not sail the Gauntlet at night. They would need to anchor soon.

"We don't know that for certain," Nikolai finally said. "We've seen imperial ships in these waters before, although not this close to the Gauntlet. Could be we just picked up an overachieving patroller in our wake. Frozen Goddess knows that's the kind of luck we've been having lately."

Dax wanted to believe that, but he knew better. "That ship didn't want to sink us," he pointed out. "And they didn't start firing on us until we cut into the Gauntlet and slipped their reach. Before that, they seemed perfectly content to just follow us and stay hidden."

Gods only know how a light bender could have kept their magic up for that long, he thought, but did not give voice to the words as he paced back to the table. They already had enough to puzzle out.

"So then, it *was* trying to follow us back to the Nest," Nikolai said. His chair creaked as he leaned forward. "Could be that the information Trystos's hunters got out of Spider's ship wasn't enough to pinpoint the

Nest."

"They must know it's in the Coral Chain," Iris mused. "That much, I'm sure they already knew, and I'd be amazed if they didn't get more from Spider's ship. I can't imagine his spies being so loyal that none of them would ever talk."

"Depends on how well he paid them," Nikolai mused.

Dax leaned heavily against the table. "We have to assume the Nest is compromised, then."

Iris's gaze was grim. "We do."

"No, we have to get there," Nikolai said, and Dax and Iris both blinked at the sudden ferocity of his words. Nikolai met their stares, but his hand shifted towards the bandage still covering his missing ear. "If there's a chance that we can beat that hunting ship to the Nest, then we need to try. We have to warn Spider."

Dax and Iris locked gazes, and he knew that under less pressing circumstances, they might have laughed. They both knew he wasn't thinking of Spider. But he did have a point; the capture of Spider's Nest would be catastrophic for everyone who sailed under a black flag, the *Southern Echo* included.

"We might be able to convince the crew to abandon the current course and head east," Dax said, "but we are not stocked for a long voyage." As the Gemheart Islands weren't too far from Spider's Nest, they'd elected to keep the hold light in favor of speed. Dax regretted that decision now, but that would not change the truth before them. "It would be best if we could get to the Nest and restock as fast as we can."

Iris nodded. "Spider still owes us money as it is, not to mention he has the drinking horn." She scraped her hair back from her face, securing the dark locks in a tight bun at the nape of her neck. "We gave up too much to just let that go."

"So it's decided, then," Nikolai said. "We're going back to the Nest?"

"We're staying the course," Iris agreed, "and even if we keep to the Gauntlet, we'll come into the Nest's harbor tomorrow afternoon at the latest." She stood up and brushed her clothes straight. "The hardest part of this will be convincing the crew that this is not going to be a pleasure stop, and we'll need to be back out at sea before the day is done."

As it turned out, however, Prince Trystos's flag carried more weight than even the Solkyrian Empire's had. Once the crew understood what they were facing, they were quick to embrace the idea of putting into port, restocking, and then leaving with as much haste as possible. The majority agreed to go east and leave the Common Sea behind, with only halfhearted objections from some of the gunners that were quickly dropped.

Dax should have been relieved by that, his job made all the easier by the unification of the crew, but his sleep was uneasy that night. In the darkness of the berth, he listened to the ship and lives around him, letting his magic track the beating of so many hearts and the quiet pulse of the dryad's spirit, and he wondered if they should just abandon Spider's Nest altogether. But the state of the stores and calculations of exactly how long their depleted supplies could last told him that was impossible. The crew would starve long before they safely made landfall again.

They did not have another choice.

When the morning came and the reef was illuminated beneath the water once more, the anchor was raised and the *Southern Echo* set off at a steady pace. They quickly found their way to one of the wider paths through the Gauntlet, and the sailing was smooth and easy after that. With Nate picking out the best winds and Liliana scouting the surrounding reefs, it was barely noon when Spider's Nest came into view.

Their position within the reef demanded that they approach from the northern side of the island, which was mostly uninhabited save for a few locals. It took some time to swing around the eastern beaches to reach the south-facing harbor, but there were no signs of other ships and Nate reported empty winds all around. Slowly, bit by bit, the *Southern Echo* crept around the familiar curve of the island, until they rounded a final bend and the harbor was suddenly in view.

It was empty, not even a rowboat at the dock.

Dax felt the shock ripple across the ship, hearts skittering as the crew took in the bizarre sight. Reflexively, he started to close the channels of his magic and block out the surge, but the jump that touched him ripped him out of his own surprise. He forced his gaze away from the harbor and took in the reactions of the crew, from the budding fear to the pervading bewilderment and the surfacing anger.

AnnaMarie and her gun crew were the source of this last bit.

Dax gripped his cutlass as he watched the gunner trade dark words and scowls with her people, tension ricocheting through them and amplifying the heart rates of each person it touched. Dax heard the names "Xander" and "the *Dragonsbane*" drift up from the group. Their hunger for vengeance was a palpable thing. He tightened his hold on his sword.

Don't do anything rash, he thought, unsure if he was directing that command at himself or the gun crew.

But then, as he watched, AnnaMarie gave an audible huff of anger, and then released her clenched fists. The fight melted out of her, and she gave a soft but firm order to her people to stand down. A couple of them looked ready to resist, but a quelling stare from their leader squashed the smallest spark of rebellion. With resigned sighs, they settled in and turned their gazes to the captain.

Iris was speaking to Nate, the young man nodding and already turning his attention to the winds beyond the harbor. The moment their conversation was done, Nate headed for the steps at the stern of the ship, grim determination set into his shoulders. Meanwhile, Nikolai had ordered the riggers to prepare to turn the *Southern Echo* around inside the harbor, but he was also readying a rowboat alongside Julian Redpool.

"What's our move, here?" Dax asked as he stepped to Iris's side.

"I want the ship ready to sail at a moment's notice," she said, her gaze nailed to the empty island.

Dax did not try to hide his surprise. "I'd have thought you would order us away now."

"I'm tempted," Iris growled. "Gods below, I am tempted. But I can't imagine Spider ever abandoning this place, and if he's here, then he deserves to know what happened to his ship." Her gaze hardened into a glare. "He also owes us money."

And we can get the horn back, Dax realized. His heart lifted at the thought, and he was glad he was the only one aboard the ship who could feel his own pulse. "I'm going ashore with you," he said.

Iris hesitated, but then she nodded. "All right. Mr. Novachak," she called, "change of plans, you're aboard."

The Northman bristled as he approached. "I'm going."

"You're not," Iris said firmly. She reached out and put her hand on his shoulder. "I need you here. If something happens..." She did not finish the thought, but when Nikolai still looked ready to protest, she gave him a small shake. "Your madame can take care of herself, but this crew comes first. Command is yours until we return."

Nikolai did not look happy in the slightest, but he finally relented. "We'll sound the ship's bells if there's trouble."

"One for each ship Nate finds," Iris said.

"Aye, Captain."

With no other ships in the harbor, the *Southern Echo* skimmed as close to the shore as she could, dramatically shortening the distance to the beach. Dax and Iris descended into the rowboat, where Julian Redpool and AnnaMarie Blueshore were already waiting at the oars. A few minutes later, Dax and the others were splashing through the cold surf as they pulled the rowboat on to the beach. The gunners stayed behind to rest and ready themselves for the return, and then Dax and Iris were moving through the empty town.

For the first time in his life, Dax wished there were more people on Spider's Nest.

It was one thing to feel the crush of too many heartbeats, his magic fighting to escape his own body no matter how hard he held on. The last time he'd set foot on the island, he'd been relieved by the thinner population, but there had still been signs of people all around. Now, there was an empty void beyond the channels of Dax's magic. It was peaceful, but Spider's Nest was not supposed to be quiet. The Nest was supposed to be alive and thriving in spite of the empire.

This perfect silence shook Dax to his core.

He focused on Iris's heart, nervous but steady, and

followed it like a beacon through the dark.

They found the first signs of life at the pleasure house, where two workers bundled into coats sat on the steps and passed a bottle of rum between them. They perked up when they saw Dax and Iris coming down the road, and one of them called a slurred but surprisingly chaste greeting. The other climbed unsteadily to her feet and stumbled her way back inside the pleasure house, giggling as she went.

There was something unhinged about the sound, and Dax felt it run up his spine like the scrape of fingernails.

Iris paused before the remaining pleasure worker. "How many of you are still here?"

"All of us, love," the worker said. She slumped against the railing and grinned manically up at Iris. "Been awful lonely without you lot." She swerved her gaze up and down Dax. "Fancy a tumble, Handsome?"

Dax did not answer. He skimmed his gaze across the upper floor of the pleasure house. The rooms were dark, not even a candle burning in any of the windows, but Dax saw a curtain rustle and a shadow move behind the glass.

"All of you are here?" Dax asked.

The pleasure worker took another swig of rum, dropping her forced cheer. "Course you'd have a favorite," she grumbled. "Who you looking for?"

"Spider," Dax and Iris said together.

The pleasure worker blinked. "You two got weird tastes," she said, then pointed the bottle at the tavern across the road.

Of course, Dax thought. He turned to go, but Iris lingered.

"You all may want to get off this island," she warned the worker.

The other woman snorted bitterly and brought the

bottle to her lips once more. "Don't have anywhere else to go." She waved them off.

Iris was troubled as they walked away. "They must know. Even if Spider didn't tell Silverdale anything, she's smart enough to figure out that something's wrong. She would've taken off long before the last ship left the Nest."

"Unless Spider convinced her to stay," Dax suggested.

"Or wouldn't let her leave," Iris said. "If Silverdale goes, that's a sizable hole in his pockets." She hesitated on the threshold of the tavern. The room inside was dark, the tables empty. There were no signs of any servers.

"I'm not sure it matters at this point," Dax said, his voice too loud in the stillness.

Iris drew her sword before she stepped inside. Dax followed her through the main room and up the stairs to Spider's office. They paused outside the door, listening to the muffled yet frantic voice on the other side. Iris traded an uneasy look with Dax, then pushed the door open.

The air in the room was close and stank of sweat and melted candle wax. The curtains were drawn over closed windows, illumination coming from dozens of candles scattered throughout the room. Papers and open books littered the floor along with dirty plates, and Dax saw a rat scurry off into a corner with something stuffed into its mouth. On the desk was the drinking horn, gleaming and resplendent in the soft light, but even with power thrumming off of the relic, Dax's attention was drawn to the wall with the painted map.

Standing before it, scribbling across the paint with a stick of charcoal and talking to himself, was Spider.

At least, Dax thought it was Spider.

If the man had been unkempt last time, it was nothing compared to his current state. His hair was lank and greasy, tied sloppily at the base of his neck. His waistcoat was discarded and his shirt was untucked, the underarms stained yellow with sweat. His feet were completely bare, the soles black with charcoal dust and dirt.

He did not turn around even as the door creaked.

Dax had a strong urge to seize the drinking horn and leave, but Iris still him with a hand on his sleeve.

"Fair winds," she said, the words like a gunshot through the room despite their softness.

Spider jerked around, charcoal falling from his fingers. His face was covered in unkempt growth, his eyes bright and wide against the black beard. "Arani," he breathed, and then he was coming across the room.

Dax had his channels open and his Skill trained on the man's erratic heartbeat by the time Iris had raised her sword.

Spider had the wherewithal to draw up short, just before he got a blade in his stomach or a squeeze around his heart. Dax kept his magic at the ready, and it became impossible to ignore the pulsing power of the relic on Spider's desk. When Dax surrendered a glance to it, the horn seemed to glow even brighter.

"You came back," Spider said, the words filled with awe. "No one else came back."

"There's a reason for that," Iris said. "A very bad one." She kept her saber raised as she dipped her free hand into her coat pocket and pulled out the flags she had retrieved from the wreck at the Ruby Shores. She shook them out and tossed them to the floor at Spider's feet. "We only found the one ship," she said, "but it was stripped bare. No ledgers, journals, or even bodies left behind." She waited, but Spider did not lift his gaze from the flags on the floor. "You were right," she continued, filling the silence with the truth. "It's Trystos's pirate hunters. One of his ships chased us into the Gauntlet. We barely escaped."

Spider did not move for so long, Dax had to tap his magic to be certain that the man's heart was still beating.

"Spider?" Iris said, pitching her voice to be gentle even as she shifted her stance and turned the edge of her sword. "Are you hearing me? Your ships are gone, and pirate hunters are coming."

Spider took a deep, shuddering breath, and then he fixed a manic smile on Iris. "It doesn't matter."

Dax felt Iris's heart rate flare.

"I'd argue it does," she said. "It's over. Everyone needs to get off this island."

Spider turned and snatched the drinking horn off his desk, sending a stack of papers tumbling to the floor. "Let them come. I have this."

Dax edged a little further into the room, shrugging off Iris's warning grip. "That is not yours," he reminded Spider. "It belongs to us."

Spider's grin stretched even wider. "If you knew what this could do, you never would have left it."

Dax reached with his magic, but the horn's power was hammering across the space between him and Spider, so much stronger than a thousand heartbeats combined. Dax winced at the flare of pain in his skull and quickly closed the channels of his Skill, locking them against the relic. When he was certain he had a firm grip on his magic, he took another step forward. "What does it do?" he asked.

Spider gave a breathy laugh. "It could break the world."

Slowly, Dax extended his hand, palm open. "Best give it here, then," he said, "before we do that by mistake."

"No," Spider said, folding his arms around the horn. "I don't know how yet."

"Dax," Iris said, her voice heavy with warning. "Leave it."

But he couldn't. This was a relic from the gods, powerful and dangerous, and Dax was not going to leave it in someone else's hands a second time. He lunged, grabbing for Spider, but the man was quicker than Dax expected.

Spider surged out of reach, knocking several candles off of his desk as he vaulted over it and leapt for the closest window. He ripped the curtain aside and smashed the drinking horn through the glass in one desperate motion, shattering the window. He dove through the hole, leaving stains of red blood on the jagged pieces left in the frame. He landed on a tree branch outside his office and launched himself at the trunk, falling more than climbing down to the ground.

Dax knocked more of the glass loose, ready to climb out and follow Spider. He had one foot up on the sill when he heard the sound coming in on the breeze.

Bells.

Hard and frantic, with no break in between one peal and the next.

One for each ship Nate finds.

He'd found a lot.

"Leave him!" Iris shouted. Her hand closed on Dax's belt and she yanked him back into the room. "We have to go!"

Dax did not argue. He bolted for the door, slipping on a few loose papers and coughing in the smoke rising up from the sheets that the fallen candles had caught. He and Iris flew down the stairs and out of the tavern. They took off down the road, bells ringing in the wind.

AnnaMarie and Julian already had the rowboat in the surf by the time Dax and Iris reached the beach.

"Come on!" AnnaMarie bellowed over the clanging ship bells as Julian launched himself into the boat and snatched up the oars.

Dax and Iris hit the water, and then they were clambering into the rowboat and helping the gunners fight the same waves that had carried them to shore. The bells stopped as the little boat angled for the *Southern Echo*, and Dax could see the crew running across the deck, sprinting to their stations under Nikolai's command. The anchor went up even before the rowboat was secured, but Dax, Iris, AnnaMarie and Julian all made it back aboard.

"How many?" Dax asked Nikolai as Iris ran to the helm.

"Too many," the Northman answered. "We stopped counting after seven."

Dax's heart leapt into his throat, but he forced his panic down. He had to take command and get the *Southern Echo* to safety, before the Solkyrian ships descended on the Nest. The pirate brig was angled correctly, and her sails were full as she charged out of the harbor. Dax knew that they had plenty of advantages on their side: speed, mobility, a scout who could read the wind.

But he was still unprepared for the sight of the ships coming in from the southwest, flying the blue flags emblazoned with the golden Solkyrian sun.

Dax's heart wasn't the only one aboard the *Southern Echo* that stuttered and skipped with fear.

CHAPTER TEN

Running the Gauntlet Reef

NATE WASN'T CERTAIN WHICH officer moved first, but his panic barely had the chance to rear its head between the moment when he recognized the Solkyrian flags bearing down on the harbor, and when his body instinctively moved in response to the roared orders to bring the ship about. The voices of the captain, quartermaster, and boatswain all blurred together, but even within that chaos, the crew of the *Southern Echo* dove into motion.

The navy may have proper wind workers, he thought as he hauled on the rigging ropes next to Theo, *but they can't catch us inside the Gauntlet.*

He kept that thought with him as the *Southern Echo* fled the harbor. Two ships began to pull ahead of the approaching navy fleet before the *Southern Echo* had plunged back into the narrower channel through the Gauntlet Reef, but Nate thought that the pirate brig had enough of a head start to get away. He still had to swallow a lump of fear as he saw that the pursuing ships were two heavily armed brigantines, either one of which would have no trouble blasting the *Southern Echo* into splinters by itself.

As if to test the idea, there was a flash from the closer brigantine as one of its forward cannons fired, but the shot went wide. AnnaMarie answered with a shot from one of the swivel guns on the main deck, although it lacked the power one of the larger cannons on the gun deck would have delivered. Still, the gunner grunted in satisfaction when she saw where the shot landed.

"They may be able to get one broadside off if they turn now," she called to Arani. "But we've already pulled out of range of their forward cannons."

"Once we're deep enough into the reef, none of their guns will matter," Arani answered. She eyed the *Southern Echo*'s sails and the water below the ship. "Keep this speed up. We know this part of the reef better than they do. We can run it!"

Nate felt his heart lift at the captain's words, and he gave a soft whoop alongside Theo. By the time the ship slid back into the embrace of the Gauntlet, already beginning the first turn that would take them safely through the reef, Nate's fear had all but evaporated.

Unsurprisingly, the brigantines followed the *Southern Echo*'s wake to the edge of the reef, their sails swollen with summoned winds that Nate did not need his Skill to see. The larger ships came on with frightening speed, but they balked at the narrow channel, dropping the wind and letting their sails hang limp. They began to turn, presenting their broadside cannons, and the gun ports snapped open along both ships.

"Keep going," Arani called in the face of dozens of cannons turning their mouths on the *Southern Echo*. "Do not let up."

But the wind began to waver in the *Southern Echo*'s sails.

Nate hesitated long enough to warn Theo that he was going to drop the rope, then thrust his consciousness into the wind. He felt the unnatural bend of the air currents as wind worker magic tugged them off course, the thorns of someone else's magic tearing holes in the blue ribbons.

"They're taking our wind, Captain!" Nate shouted as he came back into himself.

Arani jerked around at his words and tipped her gaze up at the mainsail. Sure enough, the tautness was going out of the cloth, and the flag off the stern was losing its momentum.

"Bastards," Theo growled as the rope slackened in his grip.

Nate looked over his shoulder at the dark squares in the sides of the turning ships, and his throat closed once more.

The first shot went wide, crossing the *Southern Echo*'s bow. The second fell into the water just off the port railing, and Nate ducked his head against the water that splashed over his shoulders on to the deck.

AnnaMarie's crew answered with another shot, but it fell short and the look she gave the captain was heavy with meaning.

Arani threw one quick glance from the enemy ships up to the sails, and then ran for the helm. "Furl the sails," she called to Novachak as she barreled past him, and Nate had just enough time to be surprised before the boatswain had him and the riggers carrying out the captain's order.

Nate watched Arani from the corner of his eye as he worked, and saw her heading for the helm, where Rori was stationed. Rori balked as the captain took the wheel from her, and Nate knew from the frantic gestures Arani was making and the way Rori's eyes were widening that she was being asked to use her Skill once more.

Rori was afraid, Nate could see it in the stiffness of her spine, but she nodded once and ran for the bow.

Another shot came from the enemy brig, this time piercing the *Southern Echo*'s hold and slamming through the other side of the ship. Nate and the riggers were thrown from their feet, ropes slipping through their hands, and the rigging squealed as the sails began to drop. Nate scrabbled back up almost as fast as Theo, and together they snatched at the ropes to control the sails once more. Novachak appeared next to them, hauling on one of the lines himself.

"Keep her steady!" he roared, and Nate set his jaw and pulled harder on the rope.

"Damage is above the waterline," Eric shouted from somewhere near the middle of the ship. "We can keep going."

Rori had reached the bow by then, and Nate caught a glimpse of her frantically scanning the water immediately in front of the ship. Her panic rose as she took in what she saw, and she cast a bleak look back at Captain Arani at the helm. But rather than scream for Rori to act, Arani only punched one fist into the air, her gaze locked on the Goodtide.

You can do it, Rori, Nate silently urged her.

Rori took a deep breath, and then began to work her Skill.

The currents quickened beneath the waves, sending the *Southern Echo* rocking, but the ship responded to Rori's push and danced just out of reach of the next cannon shot. The bow turned as Rori made a sweeping gesture to the right, and the ship angled deeper into the reef, gathering even more speed.

Then the keel struck coral, and Nate felt the grating rattle through his boots all the way up to his teeth.

"Rori!" Arani called, but the Goodtide was already moving again, her teeth bared in a determined snarl as she summoned a wave that lifted the *Southern Echo* over the coral, carrying the ship forward.

For a moment, it seemed to work. The *Southern Echo* sailed clear over the reaching fingers of the Gauntlet, the shallow patches of the reef flashing past in bright colors. Then the ship came down on the other side of the wave, and the jarring crash that ran through the ship was enough to throw Nate off his feet again.

Dazed, he sat up to see Rori clinging to the railing at the bow, her expression soaked with horror, but he did not have the chance to go to her. Dax was suddenly at his side, pulling Nate and the sailors around him to their feet and ordering them to get below to start bailing water out of the ship.

There was shouting all around Nate, panicked and scared, and he was swept up in it all. The next thing he knew, he was part of a line leading from the lower deck to the open hole that had been blasted through the *Southern Echo* earlier, frantically passing buckets full of water on to the next person so they could be emptied back into the sea. Across from him, another line ran the empty buckets back down to the flooding area, but Nate barely registered them as he snatched at each full pail that came his way, water sloshing over the edges and soaking his sleeves. His world shrank to that one task, taking a bucket from the person in front of him and twisting to hand it off to the next one in line, and even when his muscles began to burn in protest, he did not allow himself to slow.

Twice more, the *Southern Echo* was lifted and carried forward by waves summoned by Rori, and there were more crashing scrapes against coral that sounded like the stuff of nightmares down in the hold, but Nate and the others did not let up.

He did not know how many buckets passed through his hands, or how much time bled by before the ship came to a bumping halt. Nate feared the worst, that they had grounded themselves on a patch of coral, but Dax came through to tell the bailing line that they could stop, the captain had found a place to beach the ship for repairs.

Nate's arms shook as he let go of the last bucket, spilling water across his boots, but he barely felt it even when he collapsed to his knees in the puddle, shaking and sweating. All around him, the others were falling against the walls of the ship or sliding to the deck just like him, their breathing dense and exhausted.

But there was no time to rest.

The ship was damaged, and until she could sail again, they were trapped on whatever island or sandbar Arani had beached them on.

Nate swallowed several large gulps of air, then climbed back to his feet and headed for the stairs. When he emerged on the main deck, he saw that it was a small island that Arani had chosen, with a thin forest a ways up from its beach and a shallow cove where the ship now rested. Nate looked, but he did not see the navy brigantines anywhere around them. Just a few surrounding islands of the Coral Chain, and the shadowed teeth of the Gauntlet beneath the clear blue waves.

CHAPTER ELEVEN

As Much As She Needs

THE ONSLAUGHT OF SO many frantic heartbeats had given Dax the worst headache he'd felt in years. What was worse, though, was the elevated pulse of the dryad's spirit through the ship. The damage the *Southern Echo* had taken in the wild flight from Trystos's pirate hunters had affected her, and it was all Dax could do to keep his magic from mirroring her pain. By the time his boots touched the coarse sand of the island's narrow beach, the agate anchor against his chest had grown uncomfortably warm, but the looming threat of pain receded as soon as he was off the ship. He allowed himself a moment of relief, then assessed the damage.

The coral had left ugly scratches and scars along the sides of the *Southern Echo*, all clearly visible now that the ship's hull was mostly above the waterline. There were three definite holes that Dax could see, large and jagged, and he was certain there were more all along the keel. It was a wonder they had not sunk before reaching land.

The ship was not going to sail until that damage was fully repaired. Gods only knew how long that would take, but in the meantime, they were not safe. Rori's magic had gotten them away from the Solkyrian ships, but the damage had prevented them from going far. It was only a matter of time before the pirate hunters picked their way through the Gauntlet and found the *Southern Echo* beached and helpless.

Found all of them helpless.

And they'd lost the relic from the gods.

Dax's breath became heavy in his chest, and he pressed his hands against the sides of his head, right over the sweep of the tattoos that disguised his Skill mark.

He had always known that the day would come when he would not be able to outrun the empire. From the moment he'd stowed away on the ship that would become the *Southern Echo*, he'd known that his life was going to end in violence and blood. He'd been prepared to fight to the end. But this? Being grounded on an island with nothing to do but wait for death to find him? This was unbearable.

Dax's fingers curled, dragging his nails across the tattoos, and he felt the urge to scream bubbling up in his chest.

Then he saw the faces of the men and women disembarking from the ship, saw their eyes bright with uncertainty and fear.

He could join them. Let them bleed their fear into the sky, fall apart one by one until only those who lacked the will to meet their ends at the barrel of a pistol were left for the navy to find. Succumb to chaos and let go of everything.

Instead, he took a deep breath, lowered his hands, and stepped forward as their quartermaster.

"Repairs to the ship have to be our first priority," he called out. Gazes snapped to him, expressions clearing as the crew latched on to his voice like a lifeline. "We're going to make teams to assist Eric with the work, and anyone not on the carpentry lines will search for food and water."

People moved when he directed them, easily falling into the groups he designated. The newfound carpentry crew consisted of the strongest among the *Southern Echo*'s sailors, and Dax sent them off to take further instructions from Eric. The rest were given pistols for protection against wild gryphons and sent into the thin forest to search for fruits, running water, and game if there was any to be had. He did not know how many of them understood how dire their situation truly was, but all of them looked relieved to have something concrete to focus on.

He reached out with his magic to those who stood closest to him. He sensed fear and worry, but not the wild thrum of panic. That was all he could ask for.

There were injuries, of course, and Nikolai set himself up on the beach to tend to them as best he could. A quick assessment from the boatswain confirmed that the worst casualties were a bad sprain to AnnaMarie's wrist and a nasty crack to Julian Redpool's head. AnnaMarie waved off Nikolai's administrations and went to help the carpentry crew as much as she could with one functioning hand, and Julian was allowed to rest until his head cleared. Plenty of others had scrapes and bruises, but those things would heal.

For the first time since the *Southern Echo* had made that mad dash into the Gauntlet Reef, Dax allowed himself to hope.

Then he found Eric kneeling on the beach, scratching calculations into the sand with a stick. Iris wore a grim expression as she watched over his shoulder.

"We are going to need a lot of wood," Eric said when Dax joined them. "More than we have available for patching, if we want the ship's hull to keep its integrity in rougher waters." He raised his eyes to the trees growing only a few paces up from the waterline. "I don't like the look of those, but if we can find a thicker one, it may serve."

"How long are the repairs going to take?" Dax asked.

Eric winced. He nodded to the carpentry crew Dax had formed, already working to bring the spare wood out of the *Southern Echo*'s hold for measuring and cutting. "Even if they were all trained carpenters, we'd need a few days to properly cut and shape the wood."

"We don't have days," Dax said, sharper than he'd intended. "How quickly could you do a fast patch over the holes?" At least then they could continue to sail the Coral Chain and try to find a more defensible place to beach and repair the ship.

Eric shook his head bleakly. "That would be for a dirty patch. Proper repairs would take at least a month."

Dax swore loudly enough to draw the attention of the carpentry crew. He knew he should keep his head, but the hopeless fear was back in his chest, threatening to burst, and he couldn't maintain the facade for the crew and himself.

Iris gave him a searching glance, then pulled Eric to his feet. "Before we went into the Forbidden Sea," she said, "Tim Whitebranch told me that the damage the *Southern Echo* sustained in the navy attack seemed to be repairing itself. He left the crew before I had the chance to discuss that more fully with him, and then we had other matters in front of us." She kept her gaze fixed on the ship as she spoke. "Was that true?"

Eric hesitated, and then nodded. "I don't know how, but yes, the dryad fixed the damage on her own. She shrank the holes and mended the minor scuffs and gouges."

Iris made an interested noise that Dax immediately disliked. "No ideas as to how she did that?" she asked. "None whatsoever?"

Eric paused again, then reluctantly said, "Marcus suggested that the dryad might have fed off of the blood that had spilled during the fight with the navy, and I'm pretty sure he's right."

Dax had suspected as much when he'd seen the dryad come to life at the threshold of the Rend. Blood was powerful, used in rituals all over the world save for Solkyria, blessed as it was with its unique forms of natural magic. He wasn't surprised that the *Southern Echo*'s dryad had found a way to use the forfeited lives that had stained her decks.

He began to hate the way Iris was looking at the ship.

"Dax," she said, "may I have your knife?"

"Absolutely not," Dax growled.

Iris made a thoughtful noise, then drew her sword and slashed her hand across the blade. She was stepping into the surf and heading for the *Southern Echo*'s side before her blood had time to sink into the sand.

Dax ran after her. "Just what is it do you think you're going to do?" he demanded.

"Feed the *Southern Echo*," Iris said calmly. She reached out and pressed her bleeding palm to the ship's hull.

Dax snatched Iris's wrist, pulling her arm back. A smeared red handprint was left on the *Southern Echo*'s side, and Dax felt his anger mount as his magic stirred in the presence of her blood. "Do you know how much blood it took for her to repair those few holes?" he demanded. He gave Iris a rough shake when she tried to pull her wrist free. "Are you going to bleed yourself dry so she can do it again?"

"Of course not," the captain spat, "but I can help her."

"And how much are you going to give?"

Iris opened her mouth to respond, but before she could, the *Southern Echo* gave a low, shuddering sigh, and the bloody handprint vanished into the wood.

Dax stared at the spot where it had been. It was one thing to suspect, and quite another thing entirely to witness blood magic firsthand.

Iris pulled her wrist free. "As much as she needs," she said through gritted teeth. She pressed her bleeding hand against the ship once more.

Dax nearly grabbed Iris and hauled her off to get a bandage from Nikolai, but he knew the stern set of her shoulders and the determination burning in her gaze.

He could not stop her from doing this.

"I need to see if the supply scouts have found anything," he said, his voice a low growl, "but I'm pulling you away from this and bandaging that hand the minute I'm done with them."

Iris waved him off with her free hand, and Dax left her with a scowl.

She doesn't need the navy to get herself killed, he thought darkly, but his anger only grew as he realized that she was right. If the *Southern Echo* could be quickly and completely repaired through magic, there was no reason not to use it.

Other than the risk of our captain bleeding out, of course.

Anger made his voice jagged when he snapped for Eric to step away from the repair plans he was sketching into the sand. Eric looked a little fearful when he stood up and brushed the sand off of his knees, and Dax made a point of taking a few deep breaths to calm himself. His voice was much more level when he said, "Change of plans. The captain is seeing to the repairs herself."

Eric frowned, but his confusion cleared almost immediately and horror flooded in. He whipped around to stare at Iris as she bled against the ship. "How much is she...?"

"As much as I'll let her," Dax growled.

Eric swallowed nervously. "Do the rest of us need to, ah, make a donation?"

Some of the anger melted out of Dax, leaving a sense of bone-weary tiredness between his shoulders. "I'm not going to ask anyone to bleed for the *Southern Echo*," he said. "This is a radical solution to a bad problem. I'd rather see the rest of you as hale and healthy as possible once we're ready to sail again."

Provided we still have a captain, he added silently.

He chose to ignore the fact that, if Iris Arani could no longer hold the position, the captainship would fall to him.

"What if we still cut a few patches?" Eric suggested, yanking Dax out of his thoughts. "They'll have to be small, and they won't be shaped right, but maybe they can help a little, give the dryad something to grab on to when she goes to fix the ship."

He looked at Dax expectantly.

"I don't see how that could hurt," Dax said.

Eric hesitated. "Well, it will use up all the spare wood. If it doesn't work, then we'll have wasted it for nothing."

Dax spread his hands to encompass the tiny island and the beached ship. "At this point, I don't think that matters."

Eric nodded and turned to direct his carpentry crew on taking rough measurements and beginning the cuts.

When the supply scouts returned, they reported that they'd found several fruit trees and a small stream, although the migrating gryphons had depleted the island's game, if there had been any to begin with. Overripe fruit and water would have to do. Dax sent them off again with empty sacks and barrels from the *Southern Echo*'s hold. Nearly everyone went, including Nate and Marcus, and several gunners moved from the carpentry crew to put their strength towards bringing back the heavy water casks. They all went quickly, their fear of the navy putting speed in their strides.

Satisfied, Dax turned to his next task: stopping Iris Arani from bleeding herself dry. He hesitated when he saw Rori sitting by herself a ways down the beach, her head buried in her arms.

Dax caught Nikolai's eye and nodded towards the navigator. "She all right?"

Nikolai bared his teeth in a grimace. "Physically, yes. Mentally, emotionally, magically, not so much."

Dax frowned. "Magic burn out?" Nikolai gave him a sidelong look, and Dax suddenly understood what he'd meant. "I'll speak with her."

"Good idea," Nikolai grunted. Dax started forward, but the boatswain was not done. "They got away, right?"

Dax looked at him, confused. "Who?"

"Spider, the locals." Nikolai hesitated for a moment. "Julianna."

The last name was barely a whisper, and Dax felt his own heart twinge in sympathy despite the flare of anger at Spider's name.

The image of the man diving out the window, ripping the relic away forever, was going to haunt Dax for the rest of his life.

"I'm sure Spider got away," he said bitterly. "He's much too sly to have been caught in his own web." He made sure to soften his voice for the next words. "The same goes for Silverdale. She knows how to take care of herself. I didn't even see her at the pleasure house when Iris and I were ashore. If I had to guess, I'd say she's hiding herself and her people somewhere safe, where the empire is never going to find them."

Nikolai nodded, looking relieved.

Dax gave him a pat on the shoulder, but before he could step past Nikolai, the boatswain caught his arm.

"What's our noble, frost-touched captain doing?" he asked, jerking his chin towards the *Southern Echo*.

It was Dax's turn to grimace. "Feeding the dryad."

Nikolai was still for a moment, and then let out an explosive breath. "Northern winds take whatever's left of that woman's rational mind," he growled.

"She's going to need a bandage," Dax said mildly.

"Of course she is. What did she cut?"

"Her hand."

Nikolai all but threw his arms up, then snatched up the bandages and bottle of rum he'd been using to care for the crew's injuries and stalked into the surf, muttering darkly about infections and reckless captains.

Dax let him go and turned his attention back to Rori.

Luken was hopping around her, his pennant feathers trailing in the sand. He chirped as Dax approached, but Rori did not lift her head.

Dax felt a pang of guilt. He'd known that the journey to the Rend had been particularly rough on her, made all the more so by Xander Grayvoice's betrayal and her abduction, but too much had happened since then for Dax to sit down with Rori and talk. Iris had met with her immediately after the Vanishing Island, but then Spider had called on the captains and she, too, had been buried under new tasks and needs.

He wondered how badly all of that had hurt the poor girl.

Dax sat down on the hard sand next to Rori. He did not speak, but let Luken climb up his trouser leg to perch on his knee, where the bird gave a happy chirp and began to preen his feathers.

After a long moment, Rori asked, "What do you want, Dax?" Her voice was muffled by her arms and the sleeves of her coat, and thick with tears.

Dax let the informality pass without comment. "How did you know it was me?" he asked instead.

Rori's shoulders heaved as she sighed, but she lifted her head and rested her chin on her folded arms. "Arani would have taken a moment to move her pistols out of the way before she sat down. Novachak would have said something about cold winds or ice. Luken would have flown at Nate, Eric would have started talking immediately, and Marcus would have tried to feed me. You're the only other one who would have come over."

Dax blinked, wondering if that level of observation was a survival skill she'd picked up during her time as a pirate, or before she'd even gone to the tide working academy. She'd managed to keep her Skill hidden for a long time, after all.

"I'm sorry I didn't come sooner," he said.

Rori turned her face away and said nothing.

Dax pushed his boot through the sand. "Captain's found a way to quickly repair the ship. Once that's done and the crew is back with as much food and water as they can carry, we'll be setting off with the next tide. Are you ready for that?"

There was a long pause before Rori asked, "How could all that damage possibly be fixed that quickly?"

She wasn't with us when we discovered that the dryad draws power from blood, Dax remembered.

Rori had been a prisoner on the *Dragonsbane* then. No one had caught her up on the matter, it seemed.

So Dax told her, and directed her stunned gaze to the *Southern Echo*, where Iris was still standing with her hand pressed against the ship's side. Nikolai was next to her now, gesturing madly, but if they were yelling at each other, the wind and the gentle roll of the sea drowned out the words.

"She cut herself?" Rori whispered, her voice ragged with horror. She surged to her feet. "No one should have to bleed because of what I did."

Dax caught her and pulled her back down before she could take more than two steps towards the ship.

"Iris Arani would give her life for that ship," Dax told the girl firmly, "no matter if the *Southern Echo* was down to her last splinters or as whole as the day she first put to sea." He felt the truth of those words press down on his shoulders, and he gave another heavy sigh. "Doesn't matter how the ship was damaged. If Iris could give anything to fix it, she would." He nodded at the distant figure of the captain. "I don't like that it's her blood in this case, but she loves that ship more than life itself. I couldn't stop her, and you won't, either."

Rori sat back on her heels, fresh tears pooling in her eyes. She wiped them away with a violent brush of her sleeve. "It's my fault," she said.

"That we escaped imperial pirate hunters and lived to fight another day?" Dax asked. "Yes, that is thanks to you. We're all in your debt."

Rori shook her head. "The ship... because of my magic, she—"

Dax gave her a light but firm shake. "Your Skill lifted the *Southern Echo* over the coral and placed her out of the navy's reach. Yes, the hull was damaged, but that was going to happen no matter what."

Rori's expression was bleak.

Dax moved to kneel next to her, sending Luken to her shoulder with an indignant squawk. "Between the cannon fire and the Gauntlet, something was going to hurt the *Southern Echo*. You did the best you could, and the only way you could have done better is if there had been no reef to begin with. You think you should have put the *Southern Echo* down in clear waters, but

I'm telling you, that was impossible. We all know it, and you especially should know it, given your job aboard that ship."

Rori scrubbed her sleeve across her face again, but she was listening now, looking for that lifeline the same way the crew had when Dax had taken charge earlier.

"It's not fair that you keep getting asked to take responsibility for the safety of the entire ship and crew," Dax said, "but we're all proud of you for stepping up and doing it anyway. We wouldn't be alive without you." He gave her a gentle squeeze on the shoulder. "You saved the *Southern Echo*, Rori. Don't you dare confuse that with what you had to do in the past."

Rori took a shuddering breath and nodded.

"Good," Dax said as he rose to his feet. "Take a few minutes to calm down. I'll come find you if you're not back at the *Southern Echo* when we're ready to sail."

"Where are you going?" Rori asked. Her voice was still unsteady, but clearer than it had been a few moments ago.

"To help the captain," Dax said. He gave Rori a smile that was more confident than he truly felt, but he knew she needed that kind of strength to lean on right now. He could give it to her, if not himself.

When he splashed back into the water near the *Southern Echo*, he heard that Nikolai and Iris were indeed arguing. Nikolai wanted her to lower her hand and let him clean the wound, and Iris wanted him to back off before she took his other ear.

Nikolai's face was a deep red by the time Dax stepped between them.

"Tell this mad woman," the boatswain fumed, "that there is nothing left in her head for the northern winds to freeze!"

Iris rolled her eyes, but Dax did not like the pale cast

to her skin, or the fresh cut on the back of her hand. She had the decency to look a little ashamed when she realized that Dax was looking at the new wound. "She needed more," Iris murmured.

"Absolutely. Nothing. Left," Nikolai grunted. "Now give me your hand."

"No."

Dax eyed the steady drip of Iris's blood into the surf, where it turned a swirling, muddy pink against the pale blue of the shallows.

How much has she bled? he wondered.

He reached out and touched the *Southern Echo*'s side, searching for the dryad's pulse through the wood. He found it almost immediately, steady and quick and strong. There was no flash of pain, just the soft burn of effort as the dryad's strange magic worked to heal herself and the ship.

Dax looked back at Iris, saw the challenge in her eyes as she dared him to tell her to stop or try to pull her away from her ship. She'd fight him with everything she had in her.

So Dax drew his knife and laid the blade against the palm of his hand.

"The back!" Nikolai snapped.

Dax blinked at him, his skin still uncut.

Nikolai heaved a massive sigh. "If you're going to join her in this terrible idea, cut the back of your hand. You won't bleed out as fast and it'll be easier to clean and treat later."

Dax turned his hand around and quickly drew the knife across it before he could change his mind. He hissed against the sting of his parting skin, but as the blood welled up, he pressed it against the *Southern Echo*. The ship gave another small shudder, and Dax felt warmth radiate out from his point of contact with the ship and spread up his arm.

"Thank you," Iris murmured next to him.

Dax grunted in response. He put his knife away and then placed his other hand on Iris's shoulder. "I'm going to slow your bleeding," he informed her.

Iris looked ready to protest, but one glance down at the pink stain in the water around her boots changed her mind. "Not too much," she said. "The dryad still needs it."

Dax did not argue. He'd promised Iris a long time ago that he would never use his magic on her without her consent, and now that he had it, he was going to make sure she'd be alive to be annoyed about it later.

Reaching for Iris's heartbeat while connected to the dryad was strange. The pulse of the ship was slow compared to the captain's, exaggeratedly so thanks to the stress Iris's heart was under from the pain of her wounds, the press of the navy, and the state of her ship and crew. Dax focused on her heart, erratic in her chest, and felt his Skill gather in his own body. He waited until he had familiarized himself with the beating of Iris's heart before he pushed the magic out, feeling it flow from his arm into her shoulder. At first, he mirrored Iris's pulse with his fingers, always keeping one against her shoulder while the others fluttered in time with the rhythm of her heart. Then he began to slow the motion, and Iris's body answered, her blood slowing in her veins as her heart calmed. Dax did not push too hard against her natural rhythm, only eased it so there was not so much blood seeping out of the wounds in her hand, falling away into the nothingness of the world.

When he opened his eyes, Iris had more color in her cheeks, and she gave him a begrudgingly grateful nod.

"How long is this going to take?" Nikolai asked after a few moments of silence.

"As long as it needs to," Iris answered. "She took a lot

of blood from that fight with the navy."

Nikolai contemplated this for a moment, his mouth twisted underneath his white beard, and then he drew his own knife and laid it against the back of his arm. "I'm going to give you both hell for this," he grumbled. Then he made the cut and pressed the wound to the ship.

Eric approached them a few minutes later. He came up short when he saw all three of them bleeding against the ship. He swallowed past an obvious bit of nausea, but rallied quickly and informed them that the carpentry crew was making fast progress on the smaller plugs.

"I'm thinking I'll seal them against the edges of the holes, to close the gaps as much as I can, then she can do the rest." He nodded at the *Southern Echo*.

"Sounds like a good plan," Iris said as she shifted her hand's position against the ship.

Eric eyed the smear of blood she left behind, blanching a little, but he nodded and left them with his head held high.

When the crew returned with the supplies they could gather from the forest, Dax, Iris, and Nikolai were still feeding their blood to the dryad. Dax heard the uneasy voices of the crew as they took in the sight, but no one protested when he ordered them to stop staring and load up the ship. He could feel their eyes on his back as they moved, but the work went steadily, and he heard the creaking of the ropes as lines were fastened around the barrels to haul them up to the main deck.

Rori appeared not long after that, her eyes dry. Luken perched on her shoulder and peered curiously at the swirling water of the incoming tide. It was up to their knees now, and Dax knew they would need to be ready to leave soon if they wanted to get away from the island before sundown.

Rori was the one who voiced the question on his mind, though. "Is it almost done?"

Iris started to give her the same reply she'd given Nikolai, that the process would take as long as it needed, but she was interrupted by a loud creak and groan from the ship, followed by the largest shudder yet.

Dax nearly withdrew his hand in surprise, but when Iris pressed hers more firmly against the hull, he did the same.

A faint ripple ran through the wood, and Dax glanced up to see the figurehead shift and sway before settling once more. Then a single strong pulse rushed through the ship, hitting Dax's hand with the force of a punch, and this time, he, Iris, and Nikolai all backed away from the hull. The ship creaked again, and the holes in the hull shrank down to nothing as the wood fused itself back together around the patches Eric had cut. The different color of the new wood stood out like barely healed scars, but the transition from the old part of the hull was smooth and seamless.

Dax's hand stung from the strange hit it had taken, but the pain gradually faded to a tingle, and when he looked down at his hand, his mouth fell open. His skin had completely closed, nothing but the faintest of lines marring the back of his hand to indicate where he'd been bleeding mere moments before.

Nikolai swore quietly, but it was edged with wonder, and Dax saw that his wound had also been healed.

The cut on the back of Iris's hand had closed up as neat and clean as the others, but the one on her palm was still open. She winced as she flexed her hand around it. "I think that one was a little too deep," she said. "Feels a lot better now, though."

"Well, thank the Frozen Goddess for small miracles," Nikolai grumbled. "Now give me that hand before I do something we're both going to hate."

Iris gave him a wry smile as she finally surrendered her bleeding palm, and Nikolai fell upon it with a rag that had been soaking inside a rum bottle, waiting for this exact moment. Iris gave a sharp hiss as the alcohol soaked her open wound, but Nikolai was relentless, and it wasn't long before he was knotting off a bandage around her hand.

Dax lingered just long enough to make sure Iris wasn't going to do anything else drastic, then turned his attention to overseeing the crew as they got the last of the new supplies aboard. They were done well before the sun had begun to dip towards the horizon, and the *Southern Echo* rode the next tide out like she'd never had her hull ripped open.

The relief that flooded the ship was palpable even without Dax flexing his magic, and Rori's heart especially was light as the ship turned away from the island.

Iris had them set a course for deeper into the Coral Chain, where the Gauntlet Reef could still protect them. They planned to cut between the islands and make a dash into the east before they were anywhere near Veritia, and hope that they'd be able to evade Trystos's pirate hunters long enough to escape the Coral Chain and the Common Sea. Thankfully, Nate was more than willing to help scout for enemy vessels, and if they timed the journey correctly, Rori would not need to use her Skill to pluck them from danger again, but the girl placed a loving hand against the wood of the ship and said she would be ready.

They spent the rest of the day sailing carefully through the coral, until the sun dropped too low to illuminate the underwater maze. They lowered the anchor and settled in for a dark and quiet night, listening for the faintest hint of their predators on the wind.

Dax only heard the breathing of the crew and the

steady, contented pulse of the dryad.
The rest of the world was silent.

Chapter Twelve

Maelstrom

WAITING OUT THE NIGHT was a stretch of agony that no one aboard the *Southern Echo* could sleep through. Nate spent the darkest hours lying in his hammock, listening to the restless tossing and turning of the people around him, his thoughts warring over the only two possibilities that lay across the future.

When the sun rose, the *Southern Echo* would raise her anchor and sail once more. Then she would either slip out of the Gauntlet Reef and escape into the east, or be blown apart.

Captain Arani and Dax had both agreed that the ship could not hide in the Coral Chain forever. Dangerous as it was, the Gauntlet Reef was still passable, and it was only a matter of time before a Solkyrian ship found them. Rori's magic could not save them every time, and if the ship sustained larger damages, there was only so much blood they'd be able to give. The officers had filled the need this time, assisted by the patches Eric had cut. What if the next time was too much?

What if they were caught on the open sea and Nate failed to warn them in time?

What if, what if, what if, his anxious heart asked.

He did not sleep much that night.

The dawn was an uncompromising gray, barely a lightening of the clouds. Captain Arani regarded the iron sky as though trying to decide if it was a dire foe or something harmless. It was harder to see the reef beneath the ship without direct sunlight, but the glare off the water was gone, and Eric and Marcus both thought that the pirate hunters would not be able to pull off the trick with the light that had concealed their ship before.

"If the cloud cover holds," Eric said, "there just won't be enough light for them to bend it that way. It's always easier when the light is stronger."

"Not for me," Marcus grumbled. "Especially not now." He glanced up at the sky, and some of the disgust left his expression. "But the clouds are helping."

Eric fixed the stout Darkbend with a searching glare. "All right, *something* happened in the Rend when you went on that island."

Marcus quickly turned away. "It's nothing."

"It's not nothing!" Eric grabbed Marcus's arm and spun him roughly around. "What did you do?"

Marcus's face twisted with anger, but Nate dove between them and pushed them apart before things could escalate.

"This is not the time," Nate snapped as he shoved Eric back a step. "Leave him be."

Eric scowled, but he stalked off without another word.

Nate caught Marcus by the sleeve before the Darkbend could slip away. "Eric is right, though, isn't he? Something happened to you on the Vanishing Island."

Marcus gave him a bleak look made all the worse by the dark circles under his eyes. He had not slept much, either. "You said you felt the presence in the temple, right?"

Nate nodded, suppressing a shiver at the memory of the god's touch.

Marcus shot a frightened look in the direction Eric

had gone, confirming that the other Darkbend really had disappeared, then dropped his voice low. "Did you answer the question?"

Nate blinked at his friend. "What question?"

"The one the god asked," Marcus murmured. He searched Nate's face with such open desperation that Nate felt his heart fracture. "You didn't hear it?"

"I felt the god trying to reach me," Nate said slowly, "but no, nothing ever spoke to me." He hesitated, recalling the spirits laughing as they twisted around him before sending him into a duel with Xander, but he did not think that was what Marcus meant. "What did it ask you?"

The stout Darkbend's breath hitched. He scraped his hands along his face. "It asked me what I wanted, more than anything. And I... I wanted stronger magic."

The world went very still as all the times Marcus had complained about the light snapped into focus, the headaches he'd been suffering, the stronger anchor he'd so eagerly bought on Spider's Nest.

Nate couldn't believe he hadn't understood.

"I'm so stupid," Marcus said, and his hands clenched into fists against his forehead. "Eric's right, I'm so fucking stupid."

He began to smack his fists against his own head, and Nate reached out and seized his hands. It took considerable effort to pull them away from Marcus's face, straining as the Darkbend was, but Nate refused to let go.

"No, Marcus," Nate told him firmly. "You're not stupid. And if there's anyone in this world who could understand why you'd wish for stronger magic, it's me."

Marcus's breath hitched, but he stopped trying to tug his wrists out of Nate's grasp.

"All right, so your magic has been changing?" Nate asked.

Marcus nodded.

"Do you know what you can do with it now?"

To Nate's surprise, Marcus shook his head.

"I can feel it building inside of me," Marcus said, "but I can't bend the light any better. If anything, it's gotten worse. My magic... It's not working the way it's supposed to."

Nate frowned, his thoughts drifting to his own Skill. How many times had he used those exact words to describe his own magic? His grip tightened around Marcus's wrists as he stared at the simple Darkbend tattoo etched into the skin over the stout man's brow.

Part of Nate wanted to hope that a god had simply given his friend a gift in the shape of what he'd wished for. The rest of him knew better.

"Is the god still whispering to you?" Nate asked.

Marcus shook his head, and Nate nearly collapsed with relief.

At least that was a point in their favor.

"Think back to the Vanishing Island, when you wished for stronger magic. Did the god ask you for anything in return?" he asked.

Marcus hesitated, his breathing still uneven. "I don't remember," he whispered. He hunched over, as though collapsing in on himself. "I'm sorry."

"It's all right." Nate shifted his grip from Marcus's wrists to his shoulders, pulling his friend back up. "We're going to figure this out. We have to get away from the navy first, but as soon as we're safe, you and me are going to sit down and figure out what your magic can do. We'll talk to Dax about it, see if he can help. And Rori and Eric—"

Marcus jerked against Nate's grip. "Not Eric," he said. "Please."

Nate quickly agreed. "Not Eric. But at least Dax, yeah? His Skill is unique like mine. He'll be able to help us. Arani, too, probably. She knew how to train my Skill, maybe she'll have an idea about yours. And if you don't want to tell Rori, then we won't, but she knows what it's like to deal with the gods."

Marcus chewed his bottom lip. "What if we can't do it?" he asked. "What if my magic gets too big and just burns me from the inside out?"

"That's not going to happen," Nate said firmly. "I promise." He did not know where his certainty came from, but Nate did know that just as he was ready to help Rori fight off a god, he'd do the same for Marcus, for all of his friends, for anyone aboard the *Southern Echo*.

"You're not alone, Marcus," Nate said. "Please don't forget that."

Marcus gave a shuddering sigh, but he nodded.

A few minutes later, Marcus was steady on his feet once again. He still looked troubled as he headed off for his assigned task, but he was no longer crumbling into himself, and his usual heavy tread was solid against the deck as he walked away.

Nate wanted to follow him, make sure that his friend truly was all right, but if he was going to keep his promise, then the *Southern Echo* needed to escape the navy.

Not long after that, Nate took up a position on the poop deck, where the wind was the least obstructed but still close enough to the water line to carry the shadows of ships. The surrounding islands bent and distorted the air currents, but the breezes retained their clear purity. Once Nate confirmed that the only wind shadows in the immediate area were from birds and gryphons on their morning flights, Nate gave the all clear signal to the captain.

Arani called for the anchor to be raised, and the *Southern Echo* began the slow journey through the

Gauntlet.

Nate did not descend to help with the rigging work this time. From the elevated deck, he had a better view of the coral as the ship slid through the narrow gaps, but he barely gave the hazards below more than a passing glance. He kept his attention on the wind, ranging out while his gold ring was cool against his skin and withdrawing when the anchor grew warm. Nate forced himself to be patient rather than run out along the wind in a panic; he wouldn't help anyone if he drove himself to collapse. So he went slow and steady, trading speed for control.

His efforts were rewarded; he found three larger ships attempting to pick their way through the Gauntlet south of the *Southern Echo*'s position, back where Rori's magic had carried them away from the pirate hunters the day before. None of them were having much success, he could see. Their shadows moved slowly through the air as they prowled across the water, the magic of their wind workers restrained and tense as they fought to keep the ships at controllable speeds. He reported as much to the captain, whose expression brightened with relief before she told him to focus his efforts on whatever lay ahead of the *Southern Echo*.

The way through the Gauntlet was clear. Nate sensed no ships anywhere off the bow, no matter how far he extended the radius of his search, and without the sun glaring on the water, the lookouts had an easy time confirming that the only shapes around them were the unmoving islands.

It took the better part of the day, and despite his caution, Nate was exhausted with a rolling headache forming behind his eyes, but the *Southern Echo* finally reached the eastern edge of the Gauntlet and the Coral Chain. The ship herself seemed to hold her breath as her hull pulled free from the last of the coral and entered the deeper waters of the open sea. The horizon was unbroken ahead of them, and Nate confirmed with a final sweep that there were no hidden ships waiting to ambush them. The sails unfurled, and the *Southern Echo* began to gather speed.

Nate's relief lasted as long as it took him to move to the top of the stairs. Below on the quarterdeck, Dax was at the railing, glaring out at the horizon. He turned when he heard Nate's footsteps.

"Nothing at all?" the quartermaster asked.

"Not immediately around us," Nate confirmed.

Dax's eyes were troubled as he looked back at the dark sea. "It can't be this easy," he murmured. "They wouldn't have given up so soon."

Nate eased himself down the steps, nerves tightening in his gut. "I could range further out," he offered.

"You may have to," Dax said without hesitation. "Ask the captain which way she wants you to go."

"Aye, sir," Nate said, and quickly moved across the ship.

Up near the bowsprit, the captain had boosted herself up on the railing, one hand wrapped firmly in the lines of the jib. The wind lifted and tugged at the hem of her deep red coat, but she stood bold against it, flexing and moving with the rhythms of the ship instead of the air. "I don't like this," she said when Nate moved into the small bit of deck at the bow of the ship.

"Dax doesn't, either," Nate said. "Which way should I scout?"

Arani lifted her arm and pointed off the *Southern Echo*'s bow, into the east. She did not hesitate this time.

The fact that both officers had agreed that Nate should use his Skill without so much as a cautionary pause wound his nerves even tighter. If they were both willing to lean on his magic without qualm, something truly had them scared.

Nate took a moment to situate himself far enough from the railings that he would not pitch over the side of the ship if he passed out. The gold ring on his hand gleamed, the only spark of warmth under the gray winter clouds. A deep breath in, the wind filling his lungs, and then Nate was riding the breezes into the east, the shadow of the *Southern Echo* blurring behind him as he ranged out.

For a time, there was nothing but the blue and violet streaks of the wind around him, running on their own paths. The sea was black beneath him, an endless field that his magic could not penetrate. His instinct was to pull away from the water and soar higher through the sky, but he wasn't searching for dragons this time. He forced himself to stay close to the water, straining to pick out a shadow sitting on top of that wild void. The gold ring grew hot against his skin, calling him back to the *Southern Echo*, but Nate pressed on.

For his friends, for his captain, for his crew, he pressed on.

Pain was nibbling at the edge of his mind when he finally caught the trace of a wind shadow at the waterline, just south of his position. Nate steered himself towards it calmly, purposefully moving slow so that his headache would not sharpen into a nail driven through his skull.

There was no magic fuzzing through the shadow, so it did not take long for Nate to suss out the three masts of the ship, all rigged with massive sails that the wind dragged itself against. This was a big ship, slow but certainly armed on every possible deck. It was moving on a north-south line, forfeiting the best wind in favor of holding that position.

Nate turned himself around and pushed further

north, and it wasn't long before he came across another ship, also sailing perpendicular to the stronger winds. This one was considerably smaller than the first one, two masted, about the size of the *Southern Echo* and much more nimble.

Nate hesitated, gauging the pain at the edge of his mind and the distance sprawled between him and his body back on the *Southern Echo*, then moved past the second ship and found a third one just a little further north. This one was the smallest one yet, with only a single mast and a hull smaller than the *Southern Echo*'s, but from the size of the canvas suspended by the rigging, Nate suspected that this one could easily out-sail all the others.

Three ships sailing an unusual route did not necessarily need to be cause for alarm, especially with none of them using wind worker magic, but Nate still made a hasty retreat. He staggered when his consciousness returned to his body, wincing at the sharpened spike of pain that had been waiting to greet him, but steadying hands caught his shoulders and kept him on his feet.

"Easy now," the gruff voice of the boatswain warned him when he tried to take his own weight back, but Nate had the terrible feeling that they were long past that point.

When Nate was sure he could stand on his own, he shrugged off Novachack's hands and relayed what he'd found to the captain. She was still perched on the railing, although with her spyglass raised to her eye now, and she swept the lens northwards along the horizon as Nate described the three ships.

"Can't see them yet," Arani said, "although we've learned the hard way that doesn't mean much." She lowered the spyglass and glared into the distance. "I don't suppose you checked south, too?"

Nate shook his head sheepishly. He should have ranged south, looked for more ships. He started to gather himself to try, but the captain jumped down in front of him.

"Don't burn out," she told him. "I'm certain there are ships south, even if you didn't find them."

Novachak shifted uneasily behind Nate. "You don't think...?"

Arani gave a grim nod. "Blockade."

She stepped forward and called for their course to shift north, towards the smallest ship Nate had found.

Novachak caught Nate's confused expression. "That one is probably a sloop," the boatswain explained. "Smaller and faster than us, but nowhere near as heavily armed. If it is a blockade, that's going to be the weak point."

"And we're really going to run it?" Nate asked, unease sliding back around his heart in an unwanted embrace.

"It's that or drift around the Coral Chain until the pirate hunters find us again," Novachak said. "This way, we may actually have a fighting chance."

The *Southern Echo* turned hard into the north, until she was close to the latitude of the sloop Nate had sensed. Nate had recovered enough by then to take another journey through the wind, and he confirmed that the smaller ship was due east of them now. Arani had them swing to starboard, sails full with the best wind the riggers could capture, and they skimmed across the waves. Rori relinquished the helm to take up a place near the mainmast, ready to call upon her Skill to quicken the currents and drive the *Southern*

Echo even faster. She looked calmer on the open sea than she had in the Gauntlet Reef, more determined than wary.

Nate felt a small spike of pride at seeing Rori embracing her own magic. She wasn't doing it fearlessly, but she was closer than Nate had ever seen her. He hoped she'd taken his advice to heart and would remember that just because a god spoke in her ear, that did not mean she had to listen.

He also hoped that Marcus would be willing to speak to her about his own deal with a god, when the time was right. Maybe they would be able to help each other.

The gunners took their crews and armed their cannons long before the ships became visible on the horizon. There were several enemy vessels, stretching in a tight line into the north and south just as Arani had predicted, and Nate couldn't help but shiver as he looked at that long string of potential death. There was space between the ships, but not so much that the *Southern Echo* had a chance of slipping through unnoticed. So Arani ordered them to bear down on the sloop, easily identifiable at a glance now by its single sail.

It looked so small compared to the towering layers of the sails adorning the frigates and other battleships around it. Nate wondered how it had ended up in the blockade at all. Perhaps there had been no other large ships available with the men-of-war all engaged in the Aurora and Sunrise Seas.

The blockade ships held their positions as the *Southern Echo* approached, although once it became clear that the pirate ship was aiming straight for the lone sloop, the larger ships immediately to the north and south began to swing around, as though intending to cut them off before they could hit the tiny ship.

Nate sensed wind magic then, sparking strong on the breeze, and the massive frigates turned more easily than they should have in the water.

Nate could not answer them. But Rori did.

The current she called pushed the *Southern Echo* along, and Nate's eyes stung as the ship blasted forward. With the strong tailwind and Rori's Skill, the pirate ship was faster than the frigates even with their wind workers. Nate monitored the other ships, waiting to see if they would try to steal the wind out of the *Southern Echo*'s sails, but the imperial Skilled concentrated only on their own vessels.

The Solkyrian flag came into focus as the *Southern Echo* bore down on the sloop. The little ship turned as though it intended to meet them, but a warning shot from one of the swivel guns on the main deck was enough to send it veering away.

"Hold the main cannons," Arani called. "I want them ready to answer those frigates if they catch up. Don't waste them on the sloop."

The gun crews roared their acknowledgement of the orders.

The frigates did not catch up. Arani had chosen the right spot to crack open the blockade, and the *Southern Echo* reached the line long before the two larger ships had the chance to fully close in.

The little sloop bobbed a short distance away, and as Nate watched it slide past, he had the distinct impression that the smaller craft was like an animal watching a larger predator glide by. The ships were close enough that he could see the cannons on the sloop ready to fire, but with the *Southern Echo* ready to answer with twice as many shots, the smaller one held off.

Nate still did not breathe out until the *Southern Echo* had sailed past the sloop, and there was nothing but the open horizon ahead of them.

Cheers went up across the pirate ship, and Nate joined them, his heart light with relief and pride.

Gods above, he loved this ship.

She still had to outrun anything that tried to pursue her, however, and Nate ran to help the riggers pick out the stronger tailwinds once more. He paused when he drew level with Rori.

There was sweat on her brow and she was panting, but the motions of her arms were smooth and steady, nothing like the frantic gestures she'd made before. She was going to keep up the current for as long as she could, and Nate could help her by making sure the *Southern Echo* had the best wind in her sails, lightening the burden on the current Rori had twisted to her will.

"Keep going," he said as he stepped past her. "You've got this, Rori."

She did not speak or break her motions, but she smiled.

And then her eyes snapped wide and she gasped, stumbling on the deck.

Nate jumped to her side and caught her before she went sprawling, but she was trembling violently and her eyes were huge with fear and panic.

Before Nate could ask what happened, there was a strange sound on the wind, sudden and rushing and only growing louder.

The *Southern Echo* bucked violently, and Nate and Rori both fell, cries rising up around them. Nate's shoulder and elbow cracked against the deck. He hissed as pain bloomed beneath his skin.

"What's going on?" he cried out.

"Tide worker," Rori said through gritted teeth. She rolled unsteadily to her knees and bellowed, "Maelstrom!"

The word settled over the ship like a shroud, quelling every voice until there was only the rushing sound. Then the ship gave another horrible shudder and began to turn, and panic broke in a wave across the deck.

Between the screams and the thunder of footfalls, Nate scrambled back to his feet, only to be tossed into the starboard railing. The impact drove the breath from his chest, and he nearly choked on its absence when he beheld the massive whirlpool that had opened up in front of the *Southern Echo*. The ship tilted, already sliding into the open maw, and Nate went cold.

Someone grabbed him by the back of his shirt and threw him away from the railing, screams of "Get below!" echoing across the ship as the officers tried to save who they could. Nate stumbled down the steps, nearly colliding with Theo and Liliana on his way down. Their terror was clear even in the gloom of the lower deck, and everywhere Nate looked, he saw his own fear reflected in the faces of his crew mates.

The ship tilted even further, and Nate lost his feet as he and everyone else went tumbling through the dark. His world became nothing but panicked shouts and cries of pain, hard cracks of fresh wounds beating against his limbs and head, the roaring rush of water in the dark. The ship seemed to shriek around him, the wood groaning as though it was about to come apart. Nate added his own voice to the screams.

Maybe, if they were loud enough, the gods would take notice and intervene.

Water rushed into the *Southern Echo*, soaking Nate's clothes and jetting down his throat. He coughed and sputtered in the darkness, wondering if this was what awaited him in one of the six hells, or if he was already there, shot into eternal damnation by the maelstrom that had swallowed the *Southern Echo* whole.

And then, all at once, the shaking and the roaring stopped, and the *Southern Echo* bobbed gently on the waves, as though there had never been a maelstrom at all.

Nate's head spun, and he wasn't the only one who rolled over and vomited. The seawater that had flooded the ship washed it away, but that was a small comfort in the face of the pain and vertigo warring for control over Nate's very soul. Gradually, in the sudden stillness, he became aware of people around him, some sobbing openly and crying out for their parents, siblings, cousins, friends, anyone who could give them a scrap of comfort after what they'd just endured.

Nate coughed and retched again, his whole body shaking.

The darkness of the lower deck felt too close, the stench of vomit sharp in his nose, and Nate heaved himself to his feet. He needed to get out of that stale air, be topside again and feel the wind on his skin and see with his own eyes that the *Southern Echo* was still afloat, that they hadn't all drowned.

It took several tries before he successfully stumbled to the stairs, and then he had to crawl up them, strength leeching out of his arms and legs as he went. But there was weak sunlight ahead of him, and he pushed open the hatch to see the cloud-filled sky. Clean, fresh wind filled his lungs, and even though he shivered as it bit through his soaked clothing, he took deep, gulping breaths.

There was no rushing sound of the whirlpool, but the world was not quiet. Someone was shouting with a good deal of authority, and Nate turned his head to see that the little sloop had come up alongside the *Southern Echo*. Dully, he registered the grappling lines that were already latching the two ships together, and the people who were starting to climb on to the pirate ship. They carried swords and rifles, and it occurred to Nate that he should probably be afraid, but it did not sink in until he had lain back on the steps, completely exhausted, and saw the blue flag bearing the Solkyrian sun flying overhead.

CHAPTER THIRTEEN
The Surrender

DAX DID NOT BELIEVE for one moment that they should have survived.

The maelstrom that had opened in front of the *Southern Echo* had been frightening enough on its own, but even before Rori had collapsed, he'd known that the sucking maw had come from an incredibly powerful Goodtide. Whoever they were, they had successfully attacked Rori's current with one of their own, and then hijacked Rori's to create and maintain the maelstrom, pulling the *Southern Echo* down and incapacitating the ship.

The ship should have come apart around them, shredded by the force of the maelstrom and the pressure of the depths, but instead, she was bobbing on the surface again, a little damaged but still intact. Dax could feel the spirit of the dryad coiled tense inside the ship, shuddering instead of pulsing in her usual calm rhythm, though if she was hurt or angry, Dax could not say.

He did, however, know that everyone aboard the ship was still alive because the Goodtide who had created the maelstrom had allowed them to live.

And that meant that the pirate hunters wanted to take them alive.

Groaning, Dax rolled to his knees. He pressed his agate anchor more firmly against his chest, letting it siphon off his overly reactive magic and clear the fog in his head. He could still feel the racing hearts of everyone in the dark around him, but they were muted now and he could think again.

If they want us alive, he thought, *they must intend to make an example of us.*

There was a sudden flood of light across the lower deck, weak but blinding after the total darkness of the sealed hold. Dax blinked against it, realizing someone had opened the hatch at the top of the stairs. Through it poured fresh air and the authoritative shouts of navy sailors. Footsteps thundered on the upper deck as the navy came aboard, and Dax did not need his magic to know that there was no hope of fighting them. There were too many, and they were steady on their feet where the crew of the *Southern Echo* was groaning and convulsing.

Dax pushed himself up, wincing against the way his left knee and ankle twinged in protest. He'd lost his pistol and his knife somewhere in the hold, and it would be a miracle if the latter had not stabbed someone in the dark when the ship had been tossed about.

Whoever had opened the hatch at the top of the stairs was the first one taken. Dax heard the navy sailors drag the poor soul off the steps and on to the main deck, and then there was a confusing moment of silence as the navy milled around the top of the stairs.

Finally, a clear voice called down into the dark, "Crew of the pirate ship *Southern Echo*, surrender yourselves without a fight and you will be shown mercy. Any who resist will be cut down where they stand."

Those of us who can *stand*, Dax thought bitterly as he balanced his weight on his uninjured leg.

Through the gloom, he saw more of the crew climbing unsteadily to their feet, some looking dazed and others terrified. Nikolai was among them, one hand fumbling with the bandage that had come loose from around his head. Dax picked out the flash of red that was the feather in Iris's hat as she tugged it back on to her head, looking determined to fight to the end.

"Captain Iris Arani," the voice called down from above, and everyone in the hold froze. "His Highness Prince Trystos summons you to court in Solkyria. Do you come willingly?"

The silence that followed those words was louder than thunder.

Across the hold, Dax could see that Iris's mouth had fallen open, but her shock was giving way to anger. He could almost hear her outrage over her ship being captured, her crew threatened, and she herself called upon and expected to answer like a loyal hound. Perhaps worst of all, Prince Trystos knew her name and her ship, and he didn't just intend to make an example of her; he wanted something from her.

Dax knew that Iris would rather die than serve him.

She began to shake her head, and Dax felt the surge of defiance that ran through the crew as they watched their captain stand her ground.

But that determination was weak under their continuing pain and disorientation, and some of them did not have it at all.

Dax knew that the crew would fight for Iris and the *Southern Echo* and their already lost freedom, but in their current state, they would only be slaughtered. He locked eyes with Nikolai, and saw that the boatswain had reached the same conclusion.

If they fought, they died then and there, with only a fraction of the crew fighting.

If they surrendered, they all survived.

Dax tilted his head in a silent gesture towards Iris. Nikolai nodded.

"Do you come willingly?" the voice called again.

"No!" Iris roared at the same moment Nikolai screamed, "Aye!"

Iris turned to him, stunned, and that let the boatswain's voice prevail. "We come willingly," he shouted as he lurched across the deck, heading for the stairs. "We will not fight."

The crew exchanged glances of confusion mingled with resignation and relief, but Iris only had fury in her eyes. She drew in a sharp breath, ready to shout her defiance once more, but the navy had already begun to descend into the hold, rifles ready in their hands as they called for the *Southern Echo*'s crew to move against the walls of the ship and keep their hands above their heads and away from their weapons. Iris took one look at the defeated way the crew began to drag themselves to obey, and then she bolted for the stern of the ship, towards the private captain's cabin.

Dax went after her, his ankle threatening to give out with each step, but he forced himself to hurry. Iris was backed into a corner, and Dax had no idea what she was going to do. But he knew what she was capable of, from a final last stand armed to the teeth with pistols and her saber, to bypassing her cabin altogether to make a run for the gunpowder. He didn't think she'd ever turn her beloved ship into a flaming wreck, but she'd never been in so foregone a situation before.

He was almost relieved when he heard the door to her cabin bang open. By the time he got there and opened the door, he heard navy sailors moving through the hold, calling for Iris to surrender herself. Dax slipped inside the cabin just as Iris's heavy sea chest clicked open. She threw the lid back and seized a roll of paper that Dax recognized immediately: the copy of Mordanti's map that Rori had drawn.

Iris barely paused when she whipped around and

saw Dax limping across the room. She nearly growled at him as she stepped to her writing desk and violently struck a flint, lighting a candle.

"There's only one thing Trystos could possibly want," she said as she held the map over the tiny flame. For the briefest moment, she hesitated, regret and longing clear in her gaze. Then she lowered the map. The edge of the rolled paper smoked and caught, fire licking up its length. "I will not give it to him."

Dax reached her side just as she dropped the burning paper to the deck. Silently, they watched Mordanti's map burn to embers and ash, but Iris gave herself no time to mourn. She drew her saber.

"Nikolai said he wouldn't fight," she said as shouts from the navy sailors ricocheted beyond the cabin's door. "I will. I'm not letting them take this ship without one." She looked at Dax then, her dark eyes burning even hotter than the fire that had consumed the map. "Don't stop me."

Dax opened his mouth to respond, but then there was suddenly no more space between them as Iris crushed her lips against his, the kiss frantic and desperate. It was over in a moment, Iris pulling away first.

She gave him a small shrug. "I just wanted to do that once."

"I've wanted to do it a lot more than once," Dax said earnestly. He reached out and caught her wrist, feeling her pulse light and quick against his skin.

Iris looked at him almost tenderly when he did not let her pull away. "Dax," she began, her voice soft. Then her eyes widened as she felt his magic slip into her blood. Her anger returned tenfold. "Don't—" she snarled, but even that was faint as her eyes began to close. The saber fell from her hand and landed with a clatter on the deck, and Dax caught her before she could join it.

"I'm sorry," he murmured in her ear. His magic was firm around her heart, slowing its beating and turning her blood sluggish in her veins. "Forgive me."

Even as her consciousness slipped away, Iris's gaze was deadly.

"Or don't," Dax said, his breath ragged in his throat. "Hate me if that's what you need to stay alive. This crew still needs you, and you can't leave us yet."

Iris tried to say something, but the word was only a soft groan. She went limp against him, and that was how the navy sailors found them; Dax crouched on the floor of the captain's cabin with the unconscious Iris cradled in his arms, her sword lying useless before them and the smoking remains of a legend behind.

CHAPTER FOURTEEN

The Strength of a Goodtide

FROM HIS POSITION AGAINST the *Southern Echo*'s railing where the navy had left him with his hands bound behind his back, Nate had a clear view of the capture of his crew mates.

Novachak was the first one brought topside. His hands were also bound but left in front of him, and he was free to walk of his own accord. His icy eyes darted anxiously across the deck until they found Nate, and then the boatswain let out a held breath in a small ribbon of relief that the wind wiped away. Novachak's clothes were disheveled and the bandage had come loose from around his head, leaving the hole where his ear had been exposed to the world, but the navy sailors did not accost him further. He took up a position off to the side of the steps leading down into the *Southern Echo*, next to a prim navy sailor who came forward with a book and a pen. A younger boy held a pot of ink at the ready for the scribe, and they set to work taking down the names of everyone who emerged from the hold as Novachak spoke them aloud.

Those who came up first included Liliana and Theo. Both riggers blinked and stumbled as they were walked to the stern and ordered to sit, still disoriented from the maelstrom. Liliana gave Novachak one bitter glance, but it dissolved under his bleak expression. There were tears in her eyes as she passed Nate, but she fought against letting them fall.

Theo, for his part, just looked numb.

Marcus was in the next group that came up, which also included AnnaMarie and her gun crew. Most of the gunners darted nervous glances at the navy, having recovered enough for panic to begin to set in. Marcus looked terrified. Nate wished he could offer his friend some comfort, but all he could muster was a mirrored expression.

They're going to kill us all, Nate thought as he watched a navy sailor slam his palm between Marcus's shoulders, driving him forward.

But when the Darkbend stumbled, AnnaMarie reached out and caught him, setting him firmly back on his feet. She gave the navy sailor a cool look that was somehow more defiant than if she'd screamed a challenge to a duel. The navy sailor tightened his grip on his rifle, clearly ready to use the weapon. Anna-Marie flicked her attention away and held herself tall as she made her way to the stern of the ship and sat where she was told.

Nate let out his held breath, wondering where An-naMarie Blueshore had found her courage and if he could do the same.

He pressed his back against the *Southern Echo*'s railing, trying to feel the pulse of the dryad in the wood, but it was drowned out by more footsteps trudging up the stairs.

Eric was in the next wave of prisoners, his hands also tied behind his back. When he stepped on the main deck and heard his name entered into the ledger, he took a deep, shuddering breath, shoulders trem-bling as he held it. When he released it, he seemed to let his defiance go with it. Eric did not slump as he walked across the deck. He always had impeccable posture, and he carried himself the same way now. But his eyes were locked on his own feet, and he did not once look up, not even when Nate heard one of the navy sailors make an appreciative noise as she raked her gaze up and down Eric's body.

"I wouldn't mind guarding that one," she said to her neighbor, not at all quietly.

The other sailor chuckled, low and throaty. "You're going to have to get in line."

Anger flared in Nate's chest, hot enough for him to scrape his boots against the deck as he made to rise. He got a sharp crack on the back of his head for it, and he slid back down, dazed.

"Mind yourself, Lowwind," someone growled from above him.

Nate shut his eyes against the pain in his head, but that only made listening to the sounds of the rest of the crew being brought up so much worse. Some of them were resisting, and their struggles were answered with the meaty thumps of rifle butts slamming into stomachs and faces. When Nate opened his eyes again, he saw blood streaming down Roberto Perrani's chin from his freshly broken nose.

We were going to leave the Common Sea, Nate thought as he gently laid his head against the railing behind him. *We were so close.*

There was no point in telling the gods that this was not fair. Nate had been to the temple on the Vanishing Island, and had seen firsthand what the gods considered fair. He remembered the rough embrace of rope around his torso and the way his feet had slipped and scrambled across a tilting platform as spirits laughed and demanded that Arani make a terrible choice. He remembered dueling Xander and how the Grayvoice's words had cut deeper than his sword. He remembered losing Rori to the *Dragonsbane* and how she had not been returned to the *Southern Echo* with the rest of the crew, after they'd been removed from the temple. Nate knew that this situation now was exactly the sort of thing the gods would find amusing.

When Rori came up, there was a distinct pause where even the wind seemed to stop. She shifted uneasily as the eyes of the imperial navy scraped her Goodtide tattoo, and a few mutters rippled across the ship. One of the officers barked an order for quiet, and the navy sailors snapped to obedience, but their heads turned to follow Rori as she was pushed towards the foremast to join the others.

Even with the distance separating them, Nate could see that Rori was trembling. She desperately searched for somewhere to put her eyes that was not on a naval uniform bearing the Solkyrian sun. She finally looked up, and there was the slightest hitch in her step. Nate followed her gaze to the black flag still flying off the back of the *Southern Echo*. It waved limply in the feeble wind, but it was still there.

Nate knew the navy sailors would strip the flag from the ship and put up the Solkyrian one, but seeing the black standard with the white dragon head seemed to settle Rori. She was no longer shaking when she was made to sit next to Marcus and Eric, at least.

The last to come up were Dax and Arani, the latter of whom looked extremely groggy, as though she'd just woken up. But her anger was as clear and hot as a lightning bolt, and it was easy to see why the navy had bound her hands behind her back and assigned two sailors to flank her as she was marched across the deck. Dax, on the other hand, only had one sailor, and his hands had been secured in front of him.

Apparently, his tattoos had fooled the navy.

Nate wasn't sure if he should count that as a victory. Dax looked miserable as he was placed on the deck next to Captain Arani, who gave him a scathing glare that was only intensifying as her head seemed to clear.

As a navy sailor hauled Nate to his feet and pushed him to join the others at the stern, it occurred to him that, despite her defiance and clear desire to fight, Arani was no longer a captain.

That, more than anything, drove a spike of hopelessness through his heart.

He sat down heavily next to the other Skilled, who had all been pushed off to the side of the captured crew. He exchanged silent glances with his friends. They were all on the cusp of falling apart.

Nate did not pay much attention to the droning recitation of the crimes the *Southern Echo*'s crew had committed; apparently, they needed to be stated in completion so that everyone understood exactly why the navy had captured their ship and arrested them, as though they had not lived through it all and made those choices on their own. Hearing the *Southern Echo*'s history should have enthralled him, but in that moment, all Nate wanted was to wake sweating in his hammock, his heart racing as he came out of this nightmare.

Nothing would have been kinder.

Perhaps that was exactly why it did not happen.

Instead, Nate gradually became aware of someone calling out for the navy sailors to make way. The recitation of the *Southern Echo*'s crimes was over, and a broad gangplank had been rigged up between the pirate ship and the sloop. Two people were getting ready to come over, a man and a woman.

The man went first, stepping quick and sure across the plank. He had a sturdy build, all muscle and hard lines with salt-and-pepper hair and a neatly trimmed mustache. His uniform was decorated with the golden embellishments of a senior officer, and his hat was obnoxiously tall and feathered on top of his graying head. Luken would have loved it.

With a start, Nate realized he had not seen the bird since the maelstrom. He started to turn to Rori, expecting her to hit a similar state of alarm, but she was sitting calmly, almost eerily so.

Nate wondered if she'd fallen into a state of shock.

The man with the oversized hat jumped with heavy grace on to the *Southern Echo*. He smiled brightly as he sauntered to the captured crew, stopping only a step away from Arani so that she was forced to tilt her head back to look up at him.

"So this is *the* Iris Arani," the officer said, still grinning. "I must say, it was easier to find you than I was told it would be, but I suppose your best efforts could only take you so far, especially given that you've never come up against a true Solkyrian fighter before."

Arani looked like she wanted to say exactly what Nate was thinking, that she'd crossed paths with a few navy ships and even stolen aboard and rescued a prisoner from one of them, but she swallowed the words, refusing to rise to the bait.

The officer tilted his head and smiled into Arani's silence. "I know you Veritians aren't the swiftest boats in the fleet," he said, "but if I wait for you to fully understand me, it's going to get dark."

Arani growled then, a low and feral thing that only made the navy officer grin wider.

"I'm afraid I only speak the civilized tongue," he quipped.

"Could have fooled me," Eric breathed, so soft that Nate barely heard it, but he still glanced nervously at the navy sailors, worried one of them had caught the words.

"I'll keep this brief and use small words where I can," the officer said. "You are of special interest to Prince Trystos, may he shine bright and true."

The navy sailors echoed the affirmation.

"I, Commodore Coppermist, have been given the task of bringing you and your crew—" he said this word with such disdain, even Liliana lifted her head to frown at him, "—to Solkyria, where you will meet with the prince to discuss your future, brief as it may be." Coppermist's smile vanished as he swept his gaze across the pirate crew, lingering on no one as though he did not wish to touch them even with a glance. "Though what use he could have with vermin, I don't pretend to understand."

He focused his attention on Arani again, ready to say more, but a blob of white splattered his shoulder and began to run down the immaculate sleeve of his uniform. Coppermist stared at the bird excrement for a long moment, then raised his gaze to the rigging lines above his head.

And there was Luken, clinging to a rope directly over Coppermist and looking very pleased with himself.

Nate turned to Rori, and saw the smallest trace of a smile on her lips.

It vanished when Coppermist drew a pistol and aimed it at the bird.

"No!" Rori screamed, surging to her knees.

Nate and Eric both moved to stop her, but with their hands bound, they barely bumped her with their shoulders. And Rori didn't need full use of her hands to call the wave, anyway. It came rushing towards the *Southern Echo* and the navy ship like a hound protecting its master, growing larger by the second.

Coppermist had just enough time to look alarmed before the wave was bearing down on them, ready to crash across the decks and carry them all over the railing into the sea.

Nate braced himself.

Then the wave split down the middle, like it had been ripped apart by a god's hand. The two sides slid around the ships, flattening harmlessly back into the sea. The *Southern Echo* barely rocked in their passing.

"That will not be tolerated," a cool voice said.

Nate turned to see that the woman from the sloop had come across to the *Southern Echo*. Despite her young age, she leaned heavily on a silver-tipped cane and moved slowly as she crossed the deck, which Nate supposed was why the commodore had charged ahead of her. But her uniform was even more embellished than his, although she had forgone a monstrous hat in favor of a plainer, more functional tricorn.

That, however, did nothing to hide the deep blue Goodtide tattoo that curved over her brow and down her cheek in a sweeping pattern that was even more elaborate than Rori's.

Nate's mouth went dry even before Coppermist turned to the woman and said, "I expect you'll be teaching that little brat a lesson, Lisandra?"

Nate's older sister stepped past Coppermist, each motion calm and deliberate. She did not look at the commodore when she said, "Actually, I was referring to you. The bird is clearly the Goodtide's pet. She'll behave as long as it's kept safe, I believe." She pinned Rori with an intense stare, openly inviting a challenge.

Rori sank back on her heels and nodded mutely.

"We'll need a cage for it, of course," Lisandra said.

Rori swallowed, but said nothing.

Lisandra gave a small, satisfied nod, then turned her attention to the rest of the crew. Her gaze hitched on Nate and a faint frown creased her brow, but that was the only acknowledgment his sister gave him. Her dark eyes moved away as easily as they had settled, and she took in the others.

It had been years since Nate had last seen Lisandra. She'd still been a girl, flush with youth and ready to take on the world in service to the empire as she bid her family goodbye and went up the coast to the tide working academy. Now, she was a slender woman, still young but worn smooth and cold by the sea. Her dark hair was meticulously braided and hung down her back in a severe line, reminding Nate of an uncoiled whip. Despite her need for the cane, Lisandra held herself proud and tall, and she did not so much as flinch under Coppermist's outraged glare. In fact, most of the navy sailors seemed to be edging away from her, their expressions filled with a grudging respect.

Whatever Lisandra had been doing over the course of her navy career, she'd clearly advanced far more than Sebastian had. Nate felt his stomach turn as his sister took another few steps forward, her cane thudding against the *Southern Echo*'s deck with more finality than the fall of an executioner's blade.

"Captain Arani," Lisandra said, "Prince Trystos would very much like to meet you. As the commodore said, we've been tasked with bringing you to him, but this need not be an unpleasant voyage. If you cooperate, no harm will befall your crew." Her gaze flickered over Nate, Marcus, Rori, and Eric again before returning to Arani. "That includes your four Skilled there, and the disguised one next to you."

Dax froze even as Arani gave a startled jolt. Coppermist frowned and peered closer at Dax's twin tattoos.

"He's a Malatide," Lisandra said calmly before turning back to Arani. "He'll need special guard as with the other dangerous Skilled from your crew, but they will not be harmed in any way as long as you come willingly. You have my word on this, and I speak with the authority of Prince Trystos himself."

Coppermist opened his mouth to protest, but Lisandra held up her hand, and the commodore gave her a scathing look as he quelled the words before they could form. Lisandra ignored his glare.

"Well?" she said to Arani.

Arani took a moment to survey her captured crew. Her expression was fierce when she turned back to Lisandra, but Nate saw the exact moment when her shoulders slumped in resignation, and he suspected Lisandra did, too.

"Not one of them is harmed," Arani said, "or I swear you'll wish you'd sank my ship."

"Believe me, Captain," Lisandra said, "that is still an option."

Lisandra turned away and moved back across the deck, heading for the plank that connected the *Southern Echo* back to the navy sloop, her cane thudding on the deck. She did not look at Nate again.

CHAPTER FIFTEEN
Where Power Lies

LISANDRA'S PROMISE OF NO harm coming to Arani's crew was technically upheld. They were all transferred from the *Southern Echo* to a frigate that pulled alongside the pirate ship, but the cells they were locked in down in the navy ship's brig were far from comfortable. Nate was one of many who winced every time the motion of the ship jostled him against his neighbors, injured limbs brushing against bruises and sprains. Everyone without a Skill was allowed to enter the cell with their bindings cut and wrists freed, but that was an insultingly small gesture given how packed they were into three of the four available cells.

Marcus and Eric were released from their bonds once it was determined that their light bending posed no serious threat to anyone. Nate followed soon after, likely thanks to Lisandra informing the officers that her younger brother did not, in fact, possess a true wind working Skill. Or maybe Sebastian had spread the word a while back. Either way, before they cut the ropes around Nate's wrists, he heard a navy sailor say, "Oh, *that's* the Nowind. Thought he was dead."

Nate rubbed circulation back into his freed hands and did not react to the old nickname.

It didn't matter now. Nothing really mattered now.

Although, Nate still bristled at the way Dax and Rori were treated.

The final cell was dedicated solely to the two tide workers, who were both forced to trade their rope bonds for iron cuffs that were secured to rings in the walls. Rori had to wear another set of shackles around her ankles, but Dax was free to stand up. That was about all he could do, as there was not enough slack for him to move more than a step away from the wall. He opted to sit instead, his head thrown back against the cold, unfamiliar wood of the navy ship and his eyes shut tight against the world. Rori huddled silently against her wall, shivering a little whenever a draft blew through the ship.

They'd caught Luken and put him in a cage that they'd hung in the brig, right in Rori's line of sight. Sometimes, Nate would see a glimmer of defiance spark in Rori's eyes, but then she'd look up and see the bird, and he knew she was remembering Lisandra's words and power as a Goodtide. Then she'd lose the spark and slump a little further down against the wall.

Novachak and Arani were placed in separate cells across from each other, Arani in with Nate's group and Novachak with Marcus's. The arrangement probably saved the Northman's life. Arani glared daggers at him through the iron bars, but she could not reach him and therefore could not strangle him.

Novachak took advantage of that. "Surrendering was the only choice," he growled across the distance between the two cells. "They would have killed every-one."

"You think they won't now?" Arani shot back.

"Not if we can give Trystos what he wants."

Arani bared her teeth in a snarl, but before she could answer, three navy sailors marched into the narrow space.

"You," the leader said, pointing at Arani, "come here. The rest of you, get back."

The other two sailors had their swords drawn, ready to stab anyone who defied the order. No one did. Nate shuffled towards the back of the cell with the others, pressing as far away as he could from the door. That was two steps at most, and short ones at that.

The petty officer who had given the order eyed them all critically, but he said nothing as he went to unlock the cell door. He paused when he realized that Arani had not moved.

"What is it that you want, exactly?" Arani asked once she had his attention.

The petty officer narrowed his eyes. "It's not your concern, Veritian."

"You pointed at me," Arani snapped. "Presumably, someone has questions or wants to take a swing at me. Ergo, very much my concern."

The navy sailor made a disgusted noise and withdrew the key from the lock. "No one said it had to be you. Who was your quartermaster?"

Arani nodded at Dax's unmoving form, and there was a silent pause as the petty officer took this in.

"The Malatide?" he finally asked, disbelief clear in his voice. He stared at the imprisoned crew. "You lot willingly sailed under a Veritian captain with a Malatide quartermaster?"

"It made perfect sense at the time," Novachak quipped.

The petty officer blinked at the Northman's pale skin and icy eyes. "And you were...?"

"The boatswain."

"Of course you were," the navy sailor grumbled. Then, louder, "You'll do. Let's go."

"Where?" Arani demanded.

The petty officer turned to give her a slow, disdainful glance. "I didn't point to you this time, did I?" He banged the pommel of his sword against the iron bars, close to Arani's face. Nate and a few others jumped, but Arani barely flinched. "Not your concern."

Novachak's gaze lingered on Arani as he was removed from the cell. Nate thought that there was regret in his icy stare, maybe a plea for forgiveness or at least understanding, but Arani scoffed and turned her back to him. Novachak said nothing as his wrists were placed in iron cuffs and he was led away.

"Captain?" Liliana asked in a small, soft voice once the navy sailors and the Northman had disappeared. "What are they going to do to him?"

Arani glanced sharply at Liliana, but worry bloomed behind her anger, and the look she fixed in the direction Novachak had gone was more anxious than anything else.

Several hours passed without Novachak.

The navy sailors brought them stale water to drink and even staler hardtack to eat, just enough to take the edge off their hunger and thirst without satiating it. Nate gnawed his hardtack as quietly as the others, listening to the creaks and groans of the navy ship and the voices of the sailors as they worked.

It wasn't so different from the *Southern Echo*, and yet it was a world and a lifetime apart.

As the afternoon slid into evening, Nate tried to catch the rhythms of the drafts through the ship. He thought that, maybe, he could ride one of them back out into the open, just to find some relief from the claustrophobic cell and the darkness of the brig, but that was beyond what his Skill could do. His magic kept fumbling the wind and losing the thread of the drafts as they rushed through the interior of the ship, crashing against the bulkheads.

Nate had to resign himself to the endless waiting of a prisoner. It had been difficult when he'd been alone aboard Sebastian's ship, but at least then, he'd been able to imagine the *Southern Echo* escaping and sailing far away from his captors. This time, he had no such luxury.

His throat itched with the unasked questions he wanted to direct at Arani. *Will Novachak be okay? Will any of us be okay? Is there any chance at all that we survive this?*

But Arani had not moved from her place at the bars. She'd sat down, but she was still staring down the hall waiting for Novachak to return, and Nate knew that she did not have the answers. At least not the ones he hoped to hear.

Night's fall was marked by a deepening of the gloom of the navy ship's lower deck, so that when Novachak finally did return, his pale skin and white hair made him look like a spirit wandering through the dark. Arani scrambled to her feet, Nate and the others following her, but no one said a word as the cell opposite them was unlocked and Novachak stepped back inside.

He seemed unhurt, much to Nate's immediate relief, but he knew that there were wounds that could run underneath the skin. Still, Nate followed Arani's example and held his tongue until the navy sailors had locked the cell and disappeared.

"Well?" Arani asked the moment they were gone. Her voice was low and urgent, breathy with anticipation, or maybe dread. "Did they hurt you?"

"No," Novachak said, and Arani's relief was a solid thing in the air.

It disappeared at the Northman's next words, however.

"It's the *Southern Echo*," Novachak said.

Several people looked up at that, including Dax and Rori.

"What's wrong?" Arani asked.

"I think," Novachak began, a slow grin spreading across his face, "she's fighting them."

The night passed without incident or much sleep, but in the morning, Nate listened close to the few snatches of words that filtered down from the upper decks. Most were mundane things about the sails and rigging lines, sometimes talk of lives and families back on Solkyria, occasionally a curse as a task did not go as smoothly as it could have, but the murmurs about the slow progress they were making due to the *Southern Echo* grew louder and louder.

The pirate ship's helm was a source of frustration for the navy sailors trying to operate it. They complained of stiffness in the wheel and a rudder that was decidedly nonreactive one minute, and then swinging wildly the next.

The yards, apparently, were not cooperating either, and no one could get the sails properly aligned to catch the wind. The *Southern Echo* was dragging behind her navy escorts, slowing them all down.

Nate and the others with keen hearing relayed what they heard to the rest of the imprisoned crew, who traded quizzical looks. Even Dax listened with interest to these reports, the frown on his face as deep as the one on Rori's.

"The *Southern Echo* has never had these problems before," Dax mused.

"No," Arani agreed. "So either the Solkyrian navy is

full of completely incompetent sailors, or Nikolai is right. She's fighting them."

Novachak gave Arani a grin wide enough to show his teeth beneath his bushy beard. "Just you wait," he said with almost childlike glee. "I think she's far from done."

They did not hear much the rest of the morning, although when two sailors brought the breakfast rations of water and hardtack, Nate noticed that one of them had a bandage wrapped around her hand, and the other had a bruise on his nose. They both gave the *Southern Echo*'s crew particularly nasty looks and grumbled something about a poorly maintained ship before flinging the hardtack into the cells and taking their leave.

"Now we *know* something strange is going on," AnnaMarie said. "Never sailed with a captain more ornery than you when it comes to maintaining a boat."

There were several murmurs of agreement, and Arani's smirk was genuine. She gazed almost fondly at the cut on her palm that was still healing before asking, "What else do you hear?"

Throughout the rest of the day, Nate and the others listened close and slowly pieced together the *Southern Echo*'s rebellion.

The stairs leading up to the *Southern Echo*'s quarterdeck and the poop deck had managed to trip several people, Commodore Coppermist chief among them. Someone's foot went clean through a weak spot in one of the lower decks, leaving them with splinters in their ankle. Gun ports kept popping open and slamming shut for no apparent reason. Best of all, the door to the navigation room somehow locked itself with Coppermist and another officer inside, and no matter what anyone did, the door would not budge. It took the better part of an hour before someone found something heavy enough that could be used to bludgeon the door to pieces, but just before they swung, the door creaked open of its own accord, as though it had never been locked to begin with.

That was what brought Commodore Coppermist blustering down to the brig, accompanied by four armed navy sailors. His nose was bruised in the exact same manner as the sailor who'd brought the hardtack that morning, and Nate had to fight to hide his smirk.

Arani made no such efforts. "My, Commodore," she said brightly, "looks like you've had a nasty fall. Have your sea legs deserted you?"

Coppermist thrust his finger in front of Arani, his entire arm shaking from the fury that clenched his muscles. "I don't know what you are doing, or how," he growled, "but you are going to stop. Immediately."

"I'm not doing a thing," Arani said coolly. "I'm locked up here with my crew." She tilted her head. "Having a little trouble with my ship, perhaps?"

Coppermist's face flushed a deep red. "What is it?" he demanded. "Did you put a Veritian curse on it? Bind spirits to do your foul bidding?"

For a moment, Arani was too stunned to respond. Then she cocked an eyebrow. "Of all the things you could have guessed, that's what you're going with?"

"What did you do, you Veritian rat?" he snarled.

"The better question is, what did *you* do?" she shot back. "If my ship has decided she hates you—sound judgement on her part, by the way—then I assure you, that is entirely of your doing."

Coppermist wagged his finger. "So you did curse it," he said. "Remove it."

Arani threw up her hands. "Veritians don't have magic, you twit."

"Then what did you do to that ship?"

"Nothing!" Arani snarled. "*You* pissed off the dryad!"

There was a brief pause.

"The what?" Coppermist asked.

"The spirit of a dryad lives in the *Southern Echo*."

"That's ridiculous," Coppermist said. "Dryads don't exist."

Arani looked like she could not decide if she wanted to smack her head against the iron bars of the cell, or smack Coppermist's head against the iron bars of the cell. Across from her, Novachak shook with silent laughter while Dax watched the exchange with wide, horrified eyes. The rest of the crew looked on with varying shades of amusement while the navy sailors exchanged bewildered glances.

"So if I have this right," Arani said after a long moment, "you think that I, a full-blooded Veritian, from an island that has never once produced anyone with a drop of magic in their blood, put a curse on my ship so that you, a man from Solkyria, the *only* island in the entire known archipelago to have natural magic users, would be inconvenienced. And that is the only possible explanation, because there could not possibly be a dryad inhabiting my ship, because 'dryads do not exist.'" She shifted her stare from Coppermist to the navy sailors behind him. "How the absolute fuck is this idiot in charge?"

Coppermist reached through the bars to grab Arani by the throat. Nate and several others surged forward without thinking, shouting for the man to release their captain. Coppermist stumbled back more out of surprise than compliance, and the navy sailors stepped forward with raised swords that they thrust through the bars, stabbing indiscriminately into the cell. Nate fell back, uninjured, but Liliana had a fresh cut on her arm, and Lucien Scorvani cried out and clutched at his gut, red seeping across his clothes.

"Gods below," someone swore, and then people

were scrambling out of the way so Lucien could be lowered to the floor.

Arani was back at the bars of the cell in an instant. "You swore no harm would come to my crew!"

"*I* made no such promise," Coppermist snapped, "but that was only on the condition that you cooperated."

"Which I have," Arani snarled.

"You put a curse on your ship!"

"That is not—*argh!*" Arani let her protest dissolve into a frustrated cry, and then she whipped away from Coppermist to drop down next to Lucien. "Nikolai," she called, "what do I need to do?"

"Ideally, clean the wound," Novachak called back.

"Can't exactly do that," Arani said, ignoring Coppermist's indignant sputtering as the two spoke around him.

"Pressure, then," Novachak said. "Try to slow the bleeding."

Arani rolled up her sleeves and pressed her hands over Lucien's wound. He moaned and tried to roll away, but more sets of hands reach down to pin him in place.

"You are not to die, Mr. Scorvani," Arani said. "That is a direct order from your captain."

Coppermist scoffed, but his expression changed as the sound of uneven footsteps and the thud of a cane approached.

Nate tore his gaze away from Lucien's soaking shirt to see Lisandra drift between Coppermist and his sailors, right up to the cell door. She watched Arani struggle to contain the bleeding with an impassive expression.

"He will not survive without proper medical attention," she said after a moment.

"Thank you for your useful observation," Arani

growled as Lucien's blood seeped through her fingers. "Now get away from my crew."

Lisandra's expression did not change. "You have a dryad on your ship," she said. "We have a doctor on ours."

Arani glanced up at Nate's sister, her face caught somewhere between disgust and disbelief.

"Calm your dryad," Lisandra said, "and our doctor will treat your man."

Arani looked ready to tell Lisandra to find a creative place to stick her cane, but Lucien groaned and Arani's face fell. She took one last look at the stabbed man, his skin gone pale, and bared her teeth. "You save him first," she said.

Lisandra shifted, slow and deliberate, until she had a grip on the bars of the cell and had moved her weight off of her cane. She lifted the cane in her free hand, and Nate saw that the silver top was carved into the shape of a wave. Lisandra regarded the polished metal thoughtfully.

"Save him," Arani growled.

"We will try," Lisandra agreed. She nodded to one of the sailors, who stepped forward with the key to the cell.

Coppermist came forward, too. "You can't just—"

That was all he got out before Lisandra slammed her cane into his throat. He choked and stumbled back, falling against the bars of the other cell. Novachak and several others were there immediately, reaching through the bars to grab him. The navy sailors lifted their swords, but Lisanda held up her hand, and a tense silence fell. Even Novachak and the others were quiet as they held the struggling Coppermist.

"Commodore," Lisandra said, "do not forget that while you were given command of this particular operation, I stand in for Prince Trystos himself." She leaned in closer to him, all her weight on her un-hindered leg, and placed the silver tip of her cane under his chin. "When you disrespect my authority, you disrespect the Sun Crown. Difficult as it is with such a feeble mind as your own, try to remember that, despite this Skill mark, I have the royal decree on my side, and I will act accordingly."

Coppermist did not answer, but after a few more coughs, he closed his mouth and fell still.

Nate saw nothing but hatred burning in the officer's eyes as he looked at Lisandra.

A moment passed, and then Lisandra drew back, lowering her cane and leaning on it once more. She nodded to Novachak, who in turn nodded to the others, and they released Coppermist. The commodore stumbled forward, looking furious, but Lisandra put a hand to his shoulder and brushed off his uniform.

"Must be careful down here," she murmured. "Get too close to these pirates and who knows what may happen." She looked to each of the four navy sailors in turn. "It was a good thing we were here to get the commodore out of that nasty situation." The navy sailors nodded obediently, and she turned back to Coppermist. "Do take care not to trip again, Commodore."

Coppermist pulled away from her, his eyes still burning with fury and hate, and stalked off into the darkness. Lisandra did not watch him go.

"I do believe we'd best get that bleeding man to the doctor," she said idly, and the navy sailor with the key sprang to the door once more.

Arani helped lift Lucien Scorvani, but he was immediately taken from her hands and hoisted by two of the navy sailors. Arani started to follow them as they carried the wounded man off, but Lisandra shook her head.

"Best if you see to your ship now, Captain," she said.

Arani watched Lucien disappear, then glanced at the imprisoned crew. Her resolve hardened as she looked at them all, and she drew herself up and gave a single, silent nod before stepping down the hall in the direction Lisandra had indicated, the other two navy sailors escorting her.

Lisandra herself locked the cell and put the key in her pocket. Nate thought she might say something to them, or at least to him, and he stepped up to the bars, ready for it. But she turned and walked away without a backwards glance.

A few hours passed by Nate's reckoning before the next group of navy sailors came. He couldn't say how long for sure, but it felt like considerably less time than they'd spent waiting for Novachak to return.

At first, Nate thought that they were bringing Lucien back, but he was absent from the group, and the navy sailors were once again armed and ready to use their weapons.

Their leader, a short man with the uniform embellishments of a lieutenant, held a scrap of paper up to the sole lantern that illuminated the area. After squinting at it for a moment, he began to bark out names. "Theodore Yellowwood. Liliana Blackwater. Esmerelda Durmanti. Thomas Redfield." All riggers, Nate noted.

But there was one more. The lieutenant's voice stumbled on the final name, cutting off in confused disbelief, but he rallied quickly. "Nathaniel Lowwind."

Nate's head snapped up.

"The five of you move to the front of the cells," the man ordered. "The rest of you, step back, as far as you can go."

Nate exchanged a bewildered look with his cell mates. Liliana offered him a small shrug before climbing to her feet and extending her hand. Nate took it and felt the deceptive strength in her slender arm as she pulled him up.

That was a rigger, all right. Wiry and agile but far from weak. Nate wondered what the navy wanted with them. Surely, they had enough riggers of their own, and they knew Nate couldn't help with wind working. Not unless they wanted him to read the winds and seek out the strongest ones, as he'd done for the Southern Echo.

"Where are you taking them?" Novachak asked as the first cell door was unlocked and Theo and Esmerelda cautiously stepped out.

The navy sailors ignored the boatswain and locked the door again before moving to the next one.

Novachak wrapped his hands around the bars and tried again. "What about our injured man? The one you lot stabbed?"

The next cell door swung open, and Tom Redfield drifted out.

"Is he alive?" Novachak demanded. "At least tell us that much."

The lock clicked on Nate and Liliana's cell.

"Please."

The lieutenant hesitated before swinging the door open and gesturing for them to come forward. He quickly locked the door behind Nate before finally turning to Novachak. "I don't know what happened with your man," he said, his voice flat but not unkind. "He'll either be back with you tomorrow, or he won't survive the night. Either way, you'll find out in the morning."

Novachak's pale eyes were grim in the lantern light,

but he nodded his thanks to the lieutenant.

Then Nate was ushered through the ship with the riggers, a rifle against each of their backs, until they were driven topside. The light hurt after so much time spent below, and it took a minute before Nate could fully see again.

Navy sailors bustled around him, their uniforms crisp even where their owners smelled of sweat. Nate and the riggers were sorely out of place in their mismatched shirts and trousers with faded red and yellow bandanas holding their hair back, clothes dirty from the brig. They huddled a little closer together, and Nate was glad to be in their company as they were pushed across the deck.

The sails were furled overhead, not one extended to catch the sweet, steady breeze blowing in from the east. A perfect wind, going to waste.

The other navy ship, the sloop, had also furled its sails, although it looked ready to shake them loose and dart forward on a moment's notice. And in between the two ships, grappled to the frigate with her own sails furled, was the *Southern Echo*.

Despite everything, a flutter of joy went through Nate's heart as he looked upon the pirate ship. Arani's flag had been stripped from the stern and replaced with the Solkyrian sun, but this was still the *Southern Echo*, and not even the navy sailors on her deck could change that.

Nate and the riggers were made to cross over to the pirate ship, using the plank that had been secured between the two. The moment Nate's boots touched the *Southern Echo*'s deck, he felt that familiar warmth and steady pulse of the dryad, as though her spirit rose to greet him. Both faded after a moment, but they were always present at the very edge of Nate's awareness, and he knew the others felt it, too, when Liliana gave a happy sigh and even old Theo let out a breath of relief.

"There," a cool voice said, cutting through the warm contentment, "you have your rigging crew." Lisandra stood near the mainmast, Captain Arani right beside her. Nate's sister tilted her head in his direction, but kept her eyes locked on Arani. "Now get to it. We are horribly behind schedule."

"Allow us a moment, if you would," Arani said.

A faint frown creased Lisandra's brow, but she did not protest.

Arani quickly moved to Nate and the others, catching Liliana in a one-armed hug and gesturing the rest of them into a tight circle. "You were all they would let me have," Arani said, almost breathless as the words left her in a rushed whisper. "Novachak was right, the *Southern Echo* was resisting the navy. She's calmed down since I came aboard, and I can tell she's happy to have you few back, but let's make sure we don't sail her too well. I want to see if I can convince them that we need more of our people to fully get her to cooperate."

"Are you planning to try to fight?" Nate asked softly.

Arani hesitated, looking sorely like she wanted to say yes, but she finally shook her head. "I want them to believe that we're all necessary to the *Southern Echo*. No one is staying in those cells, if I have anything to say about it. Now come on, they want us underway." She moved to straighten up, then checked herself. "Not too fast, remember. And keep your wits about you. The dryad will throw the rudder every now and again, and I don't want any of you going overboard when that happens."

"How do you know she'll do that?" Theo asked.

Arani grinned without humor. "I used some special Veritian magic."

Theo blinked at her.

"I talked to the figurehead," Arani said. "Threw in

some nonsense words for Coppermist's sake so he'd think the curse was lifted, but other than that, it was a pretty straightforward discussion."

Nate noticed the fresh bandage on Arani's hand as she moved it off of Liliana's shoulder. He wondered if she'd bled for the dryad again. He wouldn't have bet against it.

Arani straightened up and put her fists to her waist, which was noticeably devoid of her saber and the usual array of pistols she kept in her sash. "All right, you have your assigned positions," she said clearly, letting her voice carry across the deck and over the navy sailors that were watching them with open distrust. "Let's go."

Nate hesitated, but Theo gave him a light tap on the shoulder and surreptitiously gestured for him to follow. Liliana and Tom Redfield made for the shrouds to climb up and unfurl the sails, and Esmerelda took her place below, extending the rope to Theo and Nate as they moved to join her. Everyone fell naturally into their usual roles, and Nate made sure he did the same. He ignored the points and whispers of the navy sailors as they watched him engage in manual labor instead of wind working.

Soon enough, the sails were down and the *Southern Echo* was gliding forward, easily keeping pace with the navy frigate and sloop that flanked her. True to Arani's word, the ship did not maintain her course as easily as she usually did, and Nate heard the man at the helm swear as the wheel bucked in his grip.

Arani made idle remarks about the *Southern Echo* having her favorites when it came to certain tasks, particularly navigating, and was eventually instructed to take over at the helm. The ship behaved considerably better for her, although the *Southern Echo* did lurch every now and then, as though still not satisfied with the people sailing her. Arani made soothing sounds and offered helpless shrugs to the navy sailors whenever this happened.

It was far from subtle, but it was enough to irritate the navy and convince Coppermist to allow a few more people from the *Southern Echo*'s crew out of the brig. Nate was glad to see Marcus among those who came across this time. The Darkbend held his hand up against the cloudy sky as the light flooded over him, but he flashed a weak smile that Nate returned, then was hurried off to a task of his own. Nate watched him go, wondering what it would take to get Eric and Rori back aboard the ship.

With a pang, Nate thought of the promise he'd made to Marcus, and the reading lessons Rori had promised him, and he wondered if any of that would ever come to pass now that they were under the navy's thumb. Novachak had said something down in the hold about giving Trystos what he wanted as a way to ensure their survival, and Nate wondered if that really was possible.

The thump and shuffle of Lisandra's footsteps warned him that his sister was coming up behind him. Nate quickly bent back over the knot he'd been tying, but Lisandra stopped all the same. He glanced up, but she only looked back at him impassively. She waited for him to finish the knot before she spoke.

"You'd do well to make Prince Trystos aware of your true Skill," she said once he'd fully turned to face her.

Nate stared at his sister and tried to think of what he was supposed to say in a situation like this. *I missed you,* maybe, or *It's nice to see you again.*

But he hadn't, and it wasn't, and he was pretty sure she felt the same.

"If you show yourself willing to serve him, he'll look favorably upon you," Lisandra continued, ignoring the awkwardness that stretched between them. "But be mindful of your place as a wind worker. Keep those light benders beneath you, where they belong."

That was one thing Nate knew how to respond to. "They're my friends," he said, not bothering to keep the anger out of his voice. "More than friends, actually. They're my family, more than you and Sebastian ever were."

He'd meant the words to hurt, but Lisandra only nodded.

"Which is exactly why you must keep your distance," she said. She glanced over her shoulder to the helm, where Arani was holding the wheel and looking the very picture of a proud captain despite everything that had happened over the past few days. "Your captain made a grave mistake when she showed just how much she cares for this ship and her crew. Trystos will use that against her." Lisandra turned her focus back to Nate. "If you want to protect them, don't let him do the same to you."

Nate stared at Lisandra, at the hardness of her face and the guarded blankness of her eyes. He did not remember much about his sister from her youth, but his few clear flashes of memory included a serious but proud girl who had been ferociously ready to face the world.

Somewhere, that girl had been shattered, and this woman before Nate was what the surviving pieces had been molded into.

"Is that what they did to you?" Nate asked softly.

Lisandra gave him another impassive blink. The only betrayal to her calm was the tapping of one finger against the carved silver wave at the top of her cane. "Yes," she said simply. Then she walked away, leaving Nate with a growing pit of cold dread in his gut.

CHAPTER SIXTEEN

The Right Thing

Iris's plan to get more people out of the brig was moderately successful. She got more than Dax had expected, but the navy soon put a limit on the number of *Southern Echo* sailors she could have during the day. Sometimes, they rotated, giving others a much needed break from the dank darkness of the brig. Dax was never one of them.

In his head, he knew that was because he was a Malatide, and even if the navy sailors weren't aware of his blood working abilities, they weren't going to risk letting him loose. The same went for Rori, who fared even worse than he did. Nikolai was never taken over to the *Southern Echo* again, although Dax suspected that had more to do with his authority within the crew. Similarly, some of the stronger gunners like AnnaMarie and Julian were kept in the brig.

Dax understood the strategic decisions behind who was and was not allowed to leave the brig each day, but at night, when they all came back after the anchors were dropped and the sails furled across all three ships, Iris would sit as far away from him as she could.

His heart wondered if she was punishing him for stopping her from fighting the navy.

He wasn't sorry for that. He knew she would have lost her life if she'd fought, and if her defiance had put a sour taste in the naval officers' mouths, there was a good chance they would have slaughtered some, if not most, of the *Southern Echo*'s crew, just to keep the survivors from rebelling.

And Dax had been right; the crew still needed their captain.

Whatever was waiting for them on Solkyria, whatever Prince Trystos had planned, Iris was their best chance of finding a way to keep them all together. As long as she was alive, she would not let anyone tear the *Southern Echo*'s crew apart ever again.

She'd already defied and threatened gods over as much. A prince was nothing compared to that.

No, Dax was not sorry that he'd stopped her. He'd done his duty as quartermaster, and acted in the best interest of the crew despite the captain's wishes. That was his job, and he'd been doing it for a long time.

But Dax was sorry that he'd used his magic on Iris without her consent. He had sworn to her long before he'd become quartermaster that he would never do that, and yet, in that desperate moment, he'd found that he actually was capable of betraying her.

He truly did not know if she would ever forgive him for that, and that was what twisted his heart in his chest.

She certainly would not do it before they had to face their fates. Now that the *Southern Echo* was cooperating, it wasn't going to take long for them to reach Solkyria, even with the three vessels stopping each night and emptying the pirate ship of her crew.

But even with the smoother sailing, the time Dax spent in the brig with nothing to do but worry over the crew was agony.

So he turned to Nikolai for a distraction, knowing the boatswain would welcome it.

Neither of them wanted to speculate on what Trystos could want them for, not when they were locked in the brig with most of the crew around to hear, but there was one thing that had been on both of their minds.

"We should have gotten clean away," Nikolai said. "There was no reason for that many Solkyrian ships to be blockading the Coral Chain in the east."

"No," Dax agreed. "They would have needed to call some back from the warfront."

"And a few pirates were never reason enough to do that before," Nikolai said. "Which, as I figure, can only mean that the empire is losing the war."

A soft murmur went up from the crew members that were listening to their exchange.

"How do you figure that?" Julian Redpool asked.

"Because even with his pirate hunting obsession," Dax said, "Trystos has never had those kinds of resources before. His older brother takes all the warships for battles in the east." He leaned his head back against the iron bars of the cell, trying to ignore the growing soreness in his spine. "Trystos doesn't have the authority to summon a blockade like that. If it was there, it was a coincidence he decided to take advantage of."

"And since that blockade *was* there," Nikolai said, picking up the thread, "that means those ships got pushed out of Vothienian waters. Now they're holding the line in the Common Sea." He grunted as he shifted within the uncomfortable space of the cell. "I suppose the emperor figured he'd encourage his spare son's efforts to clean up the Common Sea a bit more, now that the war is drifting closer to the imperial home."

"Why are we alive, then?" AnnaMarie asked. She stood with her arms threaded through the bars of the cells, letting it do the work of holding her up. "And why save him?" She nodded across the way to where Lucien Scorvani lay on the floor.

He'd been returned to them after the first night, pale from blood loss and moving slow with agonized pain, but expertly bandaged and stitched closed. Lucien kept his eyes shut, but he lifted one arm and shaped his fingers into a rude gesture directed at AnnaMarie.

"Not saying you're expendable," she chided him. "Just that if they were going to execute us, why bother saving one of us from bleeding out?"

Dax hesitated, parsing out the best way to approach the answer, but Rori suddenly spoke up, the first words she'd said since their capture.

"They want to use us," she said hoarsely.

After a small pause, AnnaMarie said, "Again, if we're just going to be made into an example—"

Rori's chains clinked as she rolled over to face the gunner. "We have a fast ship and a highly capable crew. If they're losing the war, they're not going to throw that away. If anything, they'll put us on the front lines and see how much damage we can do before we sink."

"Rori," Dax began.

She swung her gaze to him, exhausted but angry. "Tell them I'm wrong," she said. "Go ahead. Lie to them."

Dax held her stare for a long moment. "You're probably not wrong," he finally murmured.

That prompted another wave of groans and whimpers from the crew, but in their helpless situation, they subsided before long.

Dax caught Nikolai's eye, and the boatswain gave the smallest shake of his head.

Neither of them was going to voice their suspicion that Trystos wanted Iris and the *Southern Echo* in particular for something more than the war efforts. Some things were lining up too neatly for there to be no doubts about the empire's intentions.

And as AnnaMarie had pointed out, if the empire

intended to execute them or send them to the front lines of the war, there was no reason to keep all of them alive.

Dax was still mulling this over when the rest of the crew were brought back from the *Southern Echo* and locked in the brig once more. He turned towards Iris, but she moved to the far corner of her cell and settled between Theo and Liliana, all three of them looking exhausted and ready to drift off to sleep.

Iris rallied herself just enough to survey her imprisoned crew. "Landfall tomorrow," she said into the silence. "I'm sorry I couldn't get all of you topside, but at least we won't be locked in here much longer." She tipped her head back and shut her eyes without glancing at Dax.

No one responded to the captain. Gradually, they all settled into whatever uncomfortable sleeping position they could manage, leaning against each other instead of the iron bars of the cells. Dax put his back against the bars that separated his cell from the adjacent one, wishing he could do the same and draw some comfort from the crew. Across from him, Rori huddled against the wall, staring at Luken in that terrible small cage they'd stuffed him into until her eyes slipped closed.

Dax sighed quietly, listening to the sounds of the dozing crew. "I'm sorry, too," he whispered.

"For what?" someone whispered back, and Dax jumped a little.

He turned to see that Nate was sitting on the other side of the bars, his face turned to Dax. Nate had gone over to the *Southern Echo* more than anyone, other than Theo, Liliana, and Iris herself. There were dark circles under his eyes, but Dax was struck by the way the young man did not look afraid, only troubled, and deeply at that.

"It's nothing," Dax said, keeping his voice low so as

not to disturb the others around them. "Go to sleep, Nate."

The young man frowned. "Doesn't seem like nothing."

For a moment, Dax considered ordering Nate to drop the matter, but he was tired, and his heart was heavy, and he simply did not have it in him. "I suppose I'm thinking about all the friendships I had to break to be quartermaster," he said. "It's a job for someone the crew likes, but not their friend. Sometimes, you have to do things they don't like at all to protect them."

Nate made a thoughtful noise, but there was a note of resignation beneath it. "I suppose that's true." He was quiet for several moments. "What if it's something you really don't want to do, though?"

Dax tipped his head back and sighed. "If it's the right thing to do, it doesn't matter what you want."

Or how deep a hole it tears through you, he added silently.

He waited, but Nate did not say anything else, and eventually, sleep claimed Dax. The next thing he knew, the cell doors were being unlocked, and Iris was leading a small group out of the brig, back to the *Southern Echo* for the last day of sailing. She did not look back as she stepped away.

Nate did, and as he stared at the crew, his eyes lingering on Marcus, Eric, and Rori in particular, there was an aching longing in his gaze that he shuttered away before following the captain.

CHAPTER SEVENTEEN

Wants and Needs

NATE HAD SPENT THE past few days agonizing over Lisandra's advice. He didn't delude himself into thinking that it had come from a place of familial love; it was clear she had closed her heart off to anything like that a long time ago.

But she'd still told him in no uncertain terms how he could protect his friends from what was to come.

He had not wanted to believe her, but his brief conversation with Dax the night before had convinced Nate that she was right.

Now, Nate made a point of not looking to see if Marcus or Eric were brought up from the brig. He kept his head down around the navy sailors instead of looking them in the eye as he had the first day of their capture, and he tried to keep his face neutral whenever he heard something cruel said about the *Southern Echo* crew, or saw a navy sailor shove or even slap one of them for being in the wrong place at exactly the wrong moment.

His anger grew, however, and he did not know how long he'd be able to keep up an indifferent facade.

They might take me away from the Southern Echo *crew*, Nate realized. *Put me on a pirate hunting ship, if Trystos really does want to use my Skill.*

He bared his teeth at the irony, remembering his desire to do exactly that not so long ago.

But that had been before he'd sailed with Arani, before he'd met Marcus and Eric and Rori, before he'd found a dragon and crossed the line between worlds and seen all kinds of monsters, even within himself. All of that had taught Nate that there were people in his life that he was willing to die for, but given the choice, he would much rather live and fight and laugh and dream alongside them.

But if Nate wanted to protect those same people, he needed to make sure the empire never tried to use them against him. He had to be a good and obedient wind worker, willing to sacrifice everything for the empire and expecting nothing in return, not even his own dignity.

He did not want to go back to being that person.

If it's the right thing to do, Dax had told him, *it doesn't matter what you want.*

Nate's anger rose to a boil, and then blew away like mist on the wind. He slowly turned the gold ring on his finger until the Solkyrian crest was facing up once more. The rays of the embossed sun twinkled in the light, and Nate had never seen anything uglier in his life.

As the day wore into afternoon, Nate helped where he could with the rigging work, although he no longer spoke to Liliana or Theo beyond what was absolutely necessary. He avoided Arani's gaze even as she watched him pull away from the others, and he made sure he was busy when he saw Eric coming over to join the *Southern Echo* sailors.

Eric still managed to slide over to Nate. "You holding up all right?" he asked, and the Darkbend's voice was so easily familiar that Nate almost answered.

Then he saw Lisandra standing at the railing of the quarterdeck, gazing down at him like the emperor himself would look upon his subjects. Her stare was flat and impassive, but her warning rang in Nate's ears, and he quickly stepped away from his friend. He felt Eric's eyes on his back as he fled.

Solkyria appeared on the horizon that afternoon, growing larger and darker with each passing minute. The navy sailors moved with the easy lightness of people going home, but all Nate felt was a heavy, dreadful weight in his chest. He picked at the gold ring on his finger and tried not to look at the looming island crowned with mountains, the imperial palace glittering like a jewel set into the largest one.

When the call went up for adjustments to the sails, Nate volunteered to scale the shrouds. The navy riggers had not gone up since the *Southern Echo* had tried to throw them overboard, leaving that dangerous work predominantly for Liliana and Theo. Nate had kept his boots on the deck, but he wanted to be up the lines now, away from the navy and his crew mates equally.

Former crew mates? he wondered as he climbed up, but the give of the ratlines beneath his hands and feet distracted him before he could think too hard about what the bleak future held.

He shuffled along the yard, slower than Liliana did on her side, but he focused on his own work and gathered the rough canvas up. Once the foresail was furled, Nate clung to the rigging lines and looked past the navy ships flanking the *Southern Echo* with their gunports open and cannons ready to fire, away from Solkyria and out to the open sea. The wind blew in from the horizon, salty and pure, and Nate breathed it in deep, taking one last moment of joy from his magic before it was no longer his own. Blue ribbons of wind unfurled around him, dancing over the water and through the sky, beautiful and free.

Nate was glad he'd soared among them, when he'd

had the chance.

Messenger birds had been sent ahead of the ships' arrival, so there were plenty of people waiting on the docks when the *Southern Echo* was escorted into the harbor of Sunthrone City. Nate, Arani, and the rest of the pirates who'd sailed the *Southern Echo* that day were on the main deck when the ship bumped against the dock, their hands bound once more. Across the way, Nate could see that the rest of the crew had been brought up from the brig and placed on the frigate's deck. The moment both ships were secure, the *Southern Echo* crew was pushed off the ships and down the gangplanks to the docks, navy sailors armed with rifles at their backs. More of the navy was waiting on the docks to receive them, and they filed the pirate crew into a thin line that they then marched into the city streets.

Nate nearly staggered when his feet touched the solid ground, cooling relief sweeping through him as the entire island anchored his magic. He'd been away for so long, he'd forgotten what it was like to walk upon Solkyrian soil, no threat of magic burn or the Skill sickness anywhere in his body.

But he was under no delusions that he was coming home, especially not with the crowds lining the streets.

Nate was near the back of the line, along with the other Skilled, so he had plenty of warning before the watching crowd turned gleefully vicious.

People had come from all over the city to jeer at the parade of captured pirates. Nate saw dock and factory workers mixed in with the better dressed merchants from the upper city, along with the blue tattoos of the wind and tide workers who had been at port when the ships had come in. There were even a few glittering nobles dotting the crowds that lined the street, marked by the tall hats the men wore and the jewels that decorated the women. Their light bending and animal speaking Skilled servants hovered nearby. Some of these magic users looked upon the pirate crew with open disdain just as the weather workers had done, but most kept their eyes on the ground and stood in silence as their lords and ladies scoffed and cheered. Nate's eye caught on a young Brightbend who stared at the *Southern Echo* crew with clear disappointment and sadness on her face, as though some of her hope had died with their capture. Nate was marched on with the others, and the Brightbend soon dropped out of his sight.

The navy ignored the crowd for the most part, only stepping in to shoo children aside when they got underfoot and impeded their forward march. A few rocks were thrown at the *Southern Echo*'s crew, along with a couple of eggs and rotted vegetables, but the navy did nothing when these struck the pirates, other than snap at the poor soul who stumbled when a hunk of lettuce hit their head. Nate ducked under the egg that came his way, but the screams of "Traitors!" and calls for the pirates to swing from the gallows were impossible to dodge.

Through all of that, Arani led the line with her shoulders thrown back and her head held high. Not everyone from the *Southern Echo* had it in them to imitate her, but those who did were stoic in their bearing. Nate saw AnnaMarie take a rock to the forehead, leaving her with a bloody gash above her eye, but she shook off the pain and kept going with barely a stumble in her stride. Even Lucien, hobbling as he was with his wounded side, locked his gaze ahead and refused to acknowledge the crowd.

Eric, Rori, Marcus, and Dax walked in silence behind Nate, never once crying out or letting themselves be baited, although Marcus gnawed his lower lip bloody. He looked considerably steadier on his feet now that he was on Solkyrian soil, but that was of little comfort now.

Nate hoped that Marcus would eventually find the courage to tell Dax and Rori the things he'd confessed before the maelstrom had sunken all their hopes and plans, and find some way forward with his changing magic. Nate wouldn't be there to help him, after all, or Rori if the god kept whispering to her, or Eric, or Arani, or anyone else.

The train of *Southern Echo* pirates was turned north and taken along some of the lower streets, which Nate knew would eventually bring them to the city's prison. He'd always steered clear of that area when he'd lived in the city, but he had always known where to find it, just as he'd known where exactly in the merchant districts his parents' old coppershop had been; and which streets were more dangerous at night for the Skilled no matter the color of their tattoo; and which bakers had been kind enough to give sweet rolls to the younger wind workers who had come out of the academy with their instructors to watch the auroras in the night sky during the winter holiday. And he still knew the way to the wind working academy from here, and how to find his parents' shabby apartment, and which was the road that led away from the north end of the city up the coast to the tide working academy and beyond, all the way to the mines.

Nate watched the buildings of the city slowly slide past as he trudged along, letting these memories wash over him. They felt like they'd been made only yesterday, and they felt like they'd come from a lifetime ago. Nate could not recall if he'd ever really thought of Sunthrone City as his own, but it certainly did not belong to him now.

That was fine, he decided. He didn't really fit in the city anymore, either.

The crowd thinned out as they approached the prison, the wealthier citizens peeling off long before the building had come into sight. It was a squat, unimpressive structure made of flat gray stone. Barred windows dotted the sides, some at higher levels and a few down at the street, where the less threatening prisoners no one cared enough about to try to help were usually housed. More secure cells were located deeper inside the building, if the stories Nate had heard growing up were to be believed. Looking at the prison now, he saw no reason to think otherwise.

He wondered where the *Southern Echo* pirates would be placed.

Entering the prison was surprisingly calm, especially when compared to the journey from the docks to the building. Guards took over for the navy escort, delaying only long enough to double-check everyone's bindings and make sure there were no hidden weapons among them, and then the guards cross-checked the crew's names against the list the navy had compiled when they'd first captured the *Southern Echo*. With everyone accounted for, the guards took them to the prison's lowest level, which was dank and gloomy even with the tiny windows letting a little natural light in through their bars.

It was cold, too, and Nate shivered as his breath fogged in front of him.

They were divided into groups of four and spread among the cells, only losing their bindings when they'd stepped inside and the door was ready to be slid shut.

Nate was placed with Theo, Julian, and Eric in one of the street-side cells. The window was well above their heads, and even if they could reach it and somehow get the bars off, it was far too small for any of them to wriggle through. There was a layer of straw on the floor and a few thin blankets piled into a corner, and two wooden benches on the walls that Nate supposed could double as cots, although they were too small and narrow for more than one person to use at once.

Theo gave a single heavy sigh before stepping forward and grabbing the blankets and parsing them out. Nate wrapped his around his shoulders. He wondered briefly if he should worry about lice or other crawling things, and then decided he was too tired to care. He stood at the bars of the cell door and peered out as far as he could.

To his left and right were more cells, each holding more of the *Southern Echo*'s crew. He heard Dax's voice a couple of cells down, along with Novachak's. Across from Nate was more of the same, save for the cell one spot to the right. Captain Arani had been locked in that one, and she was alone.

She wrapped her hands around the bars, breath misting before her, and called to the crew, "Is anyone hurt?"

"A few cuts and bruises from the march," Novachak answered, "but nothing bad."

Someone grumbled from further down the cell-block.

"Other than Lucien's stab wound, I mean," Novachak amended.

Arani nodded. "Dax, are you still bound?"

"I am not," he called back.

"They released me, too," Eric said.

Next to Nate's cell, an arm stuck out between the bars and waved down the hallway, gray agate peeking out from beneath the sleeve of the dark coat. That was Rori, then. Marcus did not answer, but Nate showed his unbound wrists to the captain.

Arani nodded. "All right, so at least we have that in our favor."

Theo came up on Nate's side. "But what's that do for us?" he asked.

"I'm not sure yet," Arani said, "but Dax's Skill may help us get out of here." She shifted, pressing up against the bars of her cell and turning in the direction Dax was. "How many could you take down at once?"

The Malatide did not immediately answer. "Four, maybe," he said, "if we didn't care if they survived or not."

"We don't," Arani said. She did not smile, but her eyes were bright as a plan unfurled in her mind. "They'll likely hold us here a few days, and we can learn a lot in that time. First chance we get, we take it and get out of here. I don't know what they'll do with the *Southern Echo*, but she won't let them move her easily. If we do this right, we just may get back to the ship and make a clean escape."

"And if we do it wrong?" AnnaMarie asked from somewhere off to Nate's left.

Arani shrugged. "They want to kill us anyway, right?"

Theo and AnnaMarie both made disapproving noises, but no one voiced an argument. With nothing else to do, they settled in to wait. Nate bundled his blanket tighter and sat on one of the benches, Julian pressed against him for warmth. Eric and Theo took the bench opposite them, Eric pointedly not meeting Nate's eye.

Nate wondered if the Darkbend had guessed why he'd been snubbed on the *Southern Echo*. He knew he should explain to Eric what Lisandra had said, but he did not want to do it in front of Theo and Julian, let alone the rest of the crew. Maybe that night, before

Eric had gone to sleep, Nate could whisper the truth, and hope it was enough.

Nate resigned himself to waiting out the rest of the day and observing what he could about the guards' patterns. He knew an escape was far beyond the realm of possibility, but it gave him a feeble thread of hope to hold on to, and that was far better than nothing.

The first appearance of the guards was not what any of them expected.

A group of eight of them came, moving stoically down the hall and not looking or speaking to anyone as they passed the cells. A light frown creased Arani's brow as she watched them, and Nate saw her gaze sweep over each of the guards as though she was searching for something. The key holder, perhaps. Her frown deepened when the guards stopped in front of one of the further cells.

"You four are up first," one of the guards cracked out. The lock clicked and the heavy door ground open along its track.

"First for what?" Liliana asked, her voice anxious.

None of the guards answered her, and Nate supposed she accepted that, for he heard people climbing to their feet and cuffs locking over wrists. The guards appeared again, each pair of them flanking a single prisoner. Liliana was one of them, followed by Esmerelda Durmanti, Sarah Bluewave, and Daisy Whitegrove. The four women were taken back down the hall, past each of the cells, and Arani's calm began to break.

"Where are you taking them?" she asked. She did not get an answer, but rather than fall quiet, Arani slammed her hand against the bars of her cell. "They don't have anything to tell you that I couldn't," she yelled after the guards.

They ignored her, and Nate heard a door slam shut

from the end of the hall.

"Questioning?" Novachak asked after a few silent moments.

"Undoubtedly," Arani answered. She huffed an exasperated breath. "They're going to be really disappointed when they realize that two riggers, a swab, and a member of a gun crew don't have what they want."

"What do you think they're after?" AnnaMarie asked.

"Mordanti's map," Arani said without hesitation. "That's the only thing they could possibly want from us." She fixed her attention on the cell across from her, where Rori was. "I destroyed the copy in my cabin. They have nothing to go on."

"You didn't want to maybe barter that for our freedom?" Rori asked flatly.

Arani looked at her coolly. "You think we were ever in a position to barter?" She shook her head. "I know you're smarter than that. You know they would have taken it, and whatever and whoever they needed to follow it."

Rori did not respond, but Nate felt his gut twist.

If they all knew that it was always going to come back to Mordanti's treasure, then this was the best time to tell the crew his plan, after all.

"When they come back," he said, "I'll tell them I can track the dragon."

Arani's glare snapped to him. "You will do no such thing."

Nate stood up and moved back to the bars. "I will," he said, "and I'll tell them I'll cooperate fully if they'll let the rest of you go."

"Again, none of us are in a bargaining position," Arani said. She tapped a fingernail against one of the iron bars. "The time for that has long passed."

"Not if we do it right," Nate said. "I'll tell them that

I'm the only one they need for the dragon hunt. The rest of you don't matter."

More than a few people shifted across the cells at those words, and Nate could feel the confusion brushing against hard breaths of anger.

"If I do that," Nate continued, trying to ignore how much the words hurt, "they won't need you, so they'll let the rest of you go."

"Or execute us," Arani said, "since they won't need us." Her voice was mild, but the stare she'd fixed on Nate was smoldering with rage.

Nate shook his head vigorously. "Not if you volunteer to act as privateers for the empire." He waved his hand with the gold ring on it. "Tell them I was always loyal to Solkyria, obnoxiously so, and you're glad to be rid of me, but deep in your hearts, you were loyal, too. You just found yourselves on the wrong side of bad circumstances. Tell them that you can still do good for the empire, if they'll let you attack Votheinian ships."

Silence met those words.

"You were planning to sail east, anyway," Nate pressed on. "If the war really is going badly and Vothein is pushing into the Common Sea, the empire will welcome privateers. They've done it before and they'll do it again, because they know you'll be more useful to them alive than dead. This way, you won't be forced to hunt Mordanti's dragon again. Maybe eventually they'll even let you sail freely, and you'll have the chance to disappear, if you want." He drew in a deep breath. "Or maybe you'll decide that you like having the empire at your back instead of on your heels, and you all will keep going because you'll have made names for yourselves and you'll be alive."

Arani had shut her eyes and was massaging her temples by then. "Even if this impossible scenario could actually play out as cleanly as you seem to think," she said slowly, "what in the six hells makes you think any of us would want that?"

It doesn't matter what you want, Nate thought. Aloud, he said, "If it will keep everyone alive, then it's the right thing to do."

"Gods below, shut up!" Rori's voice snapped from the adjacent cell, and Nate jumped. She sounded like she was at the corner where the solid wall met the bars, as close to him as she could be in that moment.

"This is the only way I can protect you," Nate said. "Let me do it."

"Eric, slap him," Rori commanded. "I can't reach from here."

Eric did not move, but he was watching Nate with narrowed eyes. "You're trying so hard to be a noble protector," the Darkbend said, "but you're forgetting to actually consider us. We don't need that, and *you* don't get to decide what's right for us."

Nate stood frozen for a moment, soft murmurs of agreement filling his ears from the surrounding cells. "This could save you," he finally said.

"No, it can't," Rori snarled. "If any of us really believed that, we'd have gone back to the empire a long time ago."

"They're not going to forgive us for what we've done," Dax cut in, his deep voice drifting down the cellblock. "It's too much, and it's been going on for too long."

The people that Nate could see in the other cells nodded in grim agreement. None of them looked pleased, but they'd already accepted the situation.

"We all made our choices," AnnaMarie said.

"Not necessarily good ones," Theo added, "but our choices all the same."

Arani lowered her hands. "So, it's decided then?" she asked, her voice ringing out clearly. "No groveling, and we try to make our escape?"

Voices sounded their agreement up and down the hallway, and Nate felt the weight of their decision crush down on his heart.

"No!" he shouted, slamming his hands against the bars of his cell.

"This isn't your decision, Nate," Arani said. "Stand down."

"I can't," he gasped. "I can't let you—"

"Nate?" The soft voice that cut across his back was achingly familiar. "Is that really you?"

Nate turned and saw a woman kneeling at the little slit of a window, bent over awkwardly on the street to bring her face close to the bars. Even if she hadn't spoken, Nate would have known that face anywhere.

It belonged to his mother.

She gave a small gasp when her gaze focused on his Lowwind tattoo.

"Oh, my sweet boy," she said, and her eyes swam with tears. "What has become of you?"

"Well," Nate said after an awkward moment, during which he was very aware of his cellmates' eyes on him and his mother, "I'm alive."

His mother scrubbed her sleeve across her eyes. "Yes, you are."

Nate took half a step towards her, but stopped when he realized there was no warmth in her gaze.

"When I heard them saying the navy had caught a Lowwind with the plainest mark they'd ever seen, I couldn't believe it," she murmured. "I didn't *want* to believe it. But you're really here." Fresh tears spilled from her eyes and ran down her nose, and she roughly wiped them away again.

Julian and Theo gave Nate looks that were heavy with meaning. They expected him to go to her, to clasp her hand, to take and offer some comfort while he still could. Nate remained where he was, not moving except to breathe.

"And you—" His mother coughed, her voice hitching on the words, but she continued bravely on. "You've betrayed *everything*."

Eric stood up, turning to face her, but she only had eyes for Nate.

"Did you think for a moment about what this would do to your father and me?" she said, the words coming out as an angry hiss between her teeth. "When you didn't report to the mines, the enforcers came to our home and demanded to know where we'd hidden you. We told them that lie you'd fed us, that you were sailing with a Northman and using your Skill, but they knew how weak you are. They tried to beat the truth out of us, and now your father can't use his arm at all, and it's all because of you and your selfish lies!"

A blurred mix of shame and anger rose in Nate's chest, and he realized that his shoulders were heaving with each breath now. Then Eric stepped in front of him.

"You know, in all actuality," the elegant Darkbend said, drawn up to his full height with his voice clear and steady, "none of that was a lie."

Nate glanced up, startled.

"And are you calling your own child selfish for wanting to live?" Arani snarled, pitching her words to carry clearly to the street. "There's a special place in the sixth hell waiting for you, lady."

Nate's mother blinked and then cast a startled look around the cell at the others locked in with him, as though just realizing he was not alone. Her gaze skirted past him, and she shifted a little until she could see Arani, who had crouched down in her cell to be able to return the glare tenfold.

"Who are you?" Nate's mother demanded.

"His captain," Arani fired back.

"Well, I'm his—"

"I don't care," Arani said. "He chose to join *my* crew. I won't let you speak to him that way."

His mother was taken aback, but only for a moment. "Pirate scum, you're a prisoner of the Solkyrian Empire," she said haughtily.

"And you think that means we can't hurt you from in here?" Arani asked, and Nate's skin crawled at the familiar promise of death in her voice. "Dax!" she called sharply.

"It's his *mother*, Captain," Dax answered, sounding exasperated.

"That certainly isn't stopping *her*," Arani snapped. "And you've already broken your own rules around your Skill. What's one more?"

"Iris—"

"Don't," Nate said, feeling more tired than he ever had in his life. "Please."

He felt Arani's gaze on his back for a long moment, and the stillness of his crew mates in the cells around him, but no one spoke again.

Nate stepped around Eric, twisting the gold ring off of his hand. His mother shrank back as he approached, watching him like he was a feral animal and not her son. When Nate got to the wall of the cell, he reached up as far as he could, and tipped the ring through the bars on to the street in front of her.

"Consider that repayment," Nate said, "for all the time and money and whatever actual love you wasted on me before I left."

His mother stared at the glint of gold on the cobblestone. "Nate," she began, but he had already turned away. "Listen to me, you—"

"Gods below," Julian swore, "enough."

"Leave the boy alone," Theo agreed.

His mother hesitated. "I'm just trying to—"

"Get out of here!" Eric shouted, and that was what broke the dam holding back the rest of the crew.

Jeers and cries flew out of the other cells, driving Nate's mother away. She jumped back and became a silhouette against the light, and then she was gone, her shoes scraping over the cobblestones in her haste to get away.

Nate listened to the voices raised in defense all around him, and despite the rising warmth in his chest, his heart felt even heavier than before.

"As you can see," Arani said after the crew had begun to quiet down, "you're one of us, Nate, for better or for worse. We want you with us, as long as that's what you want, too."

Nate wrapped his hands around the iron bars of the cell door, feeling their unyielding cold. "You've saved my life in more ways than you could ever know," he said. He spoke quietly, but the crew lapsed into silence in order to hear him. "All of you," he said. He pressed his forehead against one of the bars. His voice hitched, but he pushed the last words out. "I need to do this for you."

"Gods," Rori breathed, "you are an idiot."

"We're together," Arani said, "or we're nothing at all."

Soft voices sounded their agreement.

Nate fought against the sob that rose in his throat, but it escaped all the same. He shook with violent breaths and stinging tears, until Eric caught him by the shoulder and led him back to a bench. Nate sat there leaning against his friend, slowly calming himself as his captain and his crew returned to planning an escape that would see all of them either sailing free on the *Southern Echo* once again, or dying in the streets of Sunthrone City, if they even made it that far.

After a while, Eric lifted his hand and showed Nate

the gold ring sitting in his palm. "She didn't take it," Eric said softly. "You might still need it."

Nate stared at the sun crest stamped into the metal, and his heart gave another violent twist. He turned his face away.

Eric hesitated, then stood up and moved to the cell door. "Rori, do you have a sharp bit of agate?"

"What do you need it for?"

Eric held up the gold ring in answer.

"Toss it here," Arani said, reaching up for the chain around her neck. "I've got something better."

Nate watched in silence as the gold ring flashed through the air, landing neatly in Arani's open hand. She drew her chain necklace with the dragon scales out from the collar of her shirt. She tilted her head as she took a firm grip on one of the scales, considering the sun symbol stamped into the ring, and then she began to scratch it out.

"Can I get a turn at that?" Rori asked.

Arani paused when more voices rose in agreement. "I'm not one to deny you all a small pleasure," she said. She unclasped the chain and threaded it through the golden ring, then swung the whole thing to the next cell over. "Pass it around, then."

Nate lost sight of the scales and the ring, but he heard the tinkling of the chain as it went from cell to cell, changing hands until it had come back to Nate's cell. Theo and Julian both jumped up when Eric got the chain, taking their own turns with the black scales, but when they were finished, Eric did not hand it back to Nate, even though the sun must have been completely obliterated by that point. Instead, he passed it along to Rori.

She paused when she received the ring. "I have an idea," she said softly, and then there was a more deliberate scratching sound.

The ring completed its circuit of the block, finally ending up back in Arani's hands. She took it off the chain and admired it for a moment. "Much better," she said, tossing the ring back across the hall to Eric, who finally presented it with a flourish.

Nate stared at the ring for a long time.

The Solkyrian sun was completely gone from the metal, scratched out a hundred times over, but there was a new symbol carved into the gold, a simple arrangement of three lines. It was vaguely familiar, although Nate had no idea what it meant.

"What is it?" he asked softly.

"It's an N," Rori's voice answered. "First letter of your name."

Nate's breath hitched as he gazed at the freshly scoured letter, bright and pure against the weathered gold of the ring.

"Do you want it now?" Eric asked.

Nate nodded, not trusting himself to speak, and Eric tipped the ring into his hand. Nate slid it back over his finger, making sure the N was on full display for the whole world to see.

Darkness had fallen by the time the door at the far end of the hall creaked open.

Another group of guards had come around before then, with water and what barely passed for food for the prisoners, which had been handed through the cell bars without opening the doors. No forks or spoons were given, just the shallow bowls with the brown mess, but at least the stuff was hot.

Novachak was speculating that the guards who brought the food likely did not have keys on them at all, so feigning sickness or injury was unlikely to get the cells unlocked.

"So they'd have to go get one of the others," Arani mused, "and that might bring too many for us to handle." She sat with her back against the side wall of her cell, her face tilted up to the dark ceiling. "What do we think about taking a hostage?"

Before Novachak could reply, the far door opened, and all talk of escape dropped away.

Nate heard the sharp rhythm of the guards' footsteps in the hall, but he stayed on the bench and pulled his blanket closer. His nose and ears had begun to ache with the cold, which he was sure was part of their punishment as prisoners. He could see Arani shivering as she stood up to watch at the bars of her cell, but she fixed a pleasant smile in place as the guards approached.

It died and gave way to open horror as they drew closer.

"What did you do to them?" she demanded. Her blanket fell away from her shoulders as she lunged at the door of her cell, and outrage began to burn in her eyes.

The guards ignored her, and marched Liliana, Esmerelda, Sarah, and Daisy back to their cell.

Nate's gasp caught in his throat as he saw the cuts and bruises that marked each of the women, and there was a shiny patch of skin on Daisy's cheek that looked like a burn.

Nate, Eric, Theo, and Julian rushed to the door of their own cell as the *Southern Echo* crew around them did the same. No one spoke as the four women were pushed back inside their cell and locked in. The eight guards who had brought them ignored the stares of the *Southern Echo* crew and walked easily back down the hallway, closing the heavy door behind them.

"Lily?" Arani said. "Are you...?"

She left the question dangling unfinished in the air. Not one of those women were okay.

"I'm here," Liliana croaked after a few moments. "That was bad."

Novachak strained against the bars of his cell. "Is anything broken?" he called down to Liliana and the others. "How deep are those cuts?"

There was a pause as the people in the end cell checked themselves and each other, wincing and groaning all the while.

"Nothing broken," Esmerelda reported back, her voice as hoarse as Liliana's. "Cuts aren't bad. Scabbed already."

Arani bristled in her cell. "What did they want?" she asked, low and dangerous.

Liliana drew in a few ragged breaths that hurt to hear. "Nothing," she said. "They didn't ask us anything."

"Nothing?" Arani repeated. "Not about Mordanti's map or the dragons, or even the Rend?"

"They didn't care about that," Daisy groaned. "Any of it."

Arani was silent for a long moment. "Then what did they ask about?"

"Nothing," Liliana said again. Her voice was even smaller than before. "Nothing at all."

Nate stared across the way, watching Arani's anger fade back into horror. Up and down the line of cells, Nate knew that they were all asking themselves the same thing that he was:

If they weren't after Mordanti's map and her lost treasure, and if they weren't looking to outright execute the crew, what did they want?

Nate watched Arani listen to the labored breathing from the end cell, as though she could take that pain into herself, and he remembered what Lisandra had told him about the kind of leverage Prince Trystos would look to hold over the pirate captain.

He did not sleep at all that night. He knew he was not the only one.

CHAPTER EIGHTEEN

The Prince of the Hollow Sun

A TOTAL OF THREE full days passed in the prison cells, and Dax watched Iris slowly unravel across them all.

The guards kept coming and taking people from the cells, always bringing them through that heavy door at the end of the hallway and keeping them for hours. They made no discrimination between men or women, Skilled or not, taking all equally and returning them with bruises, cuts, and occasional burns on their skin. Always shallow, never fatal, but painful and deliberate all the same.

Iris waited for them to take her, but the guards ignored her each time they came for a new group, no matter how much she goaded them. On the second day, she started shouting for the guards to take her instead of more of the crew, pointing out that she was likely know more than anyone possibly could about whatever it was Prince Trystos was after. The guards never unlocked her cell. Iris screamed after them, demanding to know what they wanted and why they wasted their time.

Not one of them answered her.

But when the *Southern Echo* men and women limped back down the hall and were paraded past her cell, they always told Iris the same thing: the guards had not asked them anything, had not sought any information.

They were simply hurting the crew because they could.

Dax fumed with rage alongside Iris, but there wasn't anything either of them could do. The guards kept coming in groups too large for him to drop all at once with his magic, and those that were left standing would surely begin shooting and stabbing into whatever cell was most convenient. More of the crew would get hurt, and it would be worse than anything that happened when the guards took them behind the door.

Other than Iris, the only people the guards left untouched were Dax himself and Nikolai. They both did what they could to help the people locked in with them. Nikolai tended to wounds as best as he was able with no supplies, and Dax slowed blood flows until the freshest cuts stopped bleeding.

They were both perplexed and unnerved to discover that the guards had treated the injuries they'd inflicted, albeit that treatment was only cursory and done without much finesse. But no matter what, the guards were always careful to never break a bone or hurt someone beyond the point of recovery.

"Are they planning on doing this over and over?" Dax asked after Nikolai's cell mates had been returned that evening.

The Northman did not look up from his examination of Marcus. "I don't know," he answered as the Darkbend flinched and shied away from Nikolai's hand against his shoulder. "I'd hate to suggest the bastards are being gentle, but that is almost what it's like."

"Didn't feel gentle," Marcus groaned. He fixed Nikolai with a bleary stare. "Why didn't they take you?"

Nikolai shrugged and shook his head. Dax was about to suggest that maybe they were saving the three main officers for last when Nate spoke up.

"Because this is how they hurt you," the young man said.

Dax glanced across the hall to where Nate stood, blanket around his shoulders and hands wrapped around the cold iron bars of the cell he shared with Theo, Julian, and Eric. The four of them had been taken first thing that morning and returned just after midday, and Nate had a smear of blood crusted across his chin. He swayed a little on his feet, but his eyes were bright beneath his untouched Lowwind tattoo as he gazed into the cell where Iris was. Dax could not see her, but he knew that she was at her own door, the muscles of her arms tensed as though ready to pry the bars apart.

"They know you care about us," Nate continued. "So they're hurting us to get to you."

Iris did not respond, but Dax could picture her shaking with silent rage, just as sure as he could feel the heavy beating of his own heart as he realized that Nate was right.

"Gods below take them," Iris finally whispered into the quiet. "Take them all."

Dax knew Iris better than to think she'd suddenly turned pious. If anything, her quiet words were more of an oath than a prayer, but that she was earnestly speaking about the gods at all told Dax that she needed something solid to hold in that moment, a lifeline to keep her anchored through the storm.

He remembered her fury when he'd sedated her on the *Southern Echo*, and her refusal to so much as look at him aboard the navy frigate. He wondered if she would accept any offer of comfort from him now.

Not that it mattered, of course. He could not reach her even if he found the courage to try.

The crew still needs you, Dax had told her as he'd

quieted her pulse and guided her into unconsciousness.

He'd been right, but he'd failed to take into account
how much Iris needed her crew, too.

On the morning of the fourth day, after nearly everyone from the *Southern Echo*'s crew had been hurt in
some form or other, the guards came in force. As they
walked through the hall and stopped in front of the
cells in groups of eight, Dax couldn't help but wonder
if there were any guards left in the prison. It certainly
seemed like they had all come for the *Southern Echo*
pirates.

Curt orders were given, and with no other choice,
Dax moved to obey along with the others. They were
far too outnumbered to try and fight, and with the
crew still in pain, most of them would have struggled to
throw a single punch. Dax's anger simmered in his gut
as he let a guard bind his wrists, but he forced himself
to cooperate out of fear that any resistance would see
someone else beaten, this time in front of everyone.

Nikolai was of a similar mind. He locked eyes with
Dax before extending his own hands to be bound, and
there was nothing but resignation in his icy gaze.

Iris was the last one they took out of the cells. For a
heart-stopping moment, she did not emerge, and from
the sudden tensing of the guards, Dax worried she
meant to fight after all. But then she stepped out, teeth
bared in a silent snarl and arms extended in surrender.
The cuffs went around her wrists without trouble, and
then she was marched down the hall, towards the
door they'd all come through a few days before, when
they'd first been imprisoned.

As had happened on that first walk through the city, Iris was made to lead the way with the rest of the crew unspooling in her wake. Dax, however, was pushed into position behind her instead of taken to the back with the other Skilled.

Briefly, he wondered if the guards had been fooled by his disguised tattoo, but the navy sailors surely would have told them about his Malatide mark.

And Nikolai was just behind Dax.

Captain, quartermaster, boatswain, Dax thought. *They know exactly what I am.*

He tried to take some comfort in the idea that his position within the crew was being acknowledged, but the realization only made him worry more.

It had been a long time since Dax had been back in Sunthrone City, but some things were still hazily familiar. With the way the guards turned the column of *Southern Echo* pirates through the streets, Dax was fairly certain they were heading for the execution block.

It seemed they'd been given false hope; the crew of the *Southern Echo* was going to be slaughtered as an example after all.

The people on the streets that stopped and stood aside to watch the procession were considerably quieter than they'd been the other day. Plenty still sneered and scoffed, but it was muted under the steady sound of boots trudging over the cobblestones. Dax supposed it was a lot less fun to jeer at downcast, whipped prisoners on their way to meet their fate than defiant pirates holding their heads high.

At least no one threw anything this time.

The sky was clear that day, and Dax tried to enjoy the bits of winter sun that brushed his skin. The air was cool, but considerably warmer than it had been in the prison, and Dax breathed it in. It stank of the city, but if these breaths were going to be among the last he ever took, he figured he may as well experience them as deeply as he could. He watched the straight line of Iris's spine just ahead of him, running down between the thrust of her shoulder blades.

He remembered her kissing him.

He remembered betraying her.

I'm sorry, he thought, willing the words to reach her.

She did not look back.

He'd say the words aloud, then, when they'd reached the execution block, before the guards pulled him and Iris apart forever. And maybe he'd say more than just an apology. His final words would go to her, and then he'd meet his death regardless of how she answered, but he would say them out loud to Iris Arani, just once.

But they never came to the execution block.

Instead, the guards turned them uphill, and they began climbing into the merchant district. They walked past the shops and finer businesses into the territory of the nobles, where the homes loomed pristine and forbidding and the streets were so clean, it almost hurt to look at them. There were very few lords and ladies out for walks or business so early in the day, but their servants bustled about, and the Skilled among them moved with a scurrying freneticism that made Dax's teeth itch. If the guards hadn't bound his hands behind his back, Dax might have started fighting then and there.

He knew where they were going now, and it was so much worse than the execution block.

Iris had figured it out, too, and she was starting to drag her feet, almost digging her heels in and refusing to move until the guards grabbed her and physically hauled her forward.

Before long, the splendor of the imperial palace

came into view.

The winding road they walked upon now was paved in gleaming white stones that matched the color of the palace itself. The home of the imperial royal family was gilded with shining gold, and blue flags with the Solkyrian sun crest blew proudly from every possible corner of the layered building. Behind it loomed the cloud-scraping silhouette of the highest mountain on Solkyria, its peak covered in snow.

The towers of the palace loomed over the *Southern Echo* crew like the teeth of a giant monster as they were marched through a gate in the border wall. Dax found himself staring at the gilded edges and the soaring opulence, wondering how much blood had gone into the white-and-gold walls of this place.

He didn't have long to think about that. The prison guards handed off their charges to palace guards dressed in livery so fine, Dax felt ridiculous standing next to it. Once the prison guards had been replaced by the blue-and-white uniforms of the palace guards with the Solkyrian sun blasted across their chests, he and the rest of the crew were ushered across a short courtyard, up a sweeping set of stairs, and through the yawning doors of the palace.

When the last pirate had stepped inside, the palace doors groaned shut, closing with a thud that reverberated through Dax's chest.

He'd never been inside the palace before, much like the majority of the Solkyrian population, and in another life, Dax might have gazed in wonder at the elegant beauty of the high-ceilinged room and the soft flutter of the silk banners hanging from the balconies. As it was, he started to squirm.

Men and women dressed in their finest clothes followed royal attendants on the upper floors, but they paused to stare down at the ragged group of pirates that had just stepped inside their perfumed space. Dax saw several of these glittering people trade whispers, but never anything loud enough for him to hear.

A sharp prod at his back told him to keep moving, and Dax brought his attention back down to the ground floor. Iris was already several steps ahead of him, making her way across the room to another door set in the far wall, one made of dark wood carved with intricate designs edged with even more gold. Dax followed, and the footsteps of the full crew and their escort thundered quietly behind him. The sound on the marble tiles of the palace floor was strange to him after so many years spent on the decks of a ship.

Another finely dressed attendant opened the ornate door for them, but only slightly, so they could not see what lay beyond until they had passed through. Iris drew a deep breath, and then crossed the threshold first. Dax followed her, and Nikolai stepped in behind him.

Dax heard the palace guards call for a halt. He looked over his shoulder to see that only he and Nikolai had been allowed through after Iris, and the rest of the crew was barred from entry. AnnaMarie was at the front of the line, and there was just enough time for her to shoot Dax a single panicked look before the door thudded shut.

"What's going on?" Dax asked at the same moment Iris spat, "Let them in."

The royal guards tensed, hands on their weapons, but a rich voice rang across the room.

"None of that, now. We have important matters to discuss."

Dax turned to see a tall man at the far end of the room, standing in front of a raised dais that held two empty yet magnificent thrones crowned with sunbursts. The man was dressed in fine white clothing edged in the same velvety blue of the Solkyrian flag, sparks of silver dancing at his shoulders and along the fringe of the blue sash wrapped elegantly across his chest. His dark hair was neatly styled into gentle waves that fell around the silver circlet he wore on his brow, which was adorned with only a simple hollow circle with a few extended lines of metal to indicate his place within the royal family.

The spare son, even more distant heir to the throne now after the birth of his older brother's third child, Prince Trystos Goldskye.

And he was smiling at Dax, Iris, and Nikolai in a way that made Dax's skin crawl.

"So these are the leaders of the *Southern Echo* pirate crew," Trystos said, his voice rolling easily through the spacious throne room.

"Yes," a woman answered, and Dax had to force his gaze away from the prince to realize that the Goodtide from the naval frigate was standing at Trystos's side, along with a small phalanx of guards. Even in their uniforms, they were all so muted compared to the prince, it was almost impossible for Dax to keep his attention on them.

Then Trystos was striding towards them, his boots silent on the lush blue rug that ran the length of the room, arms open wide in welcome. He was a lean and handsome man, with a firm jawline and a straight cut of a nose. He was older than Iris, Dax guessed, but there were no touches of gray in his thick, black hair, and his dark eyes were bright with intelligence. His smile was even and dazzling, and the most dangerous thing Dax had ever seen.

Dax took an involuntary step back, and the only thing that kept him from flushing with shame was that Iris did the same thing. Nikolai half-turned from the prince, as though trying to protect his vital organs from a frontal assault, even though Trystos himself was unarmed.

"Let's remove those cuffs," the prince said as he drew closer. One of the guards next to Iris stirred and began to protest, but Trystos waved his hand. "These brave souls are my guests. I can't imagine they'd think to repay my hospitality with violence."

For his part, Dax did consider exactly that, but he remembered the door closing between him and the rest of the *Southern Echo*'s crew. Trystos did not say it, but the threat hung over their heads like an executioner's blade all the same.

By the time Trystos was only three paces away, the restraints had been removed from Dax's wrists, along with Iris's and Nikolai's. Dax rubbed at the skin the cuffs had chafed, eyeing Trystos warily. It took every scrap of willpower for Dax not to lunge forward and shove the prince away when the man seized Iris's hands in his own.

"Captain Iris Arani," Trystos said, savoring her name as though it were a delicacy on his tongue. "I'm so pleased we finally meet. I have heard quite a lot about you these past few months, and I've been eager to see how the stories measure up to the woman herself."

Iris's response was to gently retract her hands. To Dax's surprise, Trystos let her.

"Let's see," the prince said, turning his attention to Nikolai. "You are clearly Nikolai Novachak, boatswain of the ship. Formally of the Frozen North, but a sailor of our warmer waters for quite some time now." Trystos's eyes slid to Dax. "And you, of course, are Daxton Malatide, elected quartermaster of the crew, and you've held that position almost as long as Iris has been captain. I must say, that is quite an impressive feat, considering your Skill mark. Although..." The prince studied Dax's twin tattoos for a moment before nodding. "No, that's quality work there. You almost can't even tell where the original Malatide mark is." He touched a finger thoughtfully to his chin. "Although, as I've been told, perhaps you should have received a Goodtide mark, given the true nature of your Skill."

Dax swallowed, his throat tight and dry.

"You seem to know quite a bit about my officers," Iris remarked.

Trystos fixed his smile on her once more. "Don't worry, I've made a point of learning about you, too." He clasped his hands behind his back and tilted his head, as though gazing at a particularly fascinating animal. "The Veritian sailor who inspires a loyalty so fierce in her followers, even the ones who left her crew continue to say her name with respect."

Dax frowned, not liking the way the prince had phrased that.

Then again, he did not like much about the prince to begin with.

"You've been attacking Solkyrian merchants for some time now," Trystos continued. His charming smile was still in place, but none of its warmth was reflected in his eyes. "Not with the greatest success of any pirate captain, but enough to keep your crew together through the years. You've frustrated more than a few of the navy's officers, although if I asked them, they'd say your efforts were middling at best.

"Tell me, now that you stand before a member of the royal family in the very heart of the Solkyrian Empire, do you repent your sins against the Sun Crown?"

Dax was entirely unsurprised when Iris squared her shoulders and said, "I'd rather rot in the deepest, darkest hell."

"That could still be arranged," the prince said without missing a beat. He leaned in closer to Iris, his height allowing him to look down at her, but she glared fiercely back. "I'm afraid, though, you couldn't lead the way." The smile slowly dropped from Trystos's face. "You would watch each and every member of your crew make their own descents first."

In spite of himself, Dax felt a small splinter of fear in his chest. Beside him, Nikolai drew in a shallow breath and his heart quickened. Neither of them said a word.

Iris's hands clenched into fists as she stared into the prince's eyes, but she bit back any retort she might have made. Raw fury radiated off of her, but she would not risk the lives of the crew while they rested so firmly in her hands. Her silence stretched out, but slowly, her fingers uncurled.

Satisfied, Trystos withdrew from Iris's personal space. "Believe me, Iris, I would much rather have your willing cooperation going forward. You have quite the reputation."

Despite her surrenders big and small, there was still defiance inside of Iris. "I thought I was a mediocre pirate at best," she bit out.

Trystos gave a delighted laugh. "Oh, not as of late. Certainly not after capturing the Thief's legendary black dragon." He began to pace a slow circle around the three of them, but his attention remained locked on Iris.

Dax followed the prince's motion, but made certain to keep his own face blank. They'd known that Trystos had been aware of the dragon hunt. Up until their stint in the prison, they'd been certain Mordanti's map and treasure were what the prince was after. It seemed they'd been right after all, but Dax had the uneasy feeling that there was something more.

Something worse.

"Interestingly," Trystos continued, "you let that dragon go in order to save a member of your crew. Even with your noble actions and your historically decent competence as a captain, a good number of people elected to leave your ship before your next voyage. Granted, given where you were going, I can hardly say that I blame them."

The prince completed his circle and made a beckoning gesture at the cluster of guards and the Goodtide still waiting near the back of the room. The Goodtide turned and lifted something off the floor before beginning her slow journey to answer the prince's call.

"Despite their desertion," Trystos said as he spun back to Iris, "I think you'll be quite proud to know that it took some convincing to get your former crew members to talk. The ones we were able to capture were all surprisingly reluctant to speak ill of their former captain, even if they thought her mad for sailing into the Forbidden Sea. They all talked in the end, though, and their stories matched up in the important places." Trystos put his hand on Iris's shoulder and turned her so that they formed a closed ring with Dax and Nikolai. The prince raised his other arm and slung it across Dax's shoulders, as though getting ready to conspire with them.

Dax felt the prince's heartbeat through the connection of the touch, and again he thought about how simple it would be to silence that pulse with his magic.

And then the guards will kill us all, he knew. *Slow and brutal.*

Dax took a firm grip on his magic and pulled it back, until he was barely aware of the flicker of his own heart.

"Even when they were cursing your name," Trystos continued, "they still spoke highly of you. Especially that young boy who'd served with you. What was his name, now...?" He looked thoughtfully up at the ceiling, then brightened with sudden recollection. "Kai, that was it. A spirited boy, right up until the end."

Dax nearly let his magic roar into the prince's body and kill him then and there. He held his Skill in check but looked to Iris all the same, waiting for the smallest sign that she wanted him to do it.

Iris, however, was only staring at the prince with growing horror.

Nikolai was the first to find his voice. "Whatever you did to that boy," he began, his voice a low growl, but Trystos ran over his words.

"That journey into the Forbidden Sea was certainly an interesting one," the prince said. "I am beyond impressed that so many of you survived, especially with that betrayal from one of your own."

Dax jerked back, slipping out of the prince's grasp. Almost no one outside of the *Southern Echo* knew about Xander Grayvoice's actions, and from what everyone had said, the prison guards had never once tried to glean that information.

"How do you know that?" Dax asked.

Trystos fixed him with a radiant smile. He lowered the arm that Dax had pulled out of, but he kept his other one locked around Iris's shoulders.

"Why, the Grayvoice himself told me." Trystos's smile faltered. "He's very impertinent, that one. Can't say that I like him much, but he certainly has some fascinating stories to tell."

Iris was staring at the floor now, at the thick blue carpet that could have been the open sky or the unyielding sea. Dax could see her mind racing as she slotted pieces together.

"You captured the *Dragonsbane*," she said numbly. "That's why that ship never put into port."

"Yes, very good!" Trystos said, giving her a light shake. "Although, it wasn't much of a feat, to be perfectly honest. The *Dragonsbane* was heavy with gold when my hunters took it, and moving so slowly. And," the prince leaned in again, dropping his voice to a conspiratorial level, "my hunters don't like to admit this, but the day they caught the *Dragonsbane*, that ship appeared out of nowhere, as though it had been dropped into the sea right in front of them as a gift from the gods themselves."

Dax recalled the *Southern Echo* sailing out of the Rend only to appear at the very edge of the Coral Chain. He felt cold as he wondered how close they'd been to Trystos's pirate hunters. The *Dragonsbane* had left the realm of the gods first; was that the only thing that had saved the *Southern Echo*?

From the look on Nikolai's face, the Northman was asking himself the very same question.

Trystos allowed them a moment of silent speculation before glancing over his shoulder. "Ah, speaking of gifts from the gods," he said, finally releasing Iris as he whirled away.

She stumbled in the sudden absence of his support.

Dax moved to catch her, but she recovered quickly and pulled away, not looking at him.

Not trusting him.

Dax withdrew, but he couldn't keep the pain out of his gaze as he watched Iris gather herself.

Then Trystos was back, holding a bundle of cloth that the Goodtide had presented him with. "I am quite eager to hear the story of how you got your gift from them," he said as he began to pull the cloth away, eager as a child with a present.

Iris fumbled for words. "I don't know what..."

She trailed off as the cloth fell away, leaving Trystos holding the gleaming drinking horn from the Vanishing Island. Ignoring her weak denial, he lifted the horn higher, letting the light play off its surface.

For a moment, Dax was too stunned to think. Now that the relic was free from the cloth binding, he could feel the pulse of its power, but it was muted, almost imperceptible. Dax wondered if the strange anchoring power of Solkyria was doing something to the relic, or if it was something more. Either way, Trystos was entirely unbothered as he held the drinking horn for them all to see, its metal embellishments free of tarnish and almost glowing with a life of their own.

Dax's heart gave a violent lurch as his mind flooded with an image of Spider leaping through glass, fleeing with the drinking horn clenched in his hands and a wild madness gripping his mind. Spider never would have left that horn behind, or willingly surrendered it. The man was a lot of things, but not someone who could have ever abandoned an artifact like that, especially not after the way it had affected him. If Trystos had the drinking horn, then he had Spider, too.

Dax traded a stunned glance with Nikolai, who had started tugging on his white beard in distress.

Iris looked like she had been hit in the gut by a cannonball.

Trystos turned the horn and peered into it. "This is a truly beautiful item," he mused, "made all the more alluring by its mystery. I don't suppose you've worked out what it's for, other than drinking things, of course?" He looked expectantly at them, but Dax, Iris, and Nikolai only offered him numb stares in return. The prince seemed genuinely disappointed. "I see this is one puzzle that is still missing a few pieces. A shame, but no matter."

He turned and handed the horn back to the Goodtide, who winced as she accepted it. She held it as far away from herself as she could as she shuffled back to the guards at the other end of the hall, her cane digging into the rug with each hurried step.

Trystos watched her go almost fondly. "I'm looking forward to researching that artifact more," he said absently, as though speaking with friends. "I've always had a special interest in myths and legends. You should see my private library sometime. I have a wonderful collection of history and folklore from around the world. Amazing how often they intersect."

The prince shook himself out of his reverie. "Now, back to you, Iris." He faced her squarely, his face bright with eagerness. "You are quite talented when it comes to finding impossible things. I have use for such a talent, for there are a few lost things in this world that I would like you to find."

Iris stared up at Trystos with her mouth partly open, still in shock after realizing Spider had been caught. It took a few moments for her to register the prince's words, but she closed her mouth and slowly shook her head. "No," she said simply.

Trystos made a soft noise of discomfort. "Ah, I'm afraid you're not fully understanding me. You see, I am not asking." He began to slowly walk away, towards the thrones on the dais, and there was no choice but to follow him. "The *Southern Echo* is one of my ships now. I understand that it—she?—*she* will put up quite a fight without you there to captain her, but make no mistake, she is no longer yours. I own her, just as sure as I own your life, Iris. Which hangs by a very thin thread, as I'm sure you already know."

The prince stepped up to the dais, but he did not ascend the steps. He stood gazing at the empty thrones for a long moment, golden and resplendent. "I get the sense that threats against you don't hold much weight," Trystos mused, "but I'll remind you that in addition to your life and your beloved ship, I also own your crew now." He half-turned then to give Iris a speculative look. "I'm going to need your full cooperation if you intend to keep them alive."

"You frost-touched bastard," Nikolai growled.

He started forward, and Dax managed to grab his arm just as the guards leveled their halberds at him. Nikolai's pulse raced against Dax's grip, but he stilled long enough to glare at the guards, then took a deliberate step back.

Trystos tilted his head. The silver circlet on his brow looked pitiful next to the glory of the sunburst thrones. "Well, Iris?"

Iris was shaking with rage, her hands in fists again, but she gritted out, "Fine."

Trystos smiled. "Excellent." He looked ready to say more, but Iris spoke again.

"As long as I sail the *Southern Echo* with my crew."

The Goodtide glanced up sharply, and even several of the guards let their gazes flicker to Trystos. The prince, however, only looked amused.

"I think there is a fundamental flaw in your grasp of the current circumstances," he said.

Iris drew in a deep breath, and Dax could hear how hard she was fighting to keep herself calm. "If you give me my ship and my crew," she said, "I will find whatever you want. I won't resist, and I won't undercut you or whatever officer you assign to the journey. I know you won't give us total freedom, but if you give me my ship and my people, all unharmed, then I'll sail to whatever godsforsaken edge of the map you want me to."

Trystos was no longer smiling. "Even the islands of the mimic dragons?"

Iris stiffened.

The prince waited.

"It's too dangerous to go there now," Iris said slowly. "Sirens rule those waters, and their mating season—"

"Yes, I know all about that," Trystos interrupted. "But it's not what I asked."

Iris was quiet for a long, heavy moment. She drew in

another breath as though to speak, but could not get the words out. She made herself nod instead, and Dax saw how much that small gesture hurt.

If he hadn't seen her agree with his own eyes, he never would have believed it.

"Then I will consider your request," Trystos said. Iris started to protest, but he held up a hand to silence her. "Now, I'm sure you'd like to get some rest and rejoin your crew. I understand the past several days have been quite stressful for you all, and there are a few small matters to take care of before you disembark on your first journey for me." The prince gave another radiant smile that outshone even the sun thrones. "I am looking forward to our partnership, Iris. I have high expectations of you."

He gestured to the royal guards, who came forward to surround Dax, Iris, and Nikolai once more.

"Do show them every curtesy as you take them to their rooms," Trystos said, already turning to the Goodtide to discuss another matter. "They are my guests, after all."

And with that, they were out of the prince's mind.

It was a silent trek through the palace, punctured only by their footsteps on the tiled floor and the clink of the guards' weapons. The guards had not tried to bind them again, but Dax still felt the crush of imprisonment all around him. From the way her fingers kept straying to the space above her hip where the pommel of her saber usually rested, he knew that Iris was feeling the same way.

Briefly, he thought about reaching out to take her hand, but he knew she'd pull away.

Of the three of them, Nikolai was the most attentive to their surroundings. He let his eyes rove over every doorway they passed, up and down every hall, around every room. Dax knew he should be doing the same, make an attempt to understand the layout of the palace, but all he wanted was to lie down and close his eyes.

It wouldn't be so bad if they didn't open again.

He knew better than to hope he'd wake up and realize all of this had been nothing more than a dream. A terrible one that easily would have shortened his life expectancy with all the stress it had put him through, but a dream nonetheless.

Eventually, they came to one of the plainer doors Dax had seen throughout the palace, although that only meant it was lacking the gilding and gemstones that had decorated the doors of the more public-facing rooms. This door was still covered in intricate carvings, but dark as the wood was, the depictions were difficult to make out. Dax thought he saw a fleet of ships carved into the wood, but one of the guards had the door unlocked and swinging open before he could get a closer look. Dax, Nikolai, and Iris were ushered inside, and the door snapped primly shut behind them.

The lock clicked home, but Dax barely heard it over the sudden rush of voices that crashed over him in a tidal wave of relief.

The crew's faces filled his vision as they pressed in to assure themselves that their captain, quartermaster, and boatswain were all back, and to ask what had happened after they'd been separated.

"You three just vanished," AnnaMarie said, pitching her voice to carry over the others'. "They wouldn't tell us a thing, just brought us here and dumped us."

"Could have been worse," Nikolai remarked as he

glanced around the room.

Dax waited until he'd seen everyone's faces at least once before he let himself take anything else in. The crew were all accounted for, all the way down to the swabs, and none of them were bound anymore. Even Luken was free to fly circles about the room, which, now that Dax really looked at it, was far grander than a prison had any right to be.

As with the rest of the palace, the ceilings were high, but these were painted with soft clouds and soaring birds. Plush couches and cushions were spread throughout the spacious room along with soft blankets, and a fire burned merrily in the stone fireplace set into the far wall. Chopped wood was stacked neatly by the hearth, ready to feed the blaze as needed. Two huge windows flanked the rising line of the chimney, but one glance at the view outside told Dax that they were probably too high off the ground for them to serve as a means of escape. He could see the line of the horizon from where he stood, but not a single rooftop of Sunthrone City.

Perhaps strangest of all was the table in the center of the room, piled high with an assortment of food, although there were no utensils anywhere to be found.

The serving platters could still serve as a weapon, Dax supposed, along with the logs for the fire. Anna-Marie and the other gunners would have no trouble wielding those, at least. They could probably surprise the first batch of guards and take them down, but there would certainly be casualties among the crew, and gods only knew how far they'd get before they came up against royal guards armed with even better weapons.

Those halberds most of the palace guards carried were more for show than combat, but Dax couldn't imagine the guards would be adverse to putting a perfectly good bladed edge to use when faced with escaping prisoners.

Maybe Iris had a thought about that particular problem.

But when Dax turned to her, he had to look hard to be certain it was really her.

All of the fight Iris had shown in the throne room had drained out of her, leaving her slumped and swaying on her feet. She stared at the faces of the people around her with a vacant expression that made Dax's blood turn cold.

No one else had seemed to notice. The crew was still talking with Nikolai, people interjecting various details whenever they saw fit.

"You *have* to touch one of the blankets," Esmerelda Durmanti said. "It's like holding a cloud."

"The food is amazing," Julian Redpool informed the Northman. "Better than anything Brownsand ever put out."

"Hey, now," the old cook protested, but it was half-hearted as he took a massive bite out of one of the six sausages stuffed in his hands.

Others had drifted back to the food table as well, and Dax saw that even though it had been thoroughly raided already, there was plenty left, including several delicate spun sugar sculptures that seemed like they would break if Dax looked at them for too long.

It was too much.

He turned to Iris again, but she had slowly started making her way towards one of the windows.

Dax wanted to follow her, but several people were pressing close again, asking questions that deserved answers.

"Prince Trystos wants us to work for him," Dax began.

"Not that we have much choice," Nikolai cut in, but he waved Dax on and let him quickly fill the crew in on the prince's conversation with Iris.

Dax glossed over some of the more threatening parts, but by the time he was finished, a few people had grim expressions, mostly the more seasoned members of the crew. They were weathered enough to recognize that the comfort they'd suddenly been plunged into was nothing more than a thin glaze across the surface. Not everyone seemed to realize that, however.

"Maybe it won't be so bad," Lucien suggested tentatively. He was sprawled on one of the couches, still recovering from his stab wound, but Dax was glad to see he had considerably more color in his cheeks now that he was out of the cold, although there was a fever-brightness to his eyes that Dax did not like.

"I suppose I could think of worse fates than privateering for a prince," Sarah agreed. The bruises on her face had begun to fade from purple to yellow, although it would be some time before they were fully gone.

"We're not privateering," AnnaMarie snapped, arms folded across her broad chest. "Didn't you hear what Dax said? Trystos *owns* us now."

"No, he said the prince wants us to work for him," Sarah argued.

"You think we actually have any choice in the matter? We're nothing more to Trystos than a pack of dogs."

"Well-fed dogs," Julian put in.

AnnaMarie gave him an exasperated glare.

"Enough," Nikolai said, stepping forward before anything could escalate. "We've got food, and we've got a fire. What's that door off to the side there?"

While Nikolai was shown to the smaller, private room that housed a wash stand and a few additional amenities, Dax picked his way to the windows. He clasped hands with a few people he passed and exchanged quiet words with others, taking note of those who draped themselves over the cushions and began to fall asleep like Rori, Eric, Marcus, and Nate, all finally at ease, or maybe too exhausted to stay awake anymore. People spoke in level voices and there was even an occasional laugh from those gathered around the food table, although they were short and clipped sounds that died quickly. Dax ignored the growling of his own stomach and pressed on.

He was happy to see the crew's spirits improved, no doubt because of the food and the chance to sleep on something that was not a cold floor, but he knew better than to let himself be lulled by such things. Whether the bars were iron or gold, a cage was still a cage, and they needed to break free.

Iris did not move when he came up beside her at the window. She stared out at the horizon, barely blinking.

Through the glass, Dax could now see the stretch of Sunthrone City winding its way down the mountain, all the way to the curve of the harbor. He'd been right before, when he'd thought that these windows were too high to serve as an escape route, but even if they figured out a way to lower themselves safely, they would land in the middle of a guarded courtyard.

Dax wondered if that was one more taunt from Trystos.

He was almost certain that it was.

"What do you think?" Dax asked Iris, keeping his voice low. "Is there anything we can do?"

Iris blew a hard breath out through her nose, and the glass in front of her misted over. "We can survive, I suppose," she said softly. Then she pulled back and glared at Dax, sharp and hard as the blade of a dagger. "Not that I actually have a choice in the matter."

Dax felt his own anger rise. "You would have preferred that I let you die?" he asked.

"If I was going to die fighting the Solkyrian Empire,"

Iris hissed back, "then that was exactly how it was meant to be."

"Well, you didn't," Dax said, "and I wasn't wrong. The crew still needs you. We all do."

Iris looked away, but some of the ire bled out of her gaze as she took in the people in the room.

Her people.

She sighed, weary and resigned. "You want to know what we do?" she asked. "We go wherever the prince sends us, and we go together."

She moved to step away, and Dax impulsively reached out and caught her hand.

Iris froze. She did not pull away, but the gaze she fixed on him was flat and piercing, and Dax quickly let her go.

CHAPTER NINETEEN
Who Could Be Redeemed

THEY WERE ALLOWED A full day's rest in the gilded prison.

Nate tried to take advantage of the chance to sleep and eat better than he had in several months, but even with the familiar sounds of his crew mates around him, it all felt wrong. He missed the creaks of the *Southern Echo*, the sturdy warmth of her decks and the rush of the wind through her sails. He'd managed a rough nap that afternoon, but that night, he lay awake on a cushion larger and infinitely softer than his hammock on the ship, watching the path of the twin moons through the windows and the slow turn of the stars. He held up his hand with the ring to their silver light, letting it catch on the scratches the crew had scoured across the surface and the N they'd carved deep into the metal. He listened to the deep breathing of his friends, glad they were getting some rest even though their faces were creased with unease.

When the dawn began to creep across the sky, Nate picked himself up and gingerly made his way across the room.

He wasn't the only one awake. AnnaMarie Blueshore was sitting up on a couch near the door, picking at the threads of embroidery on one of the small decorative pillows. Novachak had stationed himself next to Lucien, and was dipping a white cloth into a shallow basin of water to place on the injured man's forehead in an attempt to reduce his fever. Esmerelda Durmanti and Julian Redpool were sharing a cushion, talking quietly as they stared up at the painted ceiling. They gave Nate a cursory glance as he passed them, then went back to speculating on whether or not a fresh breakfast was going to be presented once the sun was fully up.

Nate made his way to the window, where Dax stood gazing out at the lightening sky. The fire had long since burned out and left cold ash in the hearth, so there was only the approaching dawn to illuminate the quartermaster's face.

Dax's tattoos were dark and colorless in that early light, twisting in complicated knots that completely obscured the Malatide mark on his brow, but they could not hide the pensive expression he wore. Nate hesitated, wondering if he should let the man be, but Dax looked over and gestured for Nate to join him.

Through the glass, Nate studied the dark line of the sea, remembering a time when all his dreams and hopes had rested on the other side of the horizon.

He marveled at how quickly everything could change.

"Did you sleep at all?" Dax asked softly.

Nate shook his head.

"Me neither," the quartermaster said.

"It's hard, with all of..." Nate waved his hand at the luxurious room, encompassing it all. "It's difficult to trust it."

"You're right not to," Dax told him. "We're walking a very fine line right now, the captain especially."

Nate followed the quartermaster's glance across the dark room to where Arani was dozing on a couch, her hat tilted to cover her eyes. She'd kept her boots on, not caring about the dirty prints the soles left on the creamy fabric as she sprawled, but the tightness of her arms folded across her chest betrayed her apparent nonchalance.

"If one of us steps out of line, we'll face swift punishment," Dax said as he turned back to the window. "But if *she* defies Trystos, we'll be dead."

Nate watched the captain's shallow breathing for a few moments. She was not asleep. He wondered if she was trying to listen to them, but she gave no indication either way.

"Lisandra told me that Trystos uses who you care about against you," Nate said. "My sister," he clarified at Dax's questioning look, then remembered there hadn't been a good moment for him to tell anyone about his relationship to her. "The Goodtide from the navy frigate."

Dax's brows rose, but he said nothing and waited for Nate to continue.

"She told me to make Trystos aware of how useful my Skill could really be, and to close myself off from the crew to protect them." The sky through the window was turning pink now, shading towards red across the morning clouds. Nate touched the gold ring on his hand, letting his thumb rest against the scratch marks. "I couldn't do it," he said, "even if it was the right thing." He gave a small, breathless laugh. "I'm selfish, and not strong enough to ignore what I want."

Dax shifted, a deep frown descending over his face. "Something like that takes more strength than you realize," he said. "Why would you think...?" He stopped, and Nate knew he was abruptly remembering the conversation they'd had that night in the brig. Dax scrubbed his hand over his head and turned back to the window, sending his distress through the glass instead of over Nate.

"It's all right," Nate said gently. "I made my choice." He looked across the room once more, and saw that a few more people were coming awake. Luken had roused himself and was now perched on the back of the couch Rori slept on, preening his brilliant feathers. Next to Rori's couch, Marcus and Eric snored softly on long cushions, blankets tangled across their limbs. "I still want to protect them," Nate murmured, "but I need them in my life even more."

After a long moment, Dax said, "I'd say that was the right choice, then."

Nate nodded. He took a deep breath and asked the heavy question on his mind. "You said we're on a fine line, but is there any chance at all that we can escape this?"

Dax was quiet for so long, the sun had time to vault over the horizon and blaze the world with color once more. "I wouldn't get my hopes up," he finally said.

Nate nodded again and pressed his thumb more firmly against the scratches on his ring. "I'm not ready to abandon hope just yet," he said, the words slow but strong with the truth. "As long as the *Southern Echo* sails, I'm going to have hope."

Dax did not respond, and Nate left him the same way he'd found the quartermaster: staring out the window with a thoughtful frown.

By midmorning, everyone was awake, and several people had taken full advantage of the washroom to get cleaner than they'd been in months, maybe even longer. Novachak's white hair and beard gleamed in the light once he was done, and Liliana emerged with dripping hair and a glowing freshness to her skin that made more than one person stop and stare. She smiled at each of her admirers, including AnnaMarie, who abruptly turned a delicate shade of red and became very interested in the leftover food on the table.

Marcus had his appetite back and was eating his fill while Eric and Rori both picked at a day-old roll they'd split between them. Rori fed most of her half to Luken. Nate sat with his friends and managed to eat a little food while he recounted his brief conversation with the quartermaster, along with everything Lisandra had told him.

"You know," Marcus said, pausing just long enough to do them the curtesy of swallowing, "between your brother, your mother, and now your sister, it's no wonder you threw your life away to turn pirate."

"Well," Nate said tiredly, "that and the whole, 'you can't turn the wind so we're going to stick you in the mines, good luck, try not to die too soon' thing."

"Right," Marcus said. "Did your father like you at all?"

"*Marcus,*" Eric hissed, but Nate laughed and held up his hand.

"He's the one who gave me this," he said, pointing at the ring.

Eric and Rori both went very still.

"Don't worry," Nate assured them, "you really did make it better." He turned his hand and smiled as the N caught the light. "And this way, the whole world knows you're stuck with me now."

"Good," Eric said, releasing the breath he'd been holding. "I was worried about you for a minute there."

Rori stayed quiet, but a genuine smile touched her lips, and that was more than Nate could ask for.

The morning slid into afternoon, anxiety giving way to boredom as they lounged and waited for something to happen. No one had any of their possessions other than what they'd been wearing when the *Southern Echo* had been captured, so no cards or dice came out, and no one was much in the mood for telling stories. Eventually, someone had the idea to organize a tournament of strength, which involved trying to lift a couch with an increasing number of people piled on to it. Very quickly, that came down to a battle among the gunners for first place, and even Arani smiled and laughed alongside the others as AnnaMarie finally secured her dominance, only to blush fiercely as Liliana bestowed a crown woven from pulled threads and a few spun sugar shards upon her brow. Rori had done a wonderful job crafting the victor's crown after her early elimination from the competition, and when Nate told her as much, she grinned and threatened to make him one, too.

It took a few minutes before anyone became aware of the royal guards and attendants standing in the open doorway, watching them with mild terror seeping through their carefully neutral expressions.

As the crew's voices died down, one of the attendants cleared his throat and took a tentative step into the room. "Would the three lead officers come forward, please?" he said, somehow turning the question into a command.

Nate saw Dax and Novachak exchange a glance, and Arani looked tempted to snarl something in reply, but she relented and made her way to the front of the room, the quartermaster and boatswain moving in to flank her.

The attendant swallowed visibly as the three officers came to a halt before him, then cleared his throat again. He turned and accepted a folded parcel from one of the other attendants, shaking it out to reveal a fine coat dyed deep Solkyrian blue trimmed in silver and white. The hollow sun crest of Prince Trystos was stitched over the breast, intended to rest directly on top of the heart of the wearer.

Captain Arani went very still.

"Your measurements had to be estimated," the attendant said. "The fit will be adjusted accordingly after the conclusion of today's events, when you meet with the tailor."

He waited, but Arani made no move to accept the coat.

The attendant cleared his throat once more. "Prince Trystos arranged for these himself," he said. He awkwardly stretched forward, bringing the coat closer to Arani.

She still did not move.

Seeking help, the attendant glanced at his two counterparts, who quickly stepped forward and presented larger blue coats with the same embroidered symbol to Dax and Novachak. The two men hesitated, glancing at each other over the captain's head, and Novachak gave a helpless shrug before accepting the coat. Dax took his, and the attendants shrank back immediately. The quartermaster and the boatswain did not change out their old coats for the new ones, instead watching Arani, waiting for her to move first.

Finally, she reached out and closed her hands on the coat.

Relieved, the lead attendant briskly informed the room that they would be leaving soon, and they should ready themselves by changing into their most presentable clothes. He looked severely distressed when Novachak informed him that their current state of dress was the best he was going to get.

Recognizing a lost battle, the attendant advised them to be ready for the guards to escort them, and then took his leave, scurrying off with his counterparts to some unknown depths of the palace.

A few murmurs went up as people began to wonder where they were going, but Nate kept his attention on Captain Arani.

She held the blue coat in front of her like it was a venomous animal, her grip tight and unyielding. Her eyes burned as she stared at the hollow sun symbol, mouth twisting in clear disgust. But all the same, she took a deep breath, and then slowly peeled off her own red coat. She lay it carefully across one of the couches, taking the time to fold it neatly, and then pulled on the blue coat in two rough thrusts of her arms through the sleeves and a tug at the lapels. Her fingers curled as they brushed against the hollow sun, and Nate wondered if she would try to scratch it out.

She did not.

Instead, Arani dropped her hands to her sides.

The coat was decently cut on her, but the sleeves were too long, reaching down past her knuckles. The color clashed with the red sash at her waist and the feather in her hat, but that one simple adjustment had turned her from pirate captain to imperial servant.

She looked ready to burn the world down.

Quietly, Dax and Novachak donned their own Solkyrian coats. Of the three, Novachak seemed the least disconcerted. Dax wasn't as upset as Arani, but he was clearly uncomfortable, and his hand strayed up to brush against his disguised Malatide mark.

Nate wondered if, like him, Dax had ever dreamed of wearing an imperial coat. The quartermaster had one now, but there was no mistaking this nightmare for a dream.

The morning clouds had burned away and left the sky

a pearlescent winter blue by the time the *Southern Echo* crew was taken out of the palace and back down into the city. Arani, Dax, and Novachak were made to walk at the head of the column, but the rest of the crew were given considerably more freedom of movement than they'd had on the way up, if they ignored the heavily armed guards flanking them. No one wore restraints, at least.

Well, Nate thought as he eyed the three blue coats ahead of him, *not on their wrists.*

No one spoke much as they made their way through the streets, following the curt directions the guards gave at each turn. More people began to appear as they made their way deeper into the city, but they took one look at the guards and made sure to keep their distance from the *Southern Echo* crew.

Nate was baffled.

No one from the pirate crew was armed, but he was shocked they were being allowed to walk alongside Solkyrian citizens. He also could not imagine where they were going; his best guess was the docks, but Arani had yet to be given her first assignment from the prince, so there was no reason for them to be making their way to the *Southern Echo* yet.

Nate walked over the cobblestone streets that were still so familiar to him and felt how far removed he was from his old life. He pressed his thumb against the N on his ring and made sure he held his head high as he walked alongside his crew mates, ignoring the speculative murmurs of the people they passed.

As the crowds on the street thickened, Nate began to pick out people wearing the same coats as the *Southern Echo*'s officers, right down to the hollow sun embroidered in silver over the breast. He blinked when he realized that several of their faces looked familiar, but he couldn't place them until he nudged

Theo and pointed them out to the older man.

"They're from the *Red Siren*," Theo said, his voice colored with confusion. He twisted to look around, picking out more and more of the blue coats with the hollow sun. "All of them," he amended.

Nate studied the other pirate crew, and was struck by two things.

First, each and every one of them had a bright eagerness about them. They wore their coats with easy pride, and smiled and laughed as they spoke with one another. A few even waved cheerfully when they caught sight of the *Southern Echo* pirates, pointing to the hollow suns on their own coats with wide grins.

Second, although the *Red Siren* crew had counted several Grayvoices and Darkbends among their ranks, not one of the blue-coated people walking the streets bore a Skill mark.

Nate's gut and mind twinged in uneasy harmony at that revelation.

"Iris!" a voice called out moments before a familiar man pushed through the crowd. The guards made no move to stop him as he planted himself in front of Arani, smiling wide.

Cedric Whitebrook, Nate remembered. Captain of the *Red Siren*.

"If you weren't here in front of me, I'd never believe *you'd* taken the pardon," Whitebrook crowed. "I'm so pleased we'll be sending the Vothies to hell together!" His gaze drifted over Dax and Novachak in their ill-fitting coats, and he smirked. "So eager to wear the blue you couldn't wait for the tailor?" He laughed at his own joke, but his mirth faltered when he saw the plain clothes the rest of the crew wore. When his gaze caught on Eric and Rori, followed closely by Nate and Marcus, his mouth dropped open in absolute confusion. "They let you keep your Skilled?"

"I think," Arani said tightly, "our circumstances are very different."

Whitebrook finally took notice of the guards stationed around the *Southern Echo* crew, watching him with silent but dangerous expressions.

"Clearly," Whitebrook said, moving a step back. He frowned at Arani, his hand closing over the pommel of the sword belted at his hip. "I sincerely hope you aren't the main focus of today's festivities." His frown deepened. "You aren't, right?"

"Not as far as we're aware," Novachak said mildly.

Whitebrook nodded. "Good, otherwise that would have been a particularly cruel joke." He touched his hat in a brief salute to Arani. "I'll be looking for you on the seas, dear Iris. I'm sure we'll see each other again out there."

He took his leave without waiting for a response, disappearing back into the crowd.

"So that flouncing fool got a pardon," Theo growled, "and now his crew is privateering for the empire."

"Not all of them," Nate said. "Not any of the Skilled who sailed with him."

Theo bit off his next words, gave Nate a sidelong glance, and then swallowed whatever else he'd been about to say.

The rest of the walk was uneventful, although Nate figured out fairly quickly what Whitebrook had meant about a cruel joke. They headed into the main square in the merchant district, where the gallows and execution block towered in stoic finality over the swelling crowd. Nate felt a brief spike of panic when he thought that the *Southern Echo* crew was to be executed after all, but they would not have been allowed to walk the streets even with their hands bound if that was the case. Instead, they would have been crammed into a wagon and driven to their fate. Giving them a brief final taste of freedom before killing them would have been unspeakably cruel, so much so that Nate was sure that was a line not even the empire would cross.

The guards pressed in closer as the crowd thickened, herding the *Southern Echo* crew towards a set of platforms that had been erected at the side of the square. There were two levels, the topmost of which held two elegant thrones and a few less ornate seats that were already occupied by lesser nobles. The lower level was empty without even a bench to sit upon, just a railing to enclose the space, and this was where the guards guided the pirates.

Arani went up first, followed by Dax and Novachak. The three of them moved to the center of the platform and stood at the railing, directly below the empty thrones on the higher level. The rest of the crew filed up the steps and filled the space around them. Nate ended up in the second row of people, just behind the officers, so he heard it clearly when a woman's voice called out to Novachak.

Over Arani's shoulder, Nate saw a bedraggled woman shouldering her way through the crowd, her unusual blue eyes locked on Novachak. Her clothes were little more than rags and her dark hair hung limply around her face, which seemed to have aged ten years in the short time since Nate had last seen her, but he recognized Madame Silverdale all the same.

"Julianna!" Novachak exclaimed, dropping to his knees so he could reach down and take Silverdale's reaching hand.

She clutched his fingers like they were a raft in a storm, tears spilling from her eyes. "Oh, Nikolai," she sobbed, "they made me a beggar."

Arani shifted, her posture hard and pitiless as she looked down at Silverdale. "Could have been worse," Arani said. "They could have let you rot in prison, or put you in line for the execution block."

"Either would have been kinder," Silverdale spat. "They put me in the stockades and left me there for a week, free for anyone to torment. They took everything I had, everything I'd built and saved, even my name." Her face twisted in anguish. "I'm Julianna Blanc on my papers now, until I can pay off the back taxes for years of using the Silver prefix, but I can't work. No one will take me, and if I can't pay, I'm going back into the stockades again."

Novachak closed his hands around hers. "Surely there's a factory or—"

"*No one,*" Julianna Blanc said. More tears rolled off her chin to dampen the dirty shawl she wore around her shoulders. "I've been blacklisted everywhere, even the pleasure houses. Not even the illegal ones will take me. I've walked the streets until my feet were bleeding, trying to find the smallest scrap of work, but there is *nothing*." She drew in a shuddering breath. "Not for a Blanc."

Nate stole a glimpse at the former madame's crude shoes and did not doubt that she had smeared her blood across the cobblestones of the streets. He believed her story, too. For a time, before he'd been given his Lowwind mark, Nate had been a Blanc, stripped of his family name and belonging nowhere until his Skill had been officially recognized and the tattoo inked across his brow. Nate had spent longer than anyone else at the wind working academy as a Blanc; his old teacher Tobias had been so certain that Nate would be a Highwind like his brother, and had put off giving him the Lowwind mark until Nate was nearly expelled from the academy the first time.

We can always add to it, Tobias had said after Nate's tattoo was complete, and that thin hope had carried them forward for several more years, even after the

Nowind nickname had found its foothold.

But even Nowind had been infinitely better than Blanc, a name devoid of agency.

"They can't do this to you," Novachak growled. He looked to Arani, who only shrugged.

"Not my empire," she said, but the cold indifference was gone from her voice. "I don't know how to help."

Novachak's icy gaze narrowed with fury. A horn blared suddenly, prompting a cheer from the crowd, and Novachak quickly turned back to the Blanc and took a firmer grip on her hands even as a city enforcer approached, shouting for her to get away.

"I'm going to fix this," Novachak promised her. "By the Frozen Goddess, I am not going to leave you on the streets."

Her shoulders hitched. "Nikolai," she began, but the enforcer descended then, and Julianna Blanc was shoved away, back into the sweeping press of the crowd.

Novachak was back on his feet in an instant. "I promise!" he shouted just before she was lost in the sea of faces. He stared after her, as though he could make her reappear through the sheer force of his willpower, but she was gone. He slumped over the railing and tangled his hands in his hair.

"She cut off your ear," Arani reminded him mildly after a pointed pause.

"I deserved worse," Novachak said. "For what I did to her, I deserved so much worse." He straightened up, and Nate was shocked to see that the boatswain's eyes were wet with tears.

Arani said nothing, but after a moment, she put her hand on Novachak's shoulder.

Another horn squealed, and the crowd's cheering grew louder as two unicorns with hides of pale gold came trotting into the square, a blue carriage rolling along behind them. Even without the golden sunburst painted on the carriage, the unicorns alone would have been enough to announce the arrival of the ruling monarchs.

Far finer and much more dangerous beasts than horses, the use of elegant unicorns was reserved for the highest members of the nobility alone. Even then, Nate could not remember a time in his life when anyone outside of the Goldskye family had kept them.

The two pulling the carriage were so well groomed they practically glowed in the winter sunlight, their fine manes and long tails braided with blue ribbons. Their horns thrust forth from their fetlocks like swords, pointed tips capped with short, blunt wooden sheaths as the sole concession to the safety of the public. Their sharp hooves rang against the cobblestones with each dancing step, and their pointed teeth gnashed the thick bits fixed between their jaws.

Supposedly, unicorns had even fed on dragons while they'd still inhabited the known archipelago.

Nate was suddenly grateful that the equine beasts were rare.

The unicorn-drawn carriage pulled up to the staircase that led to the higher platform. An attendant smoothly opened the door, and the emperor stepped out, followed by the empress. They were dressed in gold with long, fur-trimmed capes swirling from their shoulders. Golden sunburst crowns rested on top of their white hair.

The crowd roared as the emperor and empress raised their hands in greeting.

The *Southern Echo* crew remained silent.

The emperor and empress were not young, and it took them several minutes to climb the stairs and shuffle their way to the thrones that waited for them. The crowd cheered the entire time, and the nobles on the upper level applauded with dignified restraint as the rulers of the Solkyrian Empire settled in.

By the time they were ready, the second carriage had already rolled through the square, pulled by a mismatched pair of unicorns, one dappled silver and the other deepest black. Prince Trystos emerged from this carriage to a fresh wave of cheering, and he offered the crowd a dazzling smile and wave before climbing the steps much quicker than his parents had.

Nate was struck by how young Trystos was compared to the rest of the ruling family. He knew that the empire's second son had been born after a long string of stillbirths and miscarriages. By the time Trystos had come along, defiantly healthy in spite of what the people were starting to secretly call a curse from the gods, both the emperor and empress had gray in their hair, and their firstborn son was nearly sixteen years of age.

The Unnecessary Spare, some called Trystos, although only in whispers and never in earshot of an agent of the crown.

From the way Captain Arani was looking at him, Nate had the sense that she had even worse names in mind for the prince.

Trystos took his place at the center of the upper platform. He raised his hands, quieting the crowd, and then spoke in a rich voice that rang across the square.

"My sunlit people," he said, "today is a day of celebration. I stand before you as your humble servant, bearing news of the fruits of my labor."

Arani made a disgusted noise and braced herself against the railing.

If Trystos heard the sound, he ignored it.

"My hunters have flushed out the last pirate stronghold in our waters," he continued, radiant smile still in place. "Our glorious empire is free of this internal scourge at last."

The crowd cheered again, small flags and ribbons waving in their hands. Towards the back of the square, Nate caught sight of a cluster of blue coats where the crew of the *Red Siren* had gathered. The former pirates were clapping, their smiles genuine.

"In my pursuit of these crews," Trystos said, "I have found them to be talented sailors and ferocious fighters. To waste such abilities when the war has shifted in our enemy's favor would do us a great disservice.

"To this end, I have sought out those who could be redeemed, and granted them a royal pardon in exchange for their fealty and service to the Sun Crown."

The prince gave his audience a moment to chew on his words. A considerably lighter cheer went up this time, undercut by doubtful murmurings.

Trystos's smile did not falter. "One such crew is led by Captain Cedric Whitebrook, who will be taking the *Red Siren* into the east to fight the Votheinians alongside our noble navy."

This time, the only real cheers came from the cluster of *Red Siren* sailors themselves, and they died quickly when the crowd turned mistrustful scowls on them.

"Another crew stands before you now," Trystos continued. "Captain Iris Arani and the crew of the *Southern Echo* will be taking on a special assignment in another territory." The prince's smile turned sly. "If she is successful, this will turn the tide of the war decisively in our favor."

The crowd rumbled with confusion and intrigue, but Trystos waved them to silence once more.

"There are some, however, who are beyond redemption," he said, and the crowd's attention turned hungry. "These foul souls can only be executed for their crimes against the empire, their deaths serving as a warning to those who would be foolish enough to repeat their mistakes."

A low roar went up across the square, and people began to stamp their feet in anticipation. Nate shivered as the bloodthirsty sound washed over him.

"Let these men and women who have sinned against the Sun Crown find mercy where they deserve it," Trystos said, "and the darkness of the deepest hell where they don't."

He made a cutting gesture towards the gallows, and the executions began.

None of them were easy to watch, even though Nate only distantly recognized a couple of the names read off that day. Their crimes against the empire ranged from pillaging and murder to sacrilege against the divine right of the Sun Crown, and Nate couldn't help but wonder how Captain Arani was not up there, too.

For her part, Arani stood completely still, watching every one of the executions. Forcing herself to watch, Nate realized, and remember their names and faces after they were gone. He wanted to lift his eyes and do the same, but his gaze found the sky instead of the gallows.

He prayed the gods would grant each of those poor souls lined up a quick and easy death.

And then the final prisoner was dragged up on to the gallows. His clothes were torn and his hair and beard were wild, but there was something familiar about him that Nate could not quite place until the man's name was read out for all to hear.

"Scott Brownvalley, alias Spider."

Nate jerked in surprise, and he heard several people around him gasp. Arani's breath hissed out in a hard line between her teeth as the crowd booed and jeered.

Spider's shoulders heaved, but he held himself tall and did not say a word as his crimes were read out. His list was longer than the others and included several counts of smuggling, illegal trading, and conscription of Solkyrian ships and resources. The common thread of murder and theft were there, too, and the crowd's fervor only grew as his crimes dragged out.

Spider kept his gaze fixed above their hungry faces.

When the list of crimes was finally complete, the executioner placed the noose around Spider's neck. A priest of the sky god stepped forward to ask Spider if he would take this final chance to repent his sins.

Spider lifted his chin even higher and shot a defiant look at the royals on the upper platform. His gaze caught on the *Southern Echo* crew, and fixed on Arani. His eyes went wide, and as the executioner reached for the lever, Spider screamed, "Swallow the sun!"

Then Spider dropped on the rope, body twitching as his neck snapped and the life fled from him. The crowd cheered as he went still, never to move again.

A wave of bile rose in Nate's throat, and it was all he could do to fight it back. He was very aware of the gasps and sobs from the *Southern Echo* crew around him, and the shaking of Arani's shoulders as her fingernails dug into the wooden railing in front of her.

The guards came for them once more, shepherding them off the platform ahead of the nobles milling about on the level above. Before Nate stepped off the platform, the horns sounded again, blaring the opening notes of the Solkyrian national anthem. The crowd took up the song and began to sing.

Bring forth the sun throne's golden way
Arise brave souls and strike away

Farewell to you, as journey starts
Let courage fill your thund'ring hearts

'Cross the world you shall ring
The pride of our shining king

From bright Solkyria we sail
By flag and blade and gun
For the glory of Solkyria
We'll see the day is won

Their voices echoed in Nate's ears long after the guards had taken the crew out of the square and steered them back up to the palace. He looked back once as they were leaving, and saw Prince Trystos leaning on the railing of the upper platform, his gaze fixed on Captain Arani's receding head and the red feather bobbing on her hat.

CHAPTER TWENTY
The Way Ahead

Dax barely registered the walk back to the palace, only realizing they were inside when he, Iris, and Nikolai were suddenly being separated from the rest of the crew once again.

"It's just for the tailor!" the same harried attendant from that morning assured them as Iris lunged for one of the halberds the guards carried.

Nikolai managed to catch her and drag her back before the guard could react.

Dax drew in a deliberate breath and slowly relaxed his magic, reminding himself that he could not stop the hearts of the royal guards if he wanted the crew to remain alive.

But following that awful afternoon in the city square that had culminated in Spider's last breath, Dax's body was sluggish to respond to his racing mind.

Spider had been a fixture in Dax's life ever since the day the newly christened *Southern Echo* had first glided into the Nest's harbor. He had greeted Iris with warmth and decorum despite her young age, welcoming her and her crew to his island. Then he had twisted every last copper mark he could out of their first transaction.

Very few of those who had ever struck a deal with the man had actually liked Spider, but then, those he respected never did. He drove hard bargains and picked at every detail of an agreement because he expected the same in return. Iris had given him what he'd wanted, and then Dax once he'd become quarter-master, and then Nikolai when he'd joined the crew.

In return, Spider had given them a haven, a place to anchor their ship and see what it was like to live without the Solkyrian flag hanging over their heads.

Now the Nest was under imperial control, and Spider was gone, and there was nothing any of them could do.

Dax came swimming out of his thoughts when the royal tailor poked and prodded at him, demanding that Dax raise his arms and hold still while proper measurements were taken and pins were stuck into the heavy blue coat he now wore.

It felt like a shroud, and he was beyond relieved when the tailor took it from him to make the final alterations.

Dax, Iris, and Nikolai were brought back to the locked room immediately after the tailor was done with them. They walked side-by-side, Iris in the middle, none of them speaking but all of them feeling the lightness of their shoulders without the blue coats draped over them.

That feeling faded when Dax saw Prince Trystos coming towards them from the other end of the hall.

He met them at the door to the crew's room, still wearing a smile that went nowhere near his eyes. "'Swallow the sun,'" he said as he halted in front of Iris. "That's all my interrogators were able to pry out of that man before we put him on the gallows. I wondered if he'd say anything else when he saw you, but evidently not. Any idea as to what he meant by that?"

Iris held herself still as she stared up at the prince, but Dax could feel her heart pounding in her chest. Whether that was from fear or anger, Dax could not say. Then Iris said, "Maybe you shouldn't have killed him, if you so badly wanted to know," and Dax knew it was rage that had quickened her blood.

Trystos held her stare. "You can try keeping secrets from me," he said, "but I will have them in the end. I always do."

"I don't doubt that," Iris murmured.

Trystos made a thoughtful noise, his eyes narrowing as he studied Iris. A long minute passed, neither of them looking away, and Dax felt the unease growing in the guards surrounding them as surely as it was blossoming in himself and Nikolai.

"You don't know what he meant, do you?" the prince asked.

Iris gave a quiet sigh of resignation, but she still did not look away. "No," she answered, and it was the truth.

Trystos regarded her for another few moments. Then he abruptly rocked back on his heels, and his smile became a full smirk. "I have decided on your first assignment. You'll be heading north."

Dax wondered what that meant. The Pod, maybe, but those islands had been firmly under Solkyrian control for a long time now, and he did not like the way the prince was looking at Iris.

"Any particular destination?" she asked acidly.

Trystos's smile widened to show teeth. "I'm curious to see if you can figure it out."

Dax glanced to Nikolai, but the boatswain did not return the gesture. His gaze was locked on the prince, just like Iris's, and there was a swirling dread in his pale eyes that did nothing to ease Dax's own growing alarm.

"You also will not be taking your full crew with you," Trystos continued.

Iris stiffened and started to protest.

"I'm sending you on a mission that requires stealth," the prince said, running over her voice, "not an attack.

As such, you won't need your gunners at all." He tilted his head in that manner that Dax was beginning to identify as infuriating smugness. "Those you do take will be expected to be on their best behavior, of course, especially with the naval officers who will be accompanying you. They'll be sending reports back to me at regular intervals, and if there's so much as a whiff of trouble within their writings..." Trystos flicked his gaze to the locked door. The faint voices of the crew could be heard from the other side. "I'll determine how many need to perish based on the magnitude of the offense."

Dax felt his heart clench.

He had no idea how Iris managed to keep her voice so stable when she said, "How can I trust that you won't kill my crew no matter how much I cooperate, or that those reports will even be accurate?"

The prince shrugged. "You can't," he said, "just as I cannot trust you. So take this opportunity to prove that you are capable of acting in my best interests while keeping the *Southern Echo* and your people in line. Do that, and you may be pleasantly surprised when you return."

Iris's hands were curled into fists once more, but she did not raise them. "You said you wanted me to find things for you. What, exactly, are we looking for?"

Trystos smirked again. "I've given you a clear hint, but if you're not as clever as you think you are, I'll tell you for certain once you've decided on the eight people who will be accompanying you."

Iris sputtered. "Eight? That's not enough to sail the *Southern Echo*, and you know it!"

"I do," Trystos agreed. "Which is why the navy will be supplementing your ranks." He stepped forward, brushing between Iris and Dax like they were nothing more than morning fog. "Choose your people quickly,

Iris. The tides wait for no one."

He swept away down the hall, and the guards closed rank behind him. One of them stepped forward to unlock the door, and Nikolai took that moment to seize Dax and Iris by their arms.

"I know what he's after," Nikolai said.

His fingers dug hard enough into Dax's bicep to leave a bruise, but Nikolai's sudden panic and the wild gleam in his eyes killed any protest Dax might have voiced.

"What is it?" Iris asked softly.

The lock of the door clicked open, and Nikolai ducked his head closer, speaking urgently before the rest of the crew could overhear. "He wants impossible things. That means the Flower of the Frozen North."

Dax exchanged a sharp glance with Iris.

Or tried to.

She caught herself before completing the reflexive gesture, and focused back on Nikolai.

"You're certain?" she asked.

Nikolai shuddered. "I am," he said, "just as I know the North is never going to give that up without taking something in return. Are we willing to pay that price?"

Iris drew back and gazed at Nikolai with sad resignation as the door swung open and the voices of the crew spilled into the hall.

"We don't have a choice," she said.

She did not look at Dax, but the harshness of her voice cut him all the same.

A thousand apologies burned in his throat, but he swallowed them all. He'd done what he had to for the sake of the crew. He couldn't say that they were in a better position, but they were all still alive, and Dax was not going to apologize for that, even if he had permanently broken his relationship with Iris.

But she was still his captain, and it was still his job

as quartermaster to stop her from doing something fatally stupid, if only for the sake of the crew.

When Iris turned and walked into the gilded prison cell, Dax followed one step behind.

Catch the next voyage of the *Southern Echo*:

<u>The Shattering of the Frozen North</u>

Coming Soon

Sign up for the newsletter so you never miss an update or release and get a FREE Iris Arani prequel story!

Scan the QR code below to sign up:

About the Author

K.N. Salustro is a science fiction and fantasy author who loves outer space, dragons, and stories that include at least one of those things. When not writing, she can be found drawing and painting, designing and crafting plushies, and trying to play video games while her cat paws at the screen.

For updates, new content, and other news, visit:

www.knsalustro.com

Acknowledgements

Well. Things sure did happen in this book, didn't they?

This third installment of the *Southern Echo* series marks my ninth book overall, and comes in my tenth year as an author. Not too shabby for a first decade, and there is still so much more to come! Whether you've been with me from the start, joined me somewhere in the middle, or are just recently coming along, thank you. I hope you're looking forward to the next voyage of this dryad ship and her pirate crew.

But before we go, I have lots of people in my life that I need to thank for supporting, encouraging, and surviving my writing of this book.

First, Mom, Dad, and Jacki (and I guess Greg now gets an honorary shoutout here, too!). You all are such strong fixtures in my life, and I'm so happy that I get to share moments and make memories with you. I love you all so much. Thank you for your continued unconditional love and support, and for putting up with the occasional bouts of Writer's Block. The despair is real. But also thank you for sharing my joy and excitement for all of my projects. That means more to me than you could ever know.

A huge thank you to Susan for her continued excellence as an editor. Thank you for asking all the questions that never occurred to me, and for helping me discover all the ways to make this book and its predecessors the best they could be. I can't wait to work with you on the next one, although I apologize ahead of time for a particular something in the upcoming plot that I know you're not going to like. And that's all I'll say on that matter.

Next up, thank you to all my friends for the laughs and support this past year and beyond. You all are wonderful humans and I'm forever grateful to have you in my life.

Another special shout out to the enduring game crew and the years of delight we have found in the wackiest of adventures, and in the recent strangeness of cartography. Thank you not only for all of the excitement and your incredible imaginations, but also your compassion and kindness outside of the absolute mayhem that is our game sessions.

And, once more, thank you, dear reader, for coming on this adventure with me. I'll see you on the next one!

—K.

Books by K.N. Salustro

The Star Hunters

Chasing Shadows
Unbroken Light
Light Runner
***

The Arkin Races

Cause of Death: ???

Tales from 2020
***

The Southern Echo

The Roar of the Lost Horizon
A Whisper from the Edge of the World
A Silence Falling Dark and Deep
The Shattering of the Frozen North*

*Coming Soon